Praise for the novels of Natalie Caña

"A sizzling, emotional romance with a generous helping of family and culture."
—*Kirkus Reviews* (starred) on *A Proposal They Can't Refuse*

"This delightful mix of food, familia, and culture will leave readers hungry for more."
—*Publishers Weekly* (starred) on *A Propsosal They Can't Refuse*

"An utterly charming romance that pays homage to the importance of culture, family, and friendship, *A Proposal They Can't Refuse* is a surefire winner!"
—Mia Sosa, *USA TODAY* bestselling author of *The Worst Best Man*

"This book bursts with humor, heat, love, and family! Caña's characters leap off the page and into your heart. *A Proposal They Can't Refuse* delivers a happily ever after where familia, food, and finding what was under our nose the whole time are at the core of the story."
—Denise Williams, bestselling author of *How to Fail at Flirting*

"From a comedic cast of supporting characters to an emphasis on the importance of community... A vibrant second-chance love story about repairing community and romantic connection."
—*Kirkus Reviews* (starred) on *A Dish Best Served Hot*

Also by Natalie Caña

A Proposal They Can't Refuse
A Dish Best Served Hot

SLEEPING WITH THE FRENEMY

NATALIE CAÑA

/||MIRA

///MIRA™

ISBN-13: 978-0-7783-0546-0

Sleeping with the Frenemy

Recycling programs
for this product may
not exist in your area.

For questions and comments about the quality of this book, please contact us
at CustomerService@Harlequin.com.

TM is a trademark of Harlequin Enterprises ULC.

Mira
22 Adelaide St. West, 41st Floor
Toronto, Ontario M5H 4E3, Canada
MIRABooks.com

Printed in U.S.A.

This book is dedicated to every little girl (past, present, and future) whose father broke her heart before the world even had a chance to... It's not you. It never was. You are lovable. You deserve happiness.

PROLOGUE

THE NIGHT OF KAMILAH VEGA AND LIAM KANE'S
FIRST ENGAGEMENT PARTY

LEO VEGA ALREADY KNEW WHAT HE WAS IN STORE FOR WHEN HE knocked on the door in front of him, but he did it anyway. The situation was too important for him to ignore.

"What?" the grumpy voice said from the other side.

"It's me," he said.

"I know who it is. I have a camera doorbell." Leo could practically hear the eye roll. "What do you want?"

"We need to talk."

"I'm not really in the mood to talk."

Leo knew that he had two options if he wanted to be let in: be annoying or be cajoling. There was a fifty-fifty chance with either option. It all depended on whether the person on the other side of the door was more pissed or more hurt. His best guess was pissed because of the hurt. He went for cajoling, praying it worked. "Come on. Open the door. I just want to check on you."

There was noticeably less anger when the voice responded, "I'm fine."

"I need to see you with my own eyes."

A snort slash growl.

He moved close and put his forehead against the door. "Please, bombón," he said in a deep murmur. "Let me see you."

A hiss of annoyed breath filtered through the door, but it had obviously worked.

He heard the locks being disengaged and he stepped back when the door swung open. There she stood, still in the body-hugging dress she'd worn to his sister's disastrous engagement party. She looked almost as perfect as she had when she'd first walked in and nearly caused him to stroke out on the floor, except for one thing. All the immaculate makeup on her face was gone and her eyes were swollen and red rimmed.

He knew there was a good chance she'd push him away, but he couldn't stop his response. He stepped into the apartment and palmed her damp cheek. "Come here." He pulled her into a hug and was mildly surprised when she let him. "Ay, mi Sofi."

Sofi didn't respond, she just buried her face in his neck and squeezed him.

He tightened his hold on her and firmly told himself to ignore the way her body felt against his, but it was impossible. It always was. It had been since they were teens. Sofia Santana just did something to him on every single level. To attempt to ignore her was like trying to ignore being tased. Even if he managed to shut his thoughts down, his body wasn't going to let him not react to the inundation of sensation.

"What happened?" he asked after a few minutes of silence. "All I could understand from a blubbering Kamilah is that you left because you're mad at her."

Sofi pulled back. A scowl appeared on her face. "Of course it's all because of me, right?"

Leo frowned. "I didn't say that. I'm just trying to understand what happened." It was hard for him to believe that she hadn't known about this whole fake engagement stunt either. He'd figured that she had to be in on it too. Kamilah and Sofi did everything together from the moment they met. It was often annoying to him just how close they were.

"She lied to me," Sofi said.

"She lied to all of us," he pointed out. He was angry about that too, but Sofi wasn't the type to get so upset about something like this. At the end of the day Kamilah and Liam faking an engagement to keep their grandpas from selling the family businesses they wanted to run didn't really affect Sofi that much. It wasn't like she had a stake in either business, not like Leo did.

Sofi pushed away from him. "Not about that," she scoffed. "I knew about that stupid shit with Liam. I warned her about that blowing up in her face, but she did it anyway."

Leo suddenly remembered something else that had come up. Something that *had* affected Sofi. "You didn't know she'd turned down the scholarship in Paris," he concluded. Kamilah and Sofi had planned to move to Paris together after high school, but when their abuela got sick, Kamilah lied to everyone and told them she hadn't gotten the scholarship that would have made the move possible.

Sofi actually growled in anger. "Can you believe that bullshit?" She stalked down the short hallway into her living room. "Not only did we say we were going to do that since middle school, but we had plans. Firm plans. I had a school lined up! We were looking at apartments!"

Leo could understand how that would be frustrating at the very least, more likely heartbreaking. "Why didn't you just go anyway?"

Sofi let out a bark of unamused laugher. "Have you met my

mother? You think she was going to be okay with me going to Europe by myself? She didn't want me to go even with Kamilah, but once Kamilah wasn't an option…"

Leo knew Sofi's mother pretty well and Alicia Santana was not someone you ignored when she put her foot down. However, she wasn't an unreasonable person and she trusted her daughter. "I don't know, bombón. I think she would've come around eventually."

"You don't get it, Leo. Once Kamilah said she wasn't accepted, everything changed for me. I had to—" She cut herself off. "Forget it. That's not the point. The point is that not only did she lie to me, she kept it a secret for twelve years."

Leo wasn't exactly as upset about the situation as he could be. The truth was that he'd been keeping a secret from his sister for longer than that. So had Sofi. "I understand how learning all this would upset you, but, Sofi, come on."

She spun on her heel and gave him a look that said, *You'd better not be saying what I think you're saying*, while her mouth said, "Come on, what?"

He gestured between the two of them.

Sofi arched a brow.

"Are you really going to make me say it?"

She crossed her arms and looked him up and down. "I guess you'd better because I don't know what you're talking about."

He gave her a look. She couldn't be serious. "Sofi…"

She pursed her lips.

Leo sucked his teeth. "Sofi, we've been together on and off for how long now? Since you were like fifteen?"

"First of all, we kissed once when I was fifteen and then nothing happened again until much later. Second of all, we have never been *together*, we have sex when we are both single, bored, and horny, which is not the same thing."

Leo didn't let the hurt that statement caused distract him. "Yet, never once did you mention it to Kamilah and you forbid me from telling anyone about it, because you don't want it to get back to her."

"I don't want you telling everyone and their momma about it, because who I sleep with is nobody's fucking business but mine."

Leo had to roll his eyes at that. She was so weird about people "knowing her business." She tended to think that her life was so interesting that it was some sort of gossip fodder. It was ridiculous. She worked at her father's company, went grocery shopping with her mom every week, and liked to go dancing with her friends on the weekend. Her life was not that different from plenty of women he knew. Shit, their secret relationship (because it was a fucking relationship) was probably the most interesting thing about her life. "You never want her to find out, because you know she'll be upset about you lying to her. Sort of how you're mad now."

"Are you really throwing this in my face right now?"

"All I'm saying is that it's not easy to tell people stuff you know will hurt them, so maybe you should give her a break."

Her eyes widened. "Give her a break," she murmured to herself. When she looked at him, there was anger and shock in her expression. "You really are standing in front of me not only defending her, but trying to guilt me out of feeling my own emotions right now."

"I just think given the circumstances we both owe her—"

"I. Don't. Owe. Her. Shit." She accentuated each word with a clap of her hands then paused, screwed up her face, and shook her head as if disgusted. "I don't owe you shit either. Why am I even having this conversation with you?"

"Sof—"

"I should've known that at the end of the day you were going to pick her side over mine."

"How do you figure?"

"Because, Leo, that's how your family operates. Y'all are all open and friendly and welcoming until something happens. Then you close rank like a bunch of elephants circling around the weakest members of the herd. It happens every time Big Sam and your tía Iris break up. It happened when Chase left Kamilah. Y'all still barely talk to your tía Alba's husband after he said Puerto Rico should become a state."

"Not true," Leo argued. "He said that Puerto Ricans on the island wouldn't be able to run a country without the US, so they needed to be a state which is different than just saying that Puerto Rico should be a state. And we hardly liked his conceited and low-key racist ass before that. Plus, you were just as mad about that as the rest of us were!"

"That's not the point, Leo!" she yelled at him.

"Then what is your point," he yelled back. "Because you aren't making any fucking sense."

"My point is that I'm done. I have no interest in doing this with you, your sister, or anyone else in your family."

Leo froze. His body going cold. "What does that mean?"

"That means that I'm not making up with Kamilah. I'm not coming around El Coquí anymore." She paused and looked him right in the eyes. "I don't want you coming here anymore either."

Leo scoffed. "You always say that and then you text to ask me what I'm doing and tell me to come over."

She passed by him to open her door. "Yeah well, why don't you go home and wait for that message?"

"Sofi," he began.

"Bye, Leo. Have a nice life."

Leo growled. He hated when she pulled that dismissive shit with him and she knew it. "You have to be the most stubborn person I've ever met."

"Didn't I already tell you goodbye?"

"One of these days, you're going to push me too far and I'm not going to come back."

"Maybe I'll be lucky and today will be the day."

Annoyed that she was being so stubborn and unreasonable, Leo stormed out the door.

It closed with a snick behind him and Leo fought the urge to flip it off. Instead he stomped down the stairs to the front door of the building. He hated that Sofi did this to him. She'd push him away just to prove that she could. But she didn't actually want him to go anywhere, which was why she always called him back. She'd do it again this time too. He knew she would, because—no matter how much they fought—they couldn't live without each other.

This was not an ending. It was only an intermission.

1

ONE YEAR, SEVEN MONTHS, ONE WEEK,
AND THREE DAYS LATER

AS A STRONG BELIEVER THAT SLEEP WAS A FORM OF SELF-CARE,
Sofia Maria Rosario Santana hated being woken up. She especially hated being woken up at the butt crack of dawn by the sounds of La India belting out how the perfect revenge on the woman who stole her man was to let her keep his trifling ass. It had been the soundtrack of her Saturday mornings from birth to age eighteen when she moved into her own place. Now here she was at age thirty, back to doing her best to ignore her mother, who was purposely and passive-aggressively making enough noise to get Sofi out of bed.

Sofi lifted her head from her pillow, sat up, and glared over the back of the couch in the direction of the kitchen. The two women in the kitchen didn't notice at all. They were too busy screeching along, dancing, and cleaning various things. Her mom, Alicia, had her special cleaning gloves on as she shook her hips from side to side and scrubbed at the counter. Her grandmother, Josefina, was salsa dancing with the broom in her hand instead of sweeping.

It was clear that neither one of them had any idea how much jet lag kicked your ass. Sofi had only just arrived home from France the previous evening. She hadn't been able to sleep, so she'd stayed up thinking about everything she had to do before falling into a stress-filled and unrestful snooze.

Abuela Fina did a complicated spin move with the broom which led her to catching sight of Sofi sitting up on the couch. "Buenos dias, negrita." She took in Sofi's irritated expression. "¿Qué te pasa?"

Did she really just ask what was wrong with her? As if the fact that she had to yell her question over the music wasn't answer enough. "Do you have any idea how little sleep I got?" Sofi yelled back.

Her mom looked summarily unconcerned as she used a small remote to lower the volume of her monstrous stereo. "That's on you. Who told you to stay up all night?"

"That's not fair. There's a seven-hour time difference between Chicago and Paris."

"If life was fair, my new apartment would be on Star Island in Miami and Maluma would be my new neighbor," Abuela Fina quipped.

Sofi knew her Abuela Fina was not exactly happy to be back on the mainland instead of on her beloved island of Puerto Rico. She was even less happy about being in a place that experienced cold weather, but they hadn't exactly given her a choice. Sofi would never forget the days after Hurricane Maria when they couldn't get a hold of Abuela; the gnawing fear that prevented her and her mom from eating or sleeping, that had them both planning an emergency trip to go find her themselves if they had to. By the grace of some higher power, Abuela had been safe at home and her home had received minor wind and flood damage compared to some of her neighbors. But then the earthquakes began, the power grid became even more unreliable thanks to fucking Luma, and rolling blackouts continued to affect the island. Not to mention all of the other shady-ass shenanigans the island and US government continued to subject the Puerto Rican people to. As sad as it had been for them all, they'd had to make the tough decision to bring her to Chicago, where they would be right there to help her with anything she needed.

"Maluma? He's like thirty or something," Sofi said.

"¿Y qué? Maybe I'm a cheetah."

Sofi and her mom looked at each other in confusion. "A what?"

"A cheetah. You know, one of those fast women who hunt for younger men."

Sofi laughed while her mom just shook her head. "Ay, Mai. It's a cougar not a cheetah."

"Nah," Sofi shook her head. "Maluma is my age. That makes Abuela a straight-up saber-toothed tiger."

"¿Qué es eso?" Abuela asked. Then gave Sofi a dirty look when her mom translated. "Ya veo que amaneciste bien lucía hoy." She lifted the broom and acted like she was going to whack Sofi with it.

Mami grabbed the broom from Abuela Fina before she could make contact, but never took her eyes off her only child. "Go wash your ass instead of sitting there being lazy," she told Sofi. "You were talking about all the things you need to do, so hop to it."

"And here I thought you two missed me so much that you'd

be nice to me for at least a day or so," Sofi said as she got up and began gathering the pillows and sheet from the couch.

Abuela Fina exclaimed, "Ay bendito. Of course we missed you." She rushed Sofi and wrapped her in a hug.

Meanwhile her mom rolled her eyes. "Melodramaticas." As a trauma nurse for over twenty years, her mother was an expert at maintaining a level head. It was something she'd obviously gotten from her dad since Abuela Fina was the most over-the-top person either one of them had ever known. Sofi was no-where near as dramatic as her grandmother, but she wasn't as zen as her mom either.

"Let me go to the bathroom and then I'll help you clean," Sofi told her mom.

Mami waved her off. "We don't have much. Besides you have important things to do today, one of which is to find out what is happening with this new apartment you were supposed to get."

She'd get around to that, but her mom was right. That was only one of the things she had to do and, compared to num-ber one on her to-do list, it was the easiest. "Are you sure you don't need my help?" she asked.

Mami gave her a look that told Sofi she knew exactly what she was doing. "Go take care of your business," she said. "You've put it off long enough."

"Fine," Sofi huffed before she stalked off to get ready for the day. Which was how, an hour and a half later, she found her-self standing outside the last place she wanted to be—El Coquí.

Sofi took a deep breath and stepped through the doors of a place so familiar to her that it had basically been her second home. Except just like every facet of her life at the moment, it was just different enough for her to notice and feel awkward.

She'd been one of the main people helping when Kamilah gave El Coquí its facelift, despite her aversion to physical labor and getting dirty, yet somehow she'd completely forgotten ev-erything they'd done. It was still bright, loud, and chaotic, but in a totally different way. In a way that was supposed to be welcoming, but just kept reminding Sofi how much had changed.

Liam spotted her first. He stood behind the bar holding multiple bottles in his hands. He gave her a thorough once-over and quirked one brow at her. Kamilah had always possessed the ability to interpret his looks as if they were captions on a TV. Sofi didn't usually have that gift, but in this instance she knew exactly what he was saying. *Well, well, well. Look who we have here.* Followed quickly by a *watch yourself.* He opened his mouth to say something Sofi couldn't hear at such a distance and suddenly a head popped up right next to him.

Kamilah stared at her with wide eyes, her jaw practically resting on her chest.

Sofi took a few steps forward. She had no idea what to say, so she went with her usual snark. "Do I want to know what you were doing back there?"

Liam crossed his arms. "Is that really the first thing you're going to say to her after a year and a half?"

"Seven months," Kamilah muttered just loud enough for them to hear.

"What?" he asked.

Kamilah cleared her throat, still eyeing Sofi warily like she was a gator sunbathing in her backyard. "It's been a year and seven months. A little more than that actually." The pain was evident in her voice. Her eyes started to glisten.

Sofi felt like she'd been kicked in the chest. She'd always known that her distance had hurt Kamilah, they'd been so close for so long, but she'd assumed most of the pain had been on her end. Looking at Kamilah now, she wasn't so sure. "Hey, girl, can we talk?"

"For sure," Kamilah said immediately. She moved forward, but Liam's arm shot out to block her.

"Mila," he murmured, turning her away and pulling her close. He lowered his head and started whispering in her ear.

Kamilah was nodding and murmuring back.

Sofi was struck by the image they made. The way Liam was hunched over her and wrapped around her as if to cover her and protect her with his very being and the way that Kamilah leaned her weight against him but also met his gaze steadily. They were very obviously in love but not only that, they were a unit.

Sofi ignored the sting of jealousy she felt. She'd told herself long ago that being salty was not a good look for her and she wasn't going to do it anymore.

Kamilah lifted onto her toes and planted a kiss on Liam's lips effectively ending their conversation. "I'll be fine," she told him. "Just lock the front door for me so I don't have to worry while I'm in the office."

She walked out from behind the bar and motioned for Sofi to follow her to the office in the kitchen.

Sofi couldn't help but note the confidence in Kamilah's stride. She used to come across like one of those small dogs that always shook with nervous energy, but she now exuded a comfort in her own skin and the confidence of a woman secure in her place. It was almost emotional to see. Sofi rubbed a hand on her chest absently.

Kamilah stopped right past the swinging doors that led to the kitchen. "I forgot to ask, do you want something to drink before we go into my office? I have some jugo de parcha that I made yesterday." She knew that Sofi loved passion fruit.

"No. I'm good. Thanks," Sofi said, feeling even more awkward. Since when did they talk to each other like this? Like polite strangers who were still trying to figure out what the other one wanted.

"Okay. Then I guess we can just head in." She opened the door to the office that used to belong to her father.

Sofi sucked in a breath. She was used to it being a dark and windowless place full of heavy furniture, including a huge desk, perpetually cluttered with papers and that housed an old-ass computer. It was completely different now. While there were still no windows, the office was bright. Gone was the dingy tan paint on the walls. In its place was a crisp white with the exception of the far wall which was covered floor to ceiling in a tropical print wallpaper featuring different kinds of huge leaves in various shades of green, bright hibiscus flowers in coral, orange, and cream, and golden yellow pineapples. All of the heavy dark furniture was gone, leaving a long but simple white desk in the middle of the room with a brand-new computer and no clutter. There was a built-in storage unit against one wall and a small seating area featuring two wicker chairs along the other.

Kamilah sat in one chair and Sofi sat in the other.

It was clear that Kamilah had a man she loved and trusted, a business she was killing at running, and a place she felt safe and happy in. Meanwhile, Sofi still couldn't figure out what she wanted out of life. It was as if their roles had suddenly switched.

Sofi shifted in her seat. She had no idea how to start, but opened her mouth to try her best. Except Kamilah spoke first.

"I just wanted to tell you how sorry I am for lying to you," she began, her golden brown eyes earnest. "It was a lie I never should've told and I especially shouldn't have held on to that secret for as long as I did. You were right when you said that I probably never would've told the truth if it hadn't come out on its own." She gulped. "I was a coward and I chose to tell lies in order to avoid facing the truth. I hurt you with my selfish actions and I'm sorry for that. Truly. You've never been anything but supportive and amazing and I took advantage of that." She paused and sucked in a much-needed breath.

It seemed that not everything had changed. Kamilah still had the tendency to throw words out in tangled clusters.

Sofi held up a hand before Kamilah could start in on more

apologies. "I know my reaction seemed extreme and I finally realized that you deserve to know why."

Kamilah's head tilted to the side and her brow furrowed. "I know how you are. You value honesty over anything else and I wasn't honest with you."

Sofi winced. "Yeah that's not exactly it." She took a breath to brace herself. "There are a lot of things you don't know, because I wasn't honest with you either. At least not completely."

"What do you mean?"

Sofi looked at her hands. "I told you that I decided not to pursue nursing anymore because I wanted to actually make money. I didn't want to be living paycheck to paycheck like my mom and all stressed."

"Yes," Kamilah nodded.

"That's not the whole story. It's true that when you didn't go to Paris, my mom begged me not to go, because she didn't think I would survive without you. She always considered you the grounded one."

"If only she knew what a mess I really am."

Sofi shook her head. "No, you aren't a mess. You're a go-getter and an optimist. You're willing to take chances on your ideas, no matter how impractical, because you honestly believe that it will work out in the end." Sofi motioned around them. "And it has."

"Not completely. I lost my best friend because of my tendency to leap first and ask questions later."

"Listen, that was mostly on me. The truth is that I didn't have any backup schools like you did, so when we didn't go to Paris, I had nothing to fall back on. I was panicked. Then my dad stepped in."

Kamilah sucked in a breath. She knew what that meant for Sofi, who'd never had the best relationship with her dad.

"He said that if I went to school for business, with the understanding that I'd stay working with him, he'd get me into school and pay for it," Sofi continued. "All four years if not more. It turned out that he'd made friends with a member of a certain university's board after working on a campaign with them.

"It just made sense for me to agree. I mean what the hell else was I going to do?" Sofi asked. "Get some dead-end part-time job that would stress me out, exhaust me, and keep me broke? Some shithole I'd get stuck in working my ass off only to be putting the real money in someone else's pocket? I refused to be just like every other uneducated brown daughter of a poor single mother."

"Oh, Sofi." Kamilah shook her head. "There is nothing wrong with being a hard worker and there is nothing wrong with coming from a single parent home. There is nothing that says that your origin dictates where you end up in life." It was a conversation they'd had many times in the past, but Kamilah didn't really get it.

She came from a two-parent home where her siblings all had the same parents. And sure, she had her tan skin, curly hair, and curvy body, but Kamilah was still mostly European.

Sofi was the Black daughter of a biracial Afro-Latina who had been wined and dined by a charming rich man until he kicked her to the curb and left her with nothing. From as long as she could remember, assumptions about Sofi's future had been made by everyone who knew her upbringing. She obviously wasn't going to amount to much because, sure she was pretty, but that was all she had going for her. She'd end up as some guy's arm candy and if she was smart, she'd figure out how to cash in on that. Otherwise she'd be a formerly beautiful woman whose looks faded because she'd been forced to toil just to stay poor—like her mother. At least that's what her father had told her when she'd won her final beauty pageant.

Sofi had refused to let that happen to her. Not on her fucking watch. There was no fucking way.

"Anyway," Sofi continued. "I had no choice but to take him up on his offer which is how I've ended up there, stuck."

"I thought you loved your job," Kamilah said.

"I wanted you to think so. I wanted everyone to think so. But hearing that I went through all of that because of a lie you told to your family…" She paused and shook her head. "It made me mad. I was mad for a while. Then the sense of betrayal and injustice kicked in. Especially after I heard that you and Liam worked it out and got engaged for real, and you fixed things with your family while also getting ownership of the restaurant. Everything worked out for you, but I'm still dealing with the fallout."

"I can imagine that it felt like having salt poured in an open wound."

Especially after Leo had made it clear he was on his sister's side. Sofi had felt like she'd been betrayed by her best friend (one of the very few people she'd trusted), stuck in a job she hated because she was indebted to the very last person she wanted to feel any obligation toward, and without a love because the man she wanted to be with felt more loyalty to his manipulative family than he did toward her. "I was bitter," Sofi admitted. "I was so bitter, and it took me a while to figure out that instead of feeling some type of way toward you, I needed to look more at myself. I was the one who ultimately made those choices. I can't blame that on you."

"Is that why you left? You went on a journey to find yourself."

Sofi nodded. "I wanted to see the things I felt like I'd missed out on, and I hoped that I'd gain some sort of clarity."

"Did you?"

Not really. She'd figured out that she didn't want to continue on the path she was on and had a very vague idea about what she might want going forward. But it was all still very nebulous. "I'm still working on that."

"And how do you feel about me now?"

"Honestly? I think a part of me is still raw, but I mostly just miss my friend."

Kamilah's eyes went bright and wet. "I miss my friend too. Every single day there is something I want to tell you because I know that only you would get it. Then I remember that I can't and it hurts. It hurts like when I remember that I can't just stop upstairs and talk to my abuela or step into the distillery and bicker with Killian."

Sofi understood how losing Liam's grandfather would hurt Kamilah. Not a day went by that she didn't wish she could talk to her tío Manny or her abuelo Juan. There had already been more people-sized holes in her heart than any one person needed to have, adding a Kamilah-sized one had almost taken her out. "I'm sorry for your loss. I know how much you loved Killian."

"Thank you." Kamilah gave her a sad smile. "We're still getting used to it. Some days are better than others."

"I know. I get it." Sofi, her mom, and Abuela Fina still had bad days in regards to Tío Manny and Abuelo Juan and it had been over a decade since their fatal car crash.

"I want to be friends again," Sofi said. "I don't think it will ever be the same, but I hope it can be better even if it's different."

"I want that too," Kamilah said. She reached out a hand like she was going to grab Sofi's but she stopped. It was clear that she was unsure of whether or not they were back at the physical affection stage. Kamilah thrived on physical affection. She was always hugging, kissing, and caressing her loved ones. It hurt to see her unsure of her welcome.

Sofi reached over and pulled Kamilah into a hug.

Kamilah wrapped her arms around Sofi and squeezed with all of her might. "It's already different because now we both know the truth. There are no more secrets."

Right.

Except there was one. One big secret Sofi knew she had to tell Kamilah, especially now. It was the perfect moment, but she didn't know how. Did she just open her mouth and say, *Oh, and since we're being honest I should probably tell you that I pretty much dated your brother on and off since I was fifteen.* That would go over like gangbusters.

No. Things were still too tentative between them. She needed to understand this new Kamilah better. Then she'd know how to break the news in a way that didn't completely obliterate any chance they had to rebuild their friendship.

"I just want you to know that I value this friendship," Sofi told her. "I want to fix it."

"Sofi, we don't have a friendship. You've been family since the day we met. Nothing changed on that front. I'm just working on being better at recognizing and vocalizing my needs and intentions and accepting that when I fail it's not the end of the world. It's helping me be a more honest and straightforward communicator, which I know is a trait you really value."

Oh God. Please stop, Sofi thought desperately. She was making everything better and worse at the same time. She was saying everything that Sofi needed to hear to know that she'd made the right choice in coming, but she was making Sofi feel guilty as shit too. *I'll tell her soon*, she promised herself. *Besides, it's not like there is anything between me and Leo now, so it can wait a little bit.* That thought helped slow the steeping of guilt a little bit.

Kamilah wiped at her wet eyes. "Okay, no more sad stuff. Today is a happy day. I have my best friend back and she has tons of amazing stories about her *Emily in Paris* year abroad."

Sofi snorted. "Please. When I wasn't working, I mostly just ate, explored, and shopped."

"Did you buy that outfit overseas, because that is cute as hell." Kamilah took in Sofi's bright yellow matching skort and crop top set with a tropical plant print including pink birds of paradise flowers and deep green leaves.

"I did." Sofi spun so that Kamilah could see it in all its glory. "It gives me '90s vibes and I love it."

Kamilah made a chef's kiss gesture. "And we all know that yellow was created for brown skin."

"Yes, hunnie."

They both smiled at each other.

On the desk her Apple desktop started to ring loudly. Kamilah pulled her vibrating iPhone out of her pocket. She looked down, read the screen, and hit the accept button quickly. "This is the reception venue. I gotta take this. Don't go anywhere." She stood and faced the wall as she answered. She listened to whoever was on the other line and then suddenly gasped and collapsed.

2

IT WAS THE ONE-YEAR ANNIVERSARY OF THE DAY LEO DIED. OKAY, technically his heart had only stopped for a minute or so, but he considered it dying even if the doctors didn't. It had been a long road to what they called recovery, but Leo didn't consider himself recovered. There were still too many things he struggled to do because of the nerve damage he'd sustained after being shot while saving his family from neighborhood thugs. For example, he couldn't lift anything over a hundred and ten pounds now without pain or tingling when he used to lift triple that. Still, Leo wasn't going to stop until he felt like himself again.

A hand tapped his leg, bringing his focus back to the present and making him realize that his leg had been bouncing. Leo forced his leg to still and gave his attention to the woman in front of him, Amanda McGuire—or Mandy, as she demanded they call her—Liam's business mentor and partner.

Liam and Mandy had met when Kane Distillery had been a contestant in a national craft distillery contest and she'd been so impressed that she'd offered to guide Liam as he expanded the business into something that would grow beyond Division Street. It had taken Killian, Liam's late grandfather, a bit to come around to the idea of having anyone else involved in the family business, but he'd eventually given his blessing before he passed. Since then Mandy had stepped fully into the role of mentor, helping Liam see beyond the day-to-day aspects of whiskey distilling. She got him to realize that if he diversified his business a bit, he'd eventually have more profit to put into expanding. All of which had led to the moment they were at now, on the cusp of opening a new part of the business.

"Everything looks good so far," Mandy said to Leo and Liam. "The new lighting is in, the glass walls are up, and the old catwalk has been extended and reinforced to allow for seating."

Leo looked at everything Mandy pointed out. Kane Distillery had definitely undergone a transformation, almost as radical as the one at El Coquí, which was in the same building. Where there used to just be an open space with a bunch of machines, there were now glass walls that allowed the machines to be viewed without any rando having access to them. The main wall still displayed the original Kane Distillery logo that Liam had painted all those years ago, but it now also housed a brand-new bar with built-in shelves. In Leo's mind he could see the finished product, a trendy, new, low-key hangout where people could just come and chill while drinking artisanal drinks made with one hundred percent local products including spirits made from other local craft distilleries. Mandy had originally tried to get Liam to branch out and make gin, vodka, or even brandy, but that was a step too far for him. Liam was a whiskey distiller. Point-blank period. There was still a lot of work to do to get everything ready for the grand opening in a few weeks, but Leo was willing to put it in.

Unlike Mandy, Leo's involvement had happened accidentally. It all started because Liam needed some help and Leo had been on medical leave from the Chicago Fire Department recovering. Suddenly, Leo found himself spending more and more time at the distillery with Liam, the only person who didn't treat him like he was made of crystal. Then Leo had made an offhand comment to Mandy and Liam about how creating a bar on the distillery side would bring in more people and not just for tours. From there things just sort of happened and now Leo, who had tended bar at El Coquí part-time for years and even managed the place when his parents and sister were gone, was the head mixologist and manager at Kane Distillery's Tasting Room. It was probably what he deserved after failing, yet again, to keep his damn mouth shut, but Leo didn't always have the ability to filter his words before they came out of his mouth. He just said shit and then wondered how he'd gotten himself in trouble. Not that working with Mandy and Liam on expanding the distillery was trouble. If anything, it was one of the few things holding Leo together at the moment.

Mandy turned to Leo. "We need to finalize the drink menu soon. I want to have them printed with plenty of time to get anything fixed because there will inevitably be an error."

Leo fought a grimace. "I'm fine-tuning it." If someone had told Leo a year ago that he'd be carefully curating a drink menu for the new Kane Distillery bar, he would've laughed his ass off and then gone to tell his buddies at the fire station. Life was crazy like that.

Liam turned to look at him and raised one brow. "Fine-tuning, hmm?"

So Leo was lying. The truth was he'd barely begun and Liam knew it. "Shut up," Leo told him. "I work best under pressure anyway."

Mandy cleared her throat. "Look, I'm here to help with whatever you need. I'm not a mixologist, but I do know plenty." She'd already proved that by basically holding Leo's hand throughout the entire process. She was like his personal tutor when it came to learning how to actually manage a bar.

Leo was about to thank her when the sound of someone yelling Liam's name interrupted their meeting. Leo titled his head. That sounded like...no it couldn't be. But of course it was, because she always showed up when he least expected.

Sofia Santana came barreling around the entryway. "Liam," she panted.

"Sofi?" Leo was so shocked to see her that it took him a moment to realize how panicked she was.

"Something's wrong with Kamilah," she said before spinning on her sky-high heels and running back into El Coquí.

The three of them took off after her, booking it through the dining space and into the kitchen. They pushed through the office door in tandem, like a bunch of kids trying to be the first in the classroom, and found Kamilah sitting on the floor sobbing so hard she looked like she couldn't breathe.

Liam literally jumped over the desk to get to her and pulled her into his arms. Kamilah continued to shake and cry as he did his best to comfort her.

Leo hadn't seen Kamilah this worked up since the night she'd fought with everyone in her life and they had walked out on her, including the best friend who was now back looking like she'd just stepped off a cruise to the Bahamas. "What the fuck did you do to my sister?" Leo asked Sofi.

Sofi's eyes rounded for a moment, hurt flaring, before narrowing at him in disdain. "I didn't do anything." She turned to Liam, who was also glaring at her while he held and rocked Kamilah in his lap. "She got a call from someone about the wedding and then she just collapsed and started crying," Sofi explained. "She was trying to talk to me, but I don't understand her like this. All I got were the words 'ruined' and 'Liam,' so I figured it best to come get you."

"What happened, Coquí?" Liam muttered to Kamilah.

Kamilah held up a finger.

It took a few minutes, but eventually Kamilah calmed down enough to speak. She wiped at her face with her hands. "Our reception hall flooded," she told Liam in a waterlogged voice. "Our wedding is ruined."

"What?" Liam exclaimed. "What happened?"

Kamilah shook her head. "I don't know. Something about the plumbing from the upper floor having work done on Friday and someone not tightening a piece all the way. Sometime in the night it disconnected and no one found out because this was the one weekend they didn't have an event."

"Oh my God, Kamilah," Sofi said. "That's terrible. I'm so sorry."

More tears welled up in his sister's eyes and trickled down her cheeks. "We're getting married in less than three months, we booked this place a year ago, and now we don't have a place to hold the reception."

"They can't fix it by then?" Leo asked.

Liam shook his head. "Think about how long it took us to get permits from the city to do any kind of work in the distillery— and we aren't even considered a historical building."

Shit. They'd been forced to wait weeks just to get an engineer to come check out the space and look over their plans. That didn't include the almost two months it had taken to be seen by a city inspector. Leo couldn't imagine how much more a pain it would be to have to work with the Historic Preservation Division of the city's planning and development department. It was going to take the venue forever to get repaired unless they greased some palms and pulled off a miracle.

As if reading Leo's mind, Liam said, "I'd be surprised if they get everything done by the end of the year." He rubbed a hand up and down Kamilah's back in comfort.

Kamilah wiped at her face with the collar of her tank top. "Even worse, they were taking care of everything, the food, flowers, centerpieces, everything. I mean I was picking it, obviously, but they had the vendors." She looked up at them, her eyes red and heartbroken. "What am I going to do? Our wedding is ruined and I promised—" she paused, choking on her emotions "—I promised Killian—" She cut herself off before covering her face and beginning to cry again.

Leo hated seeing his sister like this. He and Kamilah were the closest in age with a little over a year between them. It was probably one of the reasons they fought constantly growing up, but in the last year it had also been something the two of them relied upon. It took him over thirty years, but Leo finally considered his sister his friend instead of his adversary. He was willing to do whatever it took to help her. "Just hold the reception in the distillery," Leo blurted.

Her head snapped up, surprise causing her to stop crying. "What?"

Leo cleared his throat. "Well, this building is pretty much the whole reason you two ended up together, so it makes sense to have your wedding reception here."

"We already had the engagement party here…both of them," she said.

That was before Mandy had come into the picture with her big plans. "Everything is different now though," he said. He looked at Mandy for help.

"I've told Liam that renting out the distillery for events would be a great way to bring in additional profits," Mandy said. "Hosting your reception would be a great way to work out any potential kinks."

Kamilah grimaced.

Sofi snorted. "Using her wedding reception as a dry run for

a business venture is hardly the way to convince her this is a good idea."

Leo turned his attention to Sofi and truly saw her for the first time. Leo forced his expression to remain neutral before tracking everything from Sofi's riotous natural curls to her French-tipped toes peeking through her strappy sandals. She looked fucking amazing and Leo was pissed at her for it. How dare she look like a walking wet dream when he looked like the tired and overworked mess he now was?

"Chiquita Banana over here has a point," Leo said.

Sofi glared at him and it felt like coming home.

"The last thing we want is to stress you out more," Leo told Kamilah.

Sofi let out a mock gasp and then clutched her hands over her chest like all of her prayers had been answered. "Look at this. Peter Pan appears to have grown up a little bit."

"Tell me something, Carmen Miranda, did that outfit come with a hat made of fruit that you forgot to put on?" he shot back.

She ignored him to talk to Kamilah. "Give me the number for the venue and then leave it to me," Sofi told her.

Kamilah lifted her head from Liam's chest and looked at Sofi. "What?"

Sofi put her hand on Kamilah's shoulder. "I've thrown tons of events for my job. I can plan an event for hundreds of people in a few weeks."

Kamilah immediately shook her head. "Sofi, I can't ask you to do that." She stood and Liam followed.

"You aren't asking. I'm telling you that I'm doing it."

Kamilah let out a sigh. It was mostly annoyance because everyone knew better than to argue with a determined Sofi, but Leo could hear the relief underlying the annoyance. Leo wasn't surprised his sister felt that weight lifted. If Sofi said she was going to do something, you'd better believe it would be done and to the best of her abilities. It was one of the things he liked best about Sofi. She was a shark in the body of a mermaid.

"I'll accept under one condition," Kamilah said before a brief pause. "Well, two conditions."

Sofi looked a bit taken aback that his sister was negotiating with her instead of simply giving in like she used to. "What?"

"You will not pay for anything. I mean nothing. Not a deposit. Not a sample, not a single flower."

Sofi let out an epic eye roll, but Leo understood where his sister was coming from. The minute Sofi had started making money she'd also begun throwing it around like a rapper at a strip club. She probably didn't even realize she did it, but she had the tendency to throw money at problems hoping that would make them go away.

"I'm serious, Sofi. You will not try to foot any of the bills."

"Fine. What's your second condition?"

"That you'll be my maid of honor."

Sofi froze, her eyes large, dark, and shining. She looked equal parts shocked and excited. "I figured that Lucy would—" She paused to swallow. "I don't d—" She stopped again, clearly at a loss.

Leo watched her wrestle her emotions into submission. It took every ounce of his strength to not reach out and drag her into his arms. *Stop it*, he scolded himself. *She walked away from you. You're still pissed at her.* His hands flexed at his sides, trying their best to rebel against his brain. That wasn't new. His brain and body were hardly ever in agreement, especially where Sofi was concerned.

"You are the sister of my heart," she finally said to Kamilah. "Of course, I'll be your maid of honor."

They hugged and Kamilah cried again, but this time her tears were happy ones.

Leo wanted to be happy for Kamilah. He knew how much Sofi's absence had hurt. He'd seen it firsthand. In the weeks following the shit show that was her first engagement party to Liam, Kamilah had worked her ass off to mend fences with everyone she'd hurt. She'd owned up to her wrongs, apologized for her lies, but also stuck up for herself in a way she never had before. That was when Leo had first begun to see her in a new light and respect her as a grown woman, not just his annoying little sister. She'd eventually made things right with everyone but Sofi. Not because she hadn't tried, but because Sofi hadn't given her the chance. For the months that followed he saw Kamilah bury herself in work and Liam, but every so often she'd look around with a light in her eyes. A light that would die when she realized the person she was looking for wasn't there. Leo was probably one of the only people who noticed and recognized it for what it was, because he felt the exact same way and did the same thing.

That was why he couldn't be completely happy about Sofi's return. He'd been doing his best to get over her and now here she was back in his life. He had too many things going on to add her into the mix. All of his best-laid plans and good intentions went right out the window the minute Sofi was around. It had always been that way. From the moment she'd shown up in this very office and blew his fifteen-year-old mind.

"Yo no sé qué te pasa, Leo." His father shook the history test in his face.

Leo could see the bright red F scrawled at the top all too clearly. "I'm sorry," he said.

"Sorry isn't enough. You're always sorry, but you keep doing it. We took you to the doctor's. We got you medicine for your ADHD. We help you with your homework, but we can't take tests for you too."

"I know," Leo told his father. He stared at the table in front of him. His shoulders tried to push against the guilt weighing him down, but the guilt was stronger and heavier. "I tried my best," Leo said and it was the honest truth.

"Leo, you're a smart kid. You really are. There's no reason for you to be bringing home grades like this."

"I know," he said again, but this time it was a lie. Everyone tried to tell him that he was smart, but if his grades didn't reflect that then they were obviously wrong. Leo couldn't be smart when he struggled so much to focus in school and couldn't remember the things he did learn.

"I don't know what to do for you. I don't know how else to help you, but we can't go through this again this year. You're in high school now. These grades are too important. You need to qualify for scholarships and with these grades you can't play on any teams. They won't even let you stay in band or choir."

The hopeless frustration in his father's voice was the worst. Leo only heard that particular tone when Papi spoke to him. None of his other siblings caused it to make an appearance, only him. He hated disappointing his parents. He'd prayed so many times that he could be as smart as Eddie, as confident as Cristian, as capable as Junior, or that his sweet and innocent personality made everyone overlook his failures like with Kamilah. But no. He was just Leo, the stupid Vega sibling who drove everyone crazy with his endless energy and was always getting in trouble for something or other.

But that was going to change now. Leo was going to change. He was going to do whatever it took to make his dad proud of him and not ashamed. Leo opened his mouth to tell him so.

Suddenly, a wave of girly giggles poured into the back office where he sat in front of Papi's desk.

Leo raised his head as his sister stepped into the office. He couldn't see her since he had his back to the open doorway, but he heard her steps.

"I'm home, Papi," his sister announced unnecessarily.

His dad's face changed immediately from a frown to a smile. "Hola, mi vida. How was school?"

"Good, I made a new friend in French class."

"So I see."

"This is Sofia. Her family is from Puerto Rico too, but she just moved here from Florida because her uncle was traded to the Cubs."

At that Leo's curiosity was peaked. *Sports were the one thing he excelled at, besides music, and baseball was his favorite, especially the Cubs. He turned in his seat to see this niece of a professional baseball player.*

The first thing he noticed was her height. The girl stood a few inches taller than his sister and, at thirteen, Kamilah was already about half a head taller than their five-two mother.

The second thing he noticed were her eyes. They were so dark they appeared black. He couldn't tell the iris from the pupil, but somehow they shined and sparkled. Until that moment he'd thought the term bright-eyed *meant someone with light eyes, but she proved differently. Just looking at her, he could tell that her brain was working a mile a minute, just like his. He would've bet a hundred dollars that the simple quantity of thoughts in her brain could overwhelm her just like his did.*

Finally, *his brain said.* Someone who gets us.

"What are you looking at, pretty boy?"

He felt such an immediate connection to her that it took him a minute to realize she was talking to him. "What?" *Leo asked trying to catch up, like always.*

"Why do you keep looking at me like that? Have you never seen a Black girl before?"

The question was so off-putting that he struggled to answer. Of course she wasn't the first Black girl he'd ever seen. There were plenty of Black Americans and Afro-Latinos in his neighborhood not to mention in his own family. Why would she even ask him that? Leo's brow furrowed.

"I don't know what your problem is, but you need to fix your face before I fix it for you," she said.

"Leo, stop being a jerk to my friend," Kamilah demanded.

Leo opened his mouth to defend himself, but his dad cut him off before he could.

"Leo, go clean the walk-in."

Leo's jaw dropped. "But—"

"But nothing. If you have enough time to sit here being a clown in front of your sister's new friend, then you aren't busy enough."

Leo stood. *"What about the test?"*

His dad sighed again. "I'll sign it." He scribbled his name across the top and held it out. "But, Leo, you're grounded. A ver si así se te acaban las payasadas."

Leo knew better than to argue about the injustice. All because this new girl had to open her mouth and act like he was being rude to her when she was the one with an attitude problem.

He stomped out of his dad's office not bothering to check his pace. When his shoulder slammed into Sofia and almost sent her flying, he swallowed the urge to apologize. She'd just made an enemy of the wrong guy, bright eyes or not.

That was the day their heated back and forth had begun. Now, all these years later, they were still at it. Although things between them had gotten a lot more steamy than they'd been back then. It was hard to believe that they'd been playing this make up/break up, fight/fuck game since high school and it was still a secret to almost everyone they knew. Honestly, he was sick of it. He'd gone along with it for so long because that was what Sofi wanted. But the game had gotten old a long time ago. He was in his thirties. And if there was one thing getting shot, dying for a minute, and then almost losing his arm had taught him it was that he was too old to be playing games. He had spent the last year getting his shit together. He couldn't wait around for Sofi to open her eyes and see what he was offering her. It didn't matter what he felt for her, enough was enough.

Of course, that was a lot easier said than done, especially when he was standing in front of her and she was looking like his fantasy come to life.

"Don't worry, Kamilah," Mandy was saying as she patted his sister on the back. "Leo will be around to help make sure everything with the reception goes off without a hitch."

A record scratch sounded in Leo's head.

"What?"

It took him a second to realize the word hadn't come out of his mouth, but Sofi's.

Mandy smiled like a proud mom. "Leo is the manager of the new bar, so he'll obviously be helping you organize everything here."

Sofi simply blinked. Her face didn't show it, but she was not happy about that fun fact. It was all the reason Leo needed to keep his mouth shut instead of arguing that he didn't want to do it either.

"Oh, that would be so great," Kamilah said with a hand on her chest. She turned to Sofi. "It would make me feel much better if I knew you weren't tackling this all alone." She then gave Leo a serious look. "And Leo will be on his very best behavior. Isn't that right, Leo?"

Leo rolled his eyes. "I'm a grown-ass man, Kamilah. I can do my job even if it means working with a bad-tempered Iris Chacón."

"Leo," Liam intoned—a warning to take it easy.

Fine. He'd play nice. For now. "Look, not only am I the manager, which means it's my responsibility to make sure this goes off perfectly, but I'm hardly going to ruin my little sister's wedding to be petty. I'm not an asshole."

Sofi raised a brow, but Kamilah and Liam looked chastened for even doubting him. They knew better than most how much Leo had changed.

"Come on, dear," Mandy said to Kamilah. "Let's get you cleaned up and put a drink in your hand. Meanwhile, Leo can tell Sofi about everything the Tasting Room now offers." She led his sister out with a hand on her back while Liam followed closely, pulled by the invisible rope that prevented him from going too far from Kamilah's side.

Leo continued to stare at Sofi.

"What?" she asked him with enough attitude to put him immediately on defense.

"What, what?" he asked.

"You obviously want to say something to me, so just do it already."

He had a moment alone with Sofi after over a year of silence. He wasn't going to pass up the opportunity. "What does this mean?" he asked.

"What does what mean?" she asked back.

"El gran regreso de Sofia Maria Rosario Santana," he said while lifting his hand and moving across his face like he was reading a title off a marquee. "You're here in your finest armor. You're hugging all over my sister and not only agreeing to be her maid of honor but volunteering to plan her new wedding reception even if it means working with me. That seems odd for someone who was completely done with all of the Vegas."

She crossed her arms and lifted her pointy chin. "I don't have to explain myself to you."

"Are you sure about that?" Leo asked, ignoring the way he wanted to bite that proud chin. "Because I feel like our history would warrant at least an explanation."

She drew herself up. "Our history is just that. History. I came back because I missed my best friend."

He stepped up close to her. "And what about her brother? Did you miss him too?"

"Leo," she breathed. She leaned forward as if about to step into his body. Like she was a magnet and he was the fridge.

He stepped back, breaking the connection. "Because it seems like you didn't. It seems like you went off and had yourself a grand adventure. So much so that when I was shot, you didn't even come see me in the hospital. You didn't pick up the phone to call me. Shit, you didn't even send me a text. All I got from you was one fucking email wishing me a speedy recovery like I'm some random-ass coworker you share small talk with during your break." He didn't even mention that she'd promptly blocked him afterward, because every message he tried to send kept getting shot back and labeled as undeliverable. He shook his head. "Well, don't worry. I get it. It took my stupid ass fifteen years, but I get it. I'm nothing to you. I'm just your venue contact for the reception. That's fine with me." He walked past her, careful to make sure no part of them touched, and he walked out the door with his head held high, his shoulder throbbing, and his heart twisting itself into a knot.

3

SOFI SAT ON HER BALCONY ENJOYING HER VIEW OF THE EIFFEL
Tower with a glass of truly incredible wine. It had been a few weeks
and she still couldn't believe this was her life. She was finally in Paris,
living in a cute apartment and exploring all the places she'd dreamed
of since she was a kid. The best part was that she was going to be here
for months—plenty of time to soak in the city.

On the table her open laptop began to ring. She knew who it was
without even having to look. Her mother called her at this time every
single day. Sofi set down her wine and grabbed her laptop. She placed
it on her lap and hit Accept. "Bonjour, Mami," she said as soon as
her mother's face popped up on her screen.

"Negrita." Her mom sighed her nickname in relief as if she wasn't
sure Sofi would answer.

Sofi always answered. Her mother was her other half. She was the kinder, more forgiving, and selfless Ying to Sofi's Yang. She missed her mom like crazy, so she answered every single call, text, and email. Shit. Sofi would send carrier pigeons if she could only figure out how to train one of the few hundred she saw on a daily basis.

"Are you busy?" *her mom asked. Behind her tired but beautiful face, Sofi could see the bright sun reflecting off the windows of the hospital. Her mom liked to eat lunch outside when the weather permitted.*

"I'm supposed to be memorizing my presentation for tomorrow, but I got distracted by the view and my wine." *Sofi reached over and picked up her glass to show her mom.* "Do you want to see what I'm seeing?" *She didn't wait for her mom to answer, she turned the laptop so she could also enjoy the sight of the lit-up Eiffel Tower peeking out from above the neighboring buildings.*

Her mom's voice came from the speakers. "It's so beautiful."

Sofi turned the laptop around so she could see her mom's face. "I can't wait for you to come visit. You're going to love it."

Her mom smiled again. Her mother was a beautiful woman with light brown skin, high and naturally pink cheekbones, dark brown eyes with long lashes, and dimples so deep she didn't even have to smile for them to be seen. But Sofi loved it when she did smile. It reminded Sofi of the pictures she had of when her mom was young and smiled all the time. These days she was constantly stressed, exhausted, and barely smiled. Sofi was determined to change that.

"I'm excited," *she said.* "I just got my passport in the mail and the hospital approved my days off."

"They had better," *Sofi said around the glass before taking another sip of wine.* "You never use your vacation days and you're always picking up extra shifts."

She wouldn't call her mom a workaholic, but she was definitely a hard worker. When Sofi was a kid, she'd held multiple jobs while also going to nursing school. Due to many setbacks, it had taken her mom years to finally finish her degree, but, once she had, she'd never slowed down. She always said that single moms didn't really have any other choice unless they were going to live off the state and she wasn't going to do that.

"I just picked up another one," her mom said.

Sofi shook her head. "Why? I know you get attached to your patients and want to be there for them, but you're burning yourself out. You need to take care of yourself, Mom."

Her mom looked away, her expression troubled and unsure.

Sofi's stomach flipped. She put down her wine. "What?" she asked.

Her mom looked back at her. "Huh?"

Sofi shook her head. "Don't even try that. Something is wrong. Tell me what it is. Are you okay? Is it Abuela Fina?"

"No. No. We're fine. It's nothing like that."

"What is it, then?"

Her mom sighed. "I don't know if I should tell you."

Sofi sat up straight. "You can't say that and not tell me. What is it?" she demanded.

"Leo Vega is here."

That wasn't totally unheard of. He'd gotten hurt a few times in his line of work, but it was never that serious. "Did he get hurt at work again?"

She shook her head. "He was shot last night. He got out of surgery a few hours ago, but, Sofi, he coded on the table."

Suddenly Sofi felt like the wine she'd drunk had gone straight to her head. Everything spun and she felt like she was falling. She could hear her mom talking, trying to explain what happened, but Sofi couldn't really focus on any of that.

She stood with the laptop and stumbled into her apartment, oblivious to the light herringbone floors, original detailed crown molding, and antique marble fireplace she usually admired. She bypassed it all to go right into her bedroom. She dropped the computer on her bed and rushed to her closet.

"Sofi! Sofi! Mama, what are you doing?" her mom yelled from the screen.

"I'm packing," Sofi responded, dragging her maleta behind her. She tossed it on the bed next to the computer. "I'm coming home. Right now."

"Sofi, calm down," Mami begged.

"I can't calm down. You just told me that Leo was shot and that he coded during surgery. How the hell do you expect me to calm down?" Sofi went to her dresser and scooped out a bunch of stuff. She didn't even know what it was, but she dropped it in the suitcase.

"Sofia Maria Rosario Santana, cálmate o te calmo," her mother barked in her no-nonsense voice. It was the voice Sofi heard moments before she got an ass whooping.

Sofi froze.

"Now breathe," Mami commanded. "Deep breaths."

Sofi breathed.

"Now listen to me."

Sofi listened.

"He is going to be okay," her mom said. "There is some significant nerve damage in his shoulder, but he's alive and he's pretty much out of the woods."

"I need to be there," Sofi said. Sofi could feel the emotion clogging her throat. "I need to see him."

"Ay, mi nena." Mami let out on a breath. The sympathy in her voice was what made Sofi crack.

Tears clouded her vision and streamed down her face. "I... I..." She couldn't talk.

"It's okay. I know," her mom said. She did know. Her mother was the only one who knew about Sofi and Leo's relationship and Sofi's feelings for him. She was the only one Sofi trusted with that information. She stayed on the video call with Sofi, murmuring comforting words to her while Sofi cried.

She was so scared. What if something else happened to him and she wasn't there. What if he died? What if she never got to see him again?

Sofi had no idea how long she sat there blubbering on her bedroom floor half a world away, but eventually she calmed down enough to pick herself up off the floor. "I'm going to get on the next flight," she told her mom. "I'll send you my arrival information when I have it."

"Sofi." Her mom's voice was soft. "What about your presentation tomorrow?"

"Fuck that presentation," Sofi exclaimed.

"No. Not fuck it." Her mom's voice was stronger. "You've worked your ass off for this opportunity. You're finally living your dream. I'm not going to let you sabotage that."

"But, Mami."

"'But, Mami' nothing. I know how you feel about him, but you told me yourself that you were done with him, with that whole family, and you were going to leave to find yourself. This is your time, Sofia. Do not throw that away for him."

"He was shot. He's in the hospital."

"And he's okay. He's alive, surrounded by his family, and he will get better every day. I will personally make sure of that. I'll do whatever I have to do to make sure he recovers, but you will NOT come back. You will stay there. You will give that presentation tomorrow despite how nervous I know you'll be. You will blow them all away. And then you will continue to kick ass while living your best life because you are MY daughter and my daughter is not going to throw her future away for a man. Do you understand me?"

"Mom," Sofi began.

"I said, 'Do you understand me?'"

There was nothing she could say to that besides, "Yes, ma'am." She was right. Sofi had worked too hard and sacrificed too much to leave now. Not when she was finally where she wanted to be. This was her chance to prove to herself that she actually liked her chosen career in marketing. That she hadn't made a terrible mistake by accepting her father's deal all those years ago. Because if she still felt empty while living her dream life, well, then, she didn't know what she'd do.

Plus, Sofi knew her mom. If her mom said that she was going to make sure Leo recovered, she would. As long as Leo was safe, Sofi could rest easy. Or at least that's what she told herself as she told her *mom she was right and that she'd stay put. She hung up with her mom. Then she looked at her phone. She knew that she wasn't leaving Paris, but she had to reach out to him. She had to hear his voice for herself.*

She reached for her phone and then stopped. Fuck. She'd gotten a new phone and number before she left and she'd purposefully told her carrier not to transfer over her contacts. The only numbers in her new phone beyond her immediate family were those of her new coworkers. She didn't know Leo's phone number by heart or any of the Vegas'. She didn't even know her mom's.

Double fuck, she said to herself as a thought occurred to her. There was one number she had memorized. It was the number she'd called at least once a day from ages twelve to sixteen—when Kamilah's parents had finally gotten her a cell phone for her birthday. Taking a deep breath, Sofi typed the number into her phone and hit the call button. As it rang she told herself to calm down. There was a good chance that someone she didn't know would answer, because there was no chance that the entire Vega family was not at the hospital with Leo.

The call connected. "El Coquí restaurant, home of the mayor's favorite jibarito sandwich. How can I help you?"

Sofi froze. Despite the waterlogged roughness that told her that the speaker had been crying recently, she recognized the voice. It was the voice she heard in her head commenting on the new sights and sounds Sofi experienced as she toured Paris. It was the voice of the person who was supposed to have been at Sofi's side making those same comments. The best friend who would've been there if she hadn't lied to Sofi and ruined both of their futures. Sofi hit the end button.

She flopped back onto her bed trying to figure out what to do now. She balled her fist and went to pound it on the mattress but instead hit something hard. She turned her head and saw her closed laptop next to her. Suddenly, she had another idea. She sat up, pulled her laptop onto her crossed legs, and immediately opened her email app. As soon as she typed an L, the address she was looking for popped up. She rolled her eyes like she always did when she clicked on Leo_da_Ladykiller90@yahoo.com.

She knew that he barely used the account anymore, but she hoped he'd still have it attached to his phone.

Their email history popped up on her screen, hundreds of emails between the two of them, some normal, some silly, some serious, and some sexy. Sofi ignored the final one from Leo that had been sent about two months ago. She didn't need to read it to know what it said. It was only one word. Coward.

She shushed the little voice in her head that said he was right. Instead she hit the button to compose a new email. She sat there wondering what to say. She wanted to tell him how terrified she felt and how much she wished she were there, but she knew that was the worst thing she could do. That would just start everything all over again. After starting and deleting multiple messages that revealed too much, she huffed and typed, I'm glad you're okay. Get better soon... And please take care of yourself. *She almost added "for me" but decided that was too much. Before she could second-guess herself again, she hit the send button and grimaced. That was not the best, but it was the only thing she could allow herself to say. To prevent herself from the temptation of writing again, she deleted their entire history, emptied her trash to make sure it was permanent, and blocked his email address. Then after reminding herself of her mission, Sofi went to her balcony to finish off her bottle of wine while the gorgeous sight, that only a few minutes ago had given her peace, blurred due to the tears streaming down her face.*

Back in the present, Sofi stared at her computer screen, but she wasn't processing anything she was looking at. She wasn't sure how long it had been since she'd mentally checked out, but she did know that this was happening more and more lately. She'd thought taking a year abroad to escape her drama and doing all the traveling she'd felt deprived of would cure her of this feeling, but if anything, things seemed worse. She told herself every morning that this would be the day she finally did it—quit her job. Just that morning, the day after Memorial Day, she tried to amp herself. Then she'd look at her sad bank account and remember that she needed to figure out her next step before she quit. Plus, her relationship with her dad was shaky enough. She didn't even want to imagine how bad it would be once she told him she wanted to leave the company—his company, her grandfather's company. It would blow everything up as if things weren't bad enough.

Everything seemed a little bit worse now. Even Leo's initial reaction to seeing her. Usually he couldn't hide how pleased he was to see her even when he claimed otherwise. This time it was as if he'd run into a vaguely familiar stranger. No it had been worse than that. The look of utter disregard on his face had made it seem like she was not only a stranger, but one he had no interest in getting to know.

Fucking Leo Vega, the eternal jackass and fuckboy extraordinaire.

He'd been a thorn in her side since the day they'd met and Sofi was often shocked that she'd never even attempted to junk-punch him. There had been plenty of times he'd deserved it. Like when they'd seen each other and he'd curled his lip as if disgusted to be in her presence. That had hurt. Badly. But not as badly as when he'd demanded to know what she'd done to his sister. As if Sofi would purposely hurt Kamilah like that. Even though she kind of had.

The door to her office swung open. She didn't need to look away from her screen to know who it was. There was only one person who entered her office without knocking.

"Why didn't you come see me as soon as you got back? I wanted an update on the Brimburg account right after your meeting."

Sofi randomly clicked on her mouse to make it seem like she had been hard at work. Then she lifted her gaze to her father as he strolled into the room.

Felix Rosario hardly looked his sixty-four years of age. With his smooth dark brown skin and close-cut but full, pitch-black 4C hair, there were hardly any clues that indicated his true age.

Add in the fact that he made it a point to take care of himself physically and he was frequently mistaken for someone two decades younger. Her father was a well-dressed and well-built man who still turned plenty of heads and he knew it. That was possibly one of the worst things about him. Third to his frequent delusions (number two) and his selfishness (number one).

He plopped down into the seat in front of her desk. "Dígame, mi reina. What happened? Are they signing with us?"

She tried her best not to cringe at his pet name for her. She hated when he called her that. She knew he wasn't purposefully being mocking, but it felt like it to her.

No one outside of her close family knew this, but Sofi had a speech impediment when she was little. It was so bad that even her mom struggled to understand her. When she started day care, the other kids made fun of her. Her mom immediately asked for help. Shortly after, Sofi began speech therapy, but she was still embarrassed by the way she spoke. Abuela Fina thought that beauty pageants would be a great way for Sofi to gain confidence and Mami agreed, so she entered her first one at age five. Sofi hated everything about it, but she was good. When she won her first pageant and told her dad about it. He was so proud of her and had started calling her "mi reina," because she was his little beauty queen. Sofi continued competing to make her parents proud, but her fear of making a mistake when speaking only grew. To this day, her past as a beauty queen only reminded her of her failures and never her accomplishments. Of course, her dad didn't know that, but he would've if he just took the time to get to know her at all.

Sofi shook herself mentally before she could go down that unproductive rabbit hole. No good would come of her enumerating all of the ways her father failed her. Instead she focused on the only thing they had in common: work. "They want more time before they make a decision."

That obviously wasn't what he wanted to hear. He gave her

a sharp look. Then he seemed to notice what she was wearing for the first time. He took in her hot pink blazer and white blouse before his eyes traveled down to her matching ankle trousers and nude heels through the glass top of her mostly empty desk. Then he looked back up at her natural 4A hair that she had left down and extra voluminous. "Is that a new suit?" he asked. She knew exactly what he wasn't saying. If she'd looked more conservative and professional, the clients would've signed with them.

"It is. I just figured that it's such a beautiful sunny day outside, why not celebrate the brightness."

He nodded as if in agreement, but she knew he wasn't. "You've been wearing a lot of new clothes lately."

Translation: What's with the new look?

"Yeah."

"You must've done a lot of shopping while you were overseas."

"I did."

"Esos europeos y su 'high fashion' tienen al medio mundo pareciendo payasos de circo." He shook his head.

"Are you telling me that I look like a circus clown?" she asked.

His eyes rounded and he put a hand on his chest. "Claro que no, mi reina. I just mean that a simple well-fitted suit in a neutral color is a classic for a reason. It looks good to everyone. The same thing with straight hair."

"Right," Sofi said. "Well, next time I'll look like a *Men in Black* agent with a sleek bun and hopefully that will distract them from the fact that we're trying to charge them fifteen percent more than our competitors."

He looked hurt. "There's no need for the attitude and we charge them more because we get better results."

She got better results, because *she* busted her ass to make it so and was on her team to do the same. She didn't tell him that though, because all that would do was start him in on how he was the reason she knew how to do a good job. As if it was solely his "mentorship" that had taught her how to do her job and not her own ambition. There was nothing her dad loved more than pretending like he had more to do with her life than he actually had. He'd frequently bring up the few visits they'd had when she was a kid, but make it seem like they were constant. Sofi didn't know if he really believed they spent more time together than they had or was just a very good actor. It hardly mattered, because as far as he was concerned the fact that he'd moved to Chicago and offered her a job at the company made up for everything he'd failed to do when she was a kid.

"Did you find out what happened with the company apartment I was supposed to get?"

She waited for him to admit that he'd forgotten to delegate the task to his secretary after their discussion (something she'd already investigated and confirmed), which led to her apartment going to a new out-of-state transfer, but was unsurprised when he didn't. Her father barely ever acknowledged his mistakes.

"Yo no sé qué paso." He shrugged. "But you'll find something. Don't worry."

Translation: Fix this by yourself.

The whole point of her using a company apartment was that she wouldn't have had to pay rent. Sofi was trying to save money. She'd been a bit excessive with her spending in Europe and her savings were abysmal. She needed to refill the coffers as it were. Everything she'd looked at in the last week was way too expensive, too far away, or too busted. She needed to find something soon because her body hurt from sleeping on her mom's old-ass love seat. *The joys of being almost five-ten.*

"Is there anything else you needed?" she asked. "I have to get going. I'm late to visit my abuela and traffic is going to be a pain."

"You see her a lot. Almost every day."

Sofi nodded. "My mom has a lot of late shifts this month,

so I try to stop over in the evenings when I know Abuela Fina will want company."

"It's a shame you weren't able to visit the viejos like that. They would've loved to see you more."

Sofi wanted to remind him that his parents had spent most of their adult lives in NYC before moving back to the DR a few years before they passed. Both of which meant that it had been impossible for her to visit them the way she did Abuela Fina. Still, her mother had made a point to send Sofi to visit them for a week or so every summer because it had been important to her that Sofi have a relationship with his family even if she didn't have one with him.

Her dad probably wouldn't listen anyway. He had a way of making her feel guilty for the distance between his side of the family and herself even though he was the one who'd walked away from her and her mother in Puerto Rico in order to continue feeding his ambition. Instead she just said, "That would've been nice." It was true. She'd loved her grandparents dearly and they'd loved her. She hopped up from her chair. "But I really need to get going now. My abuela Fina is waiting for me for dinner."

"Sí, sí claro. We'll have a more in-depth conversation about the account tomorrow."

"Of course." Sofi grabbed her purse out of her coat closet and rushed toward the door. "See you tomorrow."

"Oh wait," he shouted after her. "I need you to take over my meeting with the Billings Corporation tomorrow morning. I'll send everything you need to know to your email so you can look it over tonight."

Sofi grit her teeth, but just nodded. She used to ask him why he'd throw these types of things on her at the last second, but when every answer she got was vague bullshit he used to cover up his desire to just not be there she stopped asking. She just accepted the sleepless nights and moved on.

As she made her way to her car and then to her mom's place, she couldn't help but think how different that whole conversation would've gone down if she'd been talking to her tío Manny. Her uncle Manuel was her mother's younger brother. He'd been a baseball prodigy on the island and had barely been eighteen before he'd gotten picked up by the NBL. That had caused the whole family to make the move to Florida, where they'd stayed until he'd gotten traded to the Cubs. He'd excelled there too until a stupid drunk driver had taken him and her abuelo Juan Manuel away from them. But he'd been so much more than a talented baseball player lost from the game at his peak. He'd been her father figure and her best friend. Sure, her biological father popped in and out of her life at his convenience to throw money and material goods at her, but Tío Manny had been the one to teach her how to ride a bike, check under her bed for monsters, and show her how to throw a punch after some boys at school called her an ugly monkey. He'd understood her like no one else in her life had.

If he were still around, her life would've been so different. That conversation with her dad never would've happened, because she never would've worked there. Tío Manny would've made sure of that. He'd always jokingly called her his mini manager and claimed that when she got older she was going to take over the world and he'd help her. God, she missed him.

She pulled up to her mom's building and found Abuela Fina already on the stoop waiting for her. She practically hopped down the stairs like a little kid. Sofi had to smile. She rolled down the passenger-side window. "You're supposed to wait for me to park and come get you," she called.

"If I wait for you to find parking around here—" she opened the car door and slipped in "—we'd never get to leave."

Wasn't that the truth.

Sofi leaned over and kissed her abuela on the cheek. Sofi couldn't help but notice the fresh coat of red lipstick on her abuela's artificially filled lips. If she wasn't mistaken, Abuela had also curled her short silver hair. "You look cute today," she said, leaning back to take in her striped blouse and wide-leg linen pants. "Although I don't think you need the heels. We're just going to El Coquí."

Abuela Fina shot her a look. "I always look cute and of course I need my heels. That would be like leaving the house without my jewelry."

Lord knew that leaving the house without jewelry on was basically like walking out naked.

She leaned over to take in Sofi's outfit. "You have heels on," she pointed out.

"Well, I'm coming from work and I'm not the one who fell and almost broke my hip not too long ago."

"¿Y eso que? That means I'm not supposed to dress up anymore?" She snorted. "Antes muerta que sencilla."

She was definitely Abuela Fina's granddaughter, because Sofi felt that in her soul. She too would rather be dead than basic. She was extra just like her grandmother. The curse of being former beauty queens she guessed.

"I'm excited to meet your friends," Abuela said.

Sofi frowned. "You've met Kamilah before. We visited you in Puerto Rico over spring break that one time."

"That was years ago and it's not the same."

"Why not?"

"Because you two were on your best behavior around me as if I didn't know what you were both up to at night."

Sofi cleared her throat. "I don't know what you mean." It was a lie obviously. She and Kamilah had snuck out almost every night to party with cute guys in the neighborhood.

Abuela Fina barked out a laugh. "Por favor. Yo soy vieja, no tonta."

"Well, either way, we are mature adults in our thirties now, so it's not like we are going to rage or anything. We're going to discuss her wedding to the most boring guy ever."

"And what about your guy? Will I finally get to meet the infamous Leo Vega?"

Sofi jerked, almost hitting the gas and shooting them into the intersection right as the light turned yellow. Luckily she was able to course correct and hit the brake instead. The stop wasn't the smoothest she'd ever done, but they didn't get whiplash, so that was good. She turned to her grandma. "What did you just say?"

"I said do I finally get to meet this boy toy of yours, Leo Vega? That's his name right?"

Sofi blinked at her in confusion before it clicked. "Mami," she growled. Of course, her mother had told Abuela Fina about her relationship with Leo. Mami told Abuela Fina everything just like Sofi told Mami everything. She sighed. "Number one, I don't know if he'll be there. Two, he's not *my* anything. He hasn't been for a long time now. Three, and this is the most important, no one over there knows anything about our history so keep anything you know to yourself."

Abuela huffed in offense. "I'm great at keeping secrets. I never told anyone that Juana, my friend growing up, had a sexual relationship with her own cousin while she was dating someone else and then had to get married quickly because she got pregnant but never really knew which one was the father."

Sofi rolled her eyes. "You told literally everyone, Abuela. You pretty much use it as an on-dit at parties."

Abuela Fina waved her off, unconcerned at betraying her once friend. "Well, she never should have told people that I got my boobs done after I had your tío Manny." She threw her hands up in outrage. "I mean what was I supposed to do, let them keep sagging to my belly button? I looked like I had two deflated balloons on my chest. I couldn't keep your abuelo interested in me with those things."

Sofi grimaced. "Abuela! TMI!"

"¿Que es eso?"

"Too much information. I don't need to know that you got a boob job to keep my grandpa interested in you."

Abuela Fina sucked her teeth. "Ay no seas tan puritana. We are both adults now and sex is just a part of life."

"Okay, but there are still boundaries we need to maintain."

Abuela grumbled, but didn't argue.

They pulled into a parking spot in the lot next to the garage doors of Kane Distillery and Sofi had an epiphany for the wedding reception. She couldn't wait to get in there and tell Kamilah.

4

LEO STEPPED OUT OF THE GYM, FRESHLY SHOWERED, AND IMMEDI-ately began to sweat all over again. The bright sun was blocked by the plethora of trees lining the side streets, but that hardly mattered. Fucking summer in the city.

Okay fine. He loved summer in Chicago. He was just in a pissy mood because his workout hadn't gone to plan. He'd tried to do some tire flips and just about started crying when he felt that first lightning strike hit his arm. He'd immediately stopped and moved on to working out his legs and core instead. But even then, his shoulder was bouncing between shooting pain and a pins and needles sensation. Now his arm muscles were cramping. He just wanted to go home and crawl in an ice bath, but unfortunately he'd told his mom that he'd pick Abuelo

Papo up from Casa del Sol. He'd also promised Kamilah that he'd perform at El Coquí. He prayed he wouldn't have to let her down, but his fingers weren't exactly cooperating with his brain at the moment. Hopefully, everything would calm down by the time he got there.

He made his way to Casa del Sol and parked so he could go in and pick up his grandpa. He walked into the lobby, waved at Teresa—one of the front desk attendants—and dapped fists with Yendriel, the young security guard.

"Qué lo qué," said the dark-skinned Dominican man with the perfect fade.

"Na', mi pana. Just coming to get my abuelo."

"He's still at dinner," Teresa said. She was one of Abuelo Papo's favorite staff members and he was frequently hanging out with her at the front desk, so if anyone knew it would be her.

Leo looked at his watch. Dinner? It was barely 5:30 p.m. "Why would he go to dinner if he knows I'm picking him up?"

"To give the staff a hard time," Teresa said. "He was really mad about breakfast this morning. He had a whole tirade about how giving them cereal was just lazy and if they were going to be lazy the least they could do was give them something other than Raisin Bran."

Leo shook his head. His abuelo was worse than the strictest food critic. "Oh damn. Let me go get him before he ends up kicked out of the cafeteria again."

Teresa smiled. "I don't blame you. He and Benny have been going at it all day, so I wouldn't be surprised if one of them ends up wearing dinner."

Sure enough when Leo walked into the cafeteria he found Abuelo and his sometimes nemesis Benicio León in each other's faces.

"You stole my bread roll!" Benny was yelling at Abuelo.

Abuelo Papo laughed. "Tú de verdad que si eres más loco

que una cabra." He gestured to his empty plate. "You can see that I don't have your stupid roll."

"You ate it already!"

"Now I know you're lying, because there is no way in hell I'd ever put one of those rocks in my mouth!"

"Abuelo," Leo said before things got too heated. "What are you doing? We have plans at El Coquí."

His abuelo turned to face him, a wide smile breaking out on his face. "Oh good. You're here. Let's go." He began making his way toward Leo.

"Wait a minute! What about my bread?" Benny yelled after him.

Abuelo Papo waved a hand in the air like he couldn't even be bothered to respond with words. He brushed past Leo as he exited the cafeteria.

Leo took one last look at an irate Benny before turning to follow. "What did you really do with his bread?" he asked Abuelo once they were out of earshot.

Abuelo looked at him, his light green eyes bright with mischief. "Me lo comí."

Leo had to laugh because of course Abuelo Papo ate it even though he made a huge stink about not having it. Leo had done the same thing to his siblings plenty of times. Everyone said that he and his grandfather were scarily alike and he guessed it was true. They were both musical, mischief-making smart-asses with the same light green eyes. Leo could only hope that when he was in his eighties he was running everyone around him ragged with his constant shenanigans. "You really are life goals, Abuelo."

Abuelo puffed out his chest. "I know." He blew a kiss at Teresa and waved to Yendriel as they exited the building.

During the short car ride to El Coquí they harmonized to Héctor Lavoe.

"I heard Sofi is back in town and she and Kamilah finally made up," Abuelo said conversationally.

"Yep." Leo did not want to talk about Sofi. He'd spent the last week doing his best to pretend like she was still overseas, to not even think about her. He couldn't believe that she'd just shown up out of nowhere like nothing had ever happened. And to reach out to Kamilah first, of all people. He knew exactly what that meant. She'd chosen his sister over him, again. Well, Leo was sick of waiting around for her to decide that he was worth giving a real chance to. She'd made it clear that she'd only ever wanted him for his body. Years ago that hadn't bothered him, he'd been willing to play along. Things were different now. He was about to be thirty-three years old and he was essentially back at the beginning of adulthood. He wasn't going to do the same shit he'd done in the past. He didn't have time for that. He had two goals: make the new Kane Distillery Tasting Room a success and pass the Chicago Fire Department physical exam so he could be back on platoon duty. Neither one of those things involved playing will they–won't they games with Sofi.

And yet the second he and Abuelo Papo walked through the door to El Coquí his eyes found her sitting at the island-shaped table by the kitchen doors. She had an old woman sitting on one side of her and Mami on the other while Kamilah and Liam sat snuggled up across from her.

"¡Mira quien es!" Abuelo Papo shouted in excitement. "Miss Humboldt Park, it's so good to see you. The neighborhood hasn't been the same without your beautiful face."

Sofi leaned in to give Abuelo a quick hug and kiss on the cheek. "Bendiciones, Don Papo."

"Don Papo ni que Don Papo," he huffed, giving her another hug and then holding her shoulders when she pulled back. "You've called me abuelo since you were seventeen years old. There's no reason to change that now."

Meanwhile Leo walked up to his mom and gave her a kiss on the cheek. "Bendiciones, Ma."

"Hola, guapo." His mom pulled him into a surprisingly strong hug. "Te quiero tanto, mi bebé," she said while peppering his face with kisses. She'd been doing this since the moment she'd seen him in the hospital. Leo let her because, well, it was nice to be loved on by his mother. Dudes who pretended otherwise were liars.

Kamilah pulled away from Liam but intertwined their fingers. "Hey," she said with semifake offense. "I'm the baby here. Not him."

Leo threw his good arm over Mami's shoulders. "Aww, princesita. Feeling jealous?"

His sister stuck her nose in the air. "Considering the only womanly love you get lately is from your mother? I think I'm good." She gave Liam's hand a squeeze.

Well, damn. She didn't have to put his business all out there like that. Especially not in front of Sofi.

Luckily Sofi didn't seem to be paying them any attention. Instead she was introducing the older woman to Abuelo. "This is my abuela," she told him.

"I thought she died a few years ago," Leo burst out. He remembered holding Sofi while she cried when she found out.

She barely looked at him. "Not that abuela, obviously. This is my mom's mom."

"Oh, this is Miss Puerto Rico," Leo surmised.

"Miss Puerto Rico?" Abuelo Papo's voice was high with excitement.

"Yes," Sofi told him. "My abuela Fina was Miss Puerto Rico in the '60s." At her side, Sofi's grandmother preened.

Abuelo Papo tugged on the front of his light blue guayabera and ran a hand over his short hair. "I knew Sofi's grandmother had to be beautiful, but I didn't know she'd be famous too," he told her in Spanish.

Sofi's abuela tittered and fluttered her lashes, the old flirt. "Oh, that was a long time ago." She held out a hand for Abuelo to take, but she held it palm down like a queen waiting for a subject to bow over. "I'm just Josefina Santana now."

Abuelo Papo grabbed her hand and bowed over it like a gentleman of old. "Mucho gusto. Soy Ricardo Vega, pero todos me dicen Papo."

Josefina tittered again. "I'm not calling a grown man Papo, but it's nice to meet you." She turned her body slightly to the side, popped out a hip, elongated her spine, and tilted her chin just so. She was a tiny little thing. Probably only a few inches over five feet, but she stood like she was a Titan. He'd seen Sofi do that same thing many times. Many may overlook the similarities between Afro-Latina Sofi and her white European–looking grandmother but those people hadn't spent as much time studying Sofi's face as Leo had. Sofi had the same high cheekbones, pointed chin, and perfectly arched brows as her grandmother. Not to mention the mile-long lashes and ever-present spark in their dark brown eyes.

"I'm Leo," he said. "It's nice to meet you, Doña Josefina." He leaned forward and gave her a peck on the cheek like he'd been taught to do.

She waved him off. "Digame Fina."

He wasn't sure why, but he felt like he was being tested. "I couldn't disrespect you by calling you anything other than Doña," he told her in Spanish.

He must've passed because she gave him a bright smile. "At home the young ones would call me Doña Fina."

"Ya veo porque te dicen 'Fina'," Papo murmured before dropping a quick peck on the hand he still held.

Leo let out a choked sound from behind him and Abuelo turned to give Leo a dirty look.

Leo had seen Abuelo Papo charm everyone he came in contact with, but he'd never ever seen him flirt. He'd especially never heard his grandfather call a woman "fine." He was equal parts scandalized and amused.

"I don't know why you're laughing," Sofi said. "His pickup lines are as cheesy as yours."

Both Leo and Abuelo Papo shot her matching looks of offense.

"The hell they are," Leo said at the same time Abuelo Papo denied flirting.

"Just because I give a beautiful woman a compliment it doesn't mean I'm trying to pick her up."

Abuela Fina gave Sofi a look. "No seas vulgar."

"I don't use pickup lines," Leo decreed. "I don't need them."

Sofi's abuela Fina examined Leo. "With that face and those eyes? I believe you."

"Except he inevitably ruins the illusion by opening his mouth," Sofi said.

"Now, Sofi. We both know that my voice only makes things better." He was referring to the voice he used when they were in bed—the one that never failed to rev her engine—but their grandparents didn't know that. It was enough that she knew. And she did, if the scowl she shot him was any indication.

His abuelo obviously thought Leo was talking about his singing voice, because he told Sofi's abuela, "He got that voice from me, you know. I used to be the best singer in Humboldt Park."

"No me digas," she purred. "So you're both singers?"

"I'm retired," Abuelo Papo said.

"But that doesn't stop him from singing all day long despite no one asking," Leo muttered.

Abuelo shrugged, completely unconcerned. "If you don't want me to sing when you play songs I know on the guitar, then you need to do it yourself."

"You play the guitar too?" Sofi's grandmother asked him.

"A little," he said.

Her eyes lit. "¿Y eres soltero?"

"Don't even start, Abuela," Sofi butt in.

Leo noticed Abuelo Papo perk up, but he was too busy watching Sofi giving her grandmother the stare down to pay much attention. He wondered what that was about.

"What?" Doña Fina said with forced breeziness. "A man who is tall, handsome, can sing, and play the guitar? There are worse husbands to have."

"Abuela, listen to me closely when I say that I would rather be buried alive in an underwater tomb."

"Ay que exagerada eres," Doña Fina told Sofi with a huff.

"Besides, Leo isn't the marrying kind," she told her abuela. "He's a guy you have a good time with for a very short time at best, and a fuckboy at worst."

Ouch. "Meanwhile, Sofi is a she-demon who will rip a guy's heart out of his chest with her bare hands and eat it if he's stupid enough to go anywhere near her."

"Thank you," Sofi said.

He could tell she was only being partially facetious. He rolled his eyes.

"What's a fuckboy?" Mami asked suddenly. He'd forgotten she was even there. "Is that like a Game Boy?"

"Go ahead, Leo. Tell Mami what a fuckboy is."

He looked at Kamilah, who was watching everything go down with her own amused yet scandalized look. Little sisters were the worst. There was no way he was getting into that right now, especially not with his mom.

"That means that he likes to sleep around, but doesn't take any of them seriously," Abuelo Papo pointed out helpfully.

Leo dropped his head into his hand. Who the fuck kept teaching his old-ass grandpa current slang? People in their eighties were not supposed to be that in the know.

"Ay, Leo," his mom said with enough disappointment to make Leo want to drop his head farther. "You need to stop playing games and find yourself the right woman to marry."

Leo had found her a long time ago, but she didn't want him.

He wasn't going to tell his mom that though, so instead he said, "But, Mami, how can I know which one is the right one unless I try a bunch out first?"

"Cochino." She smacked him on the arm. It was something she'd done more times than either one of them could remember, but none of those times had been after his injury. They'd definitely never been after he'd already overworked the shit out of that injured arm.

Leo sucked in a pained breath as what felt like a burning electric shock radiated from his neck to the tips of his fingers and back again. His other hand immediately came up to try to rub the pain away, but it only sent more burning through his nerves. "Fuck!" He bent forward, screwing his eyes up tight.

"Oh my God, Leo," his mom exclaimed.

He felt the very lightest brush of her hand and jerked away. "Don't touch me," he grit out through his clenched teeth.

"Ven. Let's give him a minute," Abuelo Papo said.

Leo didn't have to look up to know that he was shooing everyone away.

A hand landed on his good shoulder lightly. "There's a chair right behind you. Sit down." It was Liam's voice.

Leo plopped down into the seat. He was grateful that Liam was already familiar with how the pain made Leo's legs feel weak sometimes. It had happened plenty of times when Leo was helping him around the distillery, especially at the beginning. Leo did his best to take deep breaths. He tried to focus and breathe through the pain, which was already lessening, thank God.

A few seconds later he opened his eyes and raised his head, immediately locking eyes on Sofi, who had her hands clenched at her sides like she was doing her best not to reach for him.

The worst though was the look in her eyes. She looked at him with pity.

Leo tore his eyes from hers and looked for his mom. He

knew she felt terrible and indeed when he found her standing a few feet away it was clear.

She was staring at him with the most heartbreaking look of guilt and pain on her face. "I'm so sorry," she cried, tears streamed down her face.

He stood and reached his good hand out for her.

She lurched forward, her hand meeting his although she didn't come any closer.

He tugged her to his good side and dropped a kiss on her head when she buried her face in his chest. "It's okay, Mami."

"I'm a terrible mother," she sobbed in Spanish. "I can't believe I hurt you like that."

"No," he told her. "You're the best mother. That was my fault. I went to the gym and did too much. It was already hurting."

She tipped her head up and looked at him. Everyone wanted to talk about how much like Abuelo Papo he was, but Leo knew that he looked a bunch like his mom. They had the same shaped eyes, nose, and mouth. It was why he and Kamilah also looked tons alike whereas their older brother, Saint, looked like their dad and the twins were a mix of both parents. "Are you supposed to be going to the gym?" she asked, jumping right back into Mom mode. "Did you clear it with your physical therapist first?"

"Of course." Leo did his best not to look like the liar he was. The truth was that he had...to a point. What he hadn't discussed was how he would be training to retake the CFD physical exam. He knew his body wasn't ready yet and she was always telling him not to rush the process. But he knew himself better than she did and if he didn't push himself, he would end up depressed again. He'd done his best to accept the changes in his body and in his life. He'd tried to tell himself that he was happy behind his desk in the CFD office, making drinks for the bar, and making music, but the truth was that he wouldn't be happy again until he was back actively firefighting. Only, no one in his family knew that was his plan. He didn't want any of them to know until he'd passed the Physical Ability Test or PAT. He couldn't bear disappointing them again, so he told his mom the same thing he told himself in the mirror every morning. "It's okay, Mami. Everything is going to be okay." He shot a pleading look at Kamilah and she understood what he needed right away, because sometimes his sister was awesome.

"Mami, Sofi is going to have to leave soon I'm sure, so let's finish talking about the reception."

"Yes," Sofi agreed. "I have an early and full day tomorrow, so I can't stay much longer."

Leo jumped back in. "I'm sure you don't want to just sit there listening to wedding planning," he said to Doña Fina while giving his mom a gentle nudge in Kamilah's direction. "Have you seen the distillery yet?"

"I have not," she said.

"Great," Abuelo Papo said before Leo could. "Come with us. We'll show you." He held out his elbow and she slipped her hand through the crook. "Did you know that it belonged to my best friend, Killian?" he said to her as he began leading her to the doorway that connected the two businesses.

Leo followed and together they showed Doña Fina everything they'd done to the distillery.

"One of these days you will have to play the guitar for me," she told Leo. "I miss hearing it. My husband used to play, you know."

Leo hadn't known that. "Sofi never mentioned that."

"That was before she was born. When we were young, but then he got in a bad fight in his twenties. It ruined his hand. He couldn't play after that, but he did sing. Not very well, but well enough."

Leo winced. He understood that all too well. He'd struggled to regain his dexterity after his injury. He could finally get all his fingers to move when he wanted them to, but it wasn't a smooth or graceful movement. His stupid fucking ulnar nerve was basically still shit. His radial and median nerves were mostly okay, so they picked up some of the slack. However, his fingers had the tendency to tremble like a bowl of Jell-O if he did too much.

Abuelo chimed in. "We'll sing for you. We sing together all the time."

"Really?" Doña Fina asked with a flutter of lashes. "That's so impressive."

Abuelo Papo looked ready to fall to his knees and Leo bit back a grin.

Sofi's grandma was a flirt just like her granddaughter. But where Doña Fina's flirting was all old-timey coquette, Sofi's was daring and in your face. Doña Fina coaxed attention. Sofi demanded it.

"Do you know any boleros?" she asked.

Leo smiled. "Boleros were the first kind of music I ever sang. They were my abuela's favorite."

Abuelo nodded. "Especially Daniel Santos and Julio Jaramillo." The Puerto Rican singer and composer Daniel Santos had sung one of his abuela's favorite songs, "Lamento Borincano." While Julio Jaramillo, the prolific Ecuadorian singer, was well-known all over Latin America.

"Oh yes. Do one of their songs."

Leo already knew which of the songs he wanted to sing. It was actually from both the famed singers and it was one Leo had been singing a lot lately since it was about both loving and hating someone. Leo opened his mouth and began singing the first verse. He knew that Abuelo Papo would catch on by the time he got to the chorus. "Te odio y te quiero," they sang together in perfect harmony and then Leo enumerated all the reasons why he loved and hated her from the inferno in his chest to the way she was responsible for both his hours of bitterness and also the ones of honeyed sweetness.

Abuelo picked up the verse at the part where the other man sang about how he'd like to move on, but he can't. Abuelo's version of the chorus was a bit softer and more sad whereas Leo's was more forceful and angry. No surprise there.

They sang the chorus again then concluded with a bit of a flourish.

He looked up and found Doña Fina staring at him in a way he did not like. She was looking at him like he was the second half of a map she'd been missing.

"I'm going to help you win back my granddaughter," she told him in Spanish.

Leo almost fell out of his chair. "What?" He shot a panicked look in Abuelo's direction and found him staring at Leo with a delighted smile on his face.

"Don't lie on my account," Abuelo said. "I've known about it for a while."

What could he say to that? There was no way he could pull his normal bait and switch with them. He respected them too much. "How?" he asked. "How did you know?"

Abuelo shrugged. "Rosie told me all about the argument you two had and I put it together."

Ugh. Rosie, his six-year-old niece. "That little backstabber."

"Don't blame her. She didn't know what she was sharing. Besides, I bribed her."

Of course, he did. His bribe had probably been better than Leo's. You get what you paid for and he got five dollars' worth of silence. "I knew I should've bought her the video game instead of the coloring book," Leo muttered.

"I'm her favorite abuelo. She would've told me anyway."

"Back to *my* granddaughter," Doña Fina interrupted.

Since the jig was up, Leo decided to be honest. "We do have a past, but Sofi's been done with me for a year and seven months."

Doña Fina tilted her head. "What about you? Are you done with her?"

Leo rubbed a hand over his face. He beat back the immediate urge to lie and considered her question seriously. He would love to say yes, he was done with Sofi, but he knew that was more wishful thinking than truth. He honestly didn't think there was anything she could do that would make him truly done. Hell, she'd basically told him to fuck off and then disappeared for a year and a half and he still felt a pull to her. "I should be," he told Doña Fina with complete honesty. "I was shot last year."

"Dios mio."

"I could've died. There was a moment I thought I was going to."

"Ay bendito."

"It made me realize that I needed to grow up. I need to stop playing around and actually do something with my life."

"Claro," both old people said at the same time.

"But Sofi doesn't want that. She'd rather continue to play the same game we've been playing since we were kids." Leo shook his head. "I can't do that anymore. I'm sick of the making up and breaking up. I'm sick of the hiding and sneaking around."

Abuelo Papo nodded.

"But you want to be with her," Doña pressed. "Quieres un futuro con mi negrita."

Leo paused again, considering her declaration, because it had not been a question. She'd said it like she already knew the answer. If anyone had said those words to him a year ago, Leo would've denied it with everything in his body. He'd been just as into the game as Sofi had. He'd thought the back and forth was exciting and, as someone who dreaded boredom like others feared death, he'd chased that excitement. He'd been just as prone as Sofi to do something to cause a fight. He'd thought the constant fighting was just another demonstration of their passion.

Then he'd been shot and had faced death in a way he'd never had before. He'd realized that what they'd allowed themselves to have was not only toxic but a complete waste of both of their time. Leo refused to waste his time because he finally knew just how precious it was. He'd come out of that experience determined to make his life look exactly how he wanted it to be. He was ready to do whatever he had to do to make it happen, hence his dedication to training, helping his family however he could, and making himself the type of man he really wanted to be. *And where does Sofi fit into that? Are you willing to work just as hard for a real chance with her?*

As if he could read Leo's mind, Abuelo Papo jumped in. "The question isn't whether or not you want her." He waved a hand at Leo. "I think we all know that you do. The question is, what are you willing to do to get her?" Abuelo Papo said. "Because a woman like her will take a lot of work and even more sacrifice."

"But she's worth it," Leo told him, surprising himself with the decision he'd apparently come to. "Sofi is literally the most difficult person I've ever met in my entire life. Most days she makes me want to pull out my own hair. But I've never been able to envision a future without her and I'm sick of trying. I just want her to see our future too."

Doña Fina released a huge smile. One that made her look more like her granddaughter than ever. "I was hoping you'd say that." She shuffled forward in her chair. "If you let me, I can help you get what you want."

"Me too," Abuelo jumped in to say. "You already know that I'm good at it."

That was true. Abuelo Papo had proven that he was willing to lie, cheat, and manipulate in order to help his beloved grandkids win over their significant others. First, he and Killian had blackmailed Kamilah and Liam into faking a relationship that led to them finally realizing their feelings for each other. Now the two were as close as two people could be and making it official with a wedding. Then Abuelo Papo had skillfully maneuvered Saint, Leo's serious and stubborn oldest brother, into spending time with the equally determined Lola León by starting a prank war with her grandfather. He'd pushed them together in any way he could and eventually they both figured out how to bend enough to make their relationship work. Now they were happily making a life together with little Rosie, Saint's daughter. But could he do the same for Leo and Sofi?

Was there too much history between him and Sofi for either one of them to get over? Sure they'd never done anything truly terrible to each other, but there had been so many little hurts. *Death by a thousand cuts* people called it. Was there any way Leo could revive their relationship even with the help of the two people in front of him? Worse, was that even what Sofi wanted? Leo wanted to believe that deep down it was, but he wasn't positive especially not after she'd been away so long. If he'd changed in the last year because of his experiences, it only made sense that she had too. Maybe this new Sofi wanted him even less than the old Sofi. Was he willing to risk the little bit of peace he'd gained in order to find out?

It shocked him to realize that he was. He was willing to risk it all if it meant even the smallest possibility of gaining a future with Sofi. Leo had always been a gambling man and a bit of an adrenaline junkie, but nothing compared to the feeling he felt now. He was standing at the edge of a cliff with an old parachute on his back, ready to jump. He would jump no matter what. The only thing to see now was whether the parachute would open when he needed it to or if his luck would finally run out and he'd end up smashed on the rocks below.

Leo gulped. "Okay," he told his new teammates. "Let's do it."

5

SOFI COULDN'T STOP LOOKING AT LEO. SHE WASN'T THE ONLY ONE.
Just about everyone in the restaurant had been sneaking glances
at him since the scene he and his mom had made. She could
tell that he was getting annoyed with the attention, but he was
playing it off like he wasn't.

He and Papo Vega had virtually kidnapped Abuela Fina.
They'd taken her over to see Kane Distillery and returned a
short time later looking a bit too pleased with themselves. Now
they were sitting at the bar chatting with Liam's beer-brewing
friend whose name she'd forgotten, sipping something that
looked amazing while eating a plate of shrimp-stuffed tostones.

"He's cute, no?" Kamilah's mom, Valeria, asked her.

Sofi froze before shooting a panicked look at Liam, who

Kamilah had left in charge of decision making before heading back into the kitchen for a bit.

Thankfully, Liam wasn't paying them any attention. He actually looked to be playing a game on his phone.

"I think you should ask him out," Valeria continued.

Sofi felt like she was going to puke.

"Don't make that face," Valeria said. "He's exactly your type, tall, dark, handsome, and built. With both of your backgrounds and his eyes, imagine the cute babies you'd have."

Sofi frowned. "What?"

"And according to Kamilah, he used to play professional football, so you know he's good with his body." Valeria waggled her eyebrows at her in an expression that reminded Sofi too much of her son.

Sofi released a breath. "Oh, you're talking about Liam's friend?"

It was Valeria's turn to frown. "Claro. Who did you think I was talking about? Leo?" She laughed at her own joke.

Sofi tried to join, but it sounded weird even to her own ears. "Of course not. That would be crazy."

Valeria turned to Liam. "Mira yerno, does he have a girlfriend?"

Liam looked up from his phone, his face a mask of confusion. "Who?"

Valeria pointed to the man to show Liam who she was talking about.

"Roman?" Liam's confused frown deepened. "Why would I know that?"

"Isn't he your friend?" Valeria asked.

"Yes," Liam answered immediately but his tone still held his lack of understanding.

Valeria pushed. "You don't know if your friend has a girlfriend?"

Liam gave a one-shoulder shrug. "I don't know if any of my friends have girlfriends. We don't talk about that stuff."

"Y'all don't talk about it or you don't listen?" Sofi inquired even though she had a good guess already.

"Does it matter? Either way, I don't know if Rome is dating someone." He stood up and walked to the kitchen.

Sofi and Valeria watched him go.

Valeria was shaking her head. "Ay ese muchacho...tan raro." She looked back at Sofi. "How does he not know anything about his own friends?" She sounded so genuinely flabbergasted that Sofi had to bite her lip to keep from laughing. Much like her daughter, Valeria was one of those people who wanted to know everything about everyone. She could and would talk to anyone. Before she was done, she'd know their entire life story. "Come on," she said to Sofi. "Let's go join them and we can find out."

"Valeria," Sofi drew out. "I'm not looking to date right now. I just got back and I need to get everything together before I even think about guys." That comment was as much for herself as it was for Kamilah's mom.

That still didn't stop her from checking Leo out as they walked up to the little group. He was in a tan-, olive-, and rust-colored floral button-down T-shirt and pair of snug dark khaki shorts that showed off more thigh than necessary. His hair was styled in his usual tousled waves, but his scruff seemed more scruffy than normal. The most different however was the look in his eyes. Leo normally had an ever-present spark of mischief as if he were constantly ready for a wild adventure. Now he looked...not quite serious, but more mature. Like he was grounded or something. She didn't know how she felt about that. She'd always told him that he needed to grow up, but she'd never wanted something so horrible to be what caused it.

Suddenly he threw his head back in laughter and Sofi saw her Leo. Wait not *her* Leo, but old Leo, happy-go-lucky Leo.

"Roman," Valeria practically yelled, giving the man's name

a Spanish flair it didn't actually have. "I wanted to introduce you to Sofia."

Everyone in the little group turned around, including Roman.

"We met before," he said in a pleasantly deep and slightly raspy voice. "At Kamilah's birthday party. I was a vampire and she was a unicorn."

Sofi winced at the memory of the epic hangover she'd gotten that night. "Yeah, I don't actually remember much after the party bus, so I apologize for what had to be a bad first impression."

"It definitely wasn't good," Leo said loudly, causing her to startle.

She dropped Roman's gaze immediately as if she'd been caught doing something she shouldn't. Then she remembered that she was a single woman and could do whatever she wanted. She scowled at Leo. "I didn't ask you."

Leo gave her an annoying smirk. "I'm just trying to be helpful and coax your memories out. I remember everything about that night. I can share more if you want."

She one hundred percent did not want, because one of the only things that she recalled was raving jealously at Leo for his audacity in bringing his basic-ass date to a party she'd planned. It was not one of her finer moments.

"I don't believe that at all," Abuela Fina decreed. "Mi negrita es una dama perfecta."

Leo, who'd just taken a drink of water, spit it all over the place. He started coughing and laughing at the same time.

Sofi ignored the fact that she'd asked her abuela many times to not call her "mi negrita" in front of other people. It was a nickname she only allowed her mother and grandmother to use and she didn't want anyone else to even get the idea that calling Sofi their "little Black girl" was an acceptable possibility. She didn't want to have to put anyone in check. Except for

Leo. She loved checking his ass, so she glared at him. "Are you saying that I'm not a perfect lady?"

"Yes. That's one hundred percent what I'm saying."

"Leo," Valeria said in a stern tone.

But Leo didn't appear to listen. He stared at her in a way that made her heart pick up the pace. "There are a lot of words I'd use to describe you, but *perfect lady* doesn't make the top of the list."

Her thighs clenched. She knew exactly what words he'd use, because he'd said them all to her before. Moaned them in her ear really.

"She is too the perfect lady," Abuela Fina said. "She's been sleeping on the couch because she refuses to take the bedroom from me even though it's her bedroom."

Sofi really wished she hadn't said that, but she loved her abuela for defending her honor. "It was my bedroom when I was a kid. Now it's your room."

"Why are you on the couch?" Valeria asked. "What happened to your apartment?"

Sofi shifted her feet. "I'd sublet it for a few months because originally that's how long the job in France was going to be. When I ended up staying longer, I tried to hold on to it, but the owner was in the process of selling the building anyway. I had to give it up." She didn't want it to seem like she was irresponsible so she continued explaining herself. "I was supposed to get one of our company apartments when I got back, but there was a mix-up and it ended up going to someone else, so now I'm looking for a new place."

"Stay here with Leo," Papo said.

"What?" Sofi and Leo asked at the same time.

"The apartment above the restaurant is basically empty, except for him," Papo said.

"What?" Sofi asked again, because it just wouldn't compute.

"Santos and I moved out last year," Valeria said. "Eddie built us a place at his house, so the apartment was empty."

"Expect for those few months of Lola using it with the kids," Leo said. It was clear from his tone that he liked this Lola person.

Who the fuck is Lola? Sofi grit her teeth. There was no way she was living in the apartment that Leo had shared with some girl and her kids.

"But now it's just Leo and it's a five-bedroom apartment," Valeria said. "There's more than enough room."

"Let's not call it five bedrooms," Kamilah said as she walked up to them holding Liam's hand. "Some of those are glorified walk-in closets that you used to make us sleep in." She looked around. "What are we talking about?"

"We're talking about how Sofi should move in upstairs. She doesn't have a place and is sleeping on her mom's couch," Papo said.

"Sofi and Leo sharing an apartment?" Liam shook his head. "So we're actively trying to get Leo murdered now?"

Kamilah laughed. "I just got Sofi back. I don't want to lose her to prison."

"Excuse me," Leo said with very real offense. "I'm a fantastic roommate. I keep all common areas clean, I don't make tons of noise, I share whatever I buy, and I'm no drama. Ask Ricky."

"That's not what I remember," Kamilah said.

"Please," Leo scoffed. "You were the one who was always leaving your stuff all over the place, your dirty dishes in the sink, and your hair in the bathroom drain. Ya nasty."

"He's not lying," Valeria said.

"That was when we were kids," Kamilah argued. "We're adults now. Things change."

Leo and Valeria gave each other a look. "Yeah sure," Valeria said.

"Speaking of Ricky," Sofi interjected. "Why aren't you living with him anymore?" she asked Leo. He and his cousin had been roommates since their early twenties. Meaning that Ricky was one of the only people who knew about her and Leo's relationship.

"Ricky moved to Florida with Gio," Papo said, referring to his youngest son who was a well-known DJ and producer.

"What?" Sofi couldn't believe the amount of stuff she'd missed.

"Leo was staying with Saint for a bit after he got shot because he couldn't be alone and Ricky worked long hours," Valeria said. "So Ricky moved Elena into their place."

"Yeah," Kamilah nodded sadly. "But then he found out that Elena was cheating on him and since Gio was already moving for work, Ricky decided it was time for a fresh start."

"Leaving Elena with our nice-ass rent-controlled apartment. Hence me moving in upstairs," Leo concluded.

"I can't believe she cheated on Ricky," Sofi said. Ricky was, like, the nicest guy ever. He was basically a golden retriever in a human body—sweet, loyal, cute as hell, and just the right amount of playful. "I never liked her anyway." Sofi had been one of the only ones to see through the whole girl-next-door vibe which was why she wasn't surprised every time she caught the woman checking Leo out when she thought no one was watching. She'd definitely been a wolf in sheep's clothing.

"Yeah, well, that hardly means anything. You don't like anyone," Kamilah said. "You're worse than Liam, you just hide it better."

Sofi shrugged. "And nine times out of ten, they justify my dislike." People were the worst most of the time and Sofi wasn't dumb enough to pretend otherwise. "I call it having good instincts."

"Or enough trust issues to fill Lake Michigan," Leo grumbled over the lip of his glass.

Papo smacked him on the back of the head. "What is wrong

with you?" he asked. "That's no way to convince Sofi to move upstairs with you."

Shit. She'd thought she'd successfully distracted everyone from that idea. "I have no intention of letting myself be convinced of anything."

"I don't see why not," Abuela Fina said. "You complain every morning about being too tall for the couch and too old to be living with your mom. Plus you haven't been able to find a place that you like that you can afford anyway."

Dear lord, could her grandmother make her sound any more pathetic? Sofi wished the floor would open up and swallow her whole. The feeling only got worse when, in typical Kamilah fashion, her best friend went from zero to one hundred.

"Oh my God, Sofi! Why didn't you tell me you're struggling?" She reached over and grabbed Sofi's hands. "What can I do to help? Do you want to stay with me and Liam? We technically don't have a second room anymore because we turned it into Liam's office when Mandy and Leo started working with him and needed an office to work out of too, but at least our couch is bigger than your mom's love seat. And you have to let us pay you for planning the reception. There's no reason we can't. Right, Liam?" she asked without even looking at her fiancé.

At this point Sofi knew that she was blushing. She'd felt the heat rush to her cheeks and while she knew it wasn't as noticeable on her dark skin, especially under her layers of makeup, it was still visible to those who knew her well. Case in point, Leo was staring at her with a knowing look on his face. Since he'd been one of the only causes of her blushes for over a decade, he knew she was flushed. She shot him a warning glare. He'd better not mention her situation out loud or she'd be forced to throat-punch him.

His lip curled in the corner and her flush grew. Shit. He

was going to say something obnoxious. She just knew it. His lips opened and Sofi braced herself for more embarrassment.

"You should move in," he said, shocking her to her very core.

"What?" she choked out. He must've lost his damn mind.

He raised one shoulder in a shrug. "I'm barely ever there. If I'm not sitting behind a stupid desk at the CFD headquarters or practicing with the band, then I'm in the distillery with this box of cornflakes." He used his thumb to point at Liam—who simply rolled his eyes. "I basically just sleep and shower upstairs."

Valeria decided to jump in with her two cents. She grabbed Sofi's hand. "And with as much as you work, you'd never see each other. Plus, almost everything upstairs was updated by Luís and his crew last year. It's in better shape than anything you'll find around here and definitely cheaper."

Leo snorted. "Especially since no one around here will let me pay any rent, so I don't see why they'd let you."

"Claro que no," Valeria said. She squeezed Sofi's hand. "You're family and family doesn't pay rent."

Now Sofi must be losing her damn mind, because she was actually considering this insanity. Her and Leo just being in the same room together was a terrible idea, let alone cohabitating in an apartment. However, the idea of not having to pay rent was too tempting to refuse outright.

Abuela Fina wasn't exaggerating when she said that Sofi couldn't afford any of the apartments she liked. Her bank account had dwindled to virtually nothing after a year of living and traveling abroad. Even though she was now looking at potentially having to room with fucking Leo Vega, Sofi didn't regret any of her spending. She'd told herself that she was going to live her best life in Paris and she'd done that. Besides, it wasn't like she wouldn't be able to build up her savings again even if she did quit her job. She just needed some time to figure out her next steps and put them in motion. As soon as she did, she could move out. She wouldn't have a lease tying her to the place. "If I move in, it will be short-term," she heard herself say. At the smiles of everyone around her, especially the smug one on Leo's face, she felt the need to clarify. "Very very short-term. As in I will still be looking at other options."

"Sure. That makes sense," Papo said as if he still owned the building or had any say. "No one is going to hold you hostage. And it's not like we're expecting the two of you to get married or anything." He started laughing as if he'd just made the funniest joke in the world and soon enough Kamilah, Liam, Valeria, and even Liam's friend were laughing. The only two not busting a gut were Leo and Abuela Fina, but something about the looks on their faces made Sofi gulp.

She just knew this was going to bite her in her nonexistent ass, but she honestly didn't know what other options she had. "I'll think about it," she said even though she knew she'd soon find herself under the same roof as Leo.

6

LEO STILL COULDN'T BELIEVE THAT ABUELO PAPO AND DOÑA FINA'S spur-of-the-moment plan had worked. As of this morning, less than a week after the idea had come up, he was officially living with Sofi. Sure they were only roommates, but it was only a matter of time before those lines blurred as they always did when it came to him and Sofi. Of course, he'd help it along in any way he could. To that end, he knocked on her bedroom door. She'd taken the bedroom all the way across the apartment from his, claiming that it was the only other room with windows, but he knew it was because she wanted to be as far away from him as possible and she wanted to maintain some boundaries between them…good luck with that.

Sofi opened the door. She was wearing a pair of high-waisted biker shorts, a snug crop top that left a strip of her gorgeous brown skin exposed, and an oversized jean jacket. Her perfectly made-up face was looking up at him from under the brim of her black fitted baseball cap. God, she was beautiful. "What's up?"

Leo shook himself mentally and remembered his plan. "I was thinking that we should probably go grocery shopping. I haven't been in a bit and the kitchen is basically empty."

She arched a brow. "You know I don't cook."

"But you'll need some stuff like coffee, water, snacks, breakfasty-type things for before work..." He trailed off.

"Leo." Sofi sighed. "I don't know if that's a good idea."

"Sofi, it's literally just grocery shopping. Chill out." It one hundred percent was not simply grocery shopping, but she didn't need to know that.

"Fine," she huffed, all attitude. "But I'm on my way to my barre class right now." She brushed past him and closed her door behind her.

Leo shrugged like he didn't care. "How long is your class?"

"Fifty minutes." She headed past the living room to the entry way where she sat on the small bench to put on her shoes.

"That's cool. I have some stuff to do anyway, so I'll text you where I'm at and you can meet me there."

She stood up. "Okay." She grabbed her purse and keys off the little table. "I'll see you in a little bit, then."

"Yep," Leo said, wandering back toward the living room as if he had no cares in the world.

An hour and twenty minutes later, Leo stood in the middle of the cereal aisle hedged in by a plethora of colorful boxes. He looked down at his cart. There were already two boxes of cereal in it, one a boring adult cereal that advertised heart health and extra fiber and a super sugary kids cereal with tons of marsh-mallows. A guy needed options.

Why did I come over here again?

He knew something had sent him back to this aisle but he

couldn't remember what. He already knew from experience that trying to re-create the thought process that sparked whatever idea he'd had was futile. It would most likely only send him scrambling to another aisle and another only to end up still missing things. He should've made a damn grocery list, but Leo had never been a grocery list–type shopper. He bought exactly what he needed to make what he wanted that day and went about his merry way. ADHD brain for the win!

"Why are you just standing there looking like a little kid who can't find his mom?" a warm and slightly husky voice asked from behind him.

He didn't have to turn around to know who it was. Her voice was etched into his brain like engravings on stone. "Probably because I *am* lost," he responded as he turned to face Sofi.

"You're in the grocery store," she informed him with just enough snark to make it clear she was being a smart-ass.

He narrowed his eyes at her from under the brim of his Cubs snapback cap. "Cute."

Her lips quirked. "I see you got started without me."

"Well, I felt like a weirdo just standing at the front of the store waiting."

She looked in the cart. "Beer, wine, water, and cereal. Food for champions."

"Hey, I just started. Besides, I didn't want to get stuff without talking to you first."

"Like about whether or not we're just going to split the bill?"

He nodded. "That was always the easiest way to go about it with Ricky, unless there is something one person wants that the other person doesn't eat."

"I've never actually had a roommate, so I'll defer to you on that."

Leo had forgotten about that. She'd never even lived in the dorms in college, preferring to pay rent for a tiny studio apartment. The apartment she'd stayed in by herself until leaving for France. "Great, then let's get started."

"So is there like a list or something?" She paused and shook her head. "Wait. Nevermind. I forgot who I was talking to. We'll shop based on vibes. Good vibes only, right?"

"You get it," Leo said and smiled. Of course, she didn't get it. Sofi was one of the most type A people he'd ever met. She made lists like Leo made chaos. He was positive she already had a detailed mental checklist of what she wanted organized by department, aisle, and probably brand name. Meanwhile, he still couldn't remember why he'd circled back to the cereal aisle. However, he appreciated her being flexible despite how much the lack of structure was probably making her twitchy.

"So where to next?" she asked.

Leo thought about it. "Unless there is anything you want here, we should probably start at the produce section," he replied. He was sure there were things there that they'd need. He knew for a fact that Sofi liked eating tons of fruits and vegetables and always had smoothies in the morning.

Their short walk to the produce section was silent and not necessarily tense but it wasn't comfortable either. Leo felt like he did the first time he'd entered a burning building, he was nervous and excited for the adrenaline rush, but also terrified he'd mess up. Something about this moment told him that this was his last chance with Sofi. If he took one wrong step he could crash through the burning floor and into the flames.

He searched his mind for something to say, some way to reach Sofi behind the flaming door she was locked behind. He looked around. They were already in the produce section, standing right next to the watermelons. "Hey," he told Sofi.

She looked at him.

He smirked. "What did the cantaloupe say to her date?"

Her eyebrow went up. "Are you really about to make a melon joke right now?"

"I was, but you ruined it with your joylessness."

"It's not joylessness. That was just..." She looked around and reached into a bin on the other side of the walkway. "Corny," she finished, holding up an ear of corn.

Leo snorted. "Mine was way better than that."

"You wish." She motioned to the corn, silently asking him if he wanted some.

He was cutting back on starchy stuff to get in shape for the exam, but Sofi was playing with him again. He wasn't going to let some stupid diet ruin it, so he just nodded. "Grab two of them."

They moved on and Leo examined the produce in front of him for another idea. He found it. He held up his prize. "Hey, girl," he said in an over-the-top sexy voice. "What's it gonna take for you to turnip at my place?"

Sofi scrunched her adorable nose but she looked around. She reached behind him. "I don't find that a-peel-ing." She held a bunch of bananas.

"What?" he said, faking offense. "That's bananas." He took them from her and put them in the cart.

She shook her head. "You're such a dork," she told him, but she was grinning.

"And you must be an onion, because looking at you makes me wanna cry from happiness."

She actually chuckled at that.

Leo smiled. Then he saw the perfect vegetable. He'd just reached his hand out when Sofi stopped him.

"Nope," she said, swatting his hand away. "Eggplant jokes are too easy. Do better."

"Fine," he huffed and walked on. He picked up a carton of strawberries from the end cap. "But that was berry rude."

Sofi reached into the refrigerator and pulled out a bag. "Bitch, peas," she said, tossing the sugar snap peas into the cart.

Leo laughed. "Nice," he said. He took another look around.

He zeroed in on the shelves at the end of the section, which were full of different kinds of seeds and nuts.

Sofi followed his gaze to the same area and then gave him a "don't you dare" look.

Oh. Of course, he dared. He pushed his cart over to it and casually began looking. "Lola made this salad the other day that had roasted pumpkin seeds in it. It was bomb as fuck." He pretended to look at the different pepitas options.

"Who is Lola?" Sofi asked, there was an edge to her voice that Leo was all too familiar with. It was the same tone she used when she saw him out with another woman and he was thrown for a second, until he remembered that Sofi had already distanced herself from them when Lola came back to Humboldt Park. Leo held back a pleased smile at her jealousy. "Lola is Saint's girlfriend. She works at El Vecindario. Actually, she's the director of the new El Hogar that they built together."

"Oh."

Before Sofi could start overthinking her reaction and shut down on him, he grabbed a bag of walnuts and tossed them to her. "Here, hold my nuts."

She caught them on reflex but the look she gave him was unamused. "That was unoriginal." She dropped them in the cart.

"The classics are the classics for a reason," he said.

She rolled her eyes. "Are you done?"

"With the produce puns? Yes, for now. But I know how much you love salads so lettuce grab more veggies." She shot him a look and he grinned. "Okay, now I'm done."

He followed Sofi while she grabbed tomatoes, cucumbers, and baby spinach. She'd just reached for a bag of prewashed kale when she spoke again. "So you moved into your parents' old place after living with Saint?" Sofi asked.

"Yeah. He wanted to convert his basement into a garden level terrace for me, but I was ready for my own space by then."

"What do you mean?"

"You know Saint. He wants to take care of everyone."

Sofi nodded. "It's like his superpower."

"He's a real pain in the ass about it though," Leo grumbled. "Don't get me wrong. I love my brother and I'm grateful for everything he's done. My whole family has done so much, but—" He cut himself off, unsure of how to continue.

"You feel smothered by it."

"Yes," Leo agreed with feeling. "I can't do anything without one of them trying to jump in to do it for me or reminding me to take it easy. But what am I supposed to do? Tell them to leave me alone like an ungrateful shit?"

"That must be really frustrating," Sofi said.

It really was. But Leo didn't want to talk about that anymore. He wanted to continue making Sofi laugh. They were now in the meat area so Leo pointed to the cooler next to him and said in the cheesiest pickup line voice he could muster, "Are you a roast? Because that rump is well-done."

Sofi stopped walking, so he did too.

He turned and she was covering her face with her hands and shaking her head. Her shoulders shook as she laughed. "I cannot with you," she said between chuckles.

Leo beamed. "You liked that one, huh?"

She dropped her hands and shrugged. "I mean, it's an obvious lie—" she turned to the side as if to demonstrate "—but I appreciate the wordplay."

He was probably one of very few people who knew about Sofi's body issues. She frequently disparaged her lack of curves and claimed to be shaped like a boy, but that wasn't true at all. Did she have the pronounced and voluptuous curves of a Kardashian sister in the 2010s? No. But no one would ever call her figure "boyish." She was sleek and compact like an expensive sports car.

Had Sofi been anything other than Black and Latina, she'd have appreciated the fact. However, both cultures tended to take Sir Mix-a-Lot a little too seriously when he said, "little in the middle but she got much back." According to many in the communities, the perfect woman needed to have a pronounced hourglass figure with a bubble butt and a flat tummy. Leo didn't see it that way. He'd dated women of every shape, size, and color, because ultimately the outside of a person didn't really matter. Not to say that he didn't harbor an unhealthy obsession with Sofi's outside too, but it was who she was as a person that kept him coming back. "I see you're still delusional," he told her. "That rump is grade A, top choice meat." He gave his eyebrows an over-the-top waggle.

She rolled her eyes. "Come on, douchey guy from *The Wedding Singer*." But her small smile took all the sting out of her words. She grabbed onto the side of the cart and started pulling it.

Leo practically pranced behind her like a puppy. "I've been doing high protein, lower fat meals, so I've been eating a lot of white fish, shrimp, and lean white meats. Does that work for you?"

"Yeah. Red meat tends to make me feel sluggish anyway."

Leo stocked up and they continued down the refrigerated section, picking up breakfast turkey sausage and regular thick-cut bacon because they both agreed that it was the only acceptable way to eat bacon.

They reached the dairy section and, after grabbing staples, like three kinds of butter, Leo went directly to the cheese. He grabbed a package of the slices and held it up to Sofi. "Would it be too cheesy for me to say that you make me melt?"

She snorted. "Definitely."

He looked at the shelves behind her where a bright cluster of Activia showed over her shoulder. "Well, you must be yogurt, girl, because I just want to spoon you." He walked a few feet over and picked up a tub of plain Greek yogurt.

When he turned back Sofi had a gallon of whole milk in her

hand. "I know they say milk does the body good, but, damn baby, how much do you drink?"

Leo laughed loudly. "Yes!" he crowed. "That was amazing." He grabbed the gallon from her and swapped it out for 2%; at her nod he put it in the cart.

Sofi did a small curtsy. "You're welcome." She looked around and snagged a carton of unsweetened oat milk. "So now where?"

"To the freezer section," Leo exclaimed, one finger in the air.

Sofi shook her head and led the way, a small smile curled in the corner of her generous mouth. They made their way through the rest of the store, walking up and down each aisle, and grabbing things like coffee, rice, beans, condiments, and even some sweets.

He couldn't help but notice that as they neared the end of their excursion, they both began to move slower. They were almost at a crawl. He wasn't surprised. They always enjoyed each other's company when it was just the two of them. He didn't want their camaraderie to end. Not yet. He knew that it was only a matter of time before they started bickering about something, especially once they got back to the apartment and it really sunk in for Sofi that she was living with him.

"They actually have a pretty good salad bar and deli here. Everything is fresh." He used to grab a quick lunch there when he was on duty and didn't want whatever the cook for the day prepared. Just thinking about being on duty caused a pang in his chest. He missed it. He missed his crew at the station. Especially the guys on truck with him. But he would be with them again soon if he had any say about it. "Do you want to pick something up?"

She bit her lip. "Yeah, sure."

They walked over to the deli section where workers created salads, sandwiches, and smoothies to order. Sofi had them prepare her a huge salad that had more fruit on it than veggies. Leo was not one for fruit on a salad. He ordered a chicken pesto sandwich with mozzarella and tomato along with a small Caesar salad. As they waited for their order Leo pointed to the small refrigerated enclosure. "Their sushi is really good here too."

Sofi shook her head. "I'm scared to get sushi from a grocery store. I feel like there's more chance for something to make me sick. My mom told me a story about a patient who got worms from grocery store sushi."

Leo grimaced. "Gross."

"I know."

"Well, their sushi people come in every morning and only make a small quantity for the day. They write the time and date on them. You should try one, at least."

"I'm good with the salad." Her voice was firm.

Immediately, Leo knew he'd pushed too much. Sofi did not like feeling pressured. It made her shut down. "Of course."

Suddenly the silence was weighted again. Leo scrambled for a way to bring back the lighthearted feeling from a moment ago. When his usual wit was nowhere to be found he began to panic. This was the first time they'd actually enjoyed each other's presence in over a year. He didn't want that to end. He was so in his head that he didn't even notice Sofi move closer until she was right against him.

"Hey, baby," she said in her breathy bedroom voice. "Are you sushi? Because I like it raw."

Leo knew he was supposed to laugh. She was trying to do the same thing he was, lighten the mood. But that voice of hers talking about liking it raw brought back too many memories. Skin-on-skin, toe-curling, life-changing memories. His body reacted accordingly. "That was just mean," he murmured to her.

"What?" she asked innocently. She batted her eyelashes and everything.

"You already know."

"I have no idea what you're talking about."

"You know what your voice does to me. Don't act like you don't."

Her lip curled the tiniest bit at the corner.

Devious woman.

Their names were called and they stepped back from each other. Right. They were standing in the middle of the grocery store.

Sofi hustled forward to grab their food and scooped two large waters out of a cooler. He followed her to the checkout line where they both unloaded their spoils onto the conveyor belt. "I'll send you some money after we get the total if that's cool," she said.

"Not a problem."

After he paid and they walked toward the exit, Sofi suddenly stopped, shifting from foot to foot, her water and salad in hand. "There's a little park across the street. Do you want to eat th—"

"Yes," Leo said before she'd even finished her sentence. *Dude, play it cool. You look way too eager.*

"What about the groceries? Will they spoil?"

Leo didn't give a fuck about the groceries. He'd leave the damn cart there if it wouldn't make him look like a psycho. "I'm in the parking structure, so they should be good for a little bit."

She looked unconvinced but she nodded. "Okay."

They unloaded the cart into his car and then walked out onto the street.

It was a bright and balmy summer day and Sofi tipped her face up to the sky.

"Is it good to be home?" Leo asked.

"I love Chicago. Being gone made me realize that this is my forever home," Sofi said as they crossed the street. "But it would be a lie to say that I don't miss traveling. I want to see a whole lot more of the world in the future."

Leo had never been out of the US, so he didn't know what

it was like firsthand. Plus, he hated flying with a passion. He hadn't been on a real vacation in years because of it.

"I think my next vacation will be in Asia," Sofi said, "I've always wanted to go to the place in Bali with all the monkeys and the elephant sanctuary in Thailand."

Leo loved seeing her so animated. Her eyes lit from the inside with excitement. "Tell me about your travels," he said as they took a seat at an empty bench. "What was it like finally getting to see the places you've been dying to see."

Sofi smiled. "It was amazing." She paused. "I mean the racism is real in Europe, don't get me wrong. People would stare at me like I was a street performer and I'm sure they were talking all kinds of shit about the Black girl in their midst, but I wasn't going to let that prevent me from having a good time. Although I did have to check a few people for trying to touch my hair when I wore it curly."

He never understood why people did that. Like, why would they think it was okay to just touch someone without asking, especially someone you didn't know well? He couldn't count the number of times random people thought it was totally cool to touch his arm when he'd still had it in a sling. Sure, they'd reach out like they wanted to rub it in comfort, but WTF. It was weird. "What was your favorite?" Leo asked. "France?"

"Actually, I loved Iceland. It was freaking gorgeous and the people there were very nice and chill. Of course, the food in Italy made me want to weep with joy. I did actually weep with joy when I finally saw the Eiffel Tower."

She continued talking about things she'd seen and people she'd met.

Leo couldn't help but smile. Ever since they'd met, Sofi had talked about traveling the world. Listening to her recount watching the changing of the guard in front of Buckingham Palace and swimming in the crystal clear waters off the coast of a Greek island, reminded him of the girl she'd been—full of hope and possibility.

"I'm so glad you were able to experience all of that," he said. "You deserve to see everything you want to see and go everywhere you want to go."

She just looked at him and smiled. Then she sobered. "I was already gone when you got shot," she told him.

"I figured you were away," he said. "Don't worry about it."

"No, I am worried about it because the other day you brought it up."

"I was just talking out of my ass," he tried to say, but Sofi had always seen through him.

She reached over and laid a hand on his arm. "I had already been in Paris for weeks, but I still should've done more than send you an email. I owed you that much."

Leo shook his head. "You don't owe me anything. You never have."

"I did and I do. You're important to me, Leo. Even when we're fighting. You're not nothing."

Leo closed his eyes and turned his face away before she could see the moisture build up. It had hurt when she'd sent him a damn email then blocked his ability to reply. Even now he hated that it took him getting shot for her to say that he was important to her. He wanted to be happy that he'd finally heard the words aloud, but it reminded him too much of how much everything had changed. She was different and so was he.

He cleared his throat. "Well, what's done is done. Let's not talk about that anymore."

Any other time, Sofi would push. He knew she would, so when she simply said, "Okay," he took it as more proof of change.

"Can I ask you something?" he asked after a moment of silence.

Sofi tensed. "I guess."

"What made you decide to make up with Kamilah? You were dead set against it when you left."

"Honestly, when I left I still felt super salty about everything. I was resentful, especially because she and Liam were back together living their best life like they hadn't completely blown up the foundation of everyone else's life. Meanwhile I was stuck hating my job and unsure of who I was. As time went on, I told myself to get over it, resentment wasn't a good look for me, and I needed to focus on living my own best life instead. I did and I found all of the anger melting away. Then I realized that I was at fault too. Neither one of us trusted the other like we should."

Leo knew better than most how important trust was to Sofi. She didn't trust a lot of people. He could probably count them on one hand. When she did offer it, it was a gift. His sister had basically thrown that gift in her face. He got it now. "And what about me?" he asked. "Did your sabbatical change the way you feel about me?"

"Leo." She sighed. "Can we not? This whole roommate thing is weird enough without bringing up our past and I don't want to fight with you right now. We have to get through Kamilah's wedding."

It wasn't what he wanted to hear, but she hadn't told him to fuck off, so that was good enough for him for now. He didn't say anything else. He just sat there enjoying the weather, her company, and the sweet hope of possibility.

7

SOFI HADN'T EVEN BEEN LIVING WITH LEO FOR A WEEK AND ALREADY she was losing her mind. She placed all of it solely on the head of her new roomie. She'd expected to barely see him since he'd claimed he'd be working at the CFD headquarters most days or in the distillery with Liam. On top of that, he'd had band practice with Los Rumberos every day to prepare for their set at the upcoming Puerto Rican festival. However, it felt like every time she turned around, there he was. And he was incapable of wearing a shirt. She knew the apartment didn't have central air-conditioning, but he didn't have to walk around half-naked all the damn time. She'd almost taken to hiding in her room, but fuck that. She wasn't a kid in a time-out, she was a grown-ass woman who was completely capable of keeping her eyes, hands, and other body parts to herself. If only he'd stop with the guitar playing.

She could hear him strumming in his room from her current spot at the dining room table, or as Kamilah had taken to calling it *Wedding Central*. She had her laptop, a notebook, and tons of wedding magazines in front of her. The first thing she'd learned upon getting in touch with the planner at the old reception hall was that Kamilah had been taken advantage of. The venue had added their own fees on top of those charged by the vendors they partnered with, and the quality was trash. After negotiating a full refund plus a little something extra for the last-minute inconvenience, Sofi had ditched all of their old vendors for her own. Now she felt like, at the very least, she'd gotten her friend a better deal than she'd had before. It was enough to get rid of a tiny bit of her nerves. Sure she was still having anxiety-influenced nightmares about everything going wrong, but that was a personal problem.

She heard the door to Leo's room open and a few seconds later he stepped out of the hallway, sans shirt and guitar in hand. "Oh hey," he said upon seeing her at the table. "I didn't know you were here."

"Yeah, I'm just trying to get some planning done."

"Do you mind if I sit out here and practice for a bit? My amp and mic are out here."

"Sure," Sofi said even though the last thing she needed was to be serenaded by Leo whether he knew he was doing it or not.

"Are you sure?" he asked. "Because you sound irritated."

"No, I'm fine."

"Uh-oh. Every man in the world knows that *fine* means not fine."

"Leo, just sing your songs," she told him.

He smiled. "As you wish."

Oh hell no. Now he was using *The Princess Bride* on her? He was conniving.

Things only got worse when he began to play the guitar and she immediately recognized the song he was about to sing. *Oh, that underhanded motherfucker.*

He knew how much she loved DLG. In their on-again phases, she was constantly telling him that he had a soulful voice like Huey Dunbar's. This specific song had him singing to her about a man who still wants a woman despite her saying that she doesn't want him.

As soon as he began singing the chorus Sofi had to squeeze her thighs together.

"'*Mas yo si me enamoré. Por eso no te olvide…*'" he crooned, his voice drenched in warmth, sweetness, and passion, all while maintaining eye contact with her.

Evil. Evil. Diabolical man.

He had no right to sing like that. Sofi soon fell into what basically amounted to a horny trance, as was usual whenever she listened to Leo sing. She felt hot and tingly in all of the naughty spots and couldn't focus on anything but how good listening to him made her feel. So good that it took her a long while to realize that his guitar playing was off. It was still really good by anyone's standards, but his normal smooth and embellished style was currently a bit jerky and stilted. She wasn't a musician at all, but she could tell that he was slightly off tempo and missing notes. She looked at his long fingers which usually played along the strings like a graceful kid jumping from stone to stone across a creek. Now they moved more like a toddler wearing their parent's shoes.

She looked at his face and noticed his skin was pale and covered in a thin layer of sweat. His brow was furrowed and there were lines of tension around his eyes. Usually, he looked lost in the music as if he were channeling it from some other dimension. Right now, he looked like he was fighting with it, dragging it through kicking and screaming instead of simply letting it flow.

The song ended and Leo lowered his head. He was flexing his fingers and breathing in and out a bit too quickly.

He's in pain, Sofi thought. She hated seeing him like that. "Leo," she murmured.

He shot out of his seat, practically tossing his precious guitar onto the couch next to him. "I have to use the restroom," he said and stalked down the hall.

Sofi stood and followed. "Leo," she said again, but he didn't stop. "Corazón."

At the sound of her nickname for him, he spun on his heel. "Don't." He pointed a finger at her. "Don't you dare pity me," he barked.

"I just want to make sure you're okay."

"Are you serious right now? I was shot. I almost died. I lost my dream job. I spent the last year putzing around doing a bunch of bullshit. Meanwhile, my dominant arm won't do what I want it to do when I want it to. I can't even assure my only sister that I'll be able to sing and play for her first dance like I promised her I would when we were kids." He shook his head. "My body was the only part of myself that I could count on and now I don't even have that, so no, Sofi. I'm not fucking okay." His chest rose and fell with each huffing breath. His fists were clenched at his sides as if he were preparing for a fight.

Sofi knew that he wasn't mad at her. He was mad at the situation and at himself for being upset. Since she'd first met Leo, it had been clear to her that the surplus of ideas and imagination Kamilah possessed, he contained equally in the form of positivity and humor. Leo didn't do deep thinking or philosophical conversations. He was witty, irreverent, and more than a bit impulsive. He just wanted everyone to enjoy life to the fullest and was prepared to act a clown to help them along. He was the perpetual good-time guy and a performer down to his marrow. Leo didn't struggle with existential crises, he just kept letting the good times roll. It was what caused Sofi to call him an immature man-child many times throughout the years.

To see him like this now, struggling with his place in his own life, caused her pain almost as sharp as what he had to be feeling. She didn't like seeing Leo doubting himself or his capabilities. It pained her to know that he felt like he couldn't trust himself. Sure, he was a bit forgetful about certain things. Sure, he tended to focus on the wrong things at the wrong time and had issues with impulse control. But Leo was far from untrustworthy. Leo was very loyal and honest. He didn't have the ability or patience to pretend to be anyone other than himself. It was one of the things she liked most about him even when he pissed her off. Leo was Leo in any situation and the Leo she knew was more than trustworthy.

She decided to honor his honesty with some of her own. "I'm terrified of public speaking."

"What?"

She nodded. "Whenever I have a presentation I have to prepare it well in advance because I have to memorize everything I'm going to say. I practice it over and over in the shower, the car, before I go to bed…any time I'm by myself."

"Really?"

"Yeah. I had speech problems when I was little. Barely anyone could understand me, so I had speech therapy for years before we moved to Chicago. A part of me is always scared that they'll come back when I least expect it and I'll make a fool of myself. I guess that means that it's more me being terrified of looking foolish, but having to get up in front of people and talk makes me want to hurl. Every single time."

"Why are you telling me this?"

"Because I want you to know that I get it. I understand you wanting your brain and body to do something that they refuse to do. When I'm forced to speak in front of people, especially if I haven't had the time to prepare myself, I start to tremble from head to toe, my mouth gets dry, and the words I had in perfect order start to bounce around in my brain causing my tongue to get all tangled. It gets difficult to breathe and sometimes I'll even get dizzy. It's scary and it sucks."

"Yeah." He nodded, looking down at his feet. "It really does." He looked back up at her. Then he took a few steps toward her, bringing them face-to-face. He lifted a hand to cup her cheek and slowly leaned in to give her one soft kiss.

Sofi felt all of the same shaky, trembling, and dizzying feelings she felt when she was nervous, but instead of being cold and clammy, she was warm and almost cozy. She felt the same way she did when she stepped into her mom's overly warm apartment after a trek through a windy Chicago winter night. She wasn't exactly comfortable yet, but she knew she was safe and comfort would come soon. It was more than a little alarming that Leo kissing her felt like home.

Finally he leaned back. He stared into her eyes. "Thank you for telling me and I'm sorry I was an ass."

Sofi bit her lip, but her smile formed anyway. "Leo, if you're going to start apologizing for being an ass now, we'll be here forever."

He smiled and let out a chuckle. "Facts."

Both of their smiles fell as the vibe changed. Suddenly they were in each other's arms. Their lips crashed together. He wrapped his hand around the back of her neck and pressed her up against the wall, never once letting his lips separate from hers. The moment her back hit the wall, Sofi hopped up and wound her legs around his waist. He caught her with his uninjured arm. His other one dropped to her bare thigh then slid up and under the skirt of her dress to grab her ass. She bit his full bottom lip and he bit hers back before sucking it into his mouth. Sofi groaned. This was the kind of kiss Leo usually gave her, the kind Sofi had been fiending—deep, wet, and just the tiniest bit aggressive. It was decidedly not safe, but damn was it good.

A loud knock at the door brought Sofi back to herself. She dropped her legs and pushed Leo away.

"Bombón," he groaned, looking like he was going to snatch her back.

She held up a hand.

He stopped. The look on his face was part confusion, part lust.

"Someone's at the door," she said, turning to go open it. She adjusted her dress and wiped around her lips to make sure she didn't have gloss smeared all over her face. All the while she yelled at herself, *What the fuck are you doing, you idiot? You did not just spend a year across the ocean trying your best to forget this guy just to jump right back in the sack with him as soon as you get a chance.* Exactly. The last thing she wanted to do was fall back into the toxic fuck-and-fight relationship that they'd had for over a decade. She'd done too much work on herself for that. Nope. No way. She'd told him before she left that she was done and she'd meant it.

She took a deep breath and then opened the door.

Kamilah stood on the other side in a black chef jacket and matching pants. Her hair was back in a tight bun and although she had on zero makeup she looked more like a model pretending to be a chef than an actual chef. "Hey, girl."

"What's up?" Sofi asked, stepping back to let her in.

Kamilah stayed in the hallway. "Come down. I have a surprise for you."

"For me?"

"Yes. Who else would I be talking to?"

Sofi turned to look in the direction of Leo's room, but he was nowhere in sight. "Uh. Do I need to change first?" She still had on her dress from work—a sleek satin wrap dress in a vibrant burgundy, beige, brown, and fuchsia floral print with pops of green and purple.

Kamilah checked out her outfit. "Well, you need shoes, but

other than that you look great. Unless you want to wear something more casual. You know we aren't fancy around these parts."

"This is fine," Sofi said, reaching down to grab her nude—for her skin tone—ankle strap and heeled sandals. She slipped them on.

"Is Leo home?" Kamilah asked.

"I think so," Sofi said, even though she knew very well that he was. "Maybe he's in his room?" She grabbed her keys off the table and stepped into the hall.

"You haven't smothered him in his sleep yet?" Kamilah asked.

"No, disposing of a body is too much work." Sofi followed Kamilah down the stairs. "Especially when there are always people around."

Kamilah chuckled, but sobered quickly enough. "But seriously, how has it been so far? I know this isn't what you want, but I hope it's not too bad."

"It's been fine," Sofi assured her. "Besides the times I made him show me the new things in the distillery, I hardly see him and he's been on his best behavior. It's almost like he grew up or something."

They reached the door that led to the kitchen and Kamilah reached out to grab the handle. "He really has," she told Sofi. "Leo's always been a firm practitioner of the 'work hard, play hard' credo, but now he mostly just works hard. It's kind of worrisome actually."

They bypassed the staff and machinery in the kitchen. Sofi felt a bit awkward seeing that she didn't recognize anyone when she used to know everyone including a bunch of the customers. "We all have to grow up sometime," Sofi said. "He couldn't be Peter Pan forever."

"Ain't that the truth." Kamilah paused outside the swinging

doors. "I just wish he seemed happier about it." She put a hand on Sofi's back and pushed her through the doors.

The first thing Sofi registered was a mob of colors that eventually took the shape of Vega family members. The second thing was the yelling. There were shouts of "surprise," "sorpresa," "bienvenidos," and "welcome home" all at the same time.

Kamilah closed her eyes and shook her head. "I should've given them more specific instructions."

"This is perfect," Sofi exclaimed, her hands at her chest. She blinked rapidly, because there was no way she was going to let anyone see her cry. "Thank you."

"Sofi!"

"We missed you so much!"

In a second she was enveloped in two pairs of arms. Lucy and Eliza squeezed her with all their might. Kamilah's cousin and her wife were the other two members of Sofi and Kamilah's little crew, but Sofi had abandoned them when she'd made her break from the Vegas. She felt terrible about it now. They hadn't deserved to be left on read. "I'm sorry, y'all. I should've responded to you. Cutting you out of my life wasn't fair."

Lucy waved her off. "Please, do you think we don't wish we could take a break from the family by just disappearing for a year? These people are animals."

"Besides," Liza said, "you saved us a bunch of awkwardness. Can you imagine how annoying Kamilah would've been if you'd talked to us and not her?"

"Hey!" Kamilah said.

"You know it's true, but we love you anyway," Liza said, pulling Kamilah back into the hug.

Kamilah grimaced. "It is true. I would've driven them crazy." She hugged Liza. "And I love your rude ass too, Lizzo."

"Liza," Lucy immediately corrected. She hated Kamilah's nickname for her wife even if her resemblance to the famous singer made it fitting.

Sofi didn't know why Lucy hated it so much. If she had a wife that looked like Lizzo, Sofi would tell everyone. Both she and Kamilah had said that so many times that it was basically a running joke between them all. "It's good to be back," Sofi said.

"Okay, okay. Enough hogging the guest of honor."

Sofi turned to see Kamilah's dad, Santiago, standing there.

He held out his arms. "I want to give my other daughter a hug."

Sofi pulled herself away from her friends and practically dove into his arms. She knew that he had a tendency to be a bit too hard on his kids, especially Kamilah and Leo, but Sofi loved Santos Vega. He'd always made her feel welcome and went out of his way to talk to her. He'd ask her about school, her plans, and books that they'd both read. He'd given her advice and praise. She was positive that he'd done it because he'd known she didn't have a dad around most of the time, but that just made her like him all the more.

"It's good to have you back," he told her in Spanish. "You were very missed."

Valeria stepped up beside him and Santos let Sofi go so they could hug. "It's true," she said. "No one can wrangle Kamilah and Leo like you can."

"Hey, I've been very good lately," Kamilah said.

"That's true," Valeria agreed. "That medicine has really helped you."

Sofi shot Kamilah an alert look. "Medicine? What medicine?"

Kamilah's expression said, *Well...* "I'm sure this won't come as a huge shock, but I have ADHD."

"Really?" Sofi asked, although looking back she could see a lot of the signs.

"Thankfully my therapist suggested I get tested. It took a while and then it took even longer to find the right medication and dosage, but now I'm good." She paused. "Well, not good good, but way better."

"Good for you, going to therapy and getting your mind right," Sofi told her and she honestly meant it.

"Thanks, but that's enough of that for now. Everyone wants to say hi to you."

Sofi made her way through the group, saying hello and receiving welcome from the other members of the Vega family present.

"Tití Sofi!" a little voice cried. Sofi knew the voice well. They'd spent a lot of time together on account of Kamilah practically being Rosie's surrogate mother. She ran over and jumped.

Sofi caught her mid-leap. "Rosie, baby girl, you're so big!"

"I'm six now," Rosie told her proudly. "And I know how to read."

"Do you?" Sofi asked, repositioning Rosie on her hip. "That's great. Now I can buy you a bunch of books."

"Okay," Rosie readily agreed, but at the same time Saint said, "That's not necessary. She already has a library of them all over the house."

Saint stepped up to Sofi and gave her a kiss on the cheek. "I'm glad you're here," he said.

Sofi gave him a soft smile. "Thanks, Saint." Saint had always treated Sofi like another sister and she treated him like a beloved big brother. Sometimes she'd wished that he was the brother she fell for, but he didn't deserve a hot mess like her.

"I want you to meet Lola, my girlfriend." He gestured to the woman standing slightly behind him.

Lola was pretty with intense eyes that didn't match the sprinkling of freckles across her face. She had curves for days and the kind of fashion sense that reminded Sofi of New York City street style. She liked her immediately.

"Hey, it's nice to finally meet you. I've heard a lot about

you." Lola held out a hand and Sofi maneuvered Rosie to her other hip to grab it.

Sofi was embarrassed. "I'm sure it wasn't the best."

Lola shook her head. "Nah. It's always been clear the family loves you."

"Of course we love her," Papo said, coming forward to wrap his arms around Sofi and Rosie. "She's family. Verdad, mi Rosita?"

Rosie nodded vigorously. "Want to meet my new abuelo Benny?" She asked Sofi as she wiggled to get down.

Papo huffed and muttered under his breath while another old man, who she assumed was Benny, strode over with a smug smile.

Rosie grabbed Benny's hand and tugged him forward. "This is Tití Sofi," she told him. "She was mad at us for a long time, but now she loves us again."

There was a moment of awkward silence in which no one knew what to say.

"There you are, you little lazybones," Leo's voice suddenly called out. "Get over here and give me one of your special Rosie massages. You're overdue."

Rosie let out a world-weary sigh and rolled her eyes. Then she looked at Sofi. "Tío Leo always wants me to rub his shoulder. He says that it makes his arm feel better, but I think he just likes my bubble gum lotion."

"Or maybe you two just love each other so much that being with you really does make him feel better."

Rosie appeared to give that some thought. "Papi did tell me that love is like magic and that's how he and Lola made me a baby."

"What?" Benny exclaimed. He spun around and looked at Saint and Lola, who were watching everything with wide panicked eyes. "Is it true, Lolita? Are you pregnant?"

Saint stepped forward. "We definitely didn't plan to tell everyone like this, but yes, Lola's pregnant."

Cheers of "Wepa!" sounded and applause broke out. People rushed forward to congratulate the parents-to-be. Valeria sobbed in happiness uncontrollably. Santos pounded Saint on the back and kissed Lola on the cheek. Behind her, Sofi could hear Kamilah also blubbering into Liam's chest and saying how happy she was for Saint and Lola while Liam tried to calm her.

Once again Sofi was reminded of how much had changed since she'd been gone. She didn't know why it was so jarring to her. Obviously, life didn't pause in Chicago while she was in Europe. However, it was still a lot for her to wrap her head around. There were new family members in the Vega clan, Valeria and Santos no longer lived in the neighborhood, and everyone's personality had changed the slightest bit. It was enough to make her feel like she was trying to fit into a pair of jeans that used to be her favorite but now felt off—like the seams had been altered without her knowledge. It made her question if she still belonged. Oh great. Now she'd just given herself another thing to fret about and try to fix.

Suddenly, a body pushed up close behind hers.

"Quick," Lucy's voice said near her ear. "Hide me before my mom comes to ask me how Saint is having his second kid when I don't even have one and have been married for almost a decade."

Sofi laughed. "Haven't you told her that you and Liza aren't interested in being parents?"

"Many, many times," she responded. "But she seems to think that if she brings it up enough, we'll change our minds."

"My mom is the exact same way," Liza said, coming up to stand beside her wife. "They just don't understand that we are still a complete family even without children."

Kamilah strode up shaking her head, clearly having heard what they said. "It's real funny how quickly things go from 'you better not get pregnant, because I'm not raising any more babies' to 'give me some grandbabies before I'm too old to enjoy them.'"

"Facts," Sofi said while throwing up praise hands. "My mom told me that if I didn't want to find a man and get pregnant, I could always adopt and she'd help me raise the baby. As if a lack of man is the only reason I'm not popping out offspring."

"Mothers," they all said at the same time before bursting into laughter.

"Speaking of finding men," Liza said after they'd all settled down. She gave Sofi an expectant look, eyes wide and eyebrows up.

"What?" Sofi asked.

"Obviously we want you to tell us about the sexy French men you met while in Paris," Lucy nudged her with an elbow.

"Or sexy Greek men," Liza said.

"Or sexy Italian men," Kamilah added, which started a round of them throwing out nationalities.

"Or sexy Spanish men."

"Sexy Scottish men."

"Sexy Irish men," Kamilah said with a dreamy sigh, obviously thinking of her own sexy Irishman.

Sofi jumped in before they could go through all fifty European countries. "Y'all know that white European men are really not my jam."

"Okay, but there are plenty of brown-skinned immigrants and I bet their accents are to die for," Lucy pointed out.

That was true. "Well, I did go on a few dates with this gorgeous Nigerian guy who had a British accent à la Idris Elba. And there was also this fine-ass Palestinian Chilean guy at my job who liked to flirt with me in Arabic, French, English, and Spanish."

Excited squeals abound.

"Tell us everything," Kamilah demanded. So Sofi did.

8

WHEN HE'D FIRST COME DOWN, AFTER HAVING TO TAKE A COLD shower, Leo's chest had felt warm and tight. Nothing made him happier than seeing his family surround Sofi with love and acceptance. As they'd welcomed her back into the fold, Leo had kept a discreet eye on her. She'd clearly been overjoyed to be back with his family. He'd been able to tell by the huge smile she gave everyone and the way she tossed her head back to laugh boisterously.

As the night went on, his feeling of happiness had begun to turn into annoyance. He sat there, a few feet away, listening to her, Kamilah, Lucy, and Liza gossiping together like a bunch of old biddies over a laundry line. Every time they brought up a new guy Sofi either dated or flirted with Leo's jaw clenched.

How could she blissfully bring up dating and flirting with other guys right after they'd basically dry humped against the wall? He knew what she was doing. She was putting up walls again. She was trying to tell him that kissing him had been a mistake. She had the tendency to throw other men in his face when she wanted him to think she was over him, but it never quite worked out how she wanted because he knew her too well.

"Your sister and her friend just walked in," Carlos, the main trumpet player, told him.

Leo spun around with a side smile that quickly turned into a scowl when he saw the guy helping Sofi into her stool at the high-top table. Fucking Brandon was still sniffing around, it appeared. Leo couldn't stand the guy Sofi had met in one of her summer college classes. He reminded Leo of when Steve Urkel would turn into Stefan, sure he looked better and his balls weren't squished into some tight-ass pants, but it was still clear that he was trying too hard to be something he wasn't for Laura. That's what Brandon was, a dork pretending to be someone deserving of a badass like Sofi. What was worse was that Sofi knew it, but she kept bringing him around anyway.

She'd snuggle up under his arm and flutter those ridiculous Snuffleupagus eyelashes at him while laughing at his corny-ass jokes and hanging on his every word. It was annoying as fuck because Leo knew it was fake. Sofi didn't actually like Brandon. She wanted to because he was the type of guy she thought she should be with, but she wasn't into him. Just like she wasn't into any of the guys she dated. She never would be because they weren't him. Leo knew how that sounded and, yes, he could oftentimes be overly confident when it came to his looks, but that wasn't what he meant. He and Sofi had something that she lacked with these other clowns. They were connected and not just because of her friendship with his sister. They saw each other. When everyone else only saw what they wanted people to see, he and Sofi could see each other's true self—the one they used all their ticks to hide from the world.

It pissed him off that she refused to acknowledge that. Sofi wanted to make it seem like they only had a physical attraction, one they kept giving in to by mistake. It made him feel stupid and Leo loathed feeling stupid. It brought out the worst in him. Which was probably why he turned to the band and said, "I want to change our opener." They all groaned, but they were used to Leo's last-minute switch ups, so they rolled with it.

A few minutes later, they were ready to begin their set.

Leo stood on the stage watching Sofi sip at her drink with a look of tired boredom on her face. When Brandon turned to glance at her in the middle of whatever story he was telling, she forced an interested smile on her face and nodded like she'd been listening. Leo smirked. It wouldn't be long until Brandon was kicked to the curb. And if he could help the guy along, all the better.

Marcos, the keyboard player, began the introduction to Marc Anthony's "Te Conozco Bien" and Leo stepped to the mic and waited for his cue to begin the first verse. "'Siento pena…'" he sang to the crowd, "'porque te quise de veras.'" He continued dragging his attention around the audience as he sang the first two verses about how he placed the world at her feet, how he felt bad for her because he knew she still missed him even though she tried to pretend like she wasn't miserable with some other guy. But when he got to the pre-chorus he looked right at Sofi, telling her that he knew her so well, he was willing to bet that she wouldn't last one more weekend with her new guy. At least, not without her skin missing… "'todas mis caricias.'" He dragged out the last word while building power in his voice just so that when he belted out the chorus about how he knew her so well that he knew she would come back to him, it was felt by every person in the room, but especially the stubborn woman glaring at him from the dim corner. He gave her a wink before he continued signing about how well he knew her and how he knew she'd be back because she regretted leaving him and trying to be with someone else.

In the end, it hadn't even taken another weekend for Sofi to dump Brandon and show up at Leo's door. She'd shown up that very night.

After raging at him for a bit about his audacity she'd climbed right on his lap and rode him until the only feeling felt in the both of them was an exhausted and pleasurable satisfaction. Leo was sure that would be the last time he'd have to call her out in order to get her to acknowledge what was going on between them, but he'd been wrong...like always.

"Tío Leo, are you mad at Tití Sofi again?" his niece asked, making him realize that he'd been scowling at the group for some time while he'd been lost in the past.

"Come here, you little motormouth," Leo said to Rosie. "I'm mad because I still haven't had a patented Rosie massage. You're slacking on your job." One day after watching Saint force Leo through his PT and OT routine, Rosie had decided that he needed a massage to help his shoulder and arm, so she'd ran into her room to grab her special lotion and proceeded to slather it all over his arm, shoulder, neck, back, and chest. She'd been too scared to hurt him to rub with any sort of pressure, plus she was five, so her massage had accomplished nothing except making him smell like Bubblicious gum. But Leo had let her do it every day for the entire summer anyway, because she'd wanted to help him and she was cute when she frowned in concentration, really thinking she was doing something.

"I don't have my lotion," Rosie said, climbing onto the stool next to him.

"Oh well, I guess I'll just have to wait." Leo reached over and plopped her on his lap using his good arm. Then he spun them so they were facing Liam behind the bar. "This little monkey needs a kiddie cocktail, stat," he told him.

Liam scrunched his brows. "A what?"

Rosie's eyes, so similar to his own, widened in surprise. "You don't know what a kiddie cocktail is, Tío Liam?" she asked in the same tone she'd used when he'd claimed to dislike snakes. It was like she couldn't believe her cute little ears.

Leo shook his head in mock disappointment. "The service

around here has really slid downhill since I've been gone, right, Rosie?"

"There've been fewer broken glasses too," Liam replied.

Leo smirked. "You can't entertain the masses without a few broken glasses."

"Did they teach you that in bartending class?"

"Hey, I'm a licensed mixologist now. Put some respect on my name."

"Whatever, Cocktail, just tell me how to make it."

Leo explained to Liam how to make a Shirley Temple with tons of cherries for their favorite six-year-old.

Rosie was about halfway done when Saint came up to them. "How many times have I told you not to make her those?" he scolded Leo. "Not only will she be up all night, but she'll get cavities."

"I didn't make that for her." Leo paused. "Liam did."

"Tío Leo told him how," Rosie said happily before taking a long pull from her straw.

Leo shook his head and looked at his brother. "I hope your second child knows how to keep a secret."

"You know Abuelo told me the same thing when Rosie called him out for sneaking a piece of my jibarito." He gave Leo a significant look.

Yeah he got it. He was just like Abuelo Papo.

"I'm going to teach the baby that kids are not supposed to keep secrets from their grown-ups," Rosie said. "That's like lying and lying is bad."

"Rosie, do you know what they say about snitches?" Leo asked.

Saint cut him off with a threatening look. He scooped Rosie up from the chair and cradled her against his chest. "Rosie's going to be a great big sister," Saint said, pride and love visible in almost every line in his body.

Leo was happy for his brother, he truly was, but for some

reason he just couldn't join in the revelry. He felt weird. Like his skin was too tight and he needed to move. It was a familiar sensation. His leg started to bounce and his fingers began to drum on his knees. He reached into his pocket and pulled out his ever-present exercise ball. He began to flex and release his hand, ignoring the slight pins and needles sensation that traveled up and down his arm.

"Saint, Lola says it's time for us to go," Abuelo Papo said, strolling up to them. "We all have an early day tomorrow."

The next day was the official start to the Fiestas Patronales Puertorriqueñas a huge holiday in Humboldt Park. The festival that celebrated the Puerto Rican community happened every June and was a wild time every summer. It spanned a few days and consisted of a parade, a bunch of music, and tons of activities.

"We're coming," Saint told Abuelo. "Say goodbye to your tío." He held Rosie so that she could lean over and give Leo a kiss on the cheek.

"Bye, Tío. I love you. Have a good sleep."

"I love you too, Snitch. I'll see you tomorrow and I'll make you a special drink that has even more sugar than a Shirley Temple."

"You'd better not," Saint threatened.

Leo just smiled.

They walked away, leaving Leo with Abuelo Papo only.

"What do you think you're doing?" Abuelo asked as soon as they were alone.

"What are you talking about?" Leo asked.

"You've been sitting here all night sipping on the same drink looking pissed off. Meanwhile, your sister and cousins are over there trying to get Sofi to join some dating app," he hissed.

"What?" Leo asked loudly, causing a few of the remaining customers to turn and look at him. He lowered his voice. "A dating app?"

"And she said she'd think about it," Abuelo said. "Have you been doing nothing?"

"I know what I'm doing," Leo told his grandpa. "She only said that because she's freaking out." At least that's what he was going to tell himself.

Abuelo didn't seem to believe that any more than Leo did. "Don't worry. I'm going to call Fina and we'll figure something out."

Leo wondered briefly if he should be worried that Abuelo and Doña Fina were making plans together without him, but brushed it off when he saw Sofi wave her hand at the last of his family member still present and start making her way toward the kitchen.

"Are you leaving?" Abuelo Papo asked Sofi.

"Yeah," Sofi said. "Tomorrow is going to be a long day and I need to rest up for the shenanigans."

"I'm leaving too." Leo jumped up and shoved the ball back into his pocket.

"Leo, throw out the garbage for your sister," Abuelo told him. "The bags are piling up in the kitchen and it stinks. Sofi can help you. Now I gotta go before that jerk Benny convinces them to leave me stranded." With that he walked away.

Leo turned to Sofi, who was watching Abuelo Papo leave with a surprised look on her face. Leo got it. It wasn't often his abuelo made demands of anyone, especially her. "Come on, Nelly Furtado," he said, making a subtle dig about her being a man-eater.

"After you and those extra snug jeans, Rico Suave."

"You're welcome for the view," he said as he pushed open the swinging doors.

Besides a muttered comment about how it was rude of him to have more ass than her, Sofi stayed quiet as he collected the large black trash bags and opened the back door to the alley. There was hardly a pile like his abuelo had claimed, so Leo didn't bother handing any to Sofi, but she followed anyway. The kitchen door slammed shut behind them. Leo adjusted the garbage bags over his good shoulder.

"That was really nice of Kamilah to throw me a surprise welcome back party," Sofi said.

"She missed you," Leo told her. "Everyone did."

Sofi swallowed thickly but didn't respond.

He lifted his elbow to push the gate to the dumpster enclosure open, but a loud scrambling sound from inside had him dropping the bags, hooking an arm around Sofi's waist and pulling them both away from the gate.

"What the hell was that?" Sofi asked.

Leo held up a hand. "It sounded like an animal." He took a few steps forward.

"What are you doing?" The alarm in her voice was enough to give him pause.

He shot her a look that was meant to be comforting. "It's fine. I'm just going to take a look."

"I swear to God, Leo, if you get bit by a raccoon, I'm going to let your ass get rabies."

"That sounded too big to be a raccoon."

"Too big? You mean like a coyote or something?"

He gave her a look. "Sofi, we're in the middle of the city. There are no coyotes here."

"Don't you watch the news? Coyote sightings are the highest they've been in years and we're only a few blocks from a huge park." She eyed the enclosure with trepidation.

Leo inched closer. "Then imagine the pleasure you'll get from being able to tell me that you were right and I was wrong."

"I don't have to witness you get mauled by a wild creature in order to say that. I get that pleasure on the daily since I'm always right and you're always wrong."

He had to smile at that. "Fine, then imagine how much fun

it will be to nurse me back to health. You'll probably even get to see me shirtless."

She snorted. "Please, if I wanted to see that, all I'd have to do is post up in any part of the apartment. I'm pretty sure you're allergic to shirts."

He smirked at her. "Glad you noticed. Although I'm not surprised. I am a perfect example of manhood." Leo was finally able to see around the dumpster. The problem was that whatever was back there also saw him. It let out a low growl to let him know so.

It took a moment for his eyes to adjust to the darkness, but once he did he immediately recognized it. He turned his head slightly to talk to Sofi, but didn't take his eyes off of it. "Well, you're sort of right," he told her. "It's a dog."

"You're sure it's not a coyote?"

"Unless coyotes recently evolved into pit bulls, yeah I'm sure."

"Pit bulls?" Her voice was high and nervous.

Leo eyed the big block head of the dark dog squatting in the corner of the enclosure. "Definitely a bully breed. I think it's black."

He took a step closer and the growling grew. Leo stepped back and slowly raised his hand. "It's okay," he spoke softly. "It's okay, buddy. I'm not going to hurt you."

"What do we do?" Sofi asked. "Should we call animal control?"

Leo shook his head. "I've had to deal with animal control on jobs before. They close at seven. Give me a second." He slipped his hand into his pocket and pulled out his phone. "Here. Google how to catch a stray dog."

Sofi grabbed it. "I don't know your passcode," she said.

"It's your birthday."

Silence.

"Did you hear me?" he asked.

"Yeah," she replied. There was nothing but the sound of typing for a minute. "Here's an article. It says to stay calm, don't move too fast, and don't corner it."

Well, that seemed like common sense. "It probably came in here because it's hungry." He kicked the garbage bag nearest to him. The dog growled again. "Open this bag. Maybe it will smell the food and come closer."

"You open it. I'm not touching that garbage."

"Sofi, I want to keep my eyes on it in case it tries to run past me. Just open the damn bag."

She huffed. "Fine."

Leo heard the crinkling of the garbage bag and so did the dog. It paused in its growling and lowered its head as if trying to see under the gate.

The strong scent of sofrito floated in the air. The dog began sniffing.

"You smell that, don't you?" he said to the dog. "Why don't you come check it out?" He raised his hand to motion to come and the dog shrunk back and immediately started growling again. It looked like it was going to try to sneak behind the dumpster. "Fuck," Leo muttered. "Grab something out of the bag quick and throw it in there."

"Oh hell no."

"Just do it."

"This is some nonsense," she grumbled, but a second later she told him, "Move. I have a half-eaten pork chop in my hand and I have a strong urge to throw it at the back of your big-ass head."

Leo bit his lip to keep from laughing and slid over to make room for her. "Toss it to the right. That's where it is."

"I can see it," she snipped at him. "Here. Take your stupid phone." She practically slammed it into his open hand. Then she waved the chunk of meat in the air. "Look, dog. It's food.

It's somebody's already eaten food that I'm touching with my bare hands, but I doubt you care about that."

The dog sniffed and walked forward a few steps.

"Don't throw the whole thing," Leo told her. "Break off a piece and throw it."

He was surprised when she actually did what he said without argument.

She tossed the piece of meat a few feet in front of the dog. It slunk forward and grabbed it before moving back again, never once taking its eyes off her.

"Leo," Sofi whispered. "He's just staring at me and wagging his tail, but I don't think he's happy to see me."

"It's okay, bombón. Just stay still. Let him sniff at it and come closer." He glanced down at his phone and saw a link at the bottom of the page that said, "How to identify different tail wags." He clicked on it and a graphic appeared.

"Leo," she whispered again.

He watched as the dog inched closer to Sofi, his nose in the air sniffing. "Give me one second," he said, quickly scanning the page.

"Listen, sir. I totally respect that you're not interested in dealing with humans today," Sofi told the dog in a soft but clear voice. "I don't blame you. Humans are the worst." The dog stopped and titled its head and raised its ears as if it was listening. "So let's figure out how to make this work without really having to deal with each other. I'm sure there's a solution here."

The tail wag paused for a second and the dog took a few more tentative steps in Sofi's direction when she said the word "here."

"Oh. No no, dog. Don't come over here." She tossed the rest of the meat in the dog's direction.

Again the wagging paused as the dog dove forward to grab the food. As soon as it was done the wagging started up again this time a little faster. Leo could see its dangly bits as the dog took a few more steps in Sofi's direction.

"It's a boy and I think he likes you," Leo said. He took a quick glance at his phone to skim the webpage about tail wagging. "Yeah," he said a moment later. "His tail is mostly down and wagging sort of fast but not too fast." He looked at Sofi. "Slowly hold out your hand and lower down to your haunches."

"Are you out of your damn mind?" Sofi asked him. "This is a brand-new Gucci dress."

"Who told your bougie ass to dress up just to come down here like we care about that shit?"

"This is what I wore to work and even if it weren't, I dress for myself. Get it straight."

"Just do it."

"Ugh, fine." Sofi lowered herself while holding out a hand. "We're cool, dog. You don't need to be scared and you definitely don't need to rush me and attack my face. I need it to stay pretty, okay?"

The dog stretched its neck and attempted to smell her hand. He took enough steps forward until he was only a few short feet way from Sofi.

"Just like that. Good girl," Leo murmured warmly.

Sofi shot him a quick glance before quickly turning her attention back to the dog. "I thought you said it's a boy."

"I'm talking to you."

She paused. "Oh," she breathed like he knew she would. Sofi loved it when he called her a good girl.

"Okay, now I want you to tell him to come to you."

Sofi took a deep breath. "Come here, boy."

The dog's ears perked all the way up and his tail started wagging a bit faster, but it was still low. He took a single step forward.

Sofi perked up too. "Come on, boy. Come here."

The dog walked up to her hand and started sniffing.

Sofi held perfectly still without Leo having to tell her to. "Good boy," she told the dog. She slowly turned her hand and let the dog sniff the other side. "That's a good boy. You're a pretty boy even if you are dirty as hell. Yeah, you're a handsome boy. Look at that cute face you have. Such a pretty boy." She didn't seem to notice that by the end of her monologue she was full-on using the baby voice.

The dog rewarded her with a few licks to her hand and more tail wagging.

Sofi slowly lifted her hand and placed it on the dog's head for a tiny pet. "Good boy," she told him again.

That seemed to be all the dog needed to hear, because he suddenly launched himself at her.

Sofi let out a short scream and Leo hopped forward, but their alarm was unnecessary since all the dog did was rub himself against her and attempt to lick at her face. Well, it was unnecessary on Leo's part. Sofi was still very much alarmed.

"Shit," she cried when he knocked her over and she plopped her ass onto the dirty asphalt. "He's getting dirt and slobber all over me. Stop it," she told the dog to no avail. "Get him, Leo."

"I don't think I should break this up," he told Sofi with a laugh. "He doesn't like me, but he loves you."

"Son of a bitch," she cursed again. It only seemed to amp the dog up. "Okay. Okay," she told the dog, pushing him back. "That's enough."

Amazingly that worked. He backed off a little bit, but stayed close enough to lean his body against hers. His tail was wagging so hard that his hips were wiggling.

"Aww. He loves you," Leo teased.

"Shut up," Sofi said. "You owe me a new outfit by the way."

Leo laughed and took a few steps forward. "Well, you're going to be waiting awhile for that, because I'm too broke to afford Gucci.."

The dog watched him alertly but didn't move away or stop wagging his tail.

Sofi looked up at him from her seat on the ground. There

was a smudge of dirt on her forehead and the dog had effectively licked off whatever shiny stuff she'd put on that gave her a glow. She still looked like the most beautiful woman he'd ever laid eyes on. "So now what?" she asked.

"We try to get him in the house."

"Our house? Absolutely not."

Leo ignored how much he liked hearing her say "our house." "Where else can we put him to make sure he doesn't run off?"

"I don't know. Can't we just walk him around until we find his owners?"

"That's a great plan. Why don't you put the leash on him and we can begin?"

"What leash? He doesn't even have a coll—" She paused. "Oh."

Leo smirked. "Exactly."

"Let's take him inside and see if anyone recognizes him," Sofi suggested.

"You want to take a filthy stray dog that was just eating garbage into my sister's busy restaurant kitchen?"

"But what about Liam's?"

Leo was already shaking his head. "Liam's allergic to animals."

"Of course he is," she said.

"What does that mean?"

"That means that Liam is the kind of guy who'd already own a dog if he could. You know, like the big silent guy with a big strong dog he'd talk to because it was his only friend."

Leo had to laugh. "I see that."

"So what are we going to do with him, Leo? You just said that animal control is closed. Are we supposed to just sit here with him while he eats the rest of this trash?"

"Probably not." He wanted to point out that these were all reasons he'd suggested taking him back to their place, but he knew that wasn't going to help the situation at all. Sofi needed to think it was her idea or she'd get stubborn about it.

Sofi sighed. "We're going to have to take this dog into the apartment, aren't we?"

Leo smirked. "Yep."

"Fuck."

9

SOMETIME LATER THEY WERE WALKING THROUGH THE APARTMENT door, Leo carrying the dog like a baby.

Sofi took a look around the pristine neutral-toned apartment and then at the dirty dog. "Hold up," she told Leo, who was about to walk into the living room with it. "That dog cannot just wander around. It's filthy."

Leo gave her a look. "Sofi, do you really think it's going to sit here in the entryway?"

"I don't know what to tell you, but that dog is not roaming free in the apartment when I can literally feel the oily dirt on me after sitting on the ground with it."

"Then I guess we'll have to give it a bath."

"We? What we? You mean you."

"Fine. I'll do it."

Sofi motioned down the hall toward his bathroom. "Go, I'll bring you the dish soap and a towel."

"Dish soap? Just grab some shampoo."

"The hell *I am* using my expensive shampoo on a dog," she said with enough attitude to make it very clear that she would not be doing that. "Unless you want to use yours."

"I actually ran out yesterday."

"Then dish soap it is. Besides, in the commercials they always use Dawn to take the dirt and oil off baby ducks. It'll be fine."

Leo just shook his head and took the dog down the hallway. It kept looking back at her and whining. "It's okay," she told it. "I'll be right there." She rushed to the kitchen to grab the Dawn from the sink. Then she went to the linen closet and tried to find the oldest and darkest towel Leo owned. She found a dark purple beach towel and snatched it up, then she booked it back down the hall. The bathroom door was closed. "Leo," she said. "I have the stuff."

"Give me a second," he said. A moment later the door cracked open and both of their heads popped out. Leo was clearly trying to maintain a hold of the dog. "I'm trying to figure out how to get him in the tub. He does not look like he's feeling this bath thing. We should've used yours. It has the walk-in shower."

Sofi shook her head. "Nuh-uh. I'm about to use my shower, because I smell like trash dog."

"You seriously aren't going to help me?"

"Nope. It was your idea to lure this dog into the house. You can wash it."

"And what if it gets mad and attacks me?"

Sofi eyed the dog who was now docilely sitting at Leo's feet. "I don't think that's going to be an issue—" she began backing down the hall "—but you have your phone. Call 911."

"You're so mean to me. I don't know why I like you."

"You're a masochist." Sofi threw him a kiss, then turned the corner and headed straight into her bathroom. She peeled off the most-likely-ruined outfit that had cost her a thousand dollars, turned the shower to piping hot, quickly pulled her hair into a bun on the top of her head, and then stepped in. She scrubbed her body and face at least three times before she felt clean again. When she was done she wrapped herself in a fluffy towel and went about her normal nightly routine: applying moisturizers, creams, and serums to her entire body. Then she put on a satin pajama set and a pair of fuzzy socks (her favorite). She put her hair up in her sleep bonnet and wandered back into the open space of the apartment to see how Leo had done with the dog.

When she stepped out into the living room she stopped dead in her tracks. Leo stood in their kitchen wearing nothing but a pair of basketball shorts that hung low on his hips. The dog was lying at his feet. All the other times he paraded around shirtless, she'd done her very best not to look at him—mostly because she knew he wanted her to—but now she couldn't help herself. She looked. Leo had always taken care of himself physically because of his job. But this was at a completely different level. It was as if his body was his entire focus now and it showed in the muscles that flexed in his back, shoulders, and legs as he moved things around in the fridge. "There's some leftover salmon in here, but that's Sofi's and she does not like to share."

Sofi shoved her tongue back in her mouth and swallowed until her throat no longer felt dry. "I leave for thirty minutes to take a shower and you're already bad-mouthing me to the dog?"

At the sound of her voice the dog got up and trotted over to her. He leaned his entire body weight against her and stared up at her like she was the greatest thing he'd ever seen. He was even more cute now that he was clean. He was gray with a hint of brown, but he had a white chest and one white front paw. His eyes were light brown and his face was subtly wrinkled giving him a sad look. "He looks like a dog from one of those commercials with the Sarah McLachlan song playing."

"Well, this little jerk cost me more than seventy cents a day." He closed the refrigerator door. "He got me soaked and filthy, I had to take a shower right after him. Then his ass chewed on my Jordans while I was in the shower."

Sofi bit her lip. She was kind of sad that she'd missed it. That had to have been hilarious. But then she noticed how he was holding one shoulder higher than the other and flexing his fingers. Fuck. She'd totally forgotten about his injury. He'd probably aggravated it carrying and bathing the dog. She should've stayed and helped him. She was ready to ask if he was in pain, but then she remembered how mad he'd gotten the last time she'd tried to show concern.

Tired of being ignored—or maybe he just liked the way her cocoa butter smelled—the dog began to lick her leg. "Eww. No. Stop that."

"Get her, Dumpy. Get her!" Leo cheered.

Sofi pushed the dog away and he settled. "What did you just call him?"

"I couldn't just keep calling him 'dog.' That felt wrong."

"So you named him Dumpy?"

"Well, we did find him hanging out behind a dumpster."

Sofi shook her head. "That's so messed up, Leo. You can't call the dog Dumpy. Absolutely not."

"Then you come up with something better."

It was clear that Leo had forgotten that this wasn't their pet and was already getting too attached. It was going to be up to her to maintain perspective. "We aren't naming him, Leo. He's only here for the night. For all we know he already has a name and someone is out there shouting it as they look for him."

"I don't think so. He doesn't look like a dog who lived in a house until recently. He's pretty skinny and his nails are unkempt."

"But he doesn't act like a dog who is not used to people either. I mean, he just crawled into my lap as soon as I gave him food."

"I guess we'll see tomorrow." He looked around as if unsure of what to do next. He reached up a hand and absently rubbed his shoulder. A brief grimace passed his face, but he quickly checked it.

Sofi couldn't take any more. "Leo?"

He looked at her. "Yeah?"

"I'm going to tell you something, but I don't want you to get mad at me."

He eyed her warily. "What?"

"I can't help but notice that you seem to be in pain."

He opened his mouth to respond but Sofi held up her hand. "Let me finish."

He closed his mouth.

"I feel responsible for that, because I should've stayed to help you wash the dog. I'd really like to make it up to you."

At that his eyebrow rose.

"I have a heating pad and some massage oils. Can I take care of your shoulder, please?" She wasn't even sure if her guilt stemmed from the current situation or if she still felt bad because she'd never checked on him while she was in Europe. All she knew was that she really, really wanted to help him.

He must've seen the earnestness on her face, because he nodded. "Okay. Thanks."

"Go make yourself comfortable on the couch. I'll be right back." Sofi rushed to her bathroom to grab the oils and heating pad. She tossed them on the bed and then went to grab another large towel and a smaller one. As she passed by the living room she could hear Leo having a one-sided conversation with the dog about not sniffing at his musical equipment. She smiled.

Back in her room she set everything up. The towels were spread on her bed and one pillow to protect the comforter and pillowcase, the oils were set right on the nightstand, and she'd opened up the back of the heating pad to remove the clay pellet insert so she could heat it.

She went to the kitchen and stuck the insert into the microwave for thirty seconds. As soon as the timer went off, she shoved the insert back into the pad and moseyed into the living room.

She found Leo stretched out on the couch with the dog half on his legs and half on the couch. "I don't remember giving that animal permission to be on the furniture."

"You said that he couldn't be on it without having a bath first. He had one."

Damn. That was true. "Touché."

He eyed the object in her hands with confusion and disbelief. "Why are you holding a stuffed cartoon uterus?"

"This is the heating pad. I usually use it for cramps." He looked like he was going to argue with her. "Don't be that guy," Sofi said.

"What guy?"

"The guy who gets all weird about something as perfectly normal as cramps and periods. It's so cliché."

"True. Fine. Give me the uterus."

"Here." She put it on his shoulder. "Hold it there for fifteen minutes." She moved to sit on the chair perpendicular to the couch. The dog hopped off Leo's legs immediately and tried to climb right into her lap. She held him at bay with a hand on his chest. "No, Dog. I am not that kind of animal person. Go back over there."

The dog whined. He placed one paw on her leg and just stared at her with that sad face.

"I don't care how pathetic you look," she told him. "You are not about to put your big butt in my lap."

"And here I thought since you went to the gym so much, you'd be able to handle more than thirty pounds," Leo said, grabbing the remote off the coffee table and turning on the huge mounted TV.

"You be quiet. This is between me and the dog."

As if to punctuate her point the dog let out another whine

and put his other paw on her knee. Then he outright cheated by putting his head on his paws and looking up at her with those sad eyes.

"Dammit," she groused. She reached down and lifted him. "Come on you manipulative con artist."

The dog immediately curled up in her lap and tried to hide his face between her arm and body. She began to stroke his back. "He's actually pretty soft," she said after a few minutes of companionable silence. She'd figured his fur would be coarse, but he felt like velvet.

"I'm positive he's still a puppy," Leo said from the couch. "He looks young in the face and he's obviously smaller than an adult. Although, he's pretty low-energy for a puppy."

"He's just a baby and he was living on the streets?" That was terrible. Sofi had never had a pet. Her mother had told her that they barely had enough money to feed and house themselves, there was no way that they could add another mouth to feed. However, the thought of someone purposefully allowing harm to come to the sweet little guy on her lap seemed too much. Then she noticed the scrapes, scabs, and patches of missing fur where wounds had obviously healed over. "Good thing we found him."

"Yeah. Now he gets to go live in a shelter with a bunch of other unwanted dogs."

"But someone will adopt him." Sofi was telling herself this more than she was telling him.

"I hope so," was all he said in response.

Realizing that she too was falling under the spell of two sad eyes and a scrawny little body, Sofi shook herself mentally. "I think it's been fifteen minutes. The heat needs to come off." Sofi lifted the dog into her arms and stood. He awoke from his nap and looked a bit startled before he saw her. His tail wagged and he tried to lick her face. "No," she said sternly. "No face licking." He stopped. She looked to Leo. "Follow me."

She led him to her room, puppy in her arms. When they arrived, she put the dog down. "Don't you dare pee on my rug," she told him. She thought he'd take off and begin to explore the new space but he stayed right at her feet.

Leo was staring at the setup on her bed. For once she couldn't tell what he was thinking by the look on his face, but he was flexing his fingers around the stress ball again. "Do you want me on my front or back?"

Dear lord. The images that question evoked.

He must've read her mind, because he said, "Thinking naughty thoughts in front of a baby? You dirty girl."

Sex had never been an issue between them. They didn't just *work* on every level—they excelled. They were like a line of black powder and a fuse both leading to the same pile of gunpowder and TNT. She'd never found Leo's equal and she was sure that he'd never found hers. That was what made everything that much harder. How could they give up something so damn good?

Because nothing else about us works, she reminded herself. "Lie on your back first," she said, doing her best to keep her voice level.

He did as he was told and she grabbed the bottle of oil that she used after a particularly hard workout. It had arnica, lavender, chamomile, and rosemary. She knew it wouldn't magically heal the damage caused by the bullet, but even if it helped him a fraction it was worth trying. She stood next to the bed and warmed the oil in her hands. The puppy came up next to her and settled into a ball at her feet. She looked down to find Leo eyeing her steadily. "I'm not going to use tons of pressure, but tell me if anything I do is too much."

He nodded.

Sofi took a deep breath and then put her hands on his shoulder. For the first time she allowed herself to look at it closely. There was a scar along his collarbone where the bullet had obviously gone in and the doctors after. There was another smaller one a few inches over by his deltoid and one on top of his shoulder, closer to his neck. She could only imagine what he'd gone through. He must've been so scared and in so much pain. Sofi held her breath in an attempt to keep her emotions under control as she applied the lightest of pressure against the proof of how close she'd come to losing him for good.

"Hey," he said.

She raised her eyes to his face and noticed for the first time that her vision was blurry, she could barely make out his features.

His other hand came up to her face and wiped her tears from one side, then the other.

Sofi blinked to clear her vision completely.

"Look at me," he told her, his voice was low but stern.

Her eyes met his and just like every time, the light green pulled her in like the warm sun-soaked Caribbean Sea.

"I'm here," he told her. "I'm here and I'm not going anywhere."

"I was so scared, Leo," she confessed in a whisper. "When my mom told me, I was ready to jump on the next flight." Her tears began to flow faster. "I wanted to be near you. See you. I just kept thinking, *What if I don't get to see him again?*" Her shoulders shook with the force of the sob she was trying to contain. "I don't know what I would've done if I'd lost you forever."

Suddenly his lips were on hers, rough and desperate as if he wanted to eat her words right out of her mouth. He kissed her like he owned her and he was tired of not having her. He grabbed the back of her neck and pulled her closer until she was precariously balanced over him. He bit her lip and then sucked it into his mouth. It was a punishment, this kiss. He was letting her know that he was mad at her for leaving him alone for a year.

Sofi welcomed it because she was mad too. Mad that she

just couldn't keep her distance from him. She growled into his mouth and bit him back. She lifted her knee onto the edge of the bed and threw her other leg over his hips.

He sat up, wrapped his arms around her waist, and pulled her close. They kissed until he pulled away for a second. "Get naked," he told her. His hands were already slipping up the hem of her shorts.

"Leo," she whispered tentatively.

When he felt nothing but skin under her shorts his eyes darkened. "Right fucking now, Sofi." He leaned in and put his mouth on her neck, sucking roughly like he wanted to mark her.

Her hands went to the buttons of her top. Her fingers were clumsy in her haste. As soon as she had the top open it slipped down her shoulders to pool at the small of her back where it was stopped from going farther by his hands under her shorts.

He straightened and looked down at her chest. "Coño," he breathed. "Every fucking time you amaze me."

Sofi preened. She knew she didn't have the biggest chest, she was a B cup, but Leo always looked at her like she was an abundance.

"Come here." He tugged at her so she lifted onto her knees, her chest at the perfect height for his mouth. He wasted no time putting his mouth on her.

They both groaned as he nibbled at her nipples before licking.

"Take your shorts off," he rasped.

Sofi paused. "I don't have any condoms," she told him.

When she didn't move fast enough. He reached for her shorts himself. "It doesn't matter." He grabbed her waistband and started tugging it down. "We aren't fucking right now anyway."

Sofi paused again, her hand on the other side of her shorts. "What?"

He looked at her very seriously. "I'm not fucking you again until you're ready to tell everyone you know about us." He didn't even give her a second to process that. He leaned in and sucked on a nipple. "But right now you're going to sit on my face because it's been too long since I've eaten mi bombón de caramelo."

Fuck. He played dirty. He knew she couldn't deny herself that pleasure. Sofi rose to her feet, standing on her bed, and moved to the side so she could let her shorts fall to her ankles. She watched him scoot down the bed as she stepped out of her shorts. She used her toes to flick them at his face.

He caught them and held them there for a second, breathing them in, before dropping them on the floor. "Enough." He grabbed her wrist and pulled her until she stood at the head of the bed facing the foot of it. He released her wrist and lay back, resting his head on the pillow he'd dragged with him. He looked up at her like a man starved. He licked his bottom lip. "Bájate," he told her, his voice deep and dark with need.

Her legs trembled as she followed his command despite the squats she did every other day. She placed her knees on either side of his head. When her knee bumped his injured shoulder she froze. "I don't want to hurt you," she murmured.

"I don't care if it hurts," he said. "Te voy a comer como si fueras mi última cena." Then he wrapped his arms around her thighs and pulled her down.

"Fuck," she exclaimed at the first touch of his mouth. "Leo."

His only response was to flex his hands on her thighs.

She wanted to lean forward and put her hands on his chest, but she was worried about putting her weight on him.

His big palm slapped her ass, hard. "You're thinking too much," he growled from between her thighs. "Just ride my mouth. I need it." Another smack. "Muévete."

She needed it too, so she leaned back, locked her hands behind her head, shut off her brain, and rocked her hips like they both wanted.

It was wet and messy, but neither one of them cared. They

loved it. She was positive of this because he groaned and growled and slurped at her like he was having the time of his life. She knew she was.

Her thighs were trembling, her stomach was clenched, she couldn't catch her breath, and her ability to speak had completely deserted her. All she could do was pant and moan. She watched as his hand slid down his chest to his stomach where it stopped for a second. "Do it," she breathed, her insides clenching at the thought. "I want to watch."

His hand continued its journey until it reached the waistband of his shorts where it slipped under them and tugged out his dick. He wrapped his fist around it and his moan reverberated through her.

"Yes," she hissed, rocking her hips harder. "Así. Así mismo."

His hand sped up.

Sofi couldn't take her eyes off it. She wanted him in her mouth, but then she'd have to stop grinding on his face and that was more important.

The muscles in his stomach clenched, his toes curled, and he let out a muffled "fuck" against her.

That was it.

Her eyes squeezed shut, her hips jerked uncontrollably, her entire body shook, and she cried his name over and over. When she couldn't stand it anymore she slumped to the side, letting her body fall to the mattress. She opened her eyes and his hips were in her line of sight.

His hand was still wrapped around himself, covered in his own pleasure. His stomach rose and fell quickly as he tried to catch his breath. His other hand came down, holding the small towel from the pillow. He wiped himself off and then set it aside. He sat up and looked over at her. "Sofi. Bombón." He reached out a hand and dragged it along her hip.

She sat up and turned herself around while he repositioned

himself against the headboard. Sofi scooted up until she was right next to him and then laid her head on his chest.

Leo wrapped an arm around her and pulled her close. He kissed her on the forehead.

Sofi didn't say anything. She just closed her eyes and let sleep take her, so she could stop thinking about the huge mistake she'd just made.

10

LEO WOKE TO A TONGUE LICKING HIS FACE. UNFORTUNATELY, THAT tongue did not belong to the woman next to him, but to the wiggly puppy on his chest. He opened his eyes and discovered that he was basically nose to nose with Dumpy—he didn't care what Sofi said, it was a good name. He pushed the dog off his chest. "How did you even get up here?" he whispered. The bed was too tall for him to have jumped up, which meant that Sofi had to have lifted him onto the bed. Leo smiled. As much as she tried to pretend otherwise, she was such a softy.

He looked over at her curled up on her side with her hands tucked under her cheek like a little girl. She must've gotten hot at some point, because she'd kicked off the thick white comforter and beige knit blanket. Her long, silky brown limbs were revealed almost to excess by her dark gold satin and lace sleep shorts and button-up top combo—reminding him why he called her bombón. She was like the chocolate-covered caramels he used to steal from any box of truffles he found around the apartment growing up. She was his secret pleasure, one he didn't feel the least bit guilty enjoying whenever he could. Even if it was just looking at her, like he was now.

On the bed Sofi yawned and turned on her back to stretch.

Distractedly, Leo watched her muscles flex and contract. It reminded him of the way she'd move during sex; her chest bowed off the bed, her toes curling, arms and head thrown back. He could watch it all day and never get bored.

A second later she was once again knocked out, her mouth open and everything. There was a depression in the blanket by her waist where Dumpy had obviously snuggled up.

The last thing he remembered after he'd come so hard he'd saw fucking stars was snuggling up to a quiet Sofi. It wasn't totally abnormal for her to be quiet. She was frequently lost in her own thoughts. What worried him were the thoughts that had probably run through her brain after. He knew her well enough to know that she'd been overanalyzing what they'd done. She'd most likely woken up, gotten dressed, put the puppy on the bed, and then lay there freaking out until she fell back to sleep. Leo was surprised that she hadn't woken him up and sent him on his way the moment her eyes had opened. Actually no he wasn't. If there was one thing he'd learned last night it was that she cared about him a lot more than she wanted to admit.

It started with her bringing him that uterus-shaped heating pad and ended with her shedding tears as she looked at the scars left by his brush with death. For the first time in over a year, Leo had hope. She'd told him that she'd wanted to come back just to see him. She'd told him that she'd been terrified to lose him forever. That meant that a part of her still wanted him whether she was willing to admit it or not. He might not be able to do the things he used to do, but he hadn't lost her. If he had anything to do with it, he never would.

Dumpy whined, drawing Leo's attention away from his thoughts and watching Sofi sleep. Right. He probably had to go to the bathroom. Leo slid off the bed and lifted the puppy into his arms. He was a solid boy, even if he wasn't full-grown. He carried him to his bedroom and placed him on the floor. "Behave yourself while I get dressed," he told Dumpy. "I'll be pissed as hell if you mess up another pair of my shoes." Leo grabbed his clothes and rushed to put them on. He did not like the way Dumpy was sniffing the floor in agitation. He grabbed his keys from the nightstand, his phone, and wallet. Then he remembered that the dog didn't have a leash. He needed a rope or something. He thought about the fluffy purple robe he'd seen hanging on the back of her bedroom door. He tiptoed back into Sofi's room and slipped the belt from the loops. This would just have to be Dumpy's makeshift leash. Sofi would forgive him. He picked the dog back up, hoping that it would prevent him from peeing before they made it outside, and rushed out the door.

As soon as they were out the back door, Leo raced to the first spot of green he found, which happened to be a bush at the mouth of the alleyway. The second he put Dumpy down, he took care of business. "That was a close one," he said to the dog relieving himself for an inordinate amount of time. "But you did good, buddy." Dumpy wagged his tail. "Come on, let's go find us all some breakfast." He slipped the robe belt loop over the dog's head, just in case he decided to book it.

He felt like an idiot walking a dog with a robe belt leash on and the people who saw him looked at him like such, but Leo did his best to ignore the stares and pointing. He pulled his phone out of his pocket and saw missed calls from multiple family members. Shit. He'd forgotten that he was supposed to be up early to help set up at the park. He was in big trouble.

He didn't want to listen to his parents ream him out so early in the morning. Leo called Saint first instead.

"Where the fuck are you? You were supposed to be here two hours ago, you weren't answering your phone, and we couldn't find you. All we found was garbage you were supposed to throw out strewn all over the alley you were already almost killed in," his brother growled upon answering.

Uh-oh. If Saint was dropping an f-bomb and performing monologues, things were bad.

Leo immediately began apologizing. "I'm sorry. I got busy and then I forgot."

Silence.

Okay, so he was still pissed.

Leo continued to explain himself. "Sofi and I found this dog by the dumpster. We couldn't just leave it there, so we brought it to the apartment. But you know how Sofi is, so I had to take care of it. I'm actually walking it right now looking like a jack-ass because I had to MacGyver a leash out of the belt from her robe. I'll send you a picture, if you don't believe me."

A long-suffering sigh.

That was more the norm.

"So what's the plan with this dog?" Saint asked.

"We're going to take him to animal control in a bit. Why? Do you want him?"

"Hell no," Saint said. "I have enough on my plate. You better not even mention the possibility of a pet to Rosie either or I'll sic Lola on you."

"Damn. That's just plain cold-blooded." Leo liked Lola even though she had the tendency to bitch him out. He needed it most of the time, his mouth ran away from him a lot, but sometimes she did the most when he was just playing around.

"You better call Mami and Papi. They were about to force Cristian to file a missing persons report."

Leo winced. He could only imagine the earful he was about

to receive from his parents. "Uh. My phone is at like one percent. I forgot to charge it, but I don't want them to worry. Can you tell them for me?" he asked.

"Leo…" Saint sighed. "I thought you were over being this flakey."

Ouch. That hurt.

"Look, just tell everyone that I'll be there as soon as I can. The—" Leo clicked the end button. His screen showed thirty percent battery life, but Saint didn't need to know that. He'd already left everything including the recipes he wanted to try prepped for Liam, so it wasn't like they couldn't get started without him. Therefore, Leo only felt a little bit guilty when he turned off his phone and continued to the coffee shop at the next corner. There he ordered two cold brews, his with three pumps of caramel and hers with nothing because she was weird like that, and three breakfast sandwiches: one for him, one for her, and one for Dumpy, who was already drooling everywhere. The server was nice enough to throw in a big bowl of water and a few of their homemade dog treats. He and Dumpy sat on the patio enjoying their breakfast before heading back home.

"There you are," Sofi said when they entered the apartment. "I was starting to get worried he'd run off again or something." She was already dressed in a pair of high-waisted light blue jean shorts and an off-the-shoulder crop top that was designed to look like the Puerto Rican flag with one blue sleeve that went into a blue triangle on her side and a white star over her nipple. The other side was the three red stripes interspersed with two white stripes. "I was about to go look for you." She stood in the kitchen with her hand on the counter sliding her foot into a high-heeled sandal also made to look like the Puerto Rican flag.

Leo wiped at his mouth to make sure he wasn't drooling as much as the dog had when he'd spotted the breakfast sandwich. "We stopped to grab some breakfast." He placed Sofi's coffee and the bag with her sandwich in it on the island. "Then

Dumpy decided that he had to sniff absolutely everything on the way back."

She gave him a look as she slid on her other shoe. "Stop calling him that." She straightened and adjusted her blouse so the neckline sat higher on her chest. "Let me grab my purse and then we can go." Her long hair was slicked back into a low bun at the base of her neck leaving her gorgeous face front and center. Her baby hairs were laid perfectly and she had on huge gold hoops that had the word *Boricua* written across them. She had on multiple gold necklaces, one with her name, one with a Puerto Rico medallion, and the other with an outline of the island. Her lips were painted a blood red and her skin shimmered.

Leo fought the urge to walk up to her and kiss her silly. "Are you going to eat your breakfast?"

She eyed the bag and coffee. "I'll bring it with." Apparently, the walls had come back up, because she was acting like nothing had happened last night. She waltzed off, two Puerto Rican flags on her back pockets, and came back a moment later with a Puerto Rican flag mini backpack and the towel he'd used on Dumpy last night. "I hope you know that we're taking your car because that dog will not be getting hair all over my back seat."

About twenty minutes later they were finally on their way, Sofi sat in the passenger seat with Dumpy on her lap because he'd freaked out and refused to get in the back seat. Now Dumpy was cuddled up to Sofi's chest with his head thrown over her shoulder just like a baby. It was cute as hell.

Leo knew by the way that she kept petting him from head to tail, like a mom comforting her child, that this trip to animal control was going to be a huge waste of time. There was no way that they were leaving the dog there. Still, he decided it couldn't hurt to give things a little push. "This place looks cold and sad," he said when they pulled up.

"I'm sure it's fine," Sofi replied.

The inside looked even worse. "It's like a DMV or something."

"Shh." She hushed him because the worker had just stepped up to the desk from a back room.

With her '90s mom haircut à la Meg Ryan and wide smile, the older lady looked nice enough he supposed. "Can I help you?"

"Hi, we found this dog last night." Sofi motioned to Leo standing there holding Dumpy in his arms while the big baby looked around in terror. "We wanted to bring him in just in case someone was looking for him."

"Okay. Can I ask, did you happen to find him near Humboldt Park?"

Sofi and Leo shared a look.

"Yes," Sofi replied. "Right off Division Street."

"How do you know that?" Leo asked. "Besides this Boricua Bratz Doll." He used his thumb to point to his side.

Sofi smacked his arm lightly.

The woman smiled, but it fell quickly. "There was a bust there a few nights ago. The police found thirty-four dogs of various ages. Apparently there was dogfighting happening on top of the other illegal stuff. This guy looks just like a few other puppies that were brought in. They said they weren't sure they got them all."

Leo tightened his hold on Dumpy. "Dogfighting? People still do that?"

"Sadly, yes."

"Sick fucks," Sofi growled. She looked at Leo. "That has to be why he has all those scratches and scars."

"Probably," Leo agreed. He looked at the worker. "Were the other dogs that look like him messed up too?"

She nodded. "They usually start training them more intensely at this age. They have older ones fight younger ones for rewards. The vet put this specific litter at about four months old."

Sofi waved her hand as if waving away the negativity. "We don't even know if he's part of that litter. Can you check him for a microchip first, before we go all doom and gloom?"

"Of course. Let me grab the scanner." She spun on her heel and left.

"What are we going to do if he doesn't have a chip?" Leo asked.

"What do you mean?"

"You heard her. They got in over thirty dogs just from that bust not to mention the other ones already here. These places are already underfunded and short-staffed."

The woman walked back in before Sofi answered. "Okay, put him right here." She patted the counter. "Hopefully, I'm wrong and this guy has a chip with some current owner information."

Leo stepped forward and placed Dumpy on the counter. The poor guy immediately began trembling. His ears went down and his tail tucked all the way under his body.

"It's okay, big boy," the woman crooned. "I'm not going to hurt you."

A whine escaped him as soon as the scanner brushed over the back of his neck and shoulder blades.

Before Leo could, Sofi's hand reached out and cradled Dumpy's face. He tried to get up and leap to her. Luckily the worker was done.

"As I thought, nothing," she said. "If he does have owners, which I very much doubt given the situation, they didn't chip him."

"Now what?" Leo asked.

"We'll still take him of course," she said. "It's a full house here, but we are reaching out to area rescues to see if they can help us out."

"So he'll be adopted?" Sofi asked, cuddling Dumpy to her chest the best she could even though he was the size of her torso.

"We'll do our best but pit bulls are still a hard sell for a lot of potential adopters in Chicago due to the breed restrictions a lot of buildings have in place. Especially when they come from this background. Puppies are more likely to be adopted, but as soon as they get to around three months and don't look like puppy puppies anymore, people are less likely to adopt them." She held her arms out for him, but Sofi turned away.

Sofi stared at Dumpy, a frown on her face. Leo could tell that she was struggling with what she wanted to do and what they both knew she was going to do. There was no way in hell she was going to leave him there now. Not the Sofi he knew. "Fuck," she whispered. "Why do you have to look so damn sad?" she asked him. "I can't leave you here now."

Leo smiled wide.

Sofi turned the worker. "I'm going to keep him."

The woman bit her lip to hide her own smile. "Are you sure?"

Sofi nodded. "Yes, he deserves a home and if one can't be guaranteed here, then I'll give it to him."

"I think that's a great plan," she said.

"So do I have to do anything? Fill out paperwork or something?"

The worker shook her head. "Since you never actually surrendered him, he's not in our system. There's no fees or paperwork." She reached under the desk and pulled out a booklet. "However, you may want to take a look at this to figure out the next steps, the first of which should definitely be a visit to the vet for vaccinations and a checkup. None of the other dogs tested positive for heartworms, but you never know." She leaned forward. "There are coupons for a free first visit in the folder. Tell them that Carol at CACC sent you." She winked.

Leo reached for the folder.

Sofi smiled. "Thank you, Carol."

"You're more than welcome. Thank you for having a big heart."

They exited the building, Leo smiling wide the whole time. He opened his mouth.

"Shut up, Leo," Sofi said before any sound even escaped. "I can already hear your smug, *I knew you were going to keep him as soon as you let him on your bed.*" She mimicked his voice. "Well, good for you. I'll buy you a cookie right after we go to the pet store." She took off through the parking lot toward his car. "And don't be too fucking cocky," she threw over her shoulder. "He's now half yours which means you're going to take care of him when I'm at work."

Leo kept his mouth shut and followed her. He wasn't the smartest guy, but he knew to quit while he was ahead.

11

SUMMER IN CHICAGO HAD ALWAYS BEEN SOFI'S FAVORITE AND NOTH-ing kicked it off better than Fiestas Patronales Puertorriqueñas. She still remembered how amazed she'd been during her first Puerto Rican Fest in Humboldt Park. It had been the first time she'd felt so surrounded by her culture since leaving Puerto Rico at age nine. Of course, by the time her first Boricua Fest had rolled around, she'd already been familiar with the Puerto Rican flag arches on either end of Division Street. But there was something about seeing the huge crowds of people all decked out in their favorite Puerto Rico attire walking under and past the arches that had made her eyes water. Even the cars driving along, bumping their favorite Puerto Rican artists while large flags hung out of the windows, made her emotional. When she'd gotten closer to the park itself and saw the rows and rows of vendors under tents, her heart had begun to pound with excitement. There had been everything from freshly squeezed tropical fruit juice to handmade jewelry or art and informational pamphlets announcing community resources. Almost everyone around was speaking Spanish or some version of Spanglish as they greeted family and friends, spoke to customers, and just chatted with their fellow Boricuas. Everything had reminded her of Puerto Rico, the place of her birth that she'd still missed. Now, seventeen years later, she still felt that sense of culture and community as she walked up to the El Coquí booth with Leo on one side of her and her new dog on the other. He was doing pretty well although he didn't seem to be enjoying the crowd.

After leaving animal control, they'd rushed through the pet store to pick up all the essentials including a new harness, leash, and collar. She'd even grabbed a mesh muzzle just in case. She had a collapsible water bowl in her backpack and a bag of training treats. The only thing she didn't have for the dog was a name, because she refused to call him Dumpy. That wasn't happening.

"Mira quien decidió aparecer," Valeria said when she saw Leo walking toward them. His hair was still wet from the shower he'd rushed through at the apartment while Sofi sat trying to get the dog to let her put a Puerto Rican flag bandana on his neck.

Leo's dad and siblings, including Liam, who'd been rushing around the booth in their matching El Coquí shirts trying to get things organized and set up turned to face them. They all froze at the sight before them.

"I'm sorry," Leo said. "But we had something to do."

"Umm. Whose dog is that?" Kamilah asked with the most confused look on her face.

Sofi didn't blame her. She still wasn't sure what was going on and she was the one who decided to keep the dog.

"Ours," Leo replied a bit too proudly for Sofi's liking.

Kamilah's face just became more confused. She looked at Liam, who looked back at her. They had yet another wordless conversation.

"That's the dog you found in the alley?" Saint asked.

Apparently, Leo had at least told his brother what was going on.

"Yeah," Leo answered. "We took him to animal control, but they said they thought he was from a drug bust they'd done and they'd already gotten a bunch of other dogs in from it."

"Dogfighting?" Cristian concluded.

Sofi and Leo nodded. "Neither one of us could leave him there," Sofi said. "So now we basically have a dog."

"Wait. Wait." Eddie waved his hands. "Let me get this straight. So not only are you and Leo roommates, but now you're co-parenting this dog?"

"I guess," Sofi said at the same time Leo said, "Yes."

There was a moment of silence. The only thing Sofi heard was hundreds of strangers' voices and the old-school Big Pun song about Puerto Rico. Suddenly everyone started laughing. Sofi thought Santos was going to pee his pants, he was doubled over laughing so hard.

"What's so funny?" Papo asked as he walked up holding hands with Rosie. Right behind him Lola was walking with her grandfather, her arm in the crook of his elbow as if he were guiding her when Sofi was pretty sure it was the opposite.

Liam wiped his eyes. Yes, they'd reduced the most humorless man on earth to tears of hilarity. He gestured to the dog. "Sofi and Leo just adopted a baby together."

That set everyone off even more. This time Papo joined in. While Lola and her grandpa just looked on in confusion.

Leo rolled his eyes and shook his head. "And you all tell me that I'm a clown."

"Can I pet her?" Rosie asked, already moving forward.

That sobered everyone up pretty quick.

"Wait," Saint barked out, coming around the entrance to the booth. "You can't just walk up to a dog you don't know."

"Especially one used for fighting," Cristian added.

Sofi was offended even though she knew they had a point.

Apparently Leo was too, because he said, "Dumpy is a sweetheart. He let everyone at the pet store come up and pet him."

"Dumpy?" Eddie asked.

Sofi shook her head, but Leo nodded his.

"Yeah, because we found him living behind a dumpster."

"Are you serious, Leo?" Lola demanded, crossing her arms over her chest. "That's so inappropriate and not funny."

"My dog's name is not Dumpy," Sofi told Lola while glaring at Leo.

Leo bit back his grin. "I already told you that if you don't want me to call him that, you need to come up with something better."

"I don't know," Sofi said. "What about Smokey?"

"Like the bear?" Lola asked.

"Because of his color."

Leo snorted. "Only potheads name their dog Smokey."

"That's true," Papo said with a laugh.

"You'd know wouldn't you?" Kamilah said to her abuelo, who stuck out his tongue at her.

All of a sudden Valeria's voice cut them all off. "Rosie, what are you doing?"

Everyone turned to find Saint's daughter sitting on the ground with the dog at her side. In one hand she held a half-eaten tostón and in the other a plate full of tostones that the dog was devouring with glee, his whole back end wiggling back and forth with the force of his tail.

"He was hungry," Rosie said around a mouthful. "I could tell because he was whining. And Papi and Lola said we're supposed to help people when they need it."

Everyone was quiet because what were they supposed to say to that logic.

"Well," Papo said. "I think we just found the dog's name." He paused for effect. "Tostón."

Sofi smiled. "Perfect."

As everyone started congratulating Tostón on his new name and family, Papo pulled Sofi aside. "I have something for you." He pulled a flash drive out of his pocket. "Before he died, Killian recorded this video for Kamilah and Liam. He wanted it played at the wedding since he knew he wouldn't be there in person." He placed the flash drive in her hand and then sandwiched her hand between his. "Since you're in charge of the reception, I'm giving this to you." He let her hand go.

Sofi quickly placed the flash drive in the front pocket of her mini backpack for safekeeping. "I'll protect it with my life," she told him.

He smiled. "There's no need for all that. Eddie made sure there are plenty of copies, just in case."

Sometime later, after Sofi had left the Vegas to working their food stand while she went to meet up with her mom and Abuela Fina, she was sitting on the grass enjoying a piña colada. On the bench next to her, Mami and Abuela Fina had Tostón stretched out between them, rubbing his belly and saying all kinds of stuff about how sweet and cute he was in English and Spanish.

It was hilarious because, like Sofi, neither woman was an animal person. They were especially not fans of big dogs. Mami had flat out asked Sofi if she'd lost her mind, when Sofi explained that Tostón was her dog. Of course, that could be because Sofi told her that he was also Leo's dog.

Sofi knew she was going to get a talking-to from her mom the minute they were alone. She for sure needed it. She could see herself falling into the same toxic pattern and yet she knew she was going to do it anyway. There was seriously something wrong with her.

"Sofi!" a voice called, pulling her out of her reverie.

Kamilah came bounding over with Liam. You'd think after hours and hours of manning the El Coquí stand, she'd be exhausted but she wasn't. She was like a never-ending battery. It was as if she glowed with vitality. Something that only added to her beauty.

Kamilah had giant spiral curls, light eyes, a pillowy mouth, and a body like Jennifer Lopez, if JLo also had a pair of Ds to match her jaw-dropping ass. Eyes followed Kamilah as she passed, but she hardly noticed. She was unaware of just how naturally gorgeous she was.

Liam knew it though, and he scowled at every guy eyeing his fiancée. It was sort of funny how deep in love he was.

"Hey you!" Kamilah greeted. She looked unsure of her welcome, but Mami took care of that by standing up and wrapping her in a hug.

"I'm so glad you two have made up," she told Kamilah. "I've missed having you around. I thought I was going to have to miss your wedding."

"You're family too. You've always been invited." Both Kamilah's smile and eyes were bright.

It wasn't until that second that Sofi thought about how much her distance from the Vega family had affected her mother too. Her mom had also been adopted by the family, becoming friends with Valeria and Santos, along with Rico and his wife, and a few of Santos's sisters. She worked with Santos and Rico's brother-in-law, Dr. David Hart, at the hospital as well as Kamilah's cousin Mia. It had to have been difficult for her mom to be in the middle. She owed her mom an apology and a thank-you.

She turned and found Abuela Fina flirting outrageously with

Liam, who was doing his best to be polite but also not engage fully by bending low to pet Tostón sitting at Abuela's feet.

"I thought you were allergic," Sofi said to him.

He looked up. His brow was furrowed. "What?"

"When we found Tostón, I suggested taking him to your place, but Leo told me that you're allergic to animals."

Liam didn't even get a chance to respond before it clicked. "He lied, didn't he?" Sofi asked although she knew the answer already.

"I'm not allergic to anything," Liam confirmed.

That sneaky son of a— Sofi cut herself off. "I'm going to kill him."

"To be fair, I still would've said no." Liam let Tostón put his paws on his thighs and sniff his face. "It's not sanitary to have animals in the distillery, which is why I never had any pets."

"Plus, we both work such long hours we don't have time for pets," Kamilah added. "It wouldn't be fair to them." Then she smirked, looking just like her troublemaking brother. "Besides, from what Leo said the dog chose you, not the other way around, and it's clear you already love him."

Sofi grumbled about Leo being an annoying know-it-all, but it was true. Sofi had already been second-guessing herself when they pulled into the parking lot of the animal control offices. When she'd seen him shaking in fear on the counter she'd been ready to snatch him up and run out. It was safe to say that there had been a three to five percent chance that she would've actually left him there after finding out he didn't have a microchip.

"Los Rumberos, my abuelo's old band, are playing soon," Kamilah was telling Abuela Fina. "Now it's all the original crews' kids or grandkids, but they still play every year."

"And your brother is in the band?"

Kamilah nodded. "Wait until you see him perform. Don't tell him I said this, but he's a born star. I never remember a time he wasn't wandering around singing at the top of his lungs and hitting all the notes perfectly. It used to make me so mad because when I tried I sounded like a squawking parrot."

"She has the volume, but not the skill," Liam said, earning an elbow to the stomach from Kamilah.

Sofi, Mami, and Abuela Fina laughed.

"Anyway," Kamilah said with a hard look at Liam who just grinned. "The family has a spot by the stage. Come join us."

Sofi grabbed Tostón's leash from Abuela and they all followed Liam, who used his big body to clear a path.

Once they reached the side of the stage where a large portion of the Vega family was set up with coolers and lawn chairs, Sofi and Mami greeted everyone while also introducing Abuela Fina around. Omar, Kamilah's oldest nephew—who Sofi couldn't believe was now seventeen—and his buddies volunteered to hold on to Tostón and walk him around so that Sofi could enjoy the show. It probably helped that a group of cute girls from their high school immediately descended on them to coo and pet the dog. Sofi shook her head.

"Don't worry. I've got my eye on them," Yasmeen, Cristian's wife and high school sweetheart, said to Sofi. She did not look happy about the attention her son was getting.

"Oh I do too," Valeria added. "That girl in the tube top looks like she's in college."

"Mmm-hmm," Yasmeen agreed. "She's got but one more time to put her fast little hands on my baby's bicep before I catch myself a case."

"You two are a mess," Cristian said. "It's not like he can do anything with his little brothers hanging around. Leave him be."

"And yet, whenever I brought a boyfriend around you threatened to break his arm if he so much as held my hand," Kamilah said.

"Who cares?" Cristian took a swig from his bottle. "I also punched one of your boyfriends in the face."

"What?" Kamilah screeched.

"Hey." Cristian pointed to his side where Saint sat with a napping Rosie in his lap. "Saint was the one who scared him so bad he pissed his pants."

Everyone looked at Saint, who was suddenly very interested in the stagehands doing a mic check.

"What did you do?" Kamilah demanded.

Saint pretended not to hear her, but Cristian answered for him.

"He grabbed him by the throat, lifted him with one hand, and told him, 'I know many ways to kill someone and make it hurt. If you ever put your hands on my little sister again, you'll experience them all.' Then he dropped him and walked away."

"Saint," Lola gasped, wide-eyed.

Saint looked mildly embarrassed. "That was only after I heard Kamilah tell Sofi and Lucy that he'd pushed her," he explained.

"What?" Kamilah exclaimed. "Who are you even talking about? I never once had a boy push me. I would've kicked his junk clean off his body myself."

Saint shrugged. "I don't remember his name." He looked at Cristian.

Cristian rubbed his chin. "I think his name was Martin or Marvin or something."

"Melvin?" Lucy busted out in laughter. "That little nerd?"

"There's no way." Sofi joined Lucy in laughter, remembering Kamilah's first official boyfriend ever. "He was in robotics and chess club. Didn't he skip a grade too?" He'd been a good three inches shorter than Kamilah, as thin as a pole, and about as menacing as a newly hatched duckling. "He was scared of his own shadow!" Sofi hooted.

"I know what I heard," Saint said.

Kamilah was shaking her head. "I never said that. I told them he was *being pushy* as in he was pushing me to kiss him when I wasn't ready. It was why I was going to dump him. Instead, he completely ghosted me *and* switched schools." She gave her brothers the evil eye. "Now I finally know why."

Saint and Cristian shared a look before Cristian shrugged his shoulders, completely unconcerned with the difference. "The horny little shit deserved it, then."

"I can't believe my sons are so violent," Valeria said, looking scandalized.

"Don't look at me." Eddie raised his hands. "I was at school in California when all of this happened."

"Kiss ass," Cristian coughed into his hand.

"Hood rat," Eddie returned.

"It's not like Kamilah also didn't get in plenty of fights defending her brothers too," Lucy added.

"What?" Valeria screeched. "My daughter fighting? Como una callejera!" She looked so disappointed.

"We got it from you and Papi," Kamilah said. "Should we recount what happened any time either one of you caught someone flirting with the other?"

"Shut up and mind your own business," Valeria said in Spanish while wearing a scowl. "I'm a Christian woman. There's no way I went around fighting people."

"Yeah okay, Mami," Cristian said. "When Leo gets offstage, we'll ask him about the time you beat the bricks off Olga Peña right in this park because she spanked him. It's his favorite story to tell."

"Damn," Lola said, still looking around wide-eyed. "And I thought my family was gangster."

Papo Vega held up his beer. "Thug life," he cheered.

Everyone laughed and held up their drinks.

Suddenly, the lights on the stage came on signaling the show was about to begin. Rico Vega, Santos's twin and the alderman, walked out on the stage with their youngest brother, Gio, a DJ and producer known worldwide—who never missed the event no matter where he was living in the world. Together they gave a brief speech about the importance of the Fiestas Patronales Puertorriqueñas to Humboldt Park in celebrating the culture through food, art, and music. Then talked about how Los Rumberos were a part of the celebration since the beginning. They welcomed the band to the stage with cheers from the audience.

Sofi's breath caught in her throat the minute Leo walked onto the stage. He'd changed out of his jeans and El Coquí T-shirt into a pair of khaki linen trousers, a tropical floral print shirt with the first few buttons undone leaving a part of his chest on display, and a Panama hat. He matched the rest of the band down to the loafers without socks. But somehow on him it just looked…better. It was the way he wore the outfit, with confidence and easy sex appeal, that drew everyone's attention.

The band began playing the very recognizable intro to the song almost every Puerto Rican knew by heart, made famous by Frankie Ruiz and recorded by many of the island's greatest singers after. The moment Leo held the mic to his mouth and sang the first words, "Puerto Rico," the crowd went wild. Everyone sang along and the salsa dancing started.

Sofi sang and danced right along with them. She couldn't help herself. The song filled her with so much pride and happiness and she knew that every single person around her felt the same. Especially when the background singers sang, "'Boricua soy y siempre seré,'" and Leo replied, "'Puertorriqueño y de Humboldt Park!'" and the crowd screamed. It was beautiful how so many Puerto Ricans, many who weren't born on the island or who hadn't been there for a long time, still felt such love and connection to the tiny island in the Caribbean.

"Let's move closer," Kamilah yelled to Sofi a while later. Sofi nodded her agreement and soon they were working their way toward the front of the stage with Lucy and Liza in tow. They'd just reached the front when the song the entire band had been singing together ended. The rest of the singers in the band stepped back and Leo stepped forward.

"This next song I added at the last minute," Leo said into the mic. "The guys were nice enough not to kill me for it."

The band and the crowd chuckled.

"I don't know why, but I really felt the need to sing it tonight. Maybe because there are so many beautiful women in the crowd tonight."

Sofi froze when he looked right at her. It was a brief look, but still. She had no idea how he'd even known she was there. She looked around quickly, but Kamilah hadn't seemed to notice. She was just looking at her brother with pride. Lucy and Liza were staring at each other, ignoring the rest of the world.

The horns began playing a familiar intro and Sofi gasped.

He was about to sing "Comerte a Besos," a song literally about devouring someone with kisses.

He was reminding her of what he'd done to her last night. How he'd eaten her to ecstasy, and she'd loved every single second of it. She wasn't sure how to feel about that. On the one hand, she hardly needed a reminder less than a day later. She remembered every second all too clearly. The problem was that she had told herself hundreds of times that she wasn't going to do this with Leo anymore. Sofi firmly controlled every other aspect of her life from her looks to her food and schedule. It was what she needed to feel confident and capable. However, she'd never once been able to control her feelings for Leo. At first it had been exciting and a bit freeing, but now it was just scary and toxic. They simply weren't good for each other, no matter how physically compatible they were.

The song began with him singing that he'd had to wait so long for her that he'd lost all sense of time, but he was determined to win her. It was inevitable that they'd get together be-cause she was already giving in and he wanted more.

That motherfucker.

During every previous song, Leo had been dancing around with the band and moving back and forth across the stage, but this time he stood right there in the middle, in front of her. He kept the microphone in the stand and held it with one hand while he ran the other hand down his chest to the front of his hip.

Women in the crowd screamed, but Sofi just stood there star-ing at his package like an idiot. Thinking about what it looked like, tasted like, felt like. She broke out in goose bumps even though the body heat surrounding her had them all sweating.

He moved his feet in a salsa step swinging his hips in sync and Sofi stared at this thighs. He had no right to look like that and sing like that too. It was unfair and unnatural.

The band broke it down and Leo did one of those turns à la Ricky Martin/Marc Anthony/Elvis Crespo pivoting on one foot while rolling his hips. He sang about convincing her to love him little by little, kiss by kiss. Then he had the audacity to look right at her, wink, and laugh before turning his attention to the crowd. It was a clear message to her that even though he wasn't looking at her, he was singing to her. He wanted her to know that he was coming for her heart and he'd use the rest of her body to get to it if he had to.

12

LEO OPENED THE CAR DOOR FOR TOSTÓN AND CLIPPED HIS LEASH
onto his harness before allowing him to jump down. "You're
doing well, son," he told the dog. "No one would know that just
last week you were living in the alley and eating trash to survive."

Of course, the dog didn't respond except to immediately
sniff the grass, but it was still true. In the last week, Tostón had
flourished from scared and shy to happy and sweet. He was still
the chillest puppy Leo had ever seen, content to just hang out
on the couch and frequently napping most of the day away, but
he was also down for long walks and some playful wrestling
with his new dad.

Leo and Tostón walked a short distance to the dog park
which was really just a fenced-in concrete slab, but at least they

had some kiddie pools full of water to help the dogs cool down on the hot summer day. Even better, there were only a handful of other dogs in the big dog area.

Leo walked Tostón into the space and took off his leash, but he didn't go anywhere. Tostón stayed right at his side, practically causing Leo to trip as he made his way to a short wall to sit. Leo wasn't surprised. Tostón was shy and he definitely liked people more than other dogs. The last time Leo had brought him, it took Tostón a bit to warm up but then he'd played and enjoyed himself.

Leo sat and waited for Tostón to get comfortable while also waiting for his friend to arrive. He took out his phone and texted Sofi some pictures of Tostón lying on the concrete watching the other dogs play.

Your son is as anti-social as you are.

Less than a minute later he got a response.

We aren't anti-social. We just don't waste our energy on the unworthy.

Otherwise known as being stuck-up.

It's called reclaiming your time.

Well, he's sitting here lonely, so I don't think it's the best path to take.

Es mejor estar solo que mal acompañado.

You sound like my grandma.

Good. She was a smart woman.

You got me there.

Leo, when are you going to learn that
I will always "get" you?

Sofi, when are you going to learn that
I want to be "had" by you?

Leo watched the bubble with the three dots show up and disappear a few times. HA. He'd gotten her.

She had no idea what to respond to that and he loved it. There was nothing he loved more than keeping Miss Control Freak Sofi on her toes.

"Which girl are you texting that has you smiling like that?" a voice asked, making Leo jump and look up.

His buddy Ahmad Singh stood in front of him with a slick smile on his face.

Leo stood and put his phone in his pocket. "Your mother, obviously," he told Ahmad. "She was just thanking me for last night." He grabbed Tostón's leash.

"I'm glad you showed her a good time. Now I know to step my game up for my date with your mom tonight."

It was a long-standing joke between them ever since they'd watched the Andy Samberg and Justin Timberlake "Mother-lover" skit from *Saturday Night Live* in the middle of the night during a shift years ago.

They made their way out of the dog park. Leo would've apologized to his dog, but Tostón was more than happy to leave. He practically dragged Leo out the gate. "Please, as if my mom could ever overlook that ugly mug of yours," Leo teased Ahmad.

The truth was that Ahmad's father had been a model for many years and Ahmad looked just like him. He was a good-looking guy and he knew it, just like Leo knew that his own looks were nothing to scoff at. The other guys at their station referred to them as "the calendar boys," claiming they looked more like they were from a sexy firefighter calendar than from the academy. At first it had bothered the two of them and they'd bonded over their dislike of being seen as pretty boys. But they had both proved themselves many times over since then. Everyone they worked with knew they were legit.

"Just for that I'm going to work you until you cry like a baby," Ahmad told him. He'd been putting Leo through the wringer for at least an hour three times a week. They worked out at their old coworker's gym that was a few blocks from the dog park. Their buddy Derek had his own dog he brought to work with him every day, so he had no issue letting Leo put Tostón in his office while they worked out. Leo had hoped that Derek's eleven-year-old boxer, Blue, would help bring Tostón out of his shell, but as far as Leo could tell, the two dogs basically ignored each other and napped in separate corners.

"Vega! Drop those hands or I'm going to give you weights to hold," Ahmad yelled at him.

Leo immediately dropped his hands to his sides. He already had on a sixty-pound vest. He did not want dumbbells on top of that. Not when he still had so much more left to do. He stepped off the tall wooden box only to step right back up. Box climbs were one of the easier parts of the workout because Leo had always had good stamina and endurance, but with the heavy vest tugging on his shoulders it was hard for Leo to ignore the way his arm tingled.

Ahmad and Derek had come up with a workout that was designed to mimic the movements Leo would be doing during the test. They also claimed to have made it harder than it needed to be because "then the test will feel like a breeze." Leo wasn't sure about that seeing as he had yet to make it through the entire workout without his shoulder/arm causing him to mess something up.

"Stop trying to run through the whole test in your mind," Ahmad barked. He and Derek were off to the side sitting in some janky-ass lawn chairs while drinking beers like they were at a lakefront barbecue. Bastards. "Focus only on the movement you're doing. You keep psyching yourself out by thinking too hard."

As he stepped off the box for the final time and took a few seconds to catch his breath, Leo snorted. "I think that may be the first time in my life that anyone has ever accused me of thinking too hard. Usually they beg me to think at all."

Ahmad threw his empty beer can at Leo, almost hitting him in the chest. Luckily Leo ducked. "What the fuck," Leo yelled. "You could've hit me in the face with that!"

Ahmad ignored his chiding in favor of continuing his own. "Stop doing that. You always act like you're nothing but a meathead who can carry a tune. You're one of the smartest people I know."

"That doesn't say much for the people you hang around," Leo tried to joke, but Ahmad wasn't having any of that.

He stood up and got in Leo's face. "Dude, do you know how many members of my family are doctors, lawyers, engineers, or just overall highly educated? I hang around some very smart people, but none of them can problem solve on the fly like you can. They're all super regimented and stifling to everyone including themselves." He grabbed the straps of Leo's weighted vest to give him a shake. "You see the world and people in a different way, and it allows you to get to the root of the problem. Sure, you daydream more than the average person, but it makes it easier for you to shuffle through a bunch of options quickly to find the best idea."

Leo didn't know what to say to that. He'd always viewed his tendencies to jump right in as a sign of his impulsivity. He didn't brainstorm before he acted, he just acted. Most of the time it worked in his favor and sometimes it didn't. "I appreciate that, but I think I'm just lucky."

Ahmad picked up the discarded can. "You're wrong, but I'm not going to argue with you about it. I'm not your damn therapist on top of being your free personal trainer. Now get a fucking move on instead of wasting all of our time. I know you're trying to stall."

He was right. Leo was trying to stall. He dreaded the next part of his workout—carrying two forty-pound buckets a hundred and fifty feet then back without stopping. Normally that would be nothing to him, but his grip wasn't as strong as it used to be and he struggled to maintain hold of the bucket for the entire time. Usually by the time he was done, his hand and arm had checked out at least for a few minutes. But Leo didn't have a few minutes to recover during the test. He had to make it through all of the tasks without stopping or messing up if he wanted to pass. Not for the first time, Leo wondered if he would ever be able to actually do it. Every time the workout seemed to get harder instead of easier. He knew that wasn't good. But he'd promised himself that he'd get back on platoon duty and while he had the tendency to disappoint everyone else in his life, he would never disappoint himself. So he sucked in a few more breaths, told himself to fucking man up, and ignored the pain while he continued his workout. Just like he always did.

A bit later, Leo and Tostón bypassed the front doors to Casa del Sol and instead went around to the back where the building shared a large courtyard with the clinic and the main building. There he found Abuelo Papo and Doña Fina sitting at a patio table with what looked like glasses of lemonade.

"Look who it is," Abuelo said in Spanish. "My favorite grandson."

"You told me to come over," Leo pointed out. "And just to be clear, I'm telling everyone you said that."

"I was talking about the dog," Abuelo said.

"Rude," Leo responded.

Abuelo ignored Leo and held out his hands. "Come here, Tostón. Come to your abuelo."

Tostón started wiggling in excitement, so Leo dropped the leash. Let him maul Abuelo with overexcited puppy affection. That would show him.

Except Tostón didn't go to Abuelo. He went right to Doña Fina and tried to jump in her lap. "Ay!" she yelled. "No, Tostón! Bajate!"

Since Tostón had no idea what she was saying, only the high-pitched tone of her voice, he got even more excited. He jumped and barked and licked.

Leo rushed forward to grab the leash and tug him back, but he made the mistake of using the wrong hand. Tostón gave a hard tug and pain shot down Leo's arm then back up. "Fuck," Leo shouted, immediately dropping the leash to grab his shoulder.

Abuelo shot out of his chair and stood in Tostón's path to Doña Fina. "No," he said in the deep and loud authoritative voice Leo had only ever heard a very few times in his life. It was the voice that had all of his kids and grandkids jumping to follow his orders without comment like little soldiers. Apparently, it also worked on great-grandogs because Tostón skidded to a stop right at Abuelo's feet and sat down. Abuelo calmly bent down, grabbed his leash, and walked them back to the table to sit in his chair. "Quédate aquí y pórtate bien," he told the dog with a rough pat on the side. He looked to Leo then, concern written all over his face. "Are you okay?"

Leo nodded. His arm was no longer screaming in sharp lightning-like pain, but tingling in the all-too-familiar pins and needles sensation. He continued to breathe through the feeling as he made his way to the table and plopped into one of the two empty chairs.

"Do you need an ice pack?" Doña Fina asked in Spanish.

Leo shook his head. "I'm fine."

She didn't look like she believed him. "Escucha esto, it was 1965 and I was preparing for Miss Puerto Rico. Mi mamá estaba nerviosa. I was the shortest of all the contestants. She went to the nicest boutique in San Juan and bought me the highest pair of—" she paused for a second, a look of deep thought on her face and her hands making circles next to her head as if that would make her thought clearer "—tacones," she said, apparently giving up on remembering the English word. "I mean, así de grande." She held up her thumb and forefinger in an L shape to demonstrate about a six-inch heel. "She wanted me to wear them all of the time, so I could practice walking in them, but I was still dancing every day and my feet were always sore. I didn't want to wear those shoes too, so I lied to her and told her that I wore them when really I didn't." She paused to take another sip of her lemonade. "Time passes and finally it's time to practice walking on the stage for the swimsuit competition. My mami brings me the shoes and tells me to put them on. I'm as tall as the other girls now and, because I already know that I look the best in my swimsuit, I feel amazing. I know I'm going to win. Then I take one step down the stairs y—" she made a wretching motion with her hands "—mi tobillo se dobla. I fall down the rest of the stairs and land right on my face. I mean, I thought I broke my nose." She shakes her head. "They had to carry me out and they made me miss the rest of the practice so I could stay off my feet. But you better believe that I wore those shoes every day after that. And when the day of the contest came, I was back out there in those shoes strutting up and down that stage like nothing ever happened." She waved her hand in the air while saying, "After that I discovered I had done damage to the ligaments in my foot, ankle, and knee, so I couldn't dance professionally anymore."

Leo sat there for a moment trying to figure out what that

story had to do with anything. "I'm sorry, Doña Fina, but I don't get what you're trying to tell me."

She shook her head as if sad that he was so dense. "Sometimes we have to deal with a lot of pain in order to reach our goals, but it's worth it."

"But didn't you just say that you'd damaged your ligaments and couldn't dance anymore?"

"Sí, pero gané Miss Puerto Rico and that's all that matters."

Leo frowned. He didn't see that. He saw a woman who'd ruined her chosen career in order to reach a short-term goal. "Are you telling me that it was worth getting shot and losing my career, because now I can dedicate my time to winning Sofi over?"

Her eyes widened. "No! No! Claro que no! I'm saying that sometimes things happen that we can't control and we need to find a way to make the outcome a positive one."

He still didn't see how her story demonstrated that, but he wasn't going to argue with her about it.

"We called you here to talk about the next steps of the plan," Abuelo Papo said.

Leo almost rolled his eyes. They acted like they were all on some intense secret mission. All they'd done was sit there pretending like they knew nothing of the situation while other people convinced Sofi to move in with him.

"Having the two of you adopt the dog was a good idea," Doña Fina was saying, "but Sofi now knows that your sister's fiancé isn't allergic."

"Yeah. I know. She already chewed me out for that, but I wasn't lying." Leo had honestly thought Liam was allergic to animals. He could've sworn he'd heard it somewhere, but he could not remember where or who'd said it. "And it wasn't an idea I had. It sort of just happened."

Abuelo and Doña Fina looked at each other and then away.

Doña Fina bit her lip while Abuelo looked like a cat with a stomach full of canary.

Leo got a bad feeling. "What's going on?"

"Yo no hice nada," Doña Fina said, her hands up in the air like a criminal being confronted by the cops. "I only mentioned how cute the dogs were when they came for pet therapy."

"And you said that Sofi always wanted a dog when she was little," Abuelo added.

"Abuelo," Leo intoned, rubbing at his suddenly achy temples. "Please tell me that you didn't plant Tostón in the alley for us to find."

Abuelo threw up his hands. "What was I supposed to do when I saw him sniffing around the parking lot? Leave him there so he could get hit by a car? It was a sign! Destiny! Fate, I tell you!"

"Oh. My. God." Leo closed his eyes and shook his head. "How could you have known that he'd stay in the dumpster enclosure? Or that Sofi and I would go into the alley?"

"I left him a big pile of arroz con gandules and why do you think I told you to take out the garbage?"

There were so many ways that could've gone totally wrong. The odds of it working out exactly as his abuelo had planned were so slim. Leo was astounded that it had worked. He wanted to be upset, but he was more impressed than anything. But still, he needed to put a stop to their plotting behind his back. "No more planning things that include innocent creatures that could get hurt," he said firmly. "And talk to me before you do something else."

"Claro. We didn't mean to overstep," Doña Fina said, all big eyes and pouty lips.

Leo snorted. That one was about as innocent as a three-time convicted felon serving a life sentence.

"You act like it didn't work out perfectly," Abuelo grumbled.

"We now have a dog that neither one of us planned for!" Leo pointed out.

"And you love it," Abuelo said. "Also who watches the dog when you both work?" Abuelo asked.

Leo wanted to point out that Abuelo should've thought about that before he foisted Tostón onto them, but he knew it would be a waste of time. "The number of people who've volunteered their babysitting services means that I never have to worry about that. But when I have to go anywhere, I leave him with Liam since Liam has moved his office into his place, we don't have to worry about him wandering around the distillery all day."

Abuelo nodded as if he'd figured as much. "You need to make this work for Sofi otherwise she'll get frustrated and blame you for tricking her into keeping him."

"*I* didn't trick her into anything," Leo pointed out. "That was you two."

Abuelo ignored that. "Just try to make sure you're both there waiting for Sofi when she gets home." Abuelo sat forward as he began to get excited with the ideas he was spitballing. "Cook dinner, clean, take care of stuff."

"You want me to be her housewife while working two jobs?" Sure his position at the distillery hadn't officially started yet—it was mostly just planning at the moment—and once he got back on platoon duty he would have more daylight hours available, but still, he had a lot going on.

"I want you to prove to her that you will be a good partner. That you want to make her life easier not harder."

"No woman with common sense wants a man who requires her to do more work to be with him." Doña Fina took a sip from her cup. "What purpose does he serve, then? Good sex? We can get that without a relationship. Most of us can get it without even needing the man."

"She's right," Abuelo said, patting Tostón's head as the dog leaned against his leg. "The time for all that 'women need men' nonsense is over. It's time for us men to prove that we are worthy of them, not the other way around."

Leo blinked. He didn't know what to say to that. On one hand, eww old people talking about sex. On the other, they were right. He didn't want to be a burden for Sofi. He didn't want to tie her down or hold her back, like an invasive species of ivy coiling around a flower's stem and preventing it from reaching the sunlight. He wanted them to be like two fruit trees planted in the same yard because they cross-pollinate and therefore help each other bear fruit. He wanted...to flourish together.

"I get it," he told them.

Leo was feeling pretty good about the next steps until Doña Fina threw out her next idea. "I also think she should go on that dating app her friends want her to join."

That was not going to happen. Not on Leo's watch. "Why would sending her out with other guys be a good idea?"

"Because what better way to show her that what she thinks she wants is not actually what she wants?"

"You want to purposely send her on dates with dudes just to make me look good?" Leo wasn't sure if he was more offended for these other guys or himself. Did she really think that he needed all of that to look good? And, sure, most men were trash humans who only wanted relationships as long as they didn't require any type of work or personal growth, but there were good dudes out there and Leo wasn't going to risk one of them crossing her path.

"That could work," Abuelo Papo said.

"No." Leo shook his head. "That could easily blow up in my face. She could make a real connection with someone and it would push me way back."

"That's true," Doña Fina agreed.

"Besides," Leo continued, really needing to drive home the point. "If she's spending her free time going on dates, it cuts into the little bit of time I'll have to spend with her."

Doña Fina tapped her finger on her chin, her gaze focused into the distance. "Okay, fine. We won't do that part, but I'll keep thinking about what else we can do."

Leo really didn't want them doing anything more. It was enough to get their advice. He didn't need Abuelo to start pulling more shenanigans. He knew all too well his abuelo had the tendency to go way too hard. "Listen. Let's not plan anything else until we give this a chance. I know Sofi better than anyone and she needs to be guided gently into things. You can't try to force her to do anything or she will shut you out completely." He reached for Tostón's leash before standing. "I have to get going, but I'll do what you said in terms of dinner, chores, and such. I do want her to know I can be a good partner."

It wasn't until he'd said goodbye and got in his car that Leo realized they'd never agreed not to come up with more schemes. *Shit.*

13

THE LAST THING SOFI EXPECTED WHEN SHE CAME HOME FROM
work late on Monday evening was to be swiftly corralled into
the distillery for an impromptu taste testing. According to Kamilah, the wedding party was getting together to choose a signature drink for the reception which was news to Sofi—the
planner of said reception.

Freshly changed into a casual blue romper and some flat sandals, Sofi breezed through the open garage doors of Kane Distillery where the rest of the wedding party was hanging around
laughing and listening to '90s R&B. She was immediately set
upon by her baby boy.

Tostón ran over to her, his tail wagging and tongue hanging
out of his mouth. He started doing what Sofi had begun call-

ing "tap dancing." When he got so excited that he'd do this prance-like dance. It reminded her of those videos of the charros making their horses dance. Tostón did it whenever he was really happy about something and it was the cutest thing ever.

"Hola, bebé," Sofi told him as she crouched down and gave him tons of snuggles and rubs. "Mami missed you too."

"I'm obsessed with your dog. Don't be surprised if I just slip him into my car when we leave."

Sofi looked up to see Ben, Liam's best friend, standing over her and Tostón. He was a good-looking man with dark eyes and killer cheekbones, but despite his charm he never did it for Sofi. Not that he seemed interested in her that way. He just liked to flirt and Sofi was usually more than happy to accommodate him even if it was only to piss off Leo. "You'd better not try to steal my dog. I'd have to get his dad on you." She motioned over to Leo, who was standing behind the bar giving her a dirty look. She decided to put him at ease. "You're going to have to keep a close eye on Tostón," she said, raising her voice so it carried through the open space. "This guy wants to kidnap him."

Leo's expression cleared and he let out a small smile while shaking his head. "He's going to have to fight with everyone else here." He gestured to his younger cousin Alex, who was sitting across the bar from him sipping on something that looked a soft pink. "A few minutes ago, Alex was carrying him around on her hip like a baby and dancing with him to Ginuwine."

"He's the perfect dance partner," Alex said, completely unfazed by her cousins' teasing. "But I agree with Leo, if anyone is going to abscond with that sweetie, it's going to be me. Except then I'd need to find a new place because my jerk of a landlord has made it very clear that there are no pets allowed in my apartment." She shot Saint, said landlord, a faux scowl.

Saint winked at Sofi. "You're welcome."

"Well, we own our house," Lucy said. "We can dognap

Tostón and keep him with no problems. Right, babe?" She looked at Liza, who nodded.

"And we have plenty of yard for him to enjoy," Liza added.

"Um, excuse me." Sofi stood and scooped up her baby, placing him on her own hip. He immediately began licking her ear and cheek. "This here is *my* son and he will be staying with *me*. Go find your own furbabies to adopt." She glared at Leo. "And you! What kind of father just lets people plot to steal his son right in front of him?"

Leo smiled widely. "The kind who knows his baby momma is a lioness who would put anyone who tries in their place."

Kamilah walked behind him at the bar and smacked him across the head. "Don't call Sofi your baby momma. That's weird."

"Ow," Leo yelped, rubbing at the back of his head. "Is that any way to treat your brother who, out of the goodness in his heart, decided to use his badass mixologist skills to up the ante at your wedding?"

Kamilah rolled her eyes and twisted her lips, but patted him on the head like he was the dog. "You're right. I'm sowwy I hurt your wittle feewings," she said in an overly saccharine baby voice.

Leo pushed her hand away. "See, and here everyone likes to pretend like I'm the one who's mean to you, but they don't see what a brat you truly are."

Kamilah looked at Liam. "You gonna let him call me a brat like that?"

Liam shrugged. "If the shoe fits." He took a sip from his not pink drink, because of course Liam was going to drink straight whiskey even though the whole point was to come up with a cocktail.

Kamilah gasped in shocked outrage. "Oh, I don't like this at all." She gestured between Liam and Leo. "If the two of you working together is going to lead to you ganging up on me, then we're going to have to reevaluate some things."

"It's not ganging up on you if it's true," Leo said. He was slicing what looked like fresh strawberries.

"Leave her be," Saint told him. "You always aggravate her until you get a reaction."

Leo's jaw dropped while Kamilah smiled widely, having finally gotten someone to stick up for her. "See," she said, walking over to Saint and giving him a hug and a kiss on the cheek. "That's why he's always been my favorite."

Saint grinned while Leo huffed in offense. "I don't see him making any of these drinks or taking on extra band practices in order to perform at your reception *for free.*" Leo's tone was decidedly pouty.

Kamilah giggled and Sofi bit her lip to keep from joining her. It was hilarious how much Kamilah had all four of her brothers wrapped around her finger, especially now that she was getting married. Even Cristian and Eddie had texted Sofi multiple times to ask her if there was anything they could do to help. When Sofi tried to put them off, they sent her a good chunk of money anyway. Kamilah didn't know it yet, but the twins were the reason she was going to have a glasshouse's worth of flowers at the ceremony and reception. Usually being around the Vega siblings made Sofi grateful to be an only child, but there were times like these when seeing how much they truly loved each other caused her a pang of loneliness. Luckily, she did have Kamilah and they treated each other like the sister neither of them had. At least, they had before. They'd even planned how to make their feelings a reality.

Sofi fought the urge to bop her best friend on the head with her rat-tail comb. She'd been trying to make a straight part in Kamilah's wet hair for the last five minutes and had been unable to because Kamilah wouldn't stop moving.

Sitting cross-legged on the bed in front of her, Kamilah was still going on and on about the surprise eighteenth birthday party she'd help put together for Liam. "Here, we spent all this time cooking his favorite food, making him a birthday cake, plus getting all those decorations, and he couldn't even act like he was having a good time," she complained while throwing her hands around in emphasis. Kamilah was a very animated storyteller, especially when her emotions were high. "He just sat there like a freaking ice statute who is way too cold to actually melt."

Sofi nodded as she pretended to listen, but the truth was that when it came to her ex–best friend, Kamilah was a bit of a broken record, so Sofi didn't have to pay much attention to what Kamilah was saying. She already knew it was some version of calling him rude, a jerk, cold, or—when she was feeling extra butthurt—an asshole. It always was. Sofi wanted to point out that maybe Kamilah should just stop doing things for him, but she'd already tried that when Kamilah first mentioned helping his grandfather plan Liam's party. Look where that had gotten her.

"I mean, sure, he said 'thank you' to us, but it was like the most unemotional, borderline sarcastic version ever said. Seriously, you should've heard it."

"I did hear it," Sofi said, trying to make a straight part down the middle of Kamilah's head. "I was there."

Kamilah didn't hear her. "He practically ran out as soon as he could. I mean, it was barely eight o'clock and it's not like he had other plans. He doesn't even have any friends!" She shook her head in disbelief, causing the pointy end of the comb to create a sloppy zigzag from her crown to her hairline.

Sofi had enough. "Stop moving or I swear I'm going to stab you with this." She poked Kamilah with the rattail in warning.

Kamilah blinked as if coming out of her rage fog. "Oh sorry," she said, wincing. "I totally forgot you were going to braid my hair for me." She paused for a second. "Do you think this is why my mom always whacked my head with the brush when I was little?"

"Yes," Sofi said without hesitation. "Doing your hair is like trying to shove a cooked spaghetti noodle through a straw."

"I'm not that bad!"

Sofi stared at her, unblinking.

Kamilah grimaced. "Okay fine, but I'll sit still now. I promise."

A scoff from the doorway had both of their heads swiveling to the side. Leo stood, leaning his shoulder against the doorjamb. He was in his Chicago Fire Department Academy uniform and Sofi almost choked on her own saliva when she attempted to swallow. He'd really bulked up in the last few months and Sofi wasn't sure how she'd ever keep her hands to herself now.

"You must like torture," he told Sofi with a smart-ass smirk. "My mom hated doing Kamilah's nappy hair. She was always threatening to shave Kamilah bald because she was such a pain in the ass about it. Right, Sideshow Bob?" He directed the question at his sister, who rolled her eyes.

"First of all," Kamilah said, holding up a finger, "Mami was as serious about that threat as Papi was about cutting off your sticky fingers for constantly stealing the caramel-filled chocolates from the box." She held up another finger. "Secondly, shut up and go away, you goblin." She quickly dropped her index finger and left only her middle one up.

Leo's smirk grew because he lived to get a rise out of everyone around him. "Let's see how much that sassiness lasts, princesita. Mami and Papi want to talk to you downstairs. They heard about you calling Liam un huelebicho malagradecido to his face."

Kamilah's eyes widened. Sofi's widened too, but mostly because she couldn't see her bestie saying something so rude to anyone's face, even Liam's.

"Word of advice from someone who's always in trouble with them," Leo said, stepping into the room. "Don't try to act innocent, just own up to what you did right away and apologize profusely, cry if they seem really mad, and most importantly never keep them waiting when they call for you. That just makes them madder."

Kamilah hopped off the bed so fast that she nearly fell right on her face. She ran past Leo, knocking into his shoulder and almost sending them both to the floor.

As soon as the apartment door slammed shut behind Kamilah, Leo's expression changed. He looked at Sofi like a panther stalking his prey. "Sofi," he murmured, sliding farther into the room and closing the bedroom door behind him. "You've been avoiding me."

Sofi fought the urge to shrink back against the ruffled pillows in Kamilah's bed. Instead she snorted and rolled her eyes. "Please, as if you're that important. I barely remember you exist unless you're standing right in front of me."

He moved closer. "I think I am and I think you do. In fact, I'm positive that you not only remember me when I'm not around, but you miss me."

"Well, I'm not surprised about that. Your ego has always been bigger than your brain."

He smiled. "Ouch. Someone is in a mood. What's with the attitude?" He sat at the foot of Kamilah's bed, his hip touching Sofi's knee. "I thought that I'd for sure get sweet Sofi, the one who melts for me as soon as her tongue is in my mouth." He brought his hand up and began dancing his fingers along her thigh where her sleep shorts had ridden up.

Sofi pushed his hand off. "I don't know why you thought that. If you need something to melt in your mouth, you'd better hope parents have one of those caramel chocolates around."

He chuckled and put his hand back. "But I already have one right here. Tú eres mi bombón de caramelo."

Sofi wanted to ask, if that was true, why he'd been spending so much time with his fire academy friends trolling bars for girls, but that would've told him that she was jealous. She was jealous, but she didn't want him to know that. It was bad enough that he was practically an adult now, he was so close to graduating, and she was still in high school. She didn't need to look more immature. She was wracking her brain for something to say, but she couldn't think of anything. Her mind would only process the feel of his calloused fingers on her skin.

Luckily, before she could make a fool of herself, the door swung open and an angry Kamilah stomped through.

Sofi hopped off the bed so quickly that she was sure Kamilah would call her out on her obvious guilt.

Thankfully, her friend was too busy shouting at her brother. "You jerk!" she yelled at Leo. "They had no idea I'd said that. You just made me tell on myself and now I'm grounded for the next two weeks!"

"Oops," Leo smirked. "My bad. I guess I was the one who heard you. Not Mami and Papi."

"You are literally the worst! Why do you always have to be such a tool?" She waved her hands around before he could answer. "Actually, I don't care what your answer is, just get out of my room. Go hang out with your dumb academy friends and trick girls into thinking you're an actual firefighter in hopes that they'll overlook your personality and hook up with you. Neither one of us wants you here, right, Sofi?"

Sofi immediately nodded her head. "Yeah, go away, Leo. We're too smart to fall for your charming act. We know you're nothing but an idiotic douchebag."

If she hadn't known him so well, she would've missed the flash of hurt that passed his face before he schooled it into his usual look of I don't care about anything.

He let out a fake bark of laughter. "Please, as if I actually want to hang out with two high school girls. I have better things to do. I just came to grab a few rubbers from my room, since I used the ones in my wallet already."

"Eww. TMI, you perv," Kamilah exclaimed. She began actively shoving him to the door until he was on the other side of the doorway. Then she slammed the door on his face and locked it. She spun to face Sofi and rested her back on the door. She let out a sigh of annoyance. "I know I want you to marry one of my brothers, so that we'll be real sisters one day, but promise me that it won't be Leo."

"God no," Sofi said with a fake laugh of her own. "Never in my life would I even look twice at Leo."

Kamilah nodded. "Good, because he's the absolute worst. He's a cocky jerk who thinks he's the greatest thing since Ricky Martin and he doesn't care about anyone but himself." She pushed off the door and *walked over to the bed where she plopped down on her back. "Saint would be the best choice for you, if he ever decides to come home. Otherwise, there's always Eddie. He's a dork, but he's still a good guy."*

"Or I could just hold out and see if Cristian and Yasmeen actually make their marriage work," Sofi teased.

"Gross, Sofi. He's a dad already."

"I think I'd make a good stepmom, don't you?" Sofi waggled her brows.

Kamilah whacked her in the face with a pillow. "Cut it out, you homewrecker. Just keep it in your pants until one of my single and not jerky brothers comes back."

Sofi chuckled, but she could hear how forced it sounded. "Don't worry about me. I have no interest in any of your brothers and I don't have to in order for us to be sisters."

Kamilah flipped over onto her side and Sofi turned her head to look at her. "True," Kamilah said with a blazing smile. "We're already sisters."

Sofi smiled back at her. She held out her pinky. "Ride or die." It was something they'd said to each other since the day Kamilah had claimed Sofi as her best friend. It meant that they would be by each other's side no matter what.

Kamilah wrapped her pinky around Sofi's. "Ride or die," she promised.

In her head, Sofi promised that she'd always put her friendship with Kamilah first. It wasn't like her and Leo would work out anyway. They were already moving in different directions.

Sofi shook herself out of the past only to realize everyone was staring at her. "I'm sorry, what?" she asked.

Kamilah gave her a weird look. "I said, Rome has been talking about the bachelor party and I was telling him that Liam and I weren't planning on having a bachelor or bachelorette party."

"What?" Sofi screeched. "Of course you're having a bachelorette party. I've already planned it and everything."

"I told you," Leo's smug voice said right before a dark pink drink in a short tumbler appeared in front of Sofi's face, cutting off her view of Kamilah.

Sofi blinked and grabbed the drink if only to get it out of her way. "You told me what?" she asked him.

He shook his head. "No. I told Kamilah that there was no way you were letting her get away with that and that you'd no doubt started planning it as soon as she asked you to be the maid of honor."

Unwilling to say that he was right, Sofi sniffed and took a sip of her drink which tasted like a blackberry sweet tea with a tart kick of lime, spicy ginger, and the warmth of smooth whiskey. "This is good," she told him. "A bit too boozy, but good."

"I love boozy," Alex said. "Boozy sounds perfect to us, right, Gabs?" She clicked her glass against her older sister's. Alex and Gabi were the youngest daughters of Kamilah and Leo's youngest aunt, but they were a lot closer to Kamilah than mere cousins. When their mom, Carmen, had left for New York with the oldest daughter, Eva, she'd left the younger two with their father, Luís. Kamilah's parents, along with the rest of the family, had jumped right in to help Luís raise Gabi and Alex. In some ways it was like Gabi and Alex belonged more to the elder set of Vega siblings than they did to their own mother. It wasn't surprising then that both were included in Kamilah's wedding party, they were pretty much her little sisters.

"Leo, can I ask you something?" Ben asked from the bar where he was looking over the ingredients on the counter. "Are all the drinks you make today going to be pink? If so, why?"

"I was wondering that same thing," Liam said.

"Yes," Leo responded. "And I figured they should be pink so they can match with the pink wedding stuff."

Liam blinked. "What pink wedding stuff?" His tone was dark and slightly threatening as if to say there had better not be any pink wedding stuff.

"Uh-oh," Kamilah murmured, making it clear she hadn't said anything about Sofi's changes to the color palette.

Liam's eyes locked on his fiancée. "I thought you said the colors were white, gold, and green like your ring."

Kamilah squirmed. "They are, but then Sofi pointed out that we needed something bright to balance the deep emerald green."

Sofi jumped in to defend her stance. "Exactly. Adding blush, berry, and fuchsia pink to the mix with little pops of orangy coral and sage green makes your wedding look like a summer wedding instead of a fall one."

Saint shook his head as if something just wouldn't compute. "Kamilah with a pink wedding? I just don't see it."

Sofi wasn't surprised. According to the family, Kamilah had been the quintessential tomboy until she'd met Sofi. It made sense considering she had four older brothers who always teased her whenever she did anything they considered "girlie," they still did.

Case in point Leo immediately saying, "I too was shocked when I walked into the dining room and saw a bunch of pictures of pink flowers all over the wall. Who would've thought that the same girl who wore my hand-me-down jeans and tennis shoes would want a Barbie wedding?" He turned to Liam. "You ready for all that Ken?"

Liam scowled. "I don't think I want a pink wedding."

"Well, who cares what you want," Sofi said, sounding a bit bitchier than she intended. "Kamilah wants it and that's what matters most."

Leo laughed. "I don't think it works that way. The groom is also an important part of the wedding process."

Sofi waved him off. "Yeah, well, I'm on the case now. All this bride and groom need to do is show up."

Kamilah walked up to Liam and plopped herself in his lap which seemed to lighten his mood considerably. "Besides, it's not a lot of pink and it's mostly just in the flowers."

"Fine," he huffed. "But I'm not wearing anything pink."

Ben slapped Liam on the back but looked at Sofi. "Yeah, don't put him in anything pink. It doesn't go well with his pasty white skin tone. He'll look like a raw chicken breast."

Rome, Ben's cousin and Liam's other groomsman, laughed. "Yes, leave the pink for those of us with more melanin." He gestured to his brown skin that was a few shades lighter than Sofi's. "We carry it off better."

"No one is wearing pink," Sofi said. Mentally, she corrected herself. No one *else* was wearing pink. When it became clear that she wouldn't be able to get a dress that matched the rest of the bridesmaids in time, Sofi had been forced to pivot. Luckily, she had a gorgeous fuchsia designer dress from an event she'd attended in Paris. It would match the flowers perfectly and as it was also sequined, it was close enough in style to the other bridesmaids that the overall look would still be cohesive.

Ben clapped. "Great. Now that we all have accepted the addition of pink to the wedding colors, can we get back to talking bachelor party?" He waved his phone around. "Dev, who regrets that he has to be training instead of here, has suggested Vegas." He looked at Liam. "This sweaty gym sock has already said that he doesn't care as long as there are no strippers." Ben turned his attention to Leo. "You in?" His tone was more a statement than a question because who wouldn't think that Leo'd love to party in Las Vegas. He was a party guy after all.

Except Leo didn't seem thrilled by the idea at all. He pulsed the stress ball in his hand repeatedly and Sofi could practically feel his desire to fidget. "Sounds a little cliché if you ask me," he said, he was trying to come across as nonchalant, but Sofi could hear the tension in his voice.

She frowned.

"I agree," Rome said. "That's why I suggested Catalina Island. It's still fun, but more chill which is more Liam's speed. We can hang out on the beach, hike, fish, maybe charter a yacht."

Leo was already shaking his head. "Liam doesn't do boats."

Liam's head shot up and he glared at Leo, obviously mad that Leo had brought it up. After a boating accident had claimed his father's and grandmother's lives in front of him, it was hardly surprising Liam wasn't an avid sailor. But he still didn't like it brought up and usually everyone was careful to not do so. "And Leo doesn't do planes," he said with a challenging look at Leo.

All the eyes in the room shot to Leo, who was busy glaring at Liam before he schooled his expression into something that resembled light amusement. "I went to Puerto Rico at least once a year most of my life and, guess what, I certainly didn't walk there."

"And when was the last time you've been?" Liam asked, already knowing the answer.

Leo shrugged. "It's been a few years, but I've been busy working." "A few years" was generous. From her calculations, it had been close to ten years if not more.

Slowly Sofi was beginning to put things together. She'd never understood how Leo just happened to have duty every single time his family booked a trip to the island. A few times could be called bad luck, but every single time for a decade? That wasn't coincidence. That was avoidance. "Leo's scared of flying," she said, reaching the conclusion Liam had obviously come to before. She hadn't meant to say that aloud, but when Leo's glare turned on her she realized she had.

14

LEO FELT HIS FACE HEAT. HE HATED BEING PUT ON THE SPOT. IF HE wanted attention, he sought it out. He didn't like it being forced on him as was currently happening. It reminded him too much of all the times his teachers had suddenly called on him in class just to prove that he hadn't been paying attention. As if Leo were a liar who didn't own up to his shit. He'd always been the first one to say he'd drifted off, so there was no need for the gotchas they pulled. All it did was make him look stupid in front of his classmates which then caused Leo to act out because if he was going to look like an idiot, he was going to do it on his terms.

Doing things on his own terms was sort of Leo's entire life motto. Which was exactly why Leo had stopped flying as soon as he could.

Leo fucking hated flying. He loathed it with every fiber of his being. It wasn't that he was scared of heights or anything. It wasn't even that he had visions of the plane crashing. It was the feeling of being stuck in a tiny space, unable to move, for a prolonged period of time. It was torture to him, which was why he'd used his job as an excuse not to go on trips. Sure, he'd been forced to volunteer to work holiday shifts and missed out on some family trips to Puerto Rico, but it had been worth it.

His disdain for flying began when he was young. His family used to go Puerto Rico at least once a year to spend a holiday with his mom's family. The seven of them would have to figure out the best way to travel when there were only six seats in any given row. Leo had almost always gotten stuck sitting with his dad, who constantly berated him for talking too loud, moving too much, and just being an overall pain in the ass. Of course, for a long time no one knew it was due to his ADHD, but by the time they realized it the damage had been done. Getting on a plane triggered him like nothing else. To him it felt like being strapped into a straightjacket and having his legs chained together. Flying to him was the equivalent of getting buried alive, but he'd thought he'd done a better job of hiding that fact.

If the way neither of his siblings would meet his gaze told him anything, it was that he wasn't as good of an actor as he thought. As he was prone to do when called out, Leo just rolled with it. "I'm not scared," he said. "I just hate being stuck in one small space for that long. It stresses me out."

"I feel that," Liza said. "Small spaces stress me out too, but probably for a different reason than you."

"You know you can take meds for it," his cousin Lucy said. He could tell she was trying to be helpful. "There's no reason to let your anxiety stop you from flying."

Leo scoffed. "I don't have anxiety. I have ADHD and those

meds you're talking about probably won't mix well with my ADHD meds. They're designed to do the exact opposite things."

"That's true," Kamilah said. "One's an upper and the other is a downer. Although, I'm sure a doctor would be able to help you find the right medication and dosage. If you're interested in that."

Leo wanted so badly to tell them all to mind their own business. If he needed anyone's advice, he'd ask for it. But he knew that they were only trying to help, it was what his family did. Never mind that often their helpfulness came across as pushy and had the tendency to make him feel like they were talking down to him as if he were too dumb to figure things out on his own. He knew that at least when it came to Kamilah, she wasn't judging him. His sister was probably one of the least judgmental members of the family, but that was probably because the rest of them had spent too long making her feel like she didn't have a say in anything important. Ugh, why was it so hard to have a family that was actually functional and not problematic? Sitcoms managed to do it just fine and those had to be based on some real families.

"I'm not interested," he said. "Anything I want and need is right here in Chicago. There's no reason for me to trot the globe." He hoped that his tone put an end to that discussion, but just in case he decided to change the subject too. "Now, who's ready for watermelon margaritas?"

A chorus of "me" filled the air and Leo got to work.

After the watermelon margaritas came the strawberry vodka lemonade, a classic cosmo, passionfruit mules, something called a Rosa 75 which featured Aperol, pink tequila, and cotton candy, and a spritz he concocted with rosé, a bit of gin, some hibiscus syrup, and pink grapefruit juice. By the end of the night he wasn't sure which drink had been chosen as the best or even if they'd voted at all. It wasn't because he was drunk either. After spending hours making drinks instead of drinking them, he was sadly sober. Everyone else was drunk though. Especially his lightweight sister and her equally lightweight best friend.

"I'm so happy right now," Kamilah was saying. "This is exactly what I needed. Who needs a bachelorette party when I have all of this?" She gestured around herself, sloppily causing herself to almost topple off her stool.

"Nice try, bitch," Sofi said from her side. "You're still having a bachelorette party even if I have to kidnap you to do it."

"Let's do it now. We'll help wrangle her into the car," Lucy said as she stood up and wobbled on her feet.

Leo snorted. Lucy couldn't wrangle a baby at the moment.

"It's Monday night," Alex said. "Where could we possibly go?"

"Son of a bitch," Ben groaned. "Don't remind me of the day. I have a shit ton of meetings tomorrow. I'm so fucked."

Rome helped him stand. "That's on you, dumbass. No one told you to have multiples of each drink."

"Who would've thought those girlie-ass drinks had so much alcohol in them?" Ben wailed, defending his double fisting.

"You would've if you paid any attention to Leo while he was making them," Liam said from Leo's left where he was helping clean up the bar. He too was probably sober, since he stuck to sipping his neat whiskey and switched to water once he saw how hard Kamilah was going. He'd used it as an excuse to get water into her system at regular intervals. He'd take a drink and then get her to take one too.

It was one of the many little things Leo had witnessed Liam do to take care of his sister throughout the last year and a half. It made him feel confident that Liam was the right one for her, despite their decades of fighting. It gave him hope that he and Sofi could also make it work.

Speaking of Sofi, she was currently hugging Gabi and Alex goodbye while they all swayed like sunflowers in the wind. They were so drunk.

Over their heads, Saint gave him an accusatory look, but it was ruined by his own rosy cheeks and squinty eyes.

Leo smirked at the idea of his deadly serious veteran big brother getting tipsy on a bunch of pink drinks. "I hope y'all know that I'm keeping these until tomorrow," Leo told them, gesturing to the bowl where he'd collected everyone's car keys. "I've already gotten you all rides." He looked at Rome and Ben. "Although, I didn't know where either of you live, so I put in the brewery."

Rome waved him off. "That's fine. I have a pull-out couch in my office."

"I'm not sharing a bed with you," Ben grumbled to his cousin. "What are we, six years old again?"

"We aren't sharing a bed," Rome said. "I'm leaving your ass there while I walk down the street to my apartment."

"That's some bullshit," Ben groused. "This is why I keep telling you to move out of that tiny studio and get a big-boy apartment."

"You better not leave him alone," Liam said. "He might choke on his own puke."

Ben swung around to glare at Liam but tipped into a table instead. "I never puke," he claimed.

Both Rome and Liam laughed at that.

"Y'all are assholes," Ben mumbled as he stumbled toward the door, Rome close on his heels to steady him.

Within moments everyone else followed them out, leaving only Leo, Kamilah, Liam, and Sofi behind. Kamilah and Sofi were both slumped onto each other at the bar and looking like they were ready to pass out. "Come on, you two lushes," Leo told them. "It's time to go to bed."

"Ugh," Kamilah groaned. "I'm so glad the restaurant is closed tomorrow. I know I'm going to be so hungover."

"Same," Sofi said. "I don't know whose idea it was to drink

heavily on a Monday night, but I'm going to have words with them or maybe I'll just vomit on them."

Leo stayed quiet because it had totally been his spur-of-the-moment idea, but he honestly hadn't planned for everyone to get drunk as skunks. He just thought he'd try what Abuelo and Doña Fina had suggested and create a nice way for Sofi to relax after a long day at the office. But he'd forgotten about the food portion of that plan. By the time he'd realized she was getting intoxicated and hadn't had dinner, the damage had been done and not even the pizzas he ordered could fix it.

"Oh no," Kamilah said. She reached out to pat Sofi on the back but missed and swung at the empty space between them.

"I'm okay," she told Kamilah. "Just feel like I got my bell rung like Quasimodo in *The Hunchback of Notre-Dame*." She slid to the edge of her seat. "Do you know that was my favorite movie growing up?" She grabbed the hand that Leo had extended. He pulled her up. "I wanted to be Esmeralda so bad," she continued. "But then I grew up and realized how fucked up the movie truly was." She looked at him through glassy eyes. "Did you know how messed up it is? The stereotypes and all that?" She didn't wait for him to answer. "Anyway, I was so sad that I wasn't able to see it in all its glory."

"The movie?" Kamilah asked, her face scrunched into a frown that reminded Leo of her child self.

"No the real Notre-Dame," Sofi said. "It's still under construction because of the fire and so I could only see it from the outside. That made me sad even though the story was terrible." Sofi propped herself against the bar. "But you know what made me really sad?" she asked.

Leo scooped up the rest of the unused ingredients and looked for the grocery store bag he'd brought them in. Unable to find it, he just stuck everything in one of the small fridges behind the bar.

"What?" Kamilah asked in response to Sofi's question.

"Everywhere I went, I was sad that you weren't there, because you were supposed to be there with me, but I was by myself. That made me sad."

Oh shit. The alcohol was making her extra emotional and talkative. She wouldn't like that in the morning. Especially if she continued to confess things she would never confess sober.

"I'm sorry I wasn't there," Kamilah said, gently brushing Sofi's hair out of her face. "But we'll go again when the cathedral is open and this time you will know all the tricks and tips so we won't wander around like a bunch of idiot tourists."

She smiled dreamily. "We'll be like real Parisians."

"Exactly," Kamilah agreed.

"Kamilah, I want to tell you something I should've told you a long time ago."

Fuck fuck fuck. Red alert. Leo couldn't know for sure, but something was telling him that Sofi was about to air all their business to his sister. And while he'd always been the first one to say that she needed to know, now was definitely not the time. "Drink this." He shoved an open bottle of water into Sofi's mouth, forcing her to spill, swallow, or choke. Anything to get her to shut up.

She shot him a face-melting look and snatched the bottle from his hands but continued to drink.

"You two can go. I've got her," Leo assured his sister.

"I have myself," Sofi argued when she finished her water. "I don't need anyone to take care of me. I'm fine." She took a few steps; except she didn't actually go anywhere. She went from one side to the other but didn't go forward.

"Whoa, slow down, you speed demon," Leo told her. "You're practically sprinting."

"Fuck off," she told him with an adorable scowl.

Liam laughed while Leo smiled in delight. Something was definitely wrong with Leo, because he loved her sassy side way too much. Whenever she snapped at him, he got hard. It was a real problem, but not one he was looking to fix. "Seriously," he told Liam and Kamilah. "I'm a good roommate. I'll make sure Sofi gets tucked in nice and tight."

Sofi blew a raspberry at him, but Kamilah didn't. She stared at him with eyes exactly like their mother's. Maybe that's why he felt oddly naked when she said, "I know. I honestly wouldn't entrust her to anyone else." His sister gave him a soft smile and a kiss on the cheek. She took a few steps toward Liam, who met her and scooped her up. She put her head on his shoulders and closed her eyes, content to knock out now that she knew Sofi was taken care of.

Liam looked at Leo. "Tostón is probably asleep in our bed by now. Do you want to just leave him with us for the night?"

"No," Sofi groaned. "I want my baby. I can't sleep without him anymore."

Leo gasped like an old-timey detective who just discovered the pivotal clue. "I knew you were sneaking him out of the kennel at night. That's why he cries every time I try to put him in there." He scoffed, "He just needs to get used to it, my ass."

Liam chuckled as he carried Kamilah toward the door to their place. "I would've expected her to want to make a coat out of a dog like Cruella de Vil, before she'd ever let one sleep in her bed."

That just went to show how good Sofi was at playing the part of overly ambitious, coldhearted, diva. "I'll wait for Tostón in the hallway. Just let him out once you get her settled."

As soon as they disappeared through the door, Leo spun on Sofi and scooped her up too.

"Leo," she gasped. "Your shoulder! Put me down."

"Absolutely not, bombón. If I let you walk, it will take us hours to get home even though it's next door."

"It's your fault," she grumbled, as Leo hit the light switch and walked them out of the automatic locking side door next to the closed garage doors. "You didn't need to make all those drinks and you certainly didn't have to make them so good."

"I actually do feel a little bad about that. I didn't mean for everyone to get fucked up." Leo turned the corner of the building and walked them to the back door that led to their apartment. He put her down so he could grab the keys out of his pocket.

"Can I ask you something?" Sofi asked suddenly. Her tone made him a little apprehensive, but Leo wanted to be open and honest with her.

"Shoot," he said.

She frowned at him. "That's not funny. It's too soon. It will always be too soon."

For a moment he was confused, but then he realized that she thought he was making a joke about his shooting in the alley they were standing in. He had to chuckle because normally that was totally something he'd do. "I meant go ahead," he corrected, pushing the door open. He went to scoop her up again, but Sofi took off up the stairs before he could. He followed closely so he could catch her if she fell.

"Do you really not want to see other parts of the world or did you just say that because you hate flying?" she asked.

"I guess I've had random thoughts like, *It'd be cool to go on a safari,* or *I wonder what it would be like to see the pyramids up close,* but to really make firm plans or actually look into it? No."

Sofi stopped on the stairs and turned to face him. "I used to sit in front of the TV watching all the travel and nature channels for hours and hours. When he was around and not off playing baseball, my tío Manny would watch with me. He used to ask me what places I wanted to see the most. We'd go back and forth like that, naming our top spots." She leaned against the wall and stared over her shoulder as if lost in a memory. "One day when I was like seven or eight he showed up with this map of the world. We marked all the places we'd visit together when he was done playing baseball." She gave a sad smile—

one full of nostalgia. "I still have that map. It's in a box of my tío's things in my closet."

Leo knew that to Sofi he'd just been her uncle, but to him Manuel "Maserati" Santana still seemed larger-than-life. It was weird to hear about the guy who'd been one of his idols sitting around with a little girl marking up a map of the world and making plans for after a career that others envied. "He's the reason you want to be a world traveler now?"

"I wouldn't say 'now' as if I never cared about it before, but I guess everything that happened got me thinking about opportunity and wasted time. I'd spent so much time wishing I could go places instead of just going. I don't want to run out of time like he did. I want to see the places we'd marked on that map."

Leo's heart froze. Was Sofi just going to take off again for another year? Was this what she planned to do from now on? What about him? It was obvious that something was happening between them again. What was he supposed to do while she traveled the globe?

"It's not that I don't like traveling," he said. "But I'd rather drive somewhere. Then I can stop whenever I feel the need, get out, and walk around."

"I feel like I could get into hiking," Sofi said. "And I've always wanted to go to the Grand Canyon."

"Let's do it. We'll take Tostón on a road trip," he said, relieved that she would meet him halfway.

"Sounds like a plan," she said with a smile. Although Leo still worried that one day it wouldn't be enough for her and she'd take off again.

By the time they made it to the top of the stairs, Leo heard the sound of scrambling paws. Tostón skidded around the corner of the stairwell like a car in *The Fast and the Furious: Tokyo Drift*, almost slid into the back door that led to the alley, but corrected himself at the last second and booked it up the stairs to Leo. His whole back half wiggled as he greeted Leo as if he hadn't seen him in years instead of hours.

"Hey, son." Leo shut and locked the door. "Mommy's not feeling good right now, so just be gentle okay?" He swore Tostón knew what he was saying, because he pranced over to Sofi, but didn't hop up on her like he did to Leo. Instead leaned into her legs and stared up at her in adoration.

Sofi's hand dropped and stroked his head. "There's my baby boy," she cooed. She lifted her head and looked around. "When did we get back to the apartment?" she asked.

"Just now," Leo replied, coming to stand in front of her. "Let's put you to bed."

"I'm not tired. I don't want to go to sleep," she said, reminding him of Rosie arguing with Saint and Lola.

He decided to take a page out of their book. "How about this, I'll go get you some pj's to change into and then we'll set up camp in the living room?"

"Okay," she said.

"I'll be right back," he said as he walked around the couch toward her bedroom door. "But I need you to drink the rest of that water. Then I'm going to get you another one and some painkillers."

She looked at the bottle in her hand as if surprised to see it there. She trudged over to the couch and flopped down. Tostón followed and settled his big head on her thigh. "Leo," she murmured.

He paused behind the couch. "What, bombón?"

"I don't feel good."

Leo leaned down and kissed her forehead. "I know, amor. But I'll take care of you."

Her perfect lips curled into a smile.

When he came out a few minutes later with one of her silky sleep sets, her fuzzy socks, her sleep bonnet, and her makeup removal wipes, she was knocked out. He hated to wake her, but he knew she'd be mad if she slept in her clothes and makeup, without her hair protected. He had no choice but to wake her and get her comfortable which is exactly what he did.

After getting her changed and ready, he bundled her up with her knit blanket and a shit ton of pillows. By the time he was done, Tostón was completely covered under the blanket and all that was visible of Sofi was the side of her face. Her eyes were open and looking at him like he was her hero. "I'm kind of surprised that you're so good at this."

"Good at what?" Leo asked, as he came back from tossing the wipes in the trash.

"Taking care of people," she answered, snuggling deeper into the blankets. "I mean, I know you trained as a paramedic, but I just never really saw you as a caretaker."

"Why wouldn't I be a caretaker, because I'm a man?"

She scoffed. "No, Saint is probably the biggest caretaker I know and he's a man." She turned her head to rub her face in the pillow and suddenly he couldn't see any of her face. "It's because you're like my dad and he for sure isn't a caretaker."

What? She thought he was like her father? That was the first he'd ever heard about it. Never in all of their conversations or even fights had she mentioned this before and he was glad. Leo did not like being compared to Sofi's dad. She didn't talk about him much, even though they worked together, but Leo knew enough to know that he wasn't a great father to Sofi or partner to Sofi's mom. "Why would you say that?" he asked, knowing that he was taking advantage of her vulnerable state but unable to stop himself. This was the type of question she would never answer while in her right mind and Leo had a feeling that this was information he *needed* to know if they were ever going to work out.

"You two are the same…charming and too handsome for his own good, but at the end of the day not someone I can count on. You have your own things and they're the most important to you. Which cool. I don't need someone to take care of me anyway." She yawned audibly before continuing at a slow-paced whisper. "I take care of myself."

When it was clear that she'd fallen asleep, Leo slumped back in his chair. Now that he sort of knew what she meant, he liked the comparison to her father even less. It made Leo sound like a shallow and selfish asshole who only cared about his needs and looking good to others. Leo wasn't like that. At least, he didn't think he was. He tended to do whatever he wanted to do at any given time, but he didn't think that made him self-ish. Did it? He still showed up to help whenever his friends or family needed it. Yeah sometimes it wasn't right when they needed it because he got distracted by something else for a bit first or he totally forgot what they'd asked him, but he always came to help eventually. He didn't maliciously set out to be late or forget to go at all. It was simply how he was and how he'd always been. He'd thought Sofi knew and accepted that about him unlike many members of his family.

He tried to remember any times Sofi had gotten on him for forgetting something or not doing what he'd said he'd do when he was expected to do it and came up blank. Over the years she'd called him out for many things, but never for being unre-liable. To know that she'd secretly felt that way for who knew how long, made so much sense now that he thought about it. Sofi didn't share things she thought made her look weak and admitting that he'd disappointed her would've also meant ad-mitting that she cared about their relationship—something she made every effort to not do if she could help it.

Now Leo was left with a chicken versus egg scenario. What had come first? Her not thinking she could count on him or his actions making her think he was unreliable. Did it even really matter? The main point was that she felt she couldn't trust him to be there for her, take care of her, or place her needs above his own. That was something he was going to have to change and he would. He was going to do whatever it took to make sure Sofi knew she could rely on him.

15

SOFI TITLED HER FACE UP TO THE SUN, TOOK A DEEP BREATH, AND released it. She hadn't felt so at peace for a minute. It wasn't just because of the gorgeous weather, La Lupe—the queen of Latin soul—playing from the speaker next to her, or her dog cuddled up on her lap. It was the fact that she wasn't stuck in her office juggling a bunch of projects she couldn't care less about. After a long week and a half of late nights trying to get ahead on her work projects so she could focus on the wedding without guilt, she was living for the Fourth of July weekend.

Sofi turned her head to the side to look at Abuela Fina and her mom, who were in their own lounge chairs next to hers. "This is nice. I'm glad I get to hang out on the roof with you two."

Mami was leaned back in her chair taking a drink of her

mango jalapeño margarita. "I'm happy you made me take off on my day off, because this is a definite step up from hanging out on the fire escape of our apartment building."

They were on the rooftop of the Vega/Kane building which at some point in the recent past had been changed from a place where Valeria hung clothes to dry and the family roasted pigs on a spit for their famous lechón to a casual but cozy hangout space with comfy chaise loungers, little café tables, and even a small pergola. Sofi had asked if the plan was to change this space into a rooftop bar and deck for the new Kane Distillery Tasting Room and El Coquí, but was told that this was going to remain for family use only. She loved that she, Mami, and Abuela Fina were considered family. She'd never really thought about how much the Vega family meant to her on the whole. She'd of course thought about Kamilah and Leo a lot, but at some point she'd begun to see them all as her family. It'd made it even more difficult when she'd been alone in Paris. She'd taken them all for granted and she refused to do it again. She didn't want to lose the Vegas again ever.

"I'm moving into Casa del Sol," Abuela Fina announced randomly.

Sofi shot up from her spot reclining on the chaise lounge. Nearly dropping her own margarita on Tostón's head. "What?"

Her grandmother gave her a look. "What's wrong with you? Is your brain not working from the drinking?"

She shook her head at her grandmother's question. "I'm fine," she told her abuela. "I'm just confused. Why would you want to move into Casa del Sol when you can stay with Mami?" She turned to her mom. "Did you know about this?"

Mami nodded. "She mentioned it to me."

"I've been on my own for a long time now," Abuela Fina pointed out in Spanish. "It took me a long time to get used to it. After your abuelo and tío died, I didn't know what to do with myself. But time went on and I learned to be independent.

Not only that, but I discovered that I liked it. I liked having my own space where I could do what I wanted. I liked being beholden to no one. If I wanted to walk around my house naked, I could. If I wanted to not do laundry or mop for a week, I could. I want that again."

Sofi could understand that. She knew that her grandma loved her mom, but living with someone was just not the same as living alone. "You want freedom," Sofi said.

"Exacto," Abuela Fina agreed.

Sofi looked at her mom. "You probably want yours too."

Mami nodded. "I have such crazy hours sometimes that I feel like when I am home I have to tiptoe around. Plus, I want to walk around my house naked whenever I feel like it too."

Sofi couldn't argue against that. It was one of the things she missed about living alone. She wondered briefly what it said about the three of them that they liked being nude at home. Whatever. It didn't matter. They were three badass independent women and they could do what they wanted. "I get it," Sofi said. "I'm just going to miss your cooking when I visit. Back to soggy rice and bland beans I guess."

Her abuela laughed when her mom whacked her arm with the towel she'd been using to wipe the sweat from her face as they sat in the sun. "You little brat," Mami said. "You know that's a lie."

Sofi grinned. "You know I love you, Ma. You're the Puerto Rican Barefoot Contessa." She paused. "But Abuela is the Boricua Paula Deen. Minus the racism and plus the sofrito."

Her mom simply harrumphed because she knew it was true.

Her mom was a good cook, but her abuela was better. No doubt about that.

"And who does that make you?" Abuela asked.

Mami jumped at that opportunity. "She's that muppet who doesn't talk and just throws a bunch of stuff in a pot."

She and Abuela cracked up.

"Damn, Ma. You went all the way to Swedish Chef? You couldn't even give me the rat from *Ratatouille*?"

"No, because that rat could cook."

There they went again, cackling like a duo of witches.

"See, now here I so generously brought you two up here to enjoy the beautiful day with me and you treat me like this. Que malagradecidas son."

Her mom snorted. "You should talk. I didn't sleep for the first five years of your life because your needy butt wanted to cry about anything and everything. The least you can do now is help me entertain your abuela and enjoy my time off."

"So now I'm in debt for the rest of my life because you decided to have sex without protection? Where is the justice in that?"

"That's called biblical justice," Abuela said. "It's an eye for an eye. Your mami was a pain in my ass and now I get to be a pain in hers. Just like you were a pain in her ass and now she'll be one in yours."

Sofi put her hand on Tostón's head and gave him a slow pet. "Do you hear this, Tostón?" He groaned, stretched, and sighed without ever opening his eyes.

Since Tostón didn't appear keen to join in on the conversation Sofi turned back to the humans with her. "Abuela, I know you're going to love Casa del Sol. There're plenty of caribeños there. Plus, you're so sociable that I know you'll have a group of friends in no time. Although, you already have a good friend that lives there."

"Y eso?" Mami asked.

"Oh, Abuela and Papo Vega are best friends these day. According to the grapevine they talk on the phone and everything." Sofi slipped her sunglasses down her nose and waggled her eyebrows at them.

Abuela Fina gifted her with an epic eye roll. "You need to worry about yourself. I've been here for months now and I haven't seen you do anything but go to work or hangout with friends."

"That's not fair," Sofi argued. "Of course I'm spending time with friends. I'm trying to reconnect after being distanced for over a year." She took a drink of her margarita. "And of course I'm going to be working hard. My dad counts on me. I'm basically his right hand." Just thinking about her job made her eye twitch, so she drank a bit more. Suddenly, her glass was empty. Weird. She could've sworn she'd just filled it.

Abuela Fina and Mami were looking at her oddly.

"Did I ever tell you about the time I was performing *La Bayadère* at the Teatro Tapia?" Abuela said seemingly out of nowhere.

Oh great. She was about to start one of her stories.

Abuela Fina put her cup down and rose to her feet as graceful in her late seventies as she had been in the 1970s. "Imaginalo, Viejo San Juan 1964. I was the first girl in the corps de ballet for the 'Kingdom of the Shades,' so I had to do thirty-nine perfect arabesques in just the intro. But the principal dancer kept complaining that I was stealing the show. She was right of course. Everyone kept looking at me and asking why I wasn't in the main role. She was so mad that one night during a performance she paid one of the other girls to trip me during our routine. So we get to the moment and this little tramp sticks her ankle out in front of me. I stumble half a beat, but I doubt anyone would've even noticed. Except then she puts her hand on my back and pushes. And since she was such a big cow compared to me, I went flying right off the stage. But as I was falling, I thought to myself, I'm not going to let these jealous cats make me look like I can't dance. So I extended my leg into a saut de chat, pointing my toes, and leaped. When I landed I went right into a series of fouettés, whipping around like a top. I completely improvised my own solo in the aisles which got me a standing ovation. After that, the director had me do that every night. Those two had no choice but to choke on their own resentment. But they got lucky, because shortly after that night I entered Miss Puerto Rico."

Sofi shared a look with her mom. Typical Abuela Fina, always doing THE MOST.

"Mai, what was the point of that story and what does it have to do with Sofi?" Mami asked.

Abuela gave the tiniest shoulder lift and continued in Spanish. "I'm just saying that sometimes you think you're going to do one thing, but something throws you off track and you need to pivot. As long as you make it work for you, there's nothing wrong with that. Just don't let others control the path you take."

Sofi felt like glass, completely transparent. She didn't like that at all. "Okay, well, as fun as this is, I think it's time for a refill," Sofi told them. She gently pushed Tostón off her lap and stood.

He gave her a hurt look.

Abuela Fina gave him a vigorous ear scratch. "Oh, you poor baby. She's so mean to you. Ven con Abuela." She patted the seat next to her and Tostón wasted no time climbing up and plopping down right next to her.

Sofi slid on her chanclas and headed for the door.

"Tráigale algo frio al perro," Abuela Fina called out. "It's too hot for him."

Sofi shook her head. Of course, her grandma was worried about the dog overheating even though Sofi had placed him under the umbrella, had a bowl full of ice water next to her chair, and had even frozen a wet washcloth to wipe him down.

She still couldn't believe she had a dog. She really couldn't believe that this four-month-old puppy was as well-behaved as he was. It was like he understood the words she spoke and listened. It was wild. The only time he didn't seem to understand was when she told him to get off her bed and go to his kennel. The first few times she'd tried to put him in it, he'd cried, trembled, and peed himself. It made her wonder what had happened to him that he was terrified of it. Then she remembered his background and felt so horrible she let him out. Needless to say crate training was a bust and he slept in her bed. Between her, Leo, her family, and the Vegas, Tostón was one spoiled dog, but Sofi didn't care. He deserved it.

Sofi had just stepped out of the apartment door with the rest of the pitcher of margarita and a frozen doggy enrichment bowl—both made by Leo—when she almost ran right into her mom.

"Mami," she exclaimed, trying to calm her heart rate after her startle. "What's up?"

"You tell me," her mom said, walking past her into the apartment. "You've been acting weird ever since you got back. I've been waiting for you to tell me what's going on, but you've been avoiding me."

"That's not true," Sofi lied. "We've both just been really busy."

Her mom simply stared at her.

"Okay fine. I've been avoiding you, but it's not because of anything bad," Sofi rushed to tell her. "I'm just trying to get back in the groove of things here. I didn't expect it to be like this when I got back."

"What does that mean?" her mom asked.

"I mean I was supposed to have this company apartment and that fell through," Sofi began, but her mom cut her off.

"Try again and this time give me the truth. Maybe start with why just mentioning your job has you chugging tequila like water and your abuela giving you one of her parables."

Dammit. Sofi hated how well her mom read her like a book. "I'm not happy, Mami. I haven't been for a long time, even before I left, and I don't know how to fix it. I should know, but I don't. I thought leaving was the right path but that didn't fix anything really, so I came back thinking that would help, and it has to a point, but I don't know. Something is still missing."

Her mom nodded as if Sofi were making sense and not rambling. "You've always been the type of person who makes a decision and sticks with it, so it's not hard to see how you got to this point. You're like me. Neither one of us sits around thinking about ourselves deeply. We just suck it up and keep going."

"But you're happy with your life, right, Ma? You aren't sitting around regretting all the decisions you've ever made."

"I'm not," Mami agreed. "But I'm in my fifties, amor. When I was your age and we were struggling to make ends meet, I questioned everything. I kept questioning whether I should've taken your father to court for child support, if I was being selfish in trying to go to school instead of focusing on you, if I should accept the financial help your tío was always trying to force on me, if I should've dated more in order to find myself a partner and you a better father figure."

The revelation wasn't exactly surprising. "What changed?" Sofi asked.

"I realized that I couldn't accomplish anything if I was always second-guessing myself. I needed to just do what my instincts were telling me to do. It's what I did when I decided to keep you and that was the greatest decision I ever made. Whenever I struggled, I reminded myself of that and kept going."

Sofi reached out and grabbed her mom's hand. "I don't tell you this enough, but I love you and I'm in awe of you."

Her mom smiled an adorable, crooked side smile. "I'd ask you what you want, but it's been years since you needed anything from me."

"That's not true. I'll always need my momma."

"I don't know about that. You've always been extremely independent and capable. When you were little, you'd be the one reminding me of things. You created a calendar for us to follow, do you remember that?"

Sofi did. It had been a free calendar she'd gotten from some antidrug thing in the second grade. She'd brought it home and immediately began to fill it in with Tío Manny's games, her speech therapy appointments, pageant things, and her mom's classes. Then she'd stuck it on the fridge. From then on, there had always been a calendar on the fridge with all their important to-dos. Sofi shook her head at herself. "I'm such a control freak."

"You are smart and determined," her mom countered. "You have all the skills you need to do whatever you put your mind to. I mean look at what you're doing for Kamilah." She gestured to the Wedding Central wall where everything she'd planned was pinned up along with a gigantic whiteboard. "You're putting together a wedding reception by yourself with only a few weeks to do it!"

"Well, actually, a lot of it was already done. I just had to tighten some stuff up."

Mami shook her head. "Ay, mi nena, you're always downplaying your achievements." She put a hand on Sofi's shoulder and shook it. "Listen to what I'm saying to you. You can do whatever you want to do. You don't need to ask anyone for their blessing or permission. Your only job in this life is to make yourself happy without hurting others. Do what you gotta do, bebé. Y a los que no les gusta, que se joden."

It was amazing how her mom could tell her exactly what she needed to hear. "I want to quit my job," she confessed.

At that her mom froze, probably thinking all the things Sofi already continued to agonize over. "Do you know what you'd do instead?" Her tone was going for simple curiosity, but Sofi heard the worry underneath.

"I really like event planning," Sofi said. "This feels like it takes everything I like and am good at and pushes them together in something actually high stakes." Not that the stakes weren't high for the companies she worked for, but at the end of the day that was all about money. This was about more. It was about realizing someone's dream.

"Okay," Mami said while nodding her head. "Then go for it."

"I think I am," Sofi said. "I just need to finish Kamilah and Liam's wedding, so I can make a more comprehensive plan." She paused and bit her lip. "Of course, I also have to tell my dad."

Mami winced. "Yeah. That is undoubtedly going to be one awkward conversation, but you're right that you need to have it and sooner rather than later. Sometimes your father needs extra time to wrap his head around things, especially when they're unexpected." Basically, her dad liked to have his own way and didn't like it when people didn't fall in line. One of the things Sofi respected the most about her mother was that she never bad-mouthed Sofi's dad. Even when Sofi was little and he'd disappoint her in some way, her mother would simply listen and let Sofi rage, cry, or vent and then she'd ask Sofi what she wanted to do. Mami never placed herself between Sofi and her father. If anything, she was the one who encouraged Sofi to forgive and try to move forward. Mami was really the only reason that Sofi tried as hard as she did to make things work with her dad.

"He's not going to like it," Sofi said.

"Probably not," Mami said. "But that doesn't mean that you aren't making the right choice. If this is what you feel like you need, then do it."

Sofi nodded. "Okay, Mami. Thank you."

"You're welcome, negrita." She paused for a moment before throwing Sofi a mischievous smile that reminded Sofi so much of Abuela Fina and Tío Manny. "Now, let's talk about Leo Vega."

Sofi groaned. "No, I don't want to talk about him. Besides, there's nothing to talk about. We've been done for a long time now."

"It doesn't seem like it's done," Mami commented. "Not with the way he was fussing over you before he left and making us margaritas by hand, no premade mix." She put emphasis on that last part as if that really meant something.

It really didn't, but Sofi couldn't argue with her mom about the first part. Things between her and Leo did not seem done. If anything, the more time she spent with Leo the more they seemed to be creating something different together. She wasn't exactly sure what, but she wasn't going to pretend like she didn't see the writing on the walls. "Honestly, I don't really know what's going on. This is different for us both." They were usually either fucking or fighting. This whole sharing secrets in the dark and taking care of each other was new. And that was scary because she felt like she was standing at the edge of a cliff known to crumble. Sure it seemed sturdy and exciting, but at any moment the ground could give way and send her careening to the jagged rocks below.

"Mira, I'm going to tell you something that I know you aren't going to want to listen to, but I hope you do."

Usually Sofi's answer would be that if she wanted advice, she'd ask for it. However, she would always listen to her mother's advice even if she didn't take it.

"Talk to Leo," Mami said. "For once, tell him what you're thinking and feeling. See if he's thinking or feeling the same. Then make a decision together, because I think you might be surprised by what you both want."

Sofi was already shaking her head. "There's no way, Ma. We've been through too much. Even if we did give it a try, there's no way it would last long, then I'd be right where I've been every single time, trying to keep it all a secret so that I don't lose the one family we really have left."

"You mean the Vegas?"

"Of course! I see them like family and I know you do too. When Leo and I don't work out, who do you think gets to keep them? Spoiler alert. It's not us."

"Maybe you two will make it work and maybe you won't.

Maybe it will ruin your relationship with the Vegas, maybe it won't. There's no way to ever know for sure, but at some point you need to stop hiding from anything that might hurt you, Sofia. You're too strong to spend your life hiding and you deserve to be happy." With that she turned and left, leaving Sofi standing there wondering if she should make the leap she wanted to make.

Because he could read her mind, at that moment her phone buzzed with a message from Leo.

> **Bombón, I have something I want to share with you. Meet me at our spot at 6:30.**

She knew exactly where he wanted her to meet him. The place that had been their rendezvous spot since the night of their first kiss. She remembered it well because it was the night that had changed her life.

Sofi sat on her bed doing her best to stifle the sobs wracking her frame. She didn't want Mami to hear her and wake up. She knew that Abuela Fina, who lay next to her, was down for the count thanks to the pills the doctor had given her. Sofi could jump on the bed screaming the lyrics to "America" from West Side Story *and Abuela Fina would sleep on. Sofi envied her that ability to bypass the pain by being unconscious.*

Sofi felt like her body was slowly and excruciatingly trying to turn itself inside out. Everything hurt, but her heart hurt the most. She didn't think it would ever not hurt again. The two most important men in her life, the only ones she trusted at any rate, were gone for good now. They'd died a week prior, but it hadn't seemed real until she'd watched both her mom and grandma break down when they were handed the two urns containing Tío Manny and Abuelo Juan's ashes. It was still hard for her to believe that the two cookie jar–looking containers sitting on her dresser were all that remained of them.

There was a scratch at her window and Sofi nearly jumped five feet in the air at the sound. She rushed to her closet to grab the bat Tío

Manny had given her two weeks ago. It was the one he'd used to hit his five hundredth home run, so she didn't want to have to ruin it, but the last thing they needed at the moment was for a burglar to break in.

The scratch came again, but this time it was accompanied by a voice whispering her name.

Cursing under her breath, Sofi tiptoed to her bedroom window and slowly peeled back a corner of the blinds to see, all while maintaining her grip on the bat. When she saw who was scratching at her window like a psycho from a horror movie, she was tempted to use the bat anyway. "What the hell are you doing, Leo Vega?" she whisper-yelled.

"Open the window," he whisper-yelled back. "It's windy as shit out here and I'm about to be blown away."

"That's what you get for climbing my fire escape like a stalker."

"Just open the damn window already."

"No, my abuela is in here asleep."

He huffed. "Fine, then come out. We have somewhere to be anyway."

"Why would I want to do that?"

"Just come on. I have a surprise for you."

Sofi thought of all the times Kamilah complained about the "surprises" her brothers would give her and decided she probably didn't want to risk it. Leo already did whatever he could to make her life hell. Then again it wasn't like she could be any more miserable and what else was she going to do? Stare at the urns and cry some more? At least, Leo was a distraction. "Okay, but give me a second to change." She was still in the black dress her abuela had chosen for her to wear to the funeral. It had a puffy skirt and the sleeves were supertight. There was no way she could climb down the fire escape in that.

Sofi pulled on some jeans from her dirty pile and her school hoodie. Then she slipped her feet into her gym shoes and climbed out the window to meet him. Together they climbed down the ladder and ran around to the front of her building where a familiar car was parked. It was the Toyota all three of his older brothers had previously owned. Sofi hopped in the car and within moments they were on their way.

"Where are we going?" she asked when it became clear they were leaving the neighborhood. "Are we meeting Kamilah somewhere?"

"No Kamilah, just you and me and I told you it's a surprise."

Sofi wanted to argue with him, but couldn't bring herself to. In all honesty if he planned to murder her, she'd probably not put up a fight.

The buildings started to get taller and the homes less frequent. They were heading downtown, but for the life of her she couldn't figure out why. Then they pulled up to a street right by Millennium Park and Leo found a spot to park.

"Why are we going to Millennium Park? It's closed right now."

"It's never really truly closed," Leo said, opening his car door and getting out.

"That sounds like a good way to get us in trouble," Sofi told him, exiting the car as well.

Leo reached into his back seat to pull out his guitar. "Nah. We'll only get in trouble if we get caught."

"Oh great. Now we're definitely going to get caught."

"Stop being such a worrier and come on." He led the way and Sofi followed.

She trailed Leo to The Bean, where he walked underneath the tall arch and sat right in the middle. Sofi plopped down next to him. "Now what?" she asked.

Leo rummaged around in his jacket pocket and pulled out a small box. "Here," he said, shoving it at her.

"What's this?"

"Open it," he commanded while he opened his guitar case.

Sofi lifted the lid and stared at what was inside. "Chocolates?" She knew her tone was one of confusion. Leo Vega didn't give her chocolates. He also didn't show up at her apartment in the middle of the night and whisk her away to Downtown Chicago.

"Yeah. They have caramel inside. Eat one." He grabbed one and popped the whole thing in his mouth.

"Okay…" Sofi lifted a chocolate and took a bite. It was delicious.

She couldn't remember the last time she ate. She ate the rest of that chocolate and then two more.

When she finished her last chocolate, Leo positioned the guitar on his lap. "Are you ready?" he asked.

She had no idea, but she nodded anyway.

Leo started playing a familiar song on the guitar, but it didn't click completely until he started singing. "En mi Viejo San Juan."

Oh God. She was not prepared to hear her abuelo's favorite song. It was a song about someone who left their home in San Juan for a new future. They'd always planned to go back to the place they loved, but never made it home.

As Sofi listened to Leo singing goodbyes to Puerto Rico, she couldn't help but think about how both Abuelo Juan and Tío Manny were exactly like the writer of the song. They'd always talked about going home after Tío was done playing baseball and now they'd never see their beloved Puerto Rico again. Suddenly, everything they'd done as a memorial didn't seem like enough. They needed to take them home to San Juan.

Sofi didn't even realize she was crying until Leo wrapped her in his arms and pulled her into his lap. She didn't even stop to think. She just buried her face in his neck and let it all go. She didn't know how long she sat there slobbering, blubbering, wailing, and snotting all over Leo, but eventually her sobs calmed to hiccups. She could finally hear what Leo had been murmuring in her hair the whole time.

"It's okay, Sofi. Let it out. I'm here. I've got you," he said over and over.

Sofi used her hoodie to wipe her face. Once she was reasonably sure that her face wasn't covered in snot and tears she looked up at him. "Why?" she rasped out through her sore throat.

Leo shrugged. "I knew you needed it."

Sofi's brow furrowed.

"At the service I could tell that you weren't letting yourself cry. You were trying to be strong for your mom and abuela. I get that, but you don't have to be strong now. I'm here and I'll do it for you."

"But why?" She didn't get it. Leo always treated her like he was annoyed by her presence.

"Because I know that if I didn't do this for you, no one would. They'd let you continue to push it all down and that's not fair to you. You should be able to feel whatever you want without having to worry about what other people think. Since you don't care about what I think, I was the perfect person to do it."

Unable to process everything he'd said or how she felt about it, Sofi did the only thing she could think of. She lifted her lips to his and kissed him. She expected him to pull away or something, but he didn't. He kissed her back. They stayed there for hours kissing and eating chocolates, and she listened to him sing "En mi Viejo San Juan" over and over again until she had no more tears to cry.

Back in the present Sofi took a deep breath and wiped at her wet eyes. That was the Leo she liked the best. The sweet, considerate one who saw her for who she was and wanted her anyway. It was Sofi's turn to do the same for him. She told herself to just do it. Leap off that cliff and swan dive into the water below.

16

LEO'S STOMACH WAS DOING SOMERSAULTS IN HIS TORSO. HE WAS nervous, but he was also excited. A few hours ago he'd made it through the entire practice physical exam. And the best part was that his arm wasn't useless because of it. He honestly wasn't sure when things had changed, because he felt like his training kicked his ass more often than not, but at some point in the last few weeks he'd crested the hill. He now had proof that he could and would pass the physical exam and once again be considered an active firefighter.

When he'd made it through and realized what it meant, the first person he'd wanted to tell was Sofi. But there were some other things he needed to tell her first. So here he was standing in front of the iconic *Cloud Gate* statue, more commonly known as The Bean, holding a picnic basket in one hand and his guitar case in the other. He didn't worry that she wouldn't know where to go. This was their spot. Since the night they'd shared their first kiss, they'd met up here plenty of times. They knew that it would be highly unlikely for them to be seen by anyone they knew since natives tended to give any touristy spots a wide berth.

Sofi walked up to him in a bright green dress with white polka dots. Her skin was shimmery and her hair down and wild, how he liked it. "What are you up to?" she asked him.

"Where's Tostón?" he asked at the same time.

They both paused and looked at each other patiently.

"Ladies first," he said.

"I wasn't sure if dogs were allowed here, so I left him with my mom and Abuela Fina." She gave him a look to signify that it was his turn to explain.

"I thought we could have a picnic." He held up the basket.

"But why?" she asked.

"I'll explain, but let's set up first." He led her to a grassy spot in front of the pavilion and put down the basket.

"I hear that they do different types of workouts here in the mornings," she said. "I was planning to take advantage when I moved back since my apartment would've been close, but now it feels like too much of a trek."

"We can still do it." He opened the basket and pulled out the dark blue blanket he'd bought specifically for their picnic.

Together they spread the blanket and sat. Leo began taking everything he'd prepared at Ahmad's house out of the basket. There were different dried fruits, cheeses, meats, olives, nuts, crackers, jams, a baguette that he'd sliced into thin ovals, and of course chocolate bonbons with caramel filling and sprinkles of sea salt on top.

Sofi looked impressed. "Look at you pulling out the big guns."

He smiled. "What, you think only the French can do these sharkcoochie boards right?"

Sofi laughed. "First of all, it's *charcuterie*." She emphasized the correct pronunciation. "Secondly, this is too much. You already made me margaritas; you don't have to ply me with wine too."

"Hey, I need to use what I have," he replied with a shrug. "I should have it all set up in a minute."

Sofi watch him work in silence for a moment. "Okay," she said when he pulled out a bottle of French wine and two stemmed glasses. "Now you really do need to explain yourself. What is all this?"

"I wanted to celebrate," he said. He opened the wine and put it to the side to let it breathe.

"Celebrate what?"

Leo took a deep breath and released it. *Here we go.* "I've been training in order to take the CFD physical exam, so that I can be an active firefighter again. Today I blew through the practice drills without any issues, so that means that I'm finally ready to take the real thing."

"Wow," she said. "I didn't know that was even possible. I just figured it was one of those things that when you were done, you were done."

Leo shook his head. "No way. Firefighters get injured all the time and sometimes it takes them a while to get back in shape, but if they can prove they can still do the job, they're welcomed back."

"Is that why you didn't quit? So you could go back eventually?"

"Yes, but also because I needed the health insurance, so I had to accept the desk job."

"But you don't want to keep the desk job," she concluded.

"Hell no. I hate it."

"How come you don't go back as an EMT?"

"I tried," he confessed. "Being around all the real action and not being able to help the way I used to was too hard. I felt myself shutting down, falling deeper into a dark place. When

I started wishing the bullet had just ended it for me, I knew I needed to make a change. I wasn't going to let myself get worse. So I called my psychiatrist and set up an emergency session. I decided after that to accept the desk job at least until I could go back for real."

Sofi's eyes were wide. "You miss it that much?"

"Every day."

She tilted her head as if trying to figure something out. "Why is being a firefighter so important to you?"

"When I was thirteen, we had a kitchen fire at El Coquí. I don't remember how it started but I remember being in the office ignoring Eddie as he tutored me in math. All of a sudden we heard shouting and we went running. There were huge flames all over the kitchen and the heat was intense. My mom and Kamilah were dragging my abuela out the back door. My dad and Abuelo Papo were leading people out the front door. Papi saw me and Eddie standing there and told us to get our asses outside, but before we could move the firefighters burst in the front and back doors. It was like watching superheroes descend on a villain. They led us outside, so I didn't get to actually see them put out the fire, but when we were allowed back in I remember being stunned that the damage wasn't worse. Abuela and my mom were crying all over them, thanking them for saving the place, and they acted like it was no big deal. 'We were just doing our job,' one of them said. After that Abuela told them that they were forever going to eat for free at El Coquí. They took her up on it too. It seemed like there were always firefighters around and they were cool. They answered all of my questions and didn't make me feel like a dork for basically following them around like an overeager puppy."

She smiled at his description. "And that was it? You decided to become a firefighter then?"

"Yeah. Pretty much. There was never another path for me." Until he'd been ripped off that path and dropped in a whole new setting. But he was working his way back and that was what mattered. "When I was younger I worried that I'd never find the right fit for me because I hated school and was shit at remembering to do things. I struggled so much that I couldn't even imagine a job that I could actually do. But something about being a firefighter has always just worked. It's like something in my brain just clicks and everything falls into place. The only other time that happens is with music."

"How come you never pursued that? With Gio's connections I'm sure you would've had some fantastic opportunities."

Leo paused and wondered how to put his feelings about that into words. "I love music, don't get me wrong, but I don't know, it just felt too easy if that makes sense. Everyone always says that I'm a born singer slash musician. That I got my talent from Abuelo. So I guess I just felt like I didn't want to do it only because it was expected of me or because I need to carry on Abuelo's legacy or something. I also didn't want to pursue music just because I could. I don't know, maybe I'm just too much of the rebellious youngest son, but music has always been my hobby not my passion."

"I get that," Sofi said. "I've always been impressed by your sense of self." Sofi put a hand on his thigh. "You're one of the only people I know who's always been certain of who they are. You are you in any situation and without any pretense. That's not easy."

"Is that what's going on with you?" he asked. "You're having trouble distinguishing between who you are and who you think you need to be?"

Sofi sighed. "I don't know how you always know what I'm thinking. It's annoying."

Leo took that as affirmation that he was right. Not that it had been that difficult to see. People who were happy with their life didn't just take off for a year. "What's going on, bombón?"

She threw herself back on the blanket like she was in a telenovela. She was so dramatic and Leo loved it. "I thought getting away and doing everything I'd missed out on would fix this feeling, but if anything it got worse. I know I need to quit my job." She tossed her arm over her eyes. "But also like, who the hell do I think I am, you know? My grandparents on my dad's side came from the DR with nothing but a few dollars and even fewer belongings. My abuelo Juan grew up in a freaking shack in Maricao." She took her arm off her face to wave it around in emphasis. "Here I am with a great job that just allowed me to spend an entire year abroad and it pays me so well that I can buy designer things." She began counting things off on her fingers. "I'm not drowning in debt, I have a luxury car, and I'm complaining that I'm not happy? What the fuck is wrong with me?" Leo opened his mouth but Sofi threw up a hand to signal him to stop. "And don't tell me 'money doesn't buy happiness,' because that's bullshit."

"What do you want me to say, then? You want me to say 'stop playing the poor little rich girl, pull your head out of your ass, and be the badass I know you are'?"

Sofi sucked her teeth. "I wish it were as easy as you and my mom make it seem."

"It is never easy, but it's what you need to do. Want to know my secret for always being me?"

"Yes."

"I accept myself as I am in that moment. There are a lot of things about myself that I wish I could change, but I know I can't. I'm never going to not have ADHD. I'm never going to not have nerve damage. So I have to figure out how to work around those things in order to still accomplish what I want. Like playing the guitar." He pulled his guitar out and placed it in his lap. "They told me they doubted I'd ever play again, but I refused to believe that, so I kept practicing even when it hurt, even when it sounded worse than when I started. I took it one step at a time." He began strumming. Soon it turned into one of his favorites, "Lost Without U" by Robin Thicke. He closed his eyes and started singing. He felt the blanket sink next to him. He opened his eyes and met Sofi's gaze. He continued to sing about not being able to help himself. He didn't look away as he sang about her being the perfect shape. He watched closely as her breathing accelerated. He kept singing until he finished the entire song and not once did he look away from Sofi.

"Now here you are playing better than most people," she observed. With the setting sun hitting her, she looked dusted in gold like some sort of goddess. Even her dark brown eyes looked like they were speckled with gold flakes.

Leo could stare at her forever. Instead, he responded to her comment. "Yeah. I've been practicing every day because I don't want to mess up at Kamilah's wedding." He still couldn't believe that she wanted him to sing the song for their first dance. He and José, one of the guys in the band, were going to perform acoustically with Jose's daughter and niece, who both play the violin. They'd been practicing separately, but still needed to find the time to practice together.

"I know you'll be great," Sofi told him with a smile that she then turned into a threatening scowl. "Because you have no other option."

Leo set the guitar down next to him and gave Sofi a two-fingered salute. "Yes, ma'am. Madam wedding planner, ma'am."

They grinned at each other.

"How is the planning going, by the way?" he asked as he poured the two of them wine. "I know you've cc'd me in a bunch of emails with the vendors, but if you need anything else from me, just let me know."

"Thanks, but I'm good. It's been going oddly well." Sofi spread some apricot jam on a sliver of baguette and bit into it. "I've been thinking that this might be what I want to do." She finished off her bread and jam. "Like maybe I'll open my own event planning company." She started looking through more of their spread.

"That's a great idea." Leo brushed against her as he reached for a slice of hard salami.

Sofi gasped and Leo smiled. He loved knowing that his touch, as light as it was, affected her.

She cleared her throat. "There's one big problem with that." She opened the container of blue cheese–stuffed olives and used the mini fork to pluck one out. "My dad." She placed the olive in her mouth. "When I was eighteen I agreed to work for him in exchange for his help with college, but now he wants me to take over when he retires."

"You don't owe him shit," Leo said when she finished. "He's your dad. It's his freaking responsibility to support you in getting an education. Not only that, but I can guarantee that you've made the company way more money than he spent on your schooling." It didn't matter that he'd funded both a bachelor's and master's degree for her. She was a badass businesswoman and he knew that she was worth her weight in gold.

"I probably have, but I can't help but think that if I were to tell him that I wanted to quit, it would be the end of our relationship." Sofi refilled her glass of wine and set the bottle between them. "I know it's not the best, but at least it's something." She wouldn't meet his gaze. She tried to seem like she was too focused on making a tiny sandwich with the meat, cheese, and a thin layer of jam spread on the baguette bread.

"Bombón, you're fully capable of anything you put your mind to. You are amazing and anyone who doesn't recognize and value that, who wants to put limitations on what you can do, doesn't deserve to be considered in your life decisions. The people who know the real you and truly appreciate her will stand by you no matter what you decide." *And I'm one of those people*, he wanted to add but didn't. Instead, Leo grabbed his own full glass and took a drink.

"Thank you for the life lesson, Leo." The way she looked at him, with tender warmth, made his own insides melt. "I'm going to try to take your advice and just accept that I am who I am and I want what I want."

He bit into the sandwich as she held it up to his mouth. "Stick with me, kid," he said around a mouthful. "I'll teach you all you need to know." Leo licked a bit of jam off his bottom lip.

The corner of her lip curled and she gave him a heated look through her lashes. "Maybe I will." She leaned in and kissed him as if she just couldn't help herself.

He wanted to keep things light, but he couldn't help himself either. Leo deepened the kiss, his tongue playing with Sofi's. She was so sweet. He couldn't get enough.

She twisted and lifted to her knees so she could put a leg over his lap. She lowered herself into his lap and whimpered when their bodies met.

Leo groaned and wrapped an arm around her waist to pull her closer until her chest was against his.

She dug her fingers into his hair and pulled it back so she could ravage his mouth.

Fuck. He loved it. "Mmm, bombón. Qué rica eres."

Sofi ground her core against him. "You feel so good," she whispered in his ear before nibbling on it.

Goose bumps chased the shiver down his spine and spread along his body. "You have no idea how good it feels to have you right here, on my lap, in my arms." She dragged her mouth down his neck and he just about came in his pants. "Fuck, Sofi. I missed this. I missed you."

"I missed you too. I tried to get over you once I left, because un clavo saca otro clavo."

Leo tensed, not really wanting to hear about the guys she dated or may have even slept with.

"But I couldn't even bring myself to try moving on with someone else, because I knew it wouldn't work." She shook her head. "It never worked any other time I tried it, so there was no reason to do it again."

Leo loved the sound of that even though he knew he didn't have the right to care. "No one you met interested you?"

"Unfortunately no," she grumbled. "It seems like you're the only nail I want."

Leo smiled. "You're the only one I want to screw, so it works out." He waggled his eyebrows. "You see what I did there?"

Sofi chuckled. "You are so corny. That doesn't even make sense."

"Sure it does." He could tell that she was going to continue arguing with him about it, so he kissed her to give her something else to do.

They went at it then. Their lips and hands all over each other. Each kiss, each caress, more urgent than the previous one.

"Wait, wait. Let's go home," she suggested. "Or somewhere not in the middle of the park."

Leo's lip curled. "I'd love nothing more than to push you against one of these trees and fuck you where everyone could see you come apart."

Her pupils blew wide-open. She liked that idea even though she didn't want to.

He ran his hands down her sides until he reached her ass. He knew she felt insecure about her less curvy hips and butt, she'd once told him that she was considering a Brazilian butt lift, but to him she'd always been a perfect handful. "That will have to happen another night though," he continued with a squeeze to her cheeks.

"No it won't. We don't need to get arrested for public indecency." Her lips brushed against his neck where she'd been biting at his tendon.

He groaned. "Exactly. Besides I already told you, I'm not fucking you until you tell everyone that you're mine."

She pulled back. "I'm sorry?"

"Don't worry. I'll still make you come when we get home." He reached for her, but she slapped his hands away. He frowned. "What?"

"Are you kidding me?" She crossed her arms over her chest. "You say something like that and expect me to just be fine with it?"

"I told you that before, so why are you mad about it now?"

"I was mad about it then, but I was distracted!"

"Well, let me distract you again." He reached for her.

Sofi pushed off his chest and stood. "Hell no. I'm not going to let you manipulate me with sex, Leo."

"Manipulate you?"

"What do you call this? You're trying to use my own body against me. Fuck that."

"I'm putting down a boundary, Sofi. I'm not going to fall back into the same patterns with you. I'm not trying to be your glorified booty call. I don't want that anymore."

"Then what do you want?"

"I want to be with you, Sofi! What else do I have to do to make it clear?"

"I don't know, maybe actually say it." She tossed back her head. "I've never heard you say it until right now, so forgive me for not reading your mind."

Leo paused. That couldn't be true, could it? It seemed to him like he was saying it constantly, but now that he really thought about it, he was pretty sure he hadn't. His grandmother had always told him that actions speak louder than words, but apparently not. Apparently, you needed both. "You're right," he told Sofi. "So let me say it clearly. I want to be with you. For real. No hiding. I want to call you my girlfriend and for you to call me your boyfriend. I want everyone to know that you are mine and I am yours."

"I want that too," Sofi said, the anger fading from her eyes. "That's what I came to tell you tonight."

Leo was overjoyed. He reached for Sofi, but she held up a hand.

"I need time to tell Kamilah, okay? Things are still so fragile between us and I don't want to ruin things—not when I'm in the middle of planning her wedding reception. But I will tell her. I promise I will and after that, I don't care who knows."

Leo believed her. Sofi didn't make promises she had no intention of keeping. "Okay. I'll give you time, but not too much. Deal?" He held up a pinky.

She wrapped her pinky around his. "Deal." She looked around. "Can we leave to go have sex now?"

"Hell yeah." They cleaned up in the blink of an eye and rushed back to the apartment.

17

"I REALLY WISH I'D THOUGHT ABOUT HOW FINISHING OFF A BOTTLE of wine at the park would interfere with my plans to get you home quickly," Leo grumbled in her ear.

Yeah. That was a bad move on both of their parts. Now their tipsy asses were stuck in the back seat of an Uber with a driver who was obviously not a native on account of his ignoring their suggestions and taking the most traffic heavy-way back to the apartment. "We're almost home," she whispered back.

"Thank God," Leo whispered.

Sofi wanted to agree, but the fact was that she was nervous. She'd basically just agreed to be in a relationship for the first time in years. Actually more like the first time in her adult life, because even her only serious relationship in college had been her trying to move on after breaking up with Leo. Brandon had been a great boyfriend, but he'd obviously been feeling their relationship more than her. Hence her breaking it off when she stumbled across an open tab on his browser featuring engagement rings. The truth was that she'd frequently criticized Leo's inability to maintain a relationship, but she was worse than he was. Leo at least tried over the years to have normal relationships with people. Sofi simply kept things light and fun. No commitments. No drama. Good vibes only. When things went beyond that, she would dip. She was ashamed to say that she'd ghosted multiple men throughout her life.

When they reached the apartment, Leo silently followed her up the stairs. Neither one of them spoke until they were fully inside with the door locked. "I have to go to the bathroom," Sofi said before rushing to the space and locking the door behind her. She sat on the edge of the tub and stared at the tiled floor. What was wrong with her? She'd had sex with Leo so many times that she'd lost count. Sex between them was never a problem. So why was she freaking out about it now? Was she really so much of a commitment-phobe that simply agreeing to give this relationship a try was going to ruin something good? No. No way. She wouldn't let it.

Sofi stood and looked herself in the mirror. "Get your shit together," she told her reflection firmly. "You want this." Then she turned and unlocked the door. She stepped out into the living room and followed the sound of music to the kitchen where Leo was finishing putting away their picnic leftovers. There were two new glasses of wine sitting on the island.

He turned and saw her standing there. He held out a hand. "Ven, bombón. Dance with me."

Sofi let out a breath. That she could do. She stepped forward and grabbed his hand. He used his grip to tug her around the island and into his arms. The bachata remake of a Drake and Bad Bunny superhit was about halfway through, but it didn't matter to her. She loved dancing bachata. It was quite possibly the most Dominican thing about her outside of her love for the three Ms—mangú, mamajuana, and merengue. She especially loved dancing with Leo, because they were both extra AF about it. It was only seconds before Leo was spinning her as they improvised some quick footwork. The next song was a slow bachata by Leslie Grace about dancing with a lover. Sofi and Leo danced like they were two sensual bachata teachers at one of those conferences she saw all over social media—extra close, extra hips, and extra arms and footwork. They stared at one another, their foreheads touching, as their bodies rubbed and rolled against each other.

Leo spun her before pulling her close, her back to his front. Together they moved in the familiar side-to-side steps. He placed a kiss at the juncture of her shoulder and neck. She dropped her head onto his opposite shoulder to give him more room, which he took advantage of. Suddenly he spun her again and did his own rotation around her before bringing them back together face-to-face. As the song wound down he dipped her back. She hung there like a rag doll while he trailed kisses from under her chin to her chest. "You need to stop thinking so much," he told her.

"Make me stop," she practically begged him.

He lifted his head. "That's what you want? You want me to take control?"

She nodded eagerly. She loved it when he took control. It allowed her to let go completely.

His eyes sparked with pure devious desire and his lips furled into the kind of grin that made her toes curl. "Oh, bombón. You're in for it now."

Sofi shivered at the promise in his words.

He straightened with her in his arms. "Turn around and put your hands on the counter."

Sofi spun so fast she almost tipped over. Her hands slammed

down onto the cool porcelain of the island and she widened her stance to brace herself.

"Ass out, Sofi. You know better." His voice was just the right amount of firm.

She slipped her hands farther along the island as she bent forward and arched her back. She gave her hips a little wiggle. She knew he liked the view, but really it was because she was so excited she couldn't help herself.

"Look at you pretending to be a good girl, but you're not a good girl are you, bombón?" he murmured. "You're a naughty girl who disappears for a year and leaves me with nothing but memories and a weak hand."

Sofi stayed quiet.

"Say it." He punctuated his words with a smack to her ass.

Sofi sucked in a breath. "I'm a naughty girl," she whispered, her voice dripping with lust.

His hand caressed the spot he'd just smacked. "But you want to be my good girl, don't you?"

She nodded.

Another swat. "What was that?"

"I want to be your good girl."

"Hmm, we'll see about that." He leaned in so his body just barely brushed against hers. He spoke into her ear. "A good girl would let me bend her over and fuck her against this island. Are you going to let me do that?"

Sofi began to nod, but caught herself. "Yes. I will."

"What if I want to pull your hair as I do it?"

"Pull it."

"And if I grab your throat?"

"Grab it."

"That does sound like something a good girl would say, but let's test that." His hands coasted from her shoulders to her hips. "I'm going to go grab some condoms. When I come back I want you in the same position, but wearing nothing but those heels. Do you understand?"

"I understand."

"Move quickly," he said with a tap to her ass.

Sofi moved as soon as he backed up. She unzipped her dress and lifted the halter over her head before letting it slide to the floor. She pulled down her thong and kicked both items away. Then she took up the same position she'd been in before. She dropped her head and stared at the subtle veining in the white counter as goose bumps broke out all over her skin. She was almost trembling with need, all her nerves from earlier now morphed into anticipation, her breathing already fast.

Leo's voice enfolded her from a few feet away. "Ay, bombón, qué bonita te ves así, desnuda y esperándome."

"Thank you." Her voice was soft and breathy—full of desire.

A cluster of condoms landed on the counter next to her hand. "Don't move," he directed.

Sofi didn't move. She waited to see what was coming next.

She felt his breath on the back of her neck right before she felt his lips. He kissed his way down her back. He bit her ass cheek right before he pushed her forward, spread her wide, and used his mouth on her.

Sofi groaned and moaned. "Please," she panted. "More. Please. Please." He added his fingers to the mix and Sofi cried out. "Yes!"

He didn't stop. He worked harder. Faster. He was everywhere all at once. Then his tongue hit the perfect spot at the exact same time as his fingers.

Sofi came hard. "Leo!" She slumped onto the counter. Before she could even catch her breath, he was there. She hadn't even seen him grab a condom.

He wrapped a hand around her hair, making a ponytail for him to grab onto. "Ready?"

"Yes," she panted.

"Good girl," he said before he yanked on her hair and slammed into her.

"Fuck," they both exclaimed at the same time.

"Look at you," he groaned as he worked his hips. "So perfect. My good girl."

Sofi moaned loudly.

"You love it when I call you that, don't you? My good girl taking me so well. Letting me pull your hair and spank your ass." He punctuated that with a hard smack.

Sofi cried out but pushed back into him.

"That's it," he told her. "Just like that."

Her sweaty palms slipped and slid against the counter, but she did her best to brace herself against the onslaught.

Suddenly, he pulled out of her, grabbed her hips, turned her around, and lifted her onto the counter. "I need to look at you." He slammed back into her.

She'd never been more grateful for his height. "Yes," she hissed. "More."

He put his hand on the back of her neck and pulled her face to his. "Dame esa boca." He kissed her. Using his thumb to tug her lips open. He ravaged her mouth like he was ravaging her body and she loved every second of it.

She panted against his mouth. "Más. Dame más." She wasn't sure what more she wanted but Leo knew.

He wrapped his hand around her neck and pushed her down until her back hit the counter. With his other hand he pulled her ass off the edge so he had better leverage. Then he used his hold on her neck to keep her in place as he completely destroyed her. All while maintaining eye contact. "Whose good girl are you?" he asked. "Whose pussy is this?"

Sofi opened her mouth to say his name, but she wasn't sure if any words actually came out. She had no idea what she said, where she was, how loud she was being—nothing. She was only aware of the pleasure. It filled every single space she'd once thought empty. It overwhelmed her. It was so much that her body couldn't handle it. It locked and squeezed and then began to shake uncontrollably. She shook like she was being electrocuted. She screamed like she was too.

They both slid to the floor, their bones no longer working. They slumped over at the same time, facing each other.

"Damn girl, I think you killed me." Leo panted, his chest rising and falling like he'd just done the world's most difficult workout.

Sofi let out a soft groan. "I don't know if my legs will ever work again. They've been replaced with tembleque."

He chuckled. "Oh no, not tembleque." The smile on his face was equal parts amused, pleased, and cocky.

"Usually I'd tell you not to be so smug, but go right ahead. Toot your own horn because that was fucking fantastic."

"Right back at ya," he said, rolling onto his back. He sat up and reached for her leg.

She definitely wanted to do that again, but she wasn't ready yet. "Give me a minute," she told him.

His smile grew. "I like where your head is at, but I was just going to take off your shoes."

"Oh. Okay." She lifted her foot so he could reach it easier.

He unbuckled it and slipped it off before placing a quick kiss on her foot. He did the same to the other side and Sofi's chest got all warm and fuzzy.

He stood up and held out a hand. "Come on," he said. "I need a shower and a nap before I'm ready to go again. I'm not as young as I used to be."

Sofi slid her hand into his while looking him up and down. "I don't know," she said with a grin. "You've undoubtedly gotten better with age."

"Just wait until I've had my nap." Then he pulled her into the bathroom.

18

LEO WAS STANDING IN LIAM AND KAMILAH'S KITCHEN GRABBING another beer when he was cornered by Abuelo Papo.

His abuelo was wearing a bright yellow guayabera that made his green eyes look more intense. Or maybe it was the scowl on his face. "Mira muchacho del demonio, you've been ignoring my calls."

Leo did his best not to react to getting called out on avoiding his abuelo. "I've just been super busy," he replied. It was true. His days were full of work, band practice, training, Tostón, and Sofi. Well, mostly Sofi. It had been two weeks since they'd decided to really go for it and Leo had never been happier.

"There's no excuse to disappear." Abuelo crossed his arms and stared Leo down as if he weren't half a foot shorter. "Fina and I are doing our best to help you, but we can't do anything if you don't cooperate."

Leo gave a quick look around. Luckily, Liam and the rest of the groomsmen were too busy setting up the poker table to overhear. It had finally been determined that the bachelor party would consist of a night of drinks and poker, something Liam would actually enjoy, while the bachelorette party headed out for a night of drinks and dancing, something Kamilah always enjoyed. Tonight was that night, so while the guys were downstairs prepping, the girls were upstairs doing the same.

Leo leaned closer to his abuelo.

Knowing that Leo was about to spill the tea, Abuelo's eyes gleamed as he leaned toward him. "Dime," he commanded in a whisper.

"You and Doña Fina don't have to scheme anymore," Leo whispered.

Abuelo's mouth stretched into a grin. "Does that mean what I think it means?"

Leo nodded. "Sofi and I are together. Like, for real together."

"Wepa!" Abuelo hollered, throwing his hands up and giving a salsero spin.

"Shh," Leo whisper-shouted, but it was too late. Everything around them was quiet. He looked and found everyone looking at him and Abuelo in confusion and interest. Leo cleared his throat. "I just told him that if he manages to beat me tonight, I'll give him a solo at the reception."

It was obviously a lie but leave it to his grandpa to take advantage. "You said two solos and a duet." He shook his finger at Leo as if to say, *Ah, ah, ah.*

Leo narrowed his eyes. "I don't remember that."

Abuelo shrugged. "Maybe you need to slow down on the beer. It won't be any fun kicking your butt if you're too drunk to play well."

The rest of the guys laughed and let out a chorus of "ooh" and "aw snap."

"Oh, it's on now, Abuelo," he warned. "Be prepared to feel my wrath."

Abuelo snorted. "Bring it on."

By the time they'd finished their bickering, the guys had lost interest and gone back to setting everything up. Leo lowered his voice again. "We're still keeping it quiet, so chill out and please, for the love of God, don't say anything."

Abuelo was affronted. "How dare you? I'm great at keeping secrets. You're the one who just blurts out whatever pops into your head."

Leo had nothing to say to that because it was true. Maybe he did need to slow down with the beer. The last thing he needed was to drunkenly spill the beans. Sofi would be pissed and that was the last thing he wanted. It was one thing to get her worked up on purpose. It was another to make her truly angry.

Abuelo poked him in the chest. "Hey, let me ask you something."

"What?"

"Why are you still letting her hide you? I thought you said that you were done with that."

"It's not for long." Leo took a drink from his beer before putting it on the counter next to him. "Sofi is worried about how Kamilah will react to finding everything out and neither one of us wants to jeopardize the wedding, so we agreed to wait until that's done."

Abuelo nodded. "That's a good idea. Ojitos de Oro will probably have a fit."

Leo almost rolled his eyes. Here Abuelo called Kamilah Little Golden Eyes while Leo was called devil child. So rude. "I don't know," Leo said. "I don't think she'll be that upset about it. Maybe if we were teenagers who fought constantly still, but we get along pretty well now."

"Sí, but after how much of a big deal Sofi made out of her lie, Kamilah has every right to be mad about this lie."

Leo was no longer sure that he agreed with that, but he wasn't going to discuss it with his grandpa. "Look, the point is that we're already together, so there is no reason for you and Doña Fina to keep scheming. We're good. Really good."

Abuelo let out a hum of thought. "I'll believe that when I see you two out in the open together," he said, finally. "As of right now, you basically just made it back to square one. Together in secret." With that he took Leo's beer and wandered back into the dining room where the rest of the guys were.

Leo was about to follow him when the clack of heels on the floor brought his attention to the stairs where the ladies were coming down. Kamilah was wearing a sparkly dress that wasn't exactly white, but wasn't gold either. The rest of them were wearing some version of black leather and gold accessories. Sofi had on a black lacy bodysuit that showed a lot of skin with a leather mini skirt and the highest of heels. Her straightened hair was slicked back into a tight, high ponytail. Her eyes were smoky and her lips a deep red. She looked like a dominatrix. Leo was ready to drop to his knees and follow her around like Tostón while worshipping at her feet. God, she was sexy.

"Wow, mirá qué bellas son," Abuelo Papo said as the group reached the bottom of the stairs.

"Aww, thank you, Abuelo," Kamilah said, striding forward and placing a kiss on his cheek before using her thumb to wipe her lipstick off of it.

"So where are you going again?" Saint asked, he looked ready to tell them all to go back upstairs and put on more clothes.

"That Cuban place with live bands that is super popular," Sofi said. "Plus, there's a salsa conference in town, so you know there're going to be hella professional dancers there tonight."

"Okay, sexy professional dancers," Lucy said.

Alex high-fived her. "I'm here for that. Right, Gabs and Sofi?"

Leo raised his eyebrows.

"Me?" Sofi asked.

"Duh, girl." Liza bopped her on the head. "You three are the only single women here. It's on you three to have a wild hookup."

Leo almost growled, but instead he scoffed. "We have church with the whole family tomorrow. This is not the time for wild one-night hookups."

"Wait a second now," Lucy said. "Since when did you turn into an altar boy? You used to come to church straight from the after-party or whatever girl's bed."

"Exactly," Kamilah agreed. "Don't be a hypocrite, Leo. And if anyone deserves a wild one-night stand it's my maid of honor slash wedding planner. She needs to let off some steam. Right, Sof?"

Sofi just shook her head. "I don't need a wild hookup for that. I'm here to have fun with you all."

"Sofi sowed her wild oats all around Europe for the last year," Alex said. "Chicago guys probably don't compare."

"Can we not have a group discussion about my sex life?" Sofi asked. "Especially in front of your grandpa." She gestured to Abuelo Papo, who stood to the side watching everything happen like he was watching his favorite movie. All he needed was a bucket of popcorn and he'd be set.

"Yeah, some of us plan to eat soon and aren't interested in being nauseous for the next forever," Leo said with more attitude than was probably necessary.

"Oh please," Abuelo Papo said with a laugh. "Most of you wouldn't be here if I were a prude."

"Gross," Leo exclaimed. He did not need the mental image of anything his grandparents used to do.

Abuelo patted him on the back. "Relax, Leo. This is Kamilah's night and if she wants to spend it trying to get her best friend to have a good time, let her." His smile was straight-up devious. He was having too much fun at Leo's expense.

Leo promised to stop that enjoyment in its tracks as soon as they played poker. As for his secret girlfriend, she'd better not let them talk her into flirting with any guys. The look he shot her told her exactly that. At least, he thought it did until the little minx just winked at him and walked away—her arm entangled with his sister's.

"Okay, so what's our game plan?" Lucy asked from the front seat of the private car Ben had ordered for them.

"What do you mean?" Sofi asked. "We're heading to the club."

She laughed. "I was talking to Mila and I meant the plan to get you laid."

"What?" she yelped.

Kamilah reached forward and whacked Lucy's arm. "You have a big mouth. That was a secret."

"A secret?" Sofi was trying to catch up, but she'd done too much pregaming. Her brain wasn't firing on all cylinders. "You have a secret plan to get me laid at the club?"

Behind her, in the farthest seat, Alex, Gabi, and Liza laughed.

Kamilah turned to her. "Yes. I know we were just joking before, but then I think you need it."

Sofi shook her head. "I don't."

"I don't believe that," Kamilah said. "You've been tense and jumpy as hell for at least a week now and you're usually only that stressed when you aren't getting any."

She knew what Kamilah was talking about, but it wasn't true. The truth was that she was jumpy and tense whenever she was messing around with Leo and didn't want Kamilah to know. Hence her telling Kamilah that she wasn't sleeping with anyone during those times. "I'm tense because I'm planning your wedding in a few weeks."

"Exactly," Kamilah exclaimed. "All the more reason for you to let loose tonight. Work out some of that stress."

Sofi sniffed.

"Seriously, I never realized how much of a relief a good round of sex could be until Liam. I swear it's like going from a block of ice to a puddle of warm bathwater."

Sofi was well aware. She'd been taking advantage of the fact with Leo. "What about Alex and Gabi."

"Count Gabi out. She's basically a nun now and she likes it that way," Alex said, then ducked her sister's head smack. "But don't worry about me. I'm on the stress relief train too. Trust and believe that I need it after working on the fucking theater for the last year."

Kamilah turned in her seat to face her cousin. "Was it that bad? I thought you said the damage wasn't as severe as you'd originally thought."

Alex tossed her long light brown waves over a shoulder. "The problem wasn't the building, but the owner."

"Don't tell me that Chord Bailón is an asshole," Lucy cried from the front of the car. "My Barrio Brothers stan heart couldn't take it."

Sofi had missed a lot in her time away from the Vegas. She still found it hard to believe that Alex and Gabi's Broadway-based mom, Carmen, and older sister, Evalisse, were back in Chicago specifically to work on a brand-new musical written, directed, and starring, of all people, Chord Bailón—the heart-throb of world-famous boy band the Barrio Brothers. Not only that, but he'd bought an old theater slash office building to house his masterpiece *and* the new El Hogar. She didn't know how Saint and Lola had gotten that to happen, but it made her happy to see the family thriving for the most part. Although, apparently Alex felt differently about the whole thing.

Alex scoffed at Lucy's comment. "Well, I hate to break your

heart, but he's the fucking worst. I've never met a more arrogant and annoying pain in the ass in my entire life."

"Damn. Why do the best-looking celebs always have to be assholes?" Liza shook her head as if really sad about it.

"That's not true," Kamilah said. "I've heard that Keanu Reeves is one of the nicest people ever and has actually saved someone's life."

"Keanu doesn't count," Alex said. "He's another type of being entirely. Like an angel who was sent here to give us all hope that not everything is crap."

"So he's basically Denzel in *The Preacher's Wife*?" Liza asked with a smart-ass smile.

Sofi breathed a sigh of relief as they began talking about celebrity gossip. She was positive that she'd successfully pulled off a diversion, but then they arrived at the club and Kamilah proceeded to push her at every single good-looking man she could find. There was the hot nerdy guy, the Eastern European guy who looked like a Bratva member but danced like a cast member of *Dancing with the Stars*, and the creep who gave straight-up serial killer vibes.

Sofi plopped onto her seat, out of breath after a dance with her last would-be hookup. "Dear lord, he kept spinning me like a damn dreidel. I'm dizzy." She picked up her drink and slammed it. She was so hot.

Kamilah snort laughed. "You looked like one of those drills that they use to look for oil."

Sofi glanced around. "Where is everyone else?" She had to practically yell the question because it was so loud.

"They're out there dancing." She sipped her own drink before putting it down with a plop. "Okay, he's off the list." She turned her head from side to side, searching. "Let's find someone else."

"I don't want someone else and you look like a meerkat when you do that."

"Stop being a bummer," Kamilah told her. "I'm going to find you a sexy man to at least grind on and make out with if it's the last thing I do."

If there was one thing that Sofi knew about her friend it was that once she put her mind to something she was going to pursue it doggedly. There was only one option left. Sofi was going to have to come clean. The only way to stop this farce was to tell Kamilah that she was in a relationship, but she knew all too well that it wouldn't stop there. Her friend would want to know who.

Fuck. She was too drunk for this. She stood and held her hand out to Kamilah. "Come outside to the patio with me."

Kamilah stood and grabbed her hand. "Yes. Let's cool off before we go back to our hunt."

Sofi led Kamilah through the club and to the equally packed patio area. It was barely cooler than the inside, but there was at least a little bit of a breeze. Sofi found a tiny table with one single chair in the darkest corner.

Kamilah dropped into the chair. "I forgot how much heels suck," she said, her champagne-colored sequin dress with a draped neckline, low back, and thigh-high slit sparkled even in the dark. She'd told Sofi she wanted to feel like Vanessa Williams in *Dance with Me* and Sofi was there to make all her professional ballroom dreams come true.

Sofi sat on the edge of the table. Her heart was racing. She took a deep breath and wished she were either more sober or more drunk for what was about to happen. "Kamilah, I have to tell you something, but I'm scared."

Kamilah frowned. "Scared? About what?"

"I feel like I'm going to lose you again if tell you and I just got you back." Dear lord, Sofi hated how pathetic she sounded. This was why it was never good to have deep conversations while drunk and overly sensitive. "I don't want to ruin anything."

"Sofi, you're scaring me. Just tell me."

Okay. She just needed to spit it out. "Leo and I are together. Actually it's more like back together. You see we have a bit of a history. Not a bit. More like a lot of history. Like over fifteen years of history." Then Sofi just kept talking. She told Kamilah everything from their first kiss when Sofi was fifteen to them deciding to give themselves a real shot. "And I should've told you all of this years ago, but the truth is that I'm a hypocrite. I was so mad at you for lying when I've been lying to you for much longer. I'm sorry and I hope you are more forgiving than I was." She stared at her wringing hands.

A hand appeared on top of hers. "Sofi, look at me." Kamilah squeezed Sofi's hand and gave it a little shake. "Seriously, look at me."

Sofi looked up. She was surprised to see nothing in Kamilah's gaze but earnest caring. No disgust or anger. No disappointment. She didn't get it. How could she be so cool about this?

"I know."

Sofi sucked her teeth. "Shut the fuck up. There's no way. No. There's no possible way."

Kamilah gave her one of those full body winces that all but scream, *Well…*

Sofi's jaw dropped. "There's. No. Fucking. Way."

"To be fair, until recently I only suspected. But please, you're my best friend, he's my brother, of course I knew."

Sofi sat there in silence, trying to pick up the pieces of her blown mind. "Wait," she said suddenly. "What do you mean 'until recently'?"

"I sort of walked in on you two asleep in your bed the morning of the festival. I was looking for Leo and then I heard what sounded like a dog in your room, so I had to investigate. I booked it out of there before the dog woke either of you up, but honestly, I wasn't surprised." Kamilah rolled her eyes. "I mean damn. I know I can be a bit in my own world, but y'all act like I walk around in an alternate universe."

"I just. I… Why didn't you call me out?"

"Honestly, I felt like it wasn't my business. I knew that if it ever became something important enough, you'd tell me. If I'd have known that you were both making me your scapegoat, I would've busted your asses out years ago."

"You don't get it. We have fought about telling you for literal years. Years. And this whole time he was right."

"Leo said that I knew?"

"No. He said that you wouldn't care."

"I mean I wouldn't say that I don't care, and Liam certainly had to listen to me rage about it for a few days, but I'm not upset anymore. I'm happy for you actually."

"You are?"

"Hell yeah. I know I complain about him all the time, but my brother is a really good guy. However, he's the lucky one. You are an amazing, strong, smart, sweet, beautiful but badass orchid mantis who's as majestic as a…narwhal. And you smell like springtime!"

Sofi didn't really know what the hell Kamilah was talking about, but she knew that it was said with love, because her glassy eyes were blinking up at Sofi like she'd just cured cancer or something.

"I really do love you," Sofi told her with wet eyes.

"I love you too!" Kamilah threw her arms around Sofi.

They stayed like that for a while, crying and voicing their love for each other over and over.

"What in the white girl wasted…?" Liza's voice said from the side.

Sofi and Kamilah pulled away from each other, wiping their eyes.

"Here they are! We found them!" Lucy shouted to someone out of sight.

Within moments Alex and Gabi stepped into Sofi's line of sight.

Alex's look was one of secondhand embarrassment. "Drunk crying in the club? Really?"

Kamilah gave Sofi a look that said, *Do you want to tell them or should I?*

Sofi waved her on. She didn't have the energy or mental capacity do tell the whole story again.

When Kamilah finished everyone was quiet for a moment.

"Is that what this is about?" Lucy rolled her eyes. "We've been known."

"Who's 'we'?" Liza asked. "Because I sure didn't. I'm flabbergasted."

"Yeah me too," Alex said. "I'm flabbergasted as hell."

Alex looked at Gabi, but Gabi stayed quiet. "You knew?" she asked her sister.

Gabi shrugged. "It was pretty obvious something was going on. No two people enjoy fighting that much if there wasn't something between them."

Sofi blinked. "We don't like fighting."

Everyone laughed.

"We don't."

More laughter.

Sofi's friends were assholes. "I don't know why you are all laughing like I'm doing stand-up," she groused. "Just rude as hell for no reason."

"I'm sorry," Kamilah wheezed. "It's not that we're laughing at you. It just that what you said made us laugh."

"Yeah, I think I'm done with this conversation now."

"Okay. Okay. Fine. We're sorry."

"Nope. Still done. I'm going back to the dance floor. Peace out." Sofi pulled out her phone as she left.

I told Kamilah, but jokes on me. She already knew and she's happy about it.

In less than a minute she received a mind-blown emoji. A moment after that he replied.

> Meet me at our spot. We need to celebrate ASAP

Sofi smiled as she pulled up her text chain with Kamilah.

> I love you, but I gotta go. Drink tons of water and keep an eye on Alex.

Her phone buzzed with a selfie of drunk Kamilah sticking out her tongue and flipping her off.

> If I weren't ready to go home to my sexy soon-to-be husband, I'd be pissed at you!

> Love you too!

> Tell my brother that I said he'd better be good to you or I'll tell our parents about the night he snuck Miranda Vargas into the house in high school!

Sofi growled. Fucking Miranda Vargas. She'd hated that girl. After sending Kamilah a kissy face emoji, Sofi pulled up her ride-share app and put in her request. She couldn't wait to see Leo.

19

THE NEWEST ELECTRONIC HITS OF 2013 BLARED THROUGH THE *corridors of the club, causing Leo's bones to vibrate. He tried the knob of the door marked Employees Only, praying that it would open, and then cursing when it didn't.*

"Hurry up," *Sofi said from behind him.* "They're going to wonder where we are soon."

Leo huffed out a breath. "It's not my fault that all these damn doors are locked. It's like they don't even want people to hook up in the closets of their club."

"Wow, good deductive reasoning, Sherlock. Did you figure that out all on your own?"

"I'm going to gracefully ignore the attitude," *Leo said as he turned* enough to grab her hand before continuing down the darkened hall. "I know how cranky you get when you feel deficient in vitamin D."

She smacked him in the arm. "Stop calling your dick vitamin D. That's gross."

Leo tried the next door, which had to be some sort of closet. It was also locked. Leo was beginning to think that this hookup was not going to happen. "If you weren't so picky about the bathrooms, we could already be done," he grumbled.

"I am not having sex in a club bathroom. Do you have any idea how disgusting public restrooms are? Plus, there's a freaking attendant in there!"

"And I'd tip her enough to pretend like she didn't see anything," Leo pointed out as if that would magically make Sofi agree. He knew it wouldn't, but he was getting desperate.

It had been a month since their last hookup, which ended with them fighting and Sofi kicking him out...again. All because he'd made the colossal mistake of saying that they should go out to dinner. Of course, that started their normal argument of whether or not they were dating, why they weren't, and why they would never be. Leo still didn't understand Sofi's reasoning, but he'd let it go because it was either give in or have no Sofi and he was way too much of an addict to give her up. Hence his frantic search for a place private enough to get a taste of her without getting arrested.

"Ugh," Sofi exclaimed. "I wish we had a car, we could just leave and then come back."

Up ahead a sliver of light reflected off the shiny floors, barely illuminating the dark hallway. "I think there's an open door up there," Leo told Sofi. He picked up the pace, practically dragging her behind him. He could've slowed down, knowing that she was in some sky-high heels, but he wanted to get to the door before someone wandered along and closed it. He peeked through the cracked door to make sure no one was in their new hiding place and was overjoyed to see it was a decent-sized storage closet—an empty one. Well, empty of people at least. There were rows of stacked boxes on the metal shelving units along the walls.

"Get in here." He pushed the door open and practically launched himself into the space, yanking Sofi with him.

Her body slammed into his. He didn't even let her get acclimated to the space before he'd kicked the door closed behind them and pushed her back against it, sealing their mouths together.

Sofi wasted no time wrapping her arms around his neck.

He loved that she was just as desperate as he was. She usually tried so hard to pretend that he didn't affect her in any way, but when her act slipped it was clear she wanted him as much as he wanted her. Anytime she gave in it never failed to set Leo aflame in something that was equal parts desire and triumph. She just couldn't let him go and it turned him on like nothing he'd ever experienced with anyone else. Fuck. With Sofi in the picture there never really was anyone else no matter what Leo tried to do about it. *"Turn around,"* Leo growled against her neck.

Sofi, the brat, tried to act all innocent. *"For what?"* she asked in what no doubt would've been faux confusion if she weren't panting so hard she could barely talk.

Leo wasn't in the mood for games. Not after having to search the whole entire club while trying his best to hide a raging boner. *"So I can give you the spanking you've been asking for all night."*

"The hell you will. I haven't done anything wrong." She decided to lean into the bratty role, but again, Leo was done with the games.

"I just had to sit there for two hours watching you rub your ass all over that douche in the fake Louis Vuitton," he said.

"I can dance with other guys. I don't belong to you."

Leo bit back the urge to say, *the hell you don't,* because he knew that was too far. She'd probably knee him in the balls before storming off and he'd deserve it. Instead, he called her out. *"You did it for me,"* he said. *"You wanted me like this, nearly raging with jealousy. If you didn't, you wouldn't have kept smirking at me like the brat you are. Now turn around and take your punishment like a good girl."* He watched with bated breath as Sofi slowly turned her body until she was facing away from him.

She rested her hands against the door and arched out her back. *"I *don't know why you are so obsessed with spanking me. It's not like I have enough ass to make it fun."*

Leo's eyes jumped from the brightly colored tribal print minidress she'd been teasing him with all night to the back of her head. "What?" he asked, honestly confused, because she couldn't be insinuating what he thought she was.

"I mean I'm basically as flat as a board," she said, still facing the door. "I don't have an ass and I barely have any hips. I'm pretty much shaped like a boy. Hell, I've seen guys with more ass than me." She continued a very uncharacteristic ramble which just proved how drunk she was. "You probably feel bone when you spank me. You should wear padded gloves to protect your hands." She snorted then blew out a breath. "That's why, as soon as I have money, I'm going to the DR for a BBL. At least then I'll look like an actual Latina instead of some malnourished preteen boy."

Leo stood there like an idiot unsure of which of the emotions running through him he should prioritize. On one hand, he was still horny and more than willing to prove to her how perfect she was with his body. On a second hand, he was incredulous that someone as beautiful as Sofi would look at herself as less than, especially because she was usually so confident. On another hand, he was angry. How dare someone, anyone, make her believe that she needed to change her body to fit into some stereotypical idea of what a Latina should look like? On the other hand—that had to be too many hands, but he was too drunk to go back and count—he felt an overwhelming tenderness. Sofi never let anyone see her soft spots. She was basically an armadillo with diamond armor. It was extremely rare she let anyone see her soft underbelly, especially him. That was why he let the tenderness win out. He stepped up to her back, wrapped his arms around her, and pulled her close enough that their bodies were flush. "If only you could see yourself as I see you, bombón."

"How do you see me?" she asked. There was a heavy amount of sass in her tone, but under that he heard desperation. She needed him *to tell her how much he was attracted to her. She needed someone to help her feel good about herself.*

He turned her, so she was forced to look at him. "You are way more than a pretty face," he told her. "You are so beautiful that sometimes it hurts me to look at you. It's like staring into a raging fire, so intense but enthralling at the same time. I can sit there for hours following every blazing flame of you. I mean that, Sofi. Your skin, your eyes, that mouth, your chest, hips, thighs, ass, those long legs that I want wrapped around me at every minute of every day." He shook his head at his inability to put in words what he was trying to express, but there were words strong enough to make her understand. "You're a conflagration of perfection that makes my blood burn. There isn't one part of you that doesn't call to me on every single level. Not one single thing. This room could be a hundred times bigger, pitch-black, and full of people, and I'd still be able to find you without a problem. I'd just follow your brilliance. That's how much you shine more than anyone else. So stop comparing yourself to other women, because no one can measure up. They are candles, you're an inferno."

She stared up at him in silence. "Thank you," she whispered. He thought she might throw herself at him then, but instead she leaned forward and wrapped her arms around him. He responded in kind. When she tightened her arms, he did the same. When he felt drips of moisture on his neck and collarbone, he just held her tighter. He'd always hold her together when she needed to fall apart.

Leo wasn't the most observant guy, but it had not escaped his attention that Sofi had never gone through with her desire to get a Brazilian butt lift. He couldn't help but feel like he played some part in her accepting her body as it was. It made him feel good as fuck.

"What are you thinking about with your eyes closed that put that smile on your face?" Sofi's voice came from behind him.

Leo opened his eyes and found hers in the reflection in front of him. His smile grew just looking at her. "I'm thinking about you," he said.

One of her eyebrows went up. "Really?"

"That shouldn't be surprising. I'm always thinking about you."

Her gorgeous bee-stung mouth stretched into a smile of her own.

Leo couldn't take it anymore, so he spun on his heels to face her. "Hey, bombón."

"Hi." She took a few steps forward and looked up at him through her lashes. "Sorry it took me so long to get here."

Leo leaned against the statue behind him. "No big deal. I'm sure my sister had a bunch to say about you leaving early."

Sofi shook her head. "She actually didn't." Her tone was one part awestruck and another part confusion. Apparently, she was still having trouble believing that not only did Kamilah know about them, but she was fine with it.

Leo wasn't that surprised. His sister was a lot smarter than people gave her credit for. Plus, she was incapable of holding a grudge. She really didn't have a petty bone in her body. The only thing that amazed Leo was that she hadn't ever said anything to either of them about it. Like Leo, she wasn't known for her restraint. "What made you decide to tell her? I thought you were waiting until after the wedding."

"She wouldn't stop pushing me at guys," Sofi huffed. "I needed her to just stop."

Usually, any thought of Sofi with another guy revealed a jealous streak in Leo that he wasn't exactly proud of, but seeing the annoyance on Sofi's face calmed that beast. "So you had to tell her the truth because otherwise she wouldn't let it go." Leo was familiar with that stubborn side of his sister.

Sofi leaned her forehead against his shoulder. "I was so scared. I thought for sure she was going to flip out on me, but she just goes, 'I know.' That's it! Like she hadn't just drop-kicked me in the chest!"

Leo wrapped his arms around her and pulled her close. "I

know she had more to say than that. Kamilah doesn't communicate in short sentences. Unless Liam is rubbing off on her more than any of us thought." They were a family of talkers, with very few exceptions. Why use one or two words when you could use twenty? More is better after all.

Sofi laughed. She turned he face up to him. "She did tell me to warn you that if you aren't good to me, she will share some secret dirt from high school with your parents."

Leo's brows went up. He had no idea what that dirt could be because there was way too much to try to remember any specifics. "I'd better hedge my bets, then." He leaned down and placed a kiss on her forehead. "You're about to be so spoiled that you're gonna be sick of me."

Her adorable nose wrinkled. "No thanks. You know I'm not needy like that." She looked around. "I can't believe we are the only two people here."

"Well, it's almost 2:00 a.m. Technically, the park is closed." He lifted a hand and cupped her cheek. "We aren't supposed to be here, but I used my poker winnings to pay off a duo of security guards." Her red lips beckoned. He wanted to smear that red lipstick with his own mouth and his dick, but he settled for brushing his thumb along the crease under her plump bottom lip. "We have thirty minutes of uninterrupted privacy."

Sofi nuzzled her cheek into his hand. "Hmm. And what did you plan to do with those thirty minutes."

He leaned in and brushed his nose against hers. "Last time we were here, I told you I wanted to fuck you right in the park."

She inhaled sharply and her eyes went dark with desire.

"I would've done it too," he teased. "But you had to get all paranoid about laws and stuff."

She snorted a laugh. "You mean because the place was full of people, including families with kids?"

"Potato. Potahtoe." He wrapped his hand around her ponytail and tugged, tilting her face up to his.

Her lips parted on a gasp and her breathing started accelerating.

"So, bombón," he murmured. "How do you feel about my plan? Feeling like a naughty girl tonight?"

"Never," she said. "I'm a good girl." Her pink tongue swiped along that bottom lip. "I'm your good girl."

Goddamn. That was it. He couldn't hold back anymore. He used his hold on the back of her head to drag her mouth up to his. He devoured it; smearing that red off her lips, nipping at her cupid's bow, licking that little dent in the middle of her bottom lip, sucking on her sweet tongue. He gave her no choice but to take it and she did, letting out a little whimper. He pulled back enough to say, "You like to pretend you're a good girl, but we both know you only say that because it drives me crazy and you love to make me lose my mind." He used his thumb to wipe away remnants of her lipstick. "You, bombón, are a naughty girl at heart." And he loved it.

Her lips curled up into a Cheshire cat grin, devious and a bit unhinged. "Would a naughty girl do this?" Her hand went under his T-shirt to his abs and slid quickly down under the waistband of his jeans. She wrapped those long fingers of hers around him and gave a firm squeeze.

"Oh, most definitely," Leo groaned. "But you know what a really naughty girl would do?" He stiffened further when she began to slip her hand up and down. He threw his head back.

She attached her mouth to his neck. "What would a naughty girl do?" Her breath blew across his wet skin and caused him a full body shiver. She titled her head enough to give his jaw a nip.

Leo struggled to bring his thoughts into any type of order. "She'd lift that sexy little miniskirt and show me what's mine."

"Make me," she challenged.

Leo growled. He spun them so her back was against the cool metal now. Before she could say anything else, he gripped the hem of her skirt and yanked it up. He leaned back enough to look down. "Fuck," he groaned. She looked so good. Although he had forgotten that she was wearing a bodysuit. It was blocking the view he wanted the most. "How the hell does this thing come off?"

"There are snaps," she said, reaching between them.

He could barely hear them being undone over the rushing in his ears. His hand met hers and as soon as he felt her soft wet skin under his fingers he went wild. His other hand went around her neck and he yanked her mouth to his. Meanwhile his fingers plunged inside.

She moaned loudly, not caring that they were in public. And Leo almost came in his pants. She was so perfect. Every single thing about her. She was created just for him or he was for her. It didn't matter. All that mattered was that they were meant to be together.

Between them her hands worked at the button and zipper of his jeans. As soon as she had him out, she whimpered "inside" against his lips.

Because he was incapable of denying her anything, he pulled his fingers out, slid his hand to the back of her thigh and lifted it to his hip. "You do it," he told her. "Put me where you want me, naughty girl."

She lined him up and rolled her hips until he slid right where they both wanted them. She didn't stop rocking her hips.

Keeping his hand on her throat, Leo leaned back to watch between them. "Fuck, bombón. You feel so good."

"Más," she begged. "Dame más, papi."

Oh fuck. He loved it when she called him papi. He'd never had a daddy kink before Sofi, but hearing her call him that unleashed some inner beast in him. He gave her neck one final squeeze before he dropped his hand to grab and lift her other thigh. Then he rammed into her with a snarl. Over and over. He made them both growl, moan, pant, and grunt.

Sofi let out what could only be called a scream, and a small, tiny part of his mind was worried that the security guys he paid off would think he was murdering her. The rest of him reveled in the fact that he could make her so thoroughly lose her sense of self, space, and time. He loved that, with him, she shut off her brain. She knew he would take care of her, so she just let herself go. It made him swell with pride. He wanted to pound on his chest like a fucking gorilla. He did that to her. He made the most tightly controlled woman he knew completely lose her shit. He had that power because she gave it to him. She wouldn't give it up to anyone but him because despite everything she trusted him and loved him.

That was the thought that pushed Leo over the edge. He wrapped am arm around her back and pulled them chest to chest while his other hand landed on the cool metal statute with a smack. He buried his face in her neck and groaned through his shudders. Unable to stop himself he bit down on the tendon of her neck, sending her soaring again. "Coño, bombón," he mumbled against her sweaty skin before taking a lick. His chest heaved as he tried to get oxygen into his system again. "One of these days you're going to kill me."

Her body still shook against his. "Not if you kill me first," she puffed. She nuzzled her face into his neck and Leo melted. Like, he literally plopped down onto his ass with Sofi in his lap.

He wrapped both arms around her and pulled her so close that if they weren't flesh and bone, they would've merged into one being.

She lifted her head to look at him. She looked destroyed. Her makeup had sweat off, her mascara was running down her cheeks, and her red lipstick was smeared all over, but her eyes. Those gorgeous dark eyes, shined at him like two onyx gems.

Leo's heart squeezed painfully and then exploded into sparkles of pure joy. "I love you so fucking much," he blurted out, unable to hold the words in.

Sofi froze. She stared at him unblinking for what felt like forever. Suddenly she threw herself forward, latching her mouth to his.

They sat there kissing, even though he was positive their thirty minutes were up. Leo didn't care. They'd have to come tase him and drag him away to get him to move from this spot. He was too busy enjoying the sweetness of his little caramel bonbon. Even if his mind wouldn't stop fretting about the fact that he'd confessed his love and she hadn't said anything back.

20

KILLIAN KANE SAT IN HIS BED, PERCHED UP ON TONS OF PILLOWS.
It was clear that plenty of effort had been made to help him
look put together. He was wearing a collared plaid shirt under
a black suit jacket and his hair had been freshly styled. Despite
all of that, it was apparent he was dying. His face was gaunt and
pale. There was a tension to the way he held his body that was a
poor attempt to belie the pain clear in his eyes. But worse than
all of that was that his commanding, larger-than-life energy
was gone. He looked exhausted and just done, like he wanted
it over with already.

It was difficult to see and Sofi had never even been very
close to him. Beyond his rakish charm and over-the-top com-
pliments, they hadn't talked much. To Sofi, he'd simply been

Papo's best friend and basically Kamilah's great-uncle. Yet even so, Sofi had waited as long as humanly possible to watch the video Papo had given her. But she could no longer put it off. Mostly because in the middle of the night she'd had a great idea that could get her out of having to make a toast. First she had to know if it would fit with what Killian had said.

Taking a deep breath, Sofi hit Play.

Less than two minutes later, the video was over and she was wiping her eyes and blowing her nose. She knew that once this played at the reception, everyone would be a mess. But the good news was that it would work perfectly for her plan to get everyone to record something short and quick for Kamilah and Liam. She'd get someone, probably one of Lola's teens, to edit it all together. Then everyone had the chance to say something nice and, the best part, no one would have to give a speech in person. It was genius. Sofi fought the urge to literally pat herself on the back.

"Sofi, girl, you are awesome at this," she told herself.

Wedding planning was surprisingly fun. Sofi wasn't sure if it was because she loved pretty things or organization, but she was killing it if she said so herself. The flowers were chosen, the changes to the cake had been accepted, the tent, stage, and dance floor had been rented for the outside area, and her favorite caterers had agreed to have their team use the El Coquí kitchen and dining area to prepare the originally planned meal with a few tweaks that Sofi knew would make it even better. Luckily, all of her other corporate vendors had agreed to work with her even though it was last-minute. With the exception of the DJ, but that didn't matter, because she'd reached out to Gio and he'd agreed to do it for free. He'd been a little offended that he hadn't been the first DJ considered. Sofi assured him that it was only because Kamilah wanted her family to just enjoy the wedding. She'd left out the fact that Leo and his band were performing.

As she put off actual work to spend more time checking off items for the wedding, she realized that the only times she truly liked her job were the times she was planning events, whether they were for company functions or clients. There was just something so fulfilling about seeing her vision come to fruition and witnessing the joy of the people experiencing it.

"I'm an event planner," she said out loud to herself. She liked that. It felt good. She tried something else. "Sofia Rosario Santana, event planner." Oh yes. That was really good. Perfect. Holy shit. "This is it. This is what I want." She was more sure than ever.

Sofi pushed back from her desk and spun in her chair, throwing her arms up and giggling with excitement. This was it. This was what she wanted to do. She wanted to run an event planning company. Her *own* event planning company, so that she never had to be someone's employee again. She'd be her own boss, she'd make her own rules, and she'd only take on the clients she wanted. It would be great. Now she just needed to figure out how to do it. Sofi began the only way she knew how, by digging in.

She was into her third page of notes when the door to her office opened. Sofi rushed to flip over the paper on her desk and cover it with her crossed arms.

She looked up to see her dad standing in her doorway. "What are you still doing here, mi reina? They are in the conference room waiting for you. Vamos."

"I'm sorry. What?"

"The Costa people are here. It's time for your presentation."

"What presentation?"

Her dad looked at her like she was twerking on top of her desk. "Nena, no me digas que se te olvidó."

No. She hadn't forgotten it. She had never known about it. At least she was almost positive she'd never known about it.

Sofi clicked on her calendar to double-check. "It's not on my calendar." She looked at her dad.

"I told Malorie to make sure to let you know and add it to your calendar," he told her. "You need to take over handling the Costa account for me. I have too much other stuff going on."

Sofi wasn't sure she believed that. On one hand, Malorie was the secretary she and her father shared. She was new to the position, starting there shortly before Sofi returned from Europe. She'd been hired after their old secretary, Mrs. Barnes, had retired. Sofi had no idea what Malorie's work was like prior to her return, but since she'd been back it had been clear that Malorie was struggling to juggle both Sofi and her father. Sofi had the sneaking suspicion that Malorie's organizational skills had not been the reason her dad had hired her. She was ninety-five percent sure that Malorie was one of her dad's "friends" who'd just been lucky enough to be available when the secretary position opened.

On the other hand, Sofi would not put it past her dad to spring this meeting on her at the last minute as some sort of lesson. That was totally his MO. He was the type of dad who'd throw his kid in the deep end to get them to swim. He thought a person needed to take their licks in order to learn. Having a conversation like a normal human being didn't even cross his mind.

"Well, It's not here so I had no idea about it. I don't have anything prepared." She already knew what he was going to say next.

"We can't do anything about that now. They're here and waiting."

"I'll reschedule with them," she tried to suggest, knowing it wasn't going to work.

As expected, her dad shook his head before she was even done speaking. "Absolutely not. They have been one of our biggest accounts for years and they are already on the fence about bringing us on again. There is no way we're rescheduling."

"I have nothing ready for them. What do you want me to do? Wing it?"

"This is supposed to be your account now. Besides, you've come with me to enough meetings that you know just as much as I do. You should be able to make it work."

That was absolute bullshit. Sure, she'd accompanied him to most of the meetings so she knew some basics, but he was the one who knew the details. Besides, Sofi didn't do last-minute presentations, her glossophobia wouldn't let her. "You know that I can't do that. I need to be prepared." Her dad had never understood her need to have everything planned out and memorized to a T. He was the type of guy who could go into a meeting with nothing and leave with not only a contract, but a new best friend.

"You're going to have to." He gave her a stern look. "I'll head in there first and take some time catching up, but I want you in there in five minutes. Do you understand me?"

"Yes."

He turned and left, leaving Sofi sitting at her desk panicking.

She didn't know what to do. She felt like every word she'd ever known had flown right out of her head. Fuck. She hated this feeling. Her stomach turned as sweat started to bead along her hairline. She felt like every cell in her body was shaking. Saliva flooded her mouth. *You will not throw up*, she told herself sternly. She closed her eyes and took a deep breath in through her nose and let it out through her mouth. She repeated the action over and over until she no longer felt panicked. She still felt like she was on a train that had gone off track, but at least she didn't feel like she was going to puke.

Sofi continued to tell herself that everything was going to be fine as she reached for her phone, unlocked it, and raced through her contacts until she hit the one she wanted. She held the phone to her ear as it rang and rang. "Pick up. Pick up. Pick up," she chanted. The ringing stopped and Sofi almost cried in relief, but her relief was short lived.

"You've reached Leo. Don't leave a message, because I won't listen to it. It's not 1996. Send me a text like someone who's not a psycho. Unless this is my mom. Then just call me back later."

"Fuck," Sofi exclaimed. She called back only to get the same response. "What is the point of having a boyfriend if he doesn't respond when you need him to?" she groused. She'd just hit the call button again when there was a knock at her office door.

Malorie poked her perfectly made-up, clearly unnatural platinum blond head around Sofi's door. "Your dad told me to let you know when your five minutes were up."

Of course he would tell her that, but not that Sofi had a meeting in the first fucking place. "I got it," she gritted out through her clenched jaw. "Thank you, Malorie."

The younger woman smiled. "No problem." Then she simply stood there.

"Is there anything else?"

"Umm. He wanted me to walk you there. He said to make sure you made it there and didn't disappear."

Sofi contemplated chucking her phone at her floor-to-ceiling office window then quickly realized that it would only succeed in breaking her phone. Which she needed. To call someone else for help since Leo had decided not to answer. Maybe she'd call the police to come get her after she committed patricide.

Sofi stood up from her desk and stomped her way to the door. Malorie had better move out of the way quickly, because, with the mood she was in, Sofi was willing to bowl her over. Her willingness must've shown on her face, because Malorie practically dove out of Sofi's path. During their silent walk to the conference room, Sofi kept reminding herself to breathe. She also told herself to ignore her sweaty scalp, back, underarms, and hands. *You can do this*, she repeated over and over.

Then she reached the door to the conference room and almost turned to flee. Except freaking Malorie just *had* to knock on the door to let them all know she'd arrived. Malorie was now officially her least favorite of all her dad's girlfriends—and one of them had once told Sofi that she'd never be anything but a pretty piece of arm candy for some guy to take advantage of.

"There she is!" her dad's voice rang out. "The woman of the hour."

"Sofi, dollface," Anthony Costa said as he stood to round the table. "I'm so glad to see you. This place hasn't been the same without your gorgeous face around." He pulled her into a hug without her consent. "I've had to stare at your dad's ugly mug for the last year." He let out a loud braying laugh like the ass he was.

Sofi stood there like a board. "Hello, Mr. Costa. It's nice to see you." She didn't even bother with the other people who'd accompanied him since there'd undoubtedly be a new team the next time they met. Much like her father, Tony liked to have pretty young women around. Unlike her father, he didn't have the charisma to charm them into staying around. Where her dad could win over just about every straight woman with a pulse, Tony only attracted a certain kind of woman—one who was using him as much as he was using her.

"How many times do I have to tell you to call me Tony?" He looked like a Tony. In that he looked like the guy who played Tony Soprano. He finally pulled away and Sofi fought the urge to brush herself off. He was such a sleazeball. "We're definitely on a first-name basis, especially now that we're going to be working much more closely together." He brushed his knuckle along his jawline and suddenly the urge to vomit was back.

Of course, her dad said nothing while the guy basically harassed her right in front of him. Her tío Manny would've decked him the first time he'd called her *beautiful for a Black girl*. That had been when she was barely twenty. Every time she'd seen him since then, he'd gotten more and more bold in his words and his touches.

"I see that the culture of Europe did you well." His eyes tracked down her body, pausing at her chest and groin. "Tell me, what did you think of my home country? You must've loved Italy."

It had been her least favorite place, the racism was set to blatant there, but she wasn't going to tell him that. "It was beautiful and of course the food was to die for."

He grabbed her hand and brought it to his lips. "You let me know when you want to go back. I'll take you. I have a gorgeous villa there." Something in his tone let her know that he wasn't offering out of the goodness of his heart. Payment of some kind was expected in return.

Sofi's eyes shot to her father. Surely, he'd say something now. A man older than him had just propositioned his only daughter in a room full of their colleagues. But he said nothing and the look on his face told her that she'd better not say anything either.

"Let's get started," was all he said. "Sofi has some great ideas of how we can bring Costa watches to a new level. Right, mi reina?"

Sofi stayed quiet because she obviously didn't. Until that moment, she'd forgotten what the company even sold. All that she could think of was that she wanted out. She didn't want to pull a whole presentation out of her ass. She didn't want to take over the account. She didn't want to play nice with the pervy asswipe. She didn't even want to be in the building. She was totally overwhelmed by everything she didn't want.

Her pulse, which had never slowed, rose to what had to be a dangerous level. Her vision went blurry while her fingers and toes began to tingle. She almost felt like her soul was leaving her body. Then her unsettled stomach made an incredibly loud bubbling noise, and everyone looked at her in alarm.

"Excuse me a second," she managed to eke out of her numb, cold lips. On shaky legs, she darted for the door. She heard her dad call her name in offended anger, but she didn't stop. She couldn't. As soon as she turned the corner, she started running. She was sure she scared the shit out of Malorie, if the woman's screech was anything to go by, but she didn't care. She went straight to her office, snatched her purse, notebook, and laptop off her desk and then rushed back out the door. She decided to let her dad step in and solve the problems he'd created for once.

She saw Malorie standing by the front desk wringing her hands. "Sofi, your dad—"

Sofi cut her off. "I don't care what he has to say right now. You can tell him that I quit." With that she turned to the elevator and hit the down button. She was going to go home, open a bottle of her favorite pineapple-flavored moscato, and start putting together a business plan for her event planning idea. It had become clearer to her than ever that her time at her father's company was over. She just couldn't do it anymore. She didn't have the patience. She was tired. She didn't have the energy to pretend to be something she wasn't anymore. Besides, Leo had made a really good point when he told her that she'd made the company more money than her father had spent on her education. She wasn't beholden to him anymore, even though she'd felt like she was.

It was time for her to focus on herself.

Sofi left the building and hopped in her car where she continued to call Leo. Every time it went to voicemail. By the time she'd gotten to the building she was concerned. What if something had happened and he was currently lying in a pool of his own blood somewhere? She parked and rushed up the stairs to the apartment only to find it empty. She called him again and heard buzzing. She followed the sound to the couch where his phone was peeking out from the cushions. Okay. Well, that explained why he hadn't answered her, but where the hell was he? She knew he didn't work at the CFD that day. She went to look for him at the distillery. She'd just entered the doors when she ran into Liam.

She hadn't ever spent any amount of time alone with him, so she didn't exactly know what to do around him. "Oh hi," she said.

"Hey, Sofi." He looked down at his phone and back up at her. One of his eyebrows rose.

She could guess that he was wondering why she was there so early and wanted to know if everything was okay. No. It was not. But she wasn't going to talk to him about that. She wanted to talk to Leo. "I'm just looking for Leo. He forgot his phone upstairs."

"He stopped by earlier to leave Tostón with me." He gestured toward the doors that led to his and Kamilah's place. "He said that he had something to do. He looked in a hurry."

That could mean just about anything when it came to Leo, but she figured that he must've forgotten that he was needed somewhere and had to rush out.

He gave Sofi another once-over. "Everything okay?"

Sofi was shocked that he'd asked. Liam was not the type to offer people a compassionate ear to listen or a shoulder to lean on, especially not her. They were still clearly working things out between them, not that they'd ever gotten along well anyway, but it had definitely gotten worse after Sofi's absence. He blamed her for hurting Kamilah, which cool because she blamed him for the same thing.

They were just going to have to get over it.

Sofi would get over the fact that her best friend was in love with the same guy who'd hurt her many times for over fifteen years and Liam would get over the fact that she'd ghosted his fiancée for over a year. They had to otherwise they'd make Kamilah miserable, and she didn't deserve that. To that end, Sofi accepted the olive branch Liam was extending.

"I'm having a bit of an afternoon, but I'll be fine," she said.

"Of course you'll be fine."

She wasn't sure if it was because of what just happened at work or because of who she was talking to, but that felt like an attack. "What does that mean?" she barked with more attitude than necessary.

Liam's eyes widened. "I meant that you're the type of person who will keep going no matter what. That's why I know you'll be fine."

"Oh." That was actually a really nice thing to say. "Sorry." Okay. Fine. Maybe Sofi could understand her best friend's obsession with this guy. He didn't say much, but when he wanted to he could be sweet. "And thank you, Liam. I needed to hear that." But she couldn't help but be bothered that she'd had to hear it from him, the guy she barely got along with, instead of the one she was dating.

She knew Leo hadn't purposefully forgotten his phone and she knew that he had no reason to suspect she'd need him in the middle of the day. However, she still felt like he'd let her down. Sofi was not the type of woman to look for comfort from others. She tended to keep things to herself. And yet, here she was searching for the person she'd decided to share her life with only to still be here by herself. She didn't like that feeling. It felt like neglect. Like she wasn't important. After the situation she'd just had with her dad, it was the last way she wanted to feel. Especially from her boyfriend who claimed to love her.

She knew it didn't make sense and she was very upset with herself for feeling abandoned by Leo. She also knew she was projecting her feelings about her father onto him, but she couldn't help her feelings.

As Sofi walked up the stairs to the apartment one thought was replaying in her head over and over. Was she really ready for this relationship, and if she was, then why was she constantly comparing her boyfriend to her father?

21

LEO TOOK A DEEP BREATH AND LET IT OUT. HE CENTERED HIMSELF and then opened his eyes. He was ready. Surrounding him were eight stations all featuring tasks he'd have to complete in less than ten minutes. It was like an obstacle course he'd have to maneuver around and through in order to prove his skills. He remembered the first time he saw everything laid out and thinking that it didn't look like much. He'd assumed it would be a piece of cake, but he'd quickly learned the entire endeavor was more about stamina than anything else. Now he'd conditioned himself to handle the rigors of the job. His main worry was making sure that his body didn't rebel against him and cause him to make a careless mistake that would mean no doctor's approval.

"Oh shit, Vega looks like he's about to puke," a voice said from his left.

Leo spun and found Ahmad and his other buddies from truck standing there.

"What are you doing here?" Leo asked.

Ahmad gave him the same smile that got him hit on by women at bars. "You think I put in all that work getting your ass in shape just to miss this now?"

Obi reached him first and thumped him on the back. At six-six and about 230 pounds, his thump packed a punch and nearly sent Leo sprawling. "You got this, bro," he said in his deep voice with a hint of a Nigerian accent. The man should've and could've been a professional basketball player, but he'd forgone the draft in favor of the academy.

Leo never asked him why he'd do such a thing, because the truth was that Leo had given up the opportunity to sign with Gio's manager for the same thing. Being a firefighter was just more rewarding to him than being a salsa star.

"If you do throw up, warn us first so I can take a video," Stefani said. The dick. Enzo Stefani was a Chicago native like Leo, but his family could trace their Chicagoan legacy back generations. Their firefighting legacy too. Everyone in his large Italian American family worked for the CFD in some capacity or another. Since his uncle was the commissioner, they basically ran it. Stefani acted like it too, swaggering around like he walked on water. But Leo still liked the guy. He was a good firefighter and a loyal truck-mate.

"Lieutenant Collins couldn't make it, two of his kids are sick." Ahmad held up his phone to show Leo a text, but gave him the message verbally anyway. "But he says to kill it because he's sick of having to train these would-be replacements who can't hack it."

"Chief pretty much said the same thing," Obi added. "He

also said to make sure you're one hundred percent ready to be back."

Leo was ready. He was more than ready.

"Alright, Vega," the test administrator said, calling an end to their chat. "Let's get you back to work."

Leo slipped on the fifty-pound weight vest and the added twelve-pound weighted beanbags that would go on each shoulder. First up was stair-climbing. He had to walk fifty then sixty stairs per minute for three minutes all together. He couldn't touch the rails and he couldn't fall off or stop. This was the part that tripped a lot of people up. They didn't realize how quickly they'd tire out. Leo was familiar with it though, so he just put on his helmet and his gloves before hopping on. He wasn't going to deny he was breathing a little heavy by the time he was done, but he still had more than enough gas to keep his engine revved. Even if he didn't, the cheers and chants from his crew would've pumped him up.

After the stairs came dragging the hose. He had to keep the marked spot behind him as he dragged it seventy-five feet at a run. Once he reached the designated spot he dropped to one knee and proceeded to pull the hose hand over hand until the marked spot on the back end of the hose passed the line in front of him. He hopped up and followed the line he was directed to toward the equipment shelf.

Sure, carrying two bulky saws totaling thirty pounds a distance of forty feet there and back didn't seem like much, but his arm was tired after dragging the hose. He'd dropped one of the saws multiple times during practice which would mean an immediate fail in the test. Now his arm began to tingle in a way that scared him, but he was able to maintain his grip.

Next up was the ladder raise and extension. Lifting the heavy ladder into place wasn't difficult for him as he was used to it, but he did slow down when it was time to lower the extended ladder back down as the rope had the tendency to slip when using gloves. Especially for Leo, who mostly struggled with the resistance part of lifting/lowering heavy items. Again, his arm was tingling in an unpleasant way. His fingers began to be uncooperative, but he pushed through.

The next part had him worried—the ceiling breach and pull. He had to use a long hooked pole to both thrust against the weighted "ceiling" three times and then hook it into the device to pull the ceiling down five times. This exercise had also given Leo trouble during practice on account of the reverberations, and he had to complete a series of repetitions in the correct way in order to not get an automatic fail.

Leo flew through the search portion of the exam which basically entailed crawling seventy feet through a dark space that turned and lowered unexpectedly like the play tubes at Chuck E. Cheese. While he crawled he tried to flex his hand, but it wasn't like a cramp he could work out. It was fucking nerve damage. There was nothing he could do but ignore it.

He stood and went immediately to the 165-pound mannequin lying on the ground. He had to grab onto the handles and lift it into a sitting position before dragging it fifty feet in one direction, around a barrel and all the way back across the finish line. This was about the time things started to go really wrong. Suddenly. The mannequin felt like it weighed a ton. His shoulder and arm had gotten sick of being coy. They began screaming their anger at him, but Leo clenched his teeth and kept pulling even if he'd slowed down considerably. The relief he felt when he was able to release the mannequin was short-lived.

Finally Leo arrived to the final station—he knew this was going to suck, but he was determined to see it through. Forcible entry consisted of lifting a ten-pound sledgehammer and slamming it into small square box a bunch of times in order to simulate breaking down a door. As soon as he lifted the sledgehammer he knew this wasn't going to end well. *You're too weak. Your arm is done.* Leo told his inner voice to shut the fuck up. He wasn't too weak. His arm could hold on for a few more seconds. He could do it. He was almost done and then he'd have reached his goal. He'd be a firefighter again.

He pulled the sledgehammer back and swung it forward. The minute the hammer hit the box: instant pain. The type of pain there were no words for. It was more violent than tearing, more intense than lightning, and made getting shot feel like a kiss from an angel. Leo immediately dropped the tool, not even caring that it landed on his toes. He dropped to his knees, yelling in agony and clutching his shoulder. Something was wrong. It should not be this painful. It hadn't even felt like this when he'd first began working out again.

His crew scooped him off the floor and rushed him to the ER where he was given pain meds and eventually a CT scan, but he was barely aware of any of that. Everything around him felt like it was covered in a blurry filter. It was far away from him. It was just him and his pain. There was one thing his brain focused on. He'd failed the exam. He wasn't going to be a firefighter again. He was a failure.

The door to his room opened and the doctor, an older Asian woman, slipped in with her laptop-wielding flunky behind her. "How are you feeling?" she asked him with a caring smile. "Is the pain medicine working?"

Leo grunted. The pain was still there but the medicine helped him not care about it, which he learned long ago is the most he could ask for. "It's fine," he added when it became clear she was waiting for an actual answer.

"Well, your CT scan came back. I'm afraid that I was right. Your rotator cuff is torn. You'll obviously have to get an MRI to see the full extent of the damage, but I wouldn't be surprised if this ultimately requires another surgery."

Fuck. He'd known that something was wrong, but he hadn't thought it would be so serious. He was such an idiot. He could practically hear his abuela's voice in his head saying, *Eso es lo que te pasa por pendejo*. And she'd be right. This is exactly what he deserved for being a dumbass. A colossal dumbass. Not only had he just undone everything he'd been working for in the last year, but he set himself back farther than where he'd started. He was fucking tired. He didn't think he had it in him to go through all of this again. That left him where? Off the force completely and without the ability to even comfort himself with music. So, miserable in other words. He had few options and even less hope.

"I want you to see your specialist ASAP, but until then you must baby that arm. I mean it. No lifting, no exercise, nothing. Just ice and rest. I'm giving you an immobilizer that I want you to wear all the time, even during sleep, until you get in to see your specialist."

Shit. He'd fucked up badly if she was being adamant about him doing nothing. "Yeah. I'll call my doctor tomorrow morning and I won't do anything with my arm until he tells me I can." Not that he could if he wanted to. He couldn't even flex his fingers without pain and his last two fingers were pretty much numb.

"The nurse will be in with the sling and discharge papers, including some information about icing your shoulder. I've sent your pain med prescription to your preferred pharmacy. You should pick those up before you go home, because you'll need another dose in the next two hours."

"Okay," he replied tonelessly.

She patted his leg. "I know this isn't what you want but take care of yourself. You don't want to do any more damage." The *than you already have* was clear even if it was unsaid.

Leo's head dropped. He was such a fucking idiot. Everyone had told him to take it easy, to stop rushing it, to just give his body time. Yet, he'd decided that he knew better and he'd gunned it. Now look at him, worse off than before.

Sometime later, Leo was walking toward the lobby patting his pockets with his good arm. Where was his phone? He needed it to order an Uber. He checked the other pocket, but all he felt was his wallet. Shit. He'd forgotten his phone somewhere. Now how was he going to get home? He was going to have to ask the nurses at the desk to call the only number he knew by heart, El Coquí.

"Hey, Vega," a voice called out.

Leo looked up and found Obi sitting in one of the waiting room chairs. "What are you doing here?" Leo asked.

"Since I brought you here, I figured you'd need a ride home at the very least." He stood. "I sent Ahmad and the rest to go get your car and drive it home for you. I knew you weren't going to be able to drive yourself."

Leo hadn't even realized that he didn't have his keys. God he was such a fucking mess. He shuffled from foot to foot. "Thanks."

"Come on," Obi said leading the way to the door. "Do you have to pick anything up before we get to your place?"

"I need to pick up my meds and I can't find my phone," Leo said as they stepped into the parking lot. "It must've fallen out while I was testing."

"Your phone is at home," Obi informed him. "You forgot it there."

Leo frowned. "How do you know that?"

Obi hit the button to unlock the door of his black SUV that was still a few rows away. "Ahmad said that when they got to your place with your car, your family was freaking out because they couldn't find you. They had your phone. I've been texting with them from your number."

"Fuck." Leo grimaced. He was hoping to sneak up to the apartment and put off telling his family as long as possible.

He wanted some time to lick his wounds, but of course that would've been too good to be true.

Obi helped Leo buckle his seat belt and then they were off. For once in his life, Leo wasn't in the mood to talk, so he just stared out of the window even after they picked up his meds at the drive-thru. Luckily, Obi wasn't much of a talker so he didn't require small talk. He reminded Leo a lot of Saint—the strong silent type. As a matter of fact... "Obi, have I ever told you that you remind me of my brother Saint?"

"Yes," Obi replied. "Many times."

Leo ignored that, an idea was brewing in his brain and it was distracting him from how fucked his life was, so he was going to go with it. "I think you two would be good friends. You need to meet him."

"You've said that too," Obi pointed out.

"Then why haven't you met him yet?"

"Because I'm not a little kid who needs to be set up on a play-date."

Leo ignored that too. "One of these days I'm going to have a party and I'm going to make you come so you two can meet."

"Don't try to set me up with your brother like it's a group date. That's weird."

"No, it's not. You need more friends and he needs a friend. Shit. You'd probably like my sister's fiancé, Liam too. You gotta come kick it with my family, man." Leo knew that Obi missed his family. He was currently the only member in the state, since his younger siblings had settled all over the world after college and his parents had gone back to Nigeria to care for his paternal grandparents.

"Do you invite everyone else to come kick it with your family?"

"Hell no, Collins is old and married, Ahmad is too much of a slut to let loose around any of my cousins, and Stefani would end up getting punched in the face."

Obi nodded like that made perfect sense. They turned onto Division Street and Leo knew he didn't have much longer to put his plan in motion. "But you, you'd fit right in. You're cool as shit. Plus, my mom and aunts would fawn all over you and my sister would feed you bomb-ass food until you explode like a seagull eating rice."

"I don't think that sounds how you think it does," Obi informed him.

"You should just come in with me," Leo said.

Obi snorted. "Nice try. I'm not going to be your distraction from giving your family the explanation they deserve."

Leo's brow furrowed. "How do you know I owe them an explanation?"

"Because when Ahmad explained what happened during the exam, they all had no idea that you were even taking it." His tone was even enough, but Leo could hear the censure.

He'd better get used to it now, because his family was about to tear him a new one anyway.

They pulled up to the alley of El Coquí and Leo was not at all surprised to see his parents and older brothers standing by the door. He looked at Obi. "You're really going to leave me to face them alone right now?"

Obi nodded. "Yep."

"That's not cool."

Before Obi could say anything, Leo's door was being yanked open and his mom was dipping in. "Ay, mi niño bello!" She grabbed his face in her hands. "Let me look at you. I need to see that you are okay," she wailed in Spanish.

Leo winced at the volume. "I'm okay, Mami." It was a complete lie, but he needed her to calm down.

He felt his seat belt loosen and shot a look at Obi.

Obi jerked his chin in the direction of the open door. He wanted them out. Now.

The unfeeling asshole.

Leo turned to get out and his mom backed up to give him space.

"Ven, Saint," she called over her shoulder. "Help him out."

Saint appeared before Leo could tell them that he didn't need it. He put his hand under Leo's good elbow and helped guide him out. Saint held him while they took a few steps toward the doors, but his father's voice stopped them both.

"The rest of you don't have to stay now that we know he's safe."

Oh shit. If he was trying to get Leo alone, then he was in real trouble. He stared at his boots. Behind him, he could hear Eddie thanking Obi for bringing Leo home and keeping them updated. Once Obi pulled off they all stood there. Leo was waiting for his brothers to bail like they did whenever one of the other siblings was in deep shit, but they didn't.

Suddenly the back door opened and Abuelo Papo stood there. "What are you all doing just standing here? Ven, metense." He stepped aside while holding the door so they could pass.

Leo took the opportunity to escape and darted up the stairs as fast as he could, which wasn't very quickly given the pain meds. The second he stepped through the apartment door, his eyes went directly to Sofi.

She was sitting on the couch between Kamilah and Doña Fina while Liam was on the recliner with a sleeping Tostón in his lap. In front of them on the coffee table sat two empty bottles of cheap girlie sweet wine and a scattering of glasses. Oh man, Sofi only drank that kind of wine when she was upset. She looked at him with red-rimmed eyes and an expression of concern on her face. She stood and quickly rushed over to him. She looked ready to wrap him in a hug, but she stopped short when her eyes locked on his immobilizing sling. "Are you okay?"

Leo lied again. "I'm fine."

Her eyes narrowed. "Do they put that contraption on everyone who's fine?"

"Only the special ones like me," he replied, trying for lighthearted.

"Now's not the time for jokes," his father barked. "Sit down."

Leo plopped onto the couch, sucking in a pained breath when it jerked his shoulder. But when his dad used that tone, there was no arguing to be done. There was only apologizing. "Look, I'm sorry I forgot my phone and you guys were worried," he began, but Papi cut him off.

"You think that's what we're upset about?" he asked incredulously as the rest of the family filed in behind him. "What were you thinking, Leo?" his dad said—a familiar refrain. Unsurprisingly he answered his question himself with another familiar quote. "Bueno, obviously you weren't or you wouldn't have kept it a secret this whole time."

"I knew you'd tell me not to try," Leo said. "You'd be worried about me."

"Of course we would be worried," Mami said. "The doctors told us that you couldn't go back. You'd put yourself in danger."

"I always put myself in danger, Mami. That's the job!"

"The job is about trying to be smart and keep yourself out of danger," Eddie said. "Being on duty when your body is compromised puts you, your fellow firefighters, and the people you serve in more danger."

"You think I don't know that?" Leo grit out. "I would never do that, which is why I trained so hard to pass the PAT, to have solid proof that I was ready for duty."

"Look," Cristian said. "I get how hard it is to let the job go. There are days I second-guess my decision to leave the police force, but I wasn't fit for duty anymore. For you it's physical, for me it was mental. I woke up to the harsh realities I'd been ignoring and it affected my ability to do my job. Do I still believe in justice? Yes, but I couldn't be a part of that system anymore." He dragged his hands through his hair, obviously not comfortable talking about it. "I know you want to be out there serving the community and saving lives, but, Leo, you can't."

Leo had known this was what they were going to say and he'd had enough. "I'm so sick of this!" he yelled. "I'm sick of you all sitting here and explaining everything to me like I'm too dumb to have thought about this on my own. I know I'm the stupid kid, but I do think about things before I do them."

"What?" Mami asked. "What do you mean 'the stupid kid'?"

"That's what you think. What you've always thought." Leo took on his mother's voice. *"Oh pobre, Leo with his ADHD. He can't learn like that, so just leave him be."* Leo attempted his dad's voice next. *"Leo, your brain doesn't work like everyone else's, so you need to do things differently."* He threw up his good hand. "Stop treating me like I'm broken! I'm just as capable as anyone else!"

"Really?" his dad yelled back. "Because from what I'm looking at, it doesn't seem that way. Look what you did to yourself and don't try to say you're fine, because it's clear that's a lie."

Leo froze. This is exactly what he didn't want to happen. He'd fucked up again and now here his family was looking at him with varying degrees of pity, anger, worry, and disappointment. He hated it. "Well, you can all relax now, because I failed the exam, so I'll never be a firefighter again."

Papi huffed like he was being ridiculous. "And what about your job with Liam?" his dad asked, piling on like always. "You can't do it like that. And what about your sister's wedding? Can you even play the guitar? I doubt it."

Leo dropped his gaze to the floor. He hadn't even thought about any of that. There was no way he'd be able to play the guitar in the next few weeks nor would he be mixing drinks anytime soon. "I can still sing at the wedding," he said, his voice low and ashamed.

"I just don't get it," Papi continued, ignoring him completely. "When are you going to stop doing such idiotic things?"

Leo winced.

"That's enough, Santos," Abuelo Papo decreed.

Leo's eyes snapped up and bounced between him and his dad, who looked shocked that someone had interrupted his tirade. Not many people had the gall to do such a thing, but Abuelo Papo didn't give a shit. He'd do what he wanted, when he wanted.

Abuelo shifted his shoulders as if preparing for battle. "This is not the time," he told Papi.

Papi was still visibly pissed, his nostrils were flared, his muscles were tense, and his cheeks were flushed under his tan. But he gave one single jerk of his chin.

"Eddie, why don't you take your parents home now," Abuelo continued.

"Me quedo," Mami said in a tone that brooked no argument. "My son is hurt and I'm staying here in case he needs me."

Mami had always been extra protective of him and he was sure it was because he'd been born premature which had required him to stay in the NICU for a time. However, he didn't want her to stay. He just wanted everyone to leave him alone. Everyone but Sofi that was. He looked to her for support. He wanted her to say that she'd take care of him, but she didn't say anything. She just sat there.

What was that about? It wasn't like her to sit quietly when things were going down.

"Come on, Pop," Eddie told Papi. "Let's get you home so you can get some rest."

Still red and tense, Papi turned on his heel and left without saying anything to anyone. Cristian followed them with Saint in tow since he'd offered to drop Saint off at home. Liam stood up with Tostón in his arms and said he'd take the dog for the night, so no one had to worry about him and could focus on Leo. He didn't look at Leo at all.

Leo's gut roiled with guilt. He'd really screwed Liam over

more than anyone else except for maybe Kamilah. He looked at his sister and found her staring at Sofi with a weird look on her face.

Sofi still hadn't said anything. She just sat there staring at the TV playing, what appeared to be, a documentary about the wives of the pharaohs in Ancient Egypt. It was clear she was pissed at him, but he didn't understand why. It wasn't like she didn't know about him taking the exam—unlike his family. He'd been honest with her about it. Was she mad that she couldn't get a hold of him all day? "I really am sorry I forgot my phone," he told her. "I'll be more responsible in the future."

She frowned in confusion. "Leo, I'm not your mother. I'm not going to punish you for forgetting your own stuff."

"Then why are you mad at me?" Leo asked.

"Who said I'm mad?"

Leo shook his head in bafflement. Did she really think he was that dumb or that he didn't know her? "I can tell that you're mad. You're basically treating me how you treat white women who ask you if your hair is real and try to call you 'sis.'" If she wasn't mad, then she must be disappointed too. He'd told her that he'd done the practice test and passed, so she was probably expecting him to pass this time as well. Well, fuck. No one was more upset about that than him. Besides, what right did she have to be disappointed? She'd barely said anything when he'd told her about his plan and she never encouraged him when he told her about his training. She was too busy with Kamilah's wedding. "This is some bullshit," he snapped. "I know something is wrong," he told her. "I wish you'd just tell me what it is instead of acting like it's nothing."

"Like your abuelo said, now is not the time," she replied.

Leo's frustration boiled over. He hopped up and moved to block the TV. "If you have something to say, then just say it. Don't be such a chickenshit."

The way she snapped her head in his direction, her eyes flashing, told him that he'd just poked the bear a bit too hard. Oh well, he'd never tiptoed around her moods and he wasn't going to start now. Not even when his abuelo's chastising "Leonardo" told him that he should've kept his mouth shut.

22

SOFI KNEW SHE SHOULDN'T RESPOND. LEO WAS OBVIOUSLY UPSET
and looking for a way to release it, but she also knew he wasn't
going to stop until he got what he wanted. And that thought
ticked her off more than anything. Why did his needs outweigh
hers right now? She'd had a shitty day too. She was hurt too. She
should be able to just sit there and feel what she felt in silence if
that was what she wanted. That didn't make her a chickenshit.
"Not everything is about you, Leo, so just leave it alone."

"What the fuck does that mean?" he hissed.

"It means exactly what I said," she told him.

He scowled at her and stepped into her space. "It sounds like
you're calling me selfish."

Sofi stood and put her hands on her hips. She was not about to be intimidated by Leo just because he was upset. "Leo, I swear. You don't want to do this right now."

"Guys," Kamilah began, but Leo ignored her.

"Do what?" he said to Sofi. "Call you out because you're here trying to imply that I'm a selfish asshole?"

"I'm trying to prevent a fight, but if you got something else out of it…" She purposely drifted off in hopes he'd pick up the thread in his head. She'd learned in the past that it was best to let Leo come to his own conclusion, because if she told him he'd just want to argue about it. She should've known it wouldn't work though because he clearly just wanted to fight.

"I can't believe you're acting like *I'm* the selfish one here," he said.

Whoa. Wait a damn minute. Now he was acting like she was the problem here and she was NOT the problem.

"Leo," Kamilah attempted again, but this time Sofi cut her off.

"What did you just say?" She stepped up to him.

"I mean, I'm not the one who up and bounced for a year because my feelings were hurt," he said.

Sofi pointed a finger at him. "Don't you dare downplay my putting down boundaries and doing what I had to do for my own mental health as me being selfish."

"Is that what we're calling it, putting down boundaries? I know it more as being petty, but sure."

"Óigame! Eso no," Abuela Fina said, jumping to her feet. She stepped in between Sofi and Leo and got all up in his face or as much as she could when he was a foot taller than her. "Your abuelo and I didn't help you with my granddaughter, so that you could turn around and treat her like a jerk."

Sofi froze. *What the hell were they talking about? What help?*

"Si," Papo joined in. "We didn't plan all that stuff for you to ruin it now."

Kamilah gasped. "Oh no, Abu, please tell me you didn't do what I think you did," she pleaded.

But Papo couldn't answer, because he was focused on his grandson who looked ready to explode.

"I didn't need your damn schemes," Leo growled.

Schemes? What fucking schemes? Were these three conniving against her?

"Pretty bold claim for a man she's broken up with more times than either one of us has been on a stage," Papo said.

"Exacto," Abuela agreed. "You may have her for now, but you still need to keep her. A cute face and guitar playing isn't going to work forever. Especially if you treat her like this."

They were totally in cahoots. These three were plotting ways to get her to be with Leo and had been for some time. She couldn't believe it. She felt so betrayed. They'd been playing with her mind and emotions like three evil doctors experimenting on their patient in a mental hospital.

Here she was thinking that she was doing what she needed to do to finally be happy only to find out that the moves she'd been so proud of herself for making had been part of some plot. She was just a puppet that the three of them had been operating behind the scenes. "I can't believe I was so stupid," Sofi said softly. Yet somehow everyone heard. "You've been playing me since the beginning," she decreed into the silence.

Leo froze for a second, but then his eyes swung to her, finally remembering that she was standing right there. "It's not what it sounds like."

"It's not? Because it sounds like you and our grandparents got together to come up with ways to manipulate me into being with you."

Leo winced. "So maybe it is what it sounds like, but it's not this huge plot or anything. They're mostly just giving me advice."

"Yeah," Papo agreed. "Just advice."

"Don't lie to me. Not now."

Papo must've heard how serious she was in her voice, because he started singing like a canary. "Okay, so it was our idea for you to move in with Leo and I may have something to do with you finding Tostón."

"What?" Sofi yelled.

"I told him we shouldn't do that," Abuela Fina tried.

"I did and still do feel really bad that I left him back there, but I knew I was going to send the two of you to find him." Papo looked like he really wanted her to understand, but she just couldn't.

"Oh well, as long as you feel bad about it, then I guess everything is fine," Sofi said.

"There's no need for sarcasm," Leo jumped in. "That's not going to help the situation."

Sofi closed her eyes and clenched her fists and her jaw. It was taking everything in her to battle the swarm of hurtful words that were trying to come out of her mouth. Finally, she opened her eyes. "I just found out that for the last two months you've been manipulating me with the help of two of the very few people in this world I respect. Do not talk to me about my tone."

Kamilah stepped forward and put a hand on Abuela Fina's shoulder. "I think we should step away and let them have this conversation in private," she told the others in the room.

Papo nodded and started leading the way to the door while Abuela Fina looked away from Sofi guiltily, but not Leo's mom. She was about to dig in her heels. Sofi could tell by the determined tilt to her chin.

"I'm not leaving," Valeria said. "My son just got out of the hospital. He can't even use his arm. He needs someone willing to take care of him."

While she didn't come right out and say that Sofi wasn't qualified to be that person, it was implied.

"Mami, just wait for me at Kamilah's," Leo said. "I'll call you as soon as we're done and you can come right back."

"Okay, guapo." Valeria nodded before continuing in Spanish. "Call me as soon as you need anything and I'll be here in a second. Your mother will always be here for you." She turned to go, but not before shooting Sofi a condemning, borderline threatening look.

In seconds she and Leo were alone. Sofi plopped down on the couch and rubbed a hand over her chest to ease the pressure she felt. This was exactly what she'd been afraid of. Here Leo had fucked up big-time in every regard, but somehow Sofi was still the villain. She hadn't lied to the Vega family about her future plans, she hadn't gone against doctors' orders and gotten herself hurt, nor had she plotted with two senior citizens to trick someone into dating her. Yet, she was the one who was going to end up cast out in the end. Because when it came down to it, Leo was their flesh and blood while Sofi was not. She needed to remember that the Vegas were not her family. She didn't have much of one. And one member of her tiny family had betrayed her that very day, so now it was really down to her and her mom. The thought was enough to make her eyes water, but she forced her tears back. She was not going to cry. Not again.

Sofi shook her head, still confused about this whole thing. "I just don't get how anyone thought manipulating me was a good idea." It was as if they didn't know her at all.

"Why do you keep saying *manipulate* like I'm being sneaky or something?" Shockingly, the offense in his voice was real. It was ridiculous, but still very real.

Sofi looked at him, dumbfounded. There was no way he didn't see it. "How have you not, Leo?"

"I've been very upfront about what I want."

"And what is that?"

"You. I want you. All of you."

For a moment Sofi's heart melted in her chest and she wanted to tell him that she wanted the same thing, but then she remembered that it had all been a lie. A planned-out series of events she'd been nudged into going through like an actress in a play. She got mad all over again. "If that were true then you'd know that *this shit* is not the way to go about it at all. You betrayed me."

Leo's eyes widened to near comical size. "Betrayed you? All I've ever done has been to try to get you to give me a chance, to give us a chance to have something real instead of hookups, but I should've known it wouldn't work. Of course, you'd spin this in the worst possible way. That's what you do."

"Excuse me?" Sofi frowned.

"You expect the worst out of everyone, Sofi. You sit there just waiting for them to let you down and the minute they make a mistake you use it to justify your distrust."

"You literally just lied and schemed against me to manipulate my emotions and somehow that's my fault because I won't give you blind trust? Are you fucking serious right now?"

"I'm not saying this is your fault. I'm just trying to explain why I agreed to let the viejos help when they approached me with their plan. You use every single thing I do as a reason to push me away. Every time we start to get too close, you find something negative and fixate on it until it becomes a huge issue that you can use to kick me to the curb."

"This is a huge issue, Leo. You betrayed my trust and now you're trying to make it seem like I'm being too sensitive. You just did to me exactly what my father has done to me for thirty years."

"Stop comparing me to your deadbeat dad!"

"Then stop acting like him! Stop being a selfish, manipulative, gaslighting liar like him!"

Leo froze. "Is that what you think about me? You think I'm a selfish liar?"

"You tell me, Leo. Think about what you did to me and tell me that you weren't lying to me for your own gain. Tell me that you didn't spend the last however long lying to your family for your own purposes."

He stayed quiet.

"Exactly. You can't because you know I'm right."

Leo plopped down onto the couch and rubbed his face with his working hand as if he were suddenly tired. "Sofi, let me just ask you one thing. Do you love me?"

Sofi paused. "What?"

He looked up at her. "Do you love me? Because I love you. Everything that I've done has been for you. To get your attention, to win a smile, to be the kind of man you'd take a chance on and finally let in. That's all I want, Sofi. For you to let me in. Let me love you and let yourself love me."

Sofi stood there staring at him trying to catch up. How did she become the one in the hot seat?

"I've been here loving you. It was never about just sex for me, but I was willing to accept your body since that was all you were willing to give." He swallowed. "But I can't do that anymore. I can't accept pieces. I need the whole thing. I need your body, your mind, your heart, your soul—all of you, every single centimeter. Because you already have all of me. But I need to know, is that what you want too? Because if it's not, then I don't even know what we're doing here."

"That's not fair," she told him. He didn't get to just bypass everything else and get to the heart of the situation. "I don't know if I can do it."

"You can."

She shook her head. She didn't think she could.

"You're just mad at me about the stuff with our grandparents," he told her. "But if you'd just let me prove th—"

"Even if none of this other stuff had happened, you want something from me that I don't think I can give you and I want something from you that is not realistic to ask for." She wanted him to actually look at her as a person instead of a goal to achieve. She wanted him to take her wants, dreams, and needs into consideration before he acted in his own interest. She wanted him to not just need her but respect her and support her. But she no longer thought he was capable of that, if she ever did. She put her hands up in a *What can you do about it?* gesture. "We're at an impasse."

"It's only an impasse because you're being stubborn and I get why, Sofi. I really do. You're scared to let me in, but we could be so good. I know we can. Just don't push me away. Don't lock me out," he pleaded.

"Leo, this is too much for me right now. With everything else going on. It's too much. I need a break. Give me time to think. The wedding is in two weeks. After that I'll have time."

His face fell. "Don't worry about it," Leo told her. "You just answered my question. You don't want to be with me. If you did, you wouldn't constantly be ready to sacrifice our relationship at the altar of everything else in your life. I'm not a priority for you and I never have been."

"Leo, that's not fair."

"Maybe not, but it's true all the same. I know you better than anyone else on this earth. I know that if you truly wanted this, you would put in the work to make it a success. You'd be willing to fight for it and for me, because that's what you do for the things you really want. I need to stop waiting for you to want this as much as I do. I need to accept that you don't. That's not on you. That's on me."

"So what? You're breaking up with me even though you're the one who lied and manipulated the situation to get here?"

"I was wrong. I shouldn't have done all of that. It wasn't okay and it shouldn't have felt as necessary as it did."

"You didn't answer my question," she pointed out.

"Because I don't know. I don't know what to say to you, Sofi.

Every fiber of my being tells me that you're it for me. But I don't understand why it has to be this hard. I don't know what else I can do or say to make you see it too and I'm tired. I'm tired of having to prove myself." His voice caught. His eyes filled.

Sofi's eyes filled too. She hated seeing him like this, beat down and without hope. She didn't want that for him. She wanted him to be happy, she truly did. But it was clear that she wasn't the one who would make him happy. She couldn't be who he needed just like he couldn't be hers. All they did when they tried was hurt each other. "We need to stop doing this to each other," Sofi said.

Leo nodded.

So that was it, then. They were done. "I'm going to stay at Kamilah's place tonight. And tomorrow I'll tell my mom that I'll be her new roommate. At least until I find something else."

Leo stared at his shoes. "Do what you need to do, Sofi."

She was quiet. She didn't want things to end this way. She didn't want him to not even be able to look at her. "Leo, please don't be like this. Don't hate me."

He looked at her then. "I don't hate you, Sofi. I'm not even mad at you." He sighed. "I've always been too damn willing to run into the fire even if I get burned. I need to remember that not everyone is like that."

Was he really calling her a chickenshit again? Because she wasn't willing to get hurt over and over again, suddenly she was a coward? That was some major bullshit, especially when Leo's thoughts on his bravery were skewed. He wasn't all that brave. "Oh? And what about flying? What about the fact that you only became a firefighter and fought so hard to get back because you're scared that it's the only thing you're good at? Don't talk to me about facing and fighting fears when you can't even be real with yourself. I know I don't trust people. I know I push people away out of fear they'll hurt me. That's because they do. Because they did. I know my faults. You, on the other hand, are delusional. You act like you own your faults, but you don't. You just try to distract from them."

Now Sofi wanted to fight. She wanted his reaction.

"You're absolutely right." He leaned back against the couch as if he just didn't have the energy to prop up his bones, and she felt deflated. "I have been delusional, and I need to face reality. I'm not sure what that reality entails, but I do know one thing for sure and it's that I didn't survive being shot just to keep putting myself through this torture over and over." He pushed himself to his feet, grabbed his pharmacy bag off the coffee table, and then shuffled to his room without ever once looking back.

That more than anything terrified Sofi. He'd never walked away from her like that—like he was truly done.

23

LEO HAD KNOWN THAT THERE WOULD EVENTUALLY BE A RECKONING, so he was not at all surprised when his family showed up in his apartment in the middle of the day. What astonished him was that they'd waited an entire week before they did. Maybe they pitied him because Leo still couldn't use his right arm or, more likely, they felt bad about his breakup with Sofi. Needless to say, Leo's life was in a pathetic state, so he didn't even care that they'd barged into his space in order to yell at him. They weren't going to say anything he didn't already know.

"Look, can we not do this? I already know that I messed up big-time." He looked at Kamilah. "I know how difficult it was for Liam to trust me with the tasting room. This is his first project with his new partner and, after I pretty much inserted myself into it, and I wasn't fully invested. He trusted me with his life's work and I wasn't honest about my intentions. He deserves way better than that." Leo shook his head. "Not only that, but I promised you I'd perform for your first dance and now, because of my own stupidity, I can't." Leo was about to continue enumerating his many faults, but his dad stopped him.

"Leo, we aren't here for that." Papi let out a breath. "Some things came out last week that we needed to process."

Leo nodded sadly. "I know. I disappointed you all again."

His dad's hand landed on his good shoulder. "No, Leo. You didn't. We need you to know that we've never thought you were broken or stupid."

Leo scoffed. "All you two ever did was push your other kids. You pushed them and set high expectations for them, but you stopped doing that with me. As soon as you were told I had ADHD, you didn't expect the same things of me as you did the others. Whenever I did anything wrong you'd just sigh in disappointment and move on, as if I'm not even worth the time or effort."

Mami looked close to tears. "Leo, we never pushed you, because we never had to. When it was important enough to you, you pushed yourself. You always have. From the minute you came into this world too early, you've pushed yourself."

"You've always stood firm in who you are and what you want," Papi said. "We wanted to respect that. If we didn't always get on you over your grades, especially later, it was because we finally understood that it was the fault of the education system, not you. You were smart and capable, but only when you wanted to be, not when anyone told you to be."

"Leo, you are not the dumb one," Saint said. "You're the brave one."

Leo snorted in disbelief. Yeah, Saint was a whole war hero with a medal, but Leo was the brave one. Right.

"You are," he emphasized. "You have always just gone for

things. Put yourself out there. It doesn't matter what anyone says or thinks. You're going to do it because you're confident in your ability to handle whatever comes next. That's brave."

"I've always been jealous of you for that," Eddie said. "I envy the way you just go for it and believe that everything will work out how you want it to. I always have to think, and plan, and think some more. Most of the time I end up picking the safest option because I'm scared of the risk. Not you. You are willing to take the risk."

Leo just stared at his brother, wide-eyed and slack-jawed. He couldn't believe that Eddie envied him anything. He was an actual genius, with a high six-figure job, a beautiful and equally successful wife, and two already high-performing kids. He had everything. It was difficult to grasp that he would want to be anything like Leo.

"Leo, you taught yourself to read music and play the guitar by age five," Papi pointed out. "Then you retaught yourself to play after your injury."

"You're a force to be reckoned with, little brother," Cristian said. He gave Leo's head a rub like Leo was a Saint Bernard. "You always have been. *You* are the one *we* want to be more like." He smirked. "Except for your propensity to stick your foot in your mouth. You can keep that."

"Please. I have that issue too and it's not as bad as it seems," Kamilah joked.

Leo fought his own smile. "I don't stick my foot in my mouth. I mean what I say and say what I mean. Even when it gets me in trouble."

Mami stood from her spot and went to crouch next to him. She grabbed his hand in hers and looked into his eyes. "You, mi amor, are my miracle," she told him in Spanish. "Every day I am proud of you and everything you have accomplished. I'm sorry for ever making you think otherwise. And if you want to become a firefighter again, then I will believe you and support you, because you've never failed at anything."

His father gave his shoulder a solid pat. "You, son, are the strongest of us all and I'm sorry I made you feel like you were a weak link. You're a survivor and I will choose to believe that you will survive this too."

"I hope you all know that I'm going to remember all of this and bring it up constantly."

His family started laughing.

"This from the guy who forgot his own birthday last year?" Papi snorted. "I doubt it."

"Hey, I was on a lot of painkillers last summer!"

"And what's your excuse for forgetting you were supposed to pick up Abuelo for a doctor's appointment three days ago?" Saint asked.

"Uhh... I'm sad?"

"Okay," Kamilah said, standing up. "I'm glad we all had this talk and now Leo knows exactly how valued he is to us, but I still need to talk to him and you are distracting us, so off you go." She made a shooing motion with her hands.

Papi grumbled. "I'm still half owner of this building."

Kamilah crossed her arms. "And the man who's going to be my husband in a week is the other owner which basically means I am too. What's your point?"

"Ooph. Someone is cranky," Eddie said. "We'd better get out of here before she goes full bridezilla."

Kamilah just smirked. "There are some new starters I'm trying out waiting for you downstairs. Let me know what you think."

Suddenly, Papi and their brothers couldn't leave fast enough. The only person who stayed was Mami.

She was looking at Leo with love and worry. "Are you sure we're okay?" she asked.

Leo nodded. "We're more than okay. You know you'll always be my number one girl."

Her eyes filled. "I meant every word I said. I love you and I'm proud of you."

"I love you too, Mami. Now go, so Kamilah can yell at me in peace."

Mami looked at Kamilah. "You take it easy on your brother. He got shot and dumped."

Kamilah rolled her eyes. "Yes, Mami. I won't berate your baby boy."

"Good." After a decisive nod, she left.

Kamilah shook her head and looked at him. "Here I always thought Eddie was her favorite."

Leo smirked. "You heard her. I'm her miracle."

"You'd think she'd remember that I too was born early all thanks to your diva-ass causing an emergency cesarian less than two years earlier."

"Don't blame that on me, she wanted you born early so you wouldn't come out a Halloween demon baby. Too bad she waited too long and it happened anyway."

Kamilah stuck her tongue out at him, her go-to move when she couldn't think of a comeback.

"About Liam," he said, getting serious. "I know it seems like I'm not taking the bar seriously, but I am. I will make sure that I hire someone great to bartend until I can do it, but I'll still develop the menu, talk to the vendors, and basically manage everything like I promised. Making this bar successful is my priority." It was the only thing he had going for him, so it had to be his priority.

"Good," she said, both sounding and looking like their mother, especially because she gave the same quick nod. "But that's not actually why I wanted to talk to you alone."

Leo dropped his head back. "Ugh." He lifted it and shot Kamilah a look. "Please tell me that this isn't about Sofi."

"Of course it is." Kamilah came around and sat on the edge of the coffee table in front of him. She leveled him with a no-nonsense look. "What happened after we left, Leo?"

"You mean she didn't tell you everything when she went to stay at your house?"

"No, she refused to talk about it. She said that she didn't want me to be in the middle."

"Then maybe listen to her and stay out of it." He looked at the expression on his sister's face. "Right. I forgot who I was talking to. You couldn't stay out of it even if we dropped you in a cage in the ocean."

She shrugged nonchalantly. "This is true."

Leo sighed, but let it out anyway. "We argued some more, obviously, and I flat out asked her if she wanted to be with me. She couldn't answer. I told her that I loved her and she told me that we're doomed because I want what she can't give me. Then I basically told her that I was done trying to make things work with her."

"And are you?"

"Am I what?"

"Done with her?"

Leo scrubbed a hand over his face. "I'm tired, Sideshow Bob. I've been trying to get her to give me a chance since we were teens. I don't want to keep doing this for the rest of my life. After I got shot, I promised myself that I wouldn't fall into the same patterns. That I'd make my second chance worth it."

"Leo, I'm going to give you some hard-learned advice."

"Look, I know she's your best friend and you know her very well, but trust me I know her better."

"First of all, eww because I know what you were trying to say there. Second of all, this advice I gleaned from dealing with Liam not Sofi." She paused and her face scrunched in thought. "Even though the two of them are scary similar."

"No duh," Leo said. "You're basically marrying a male Sofi with less style and more facial hair."

Kamilah put a hand on her heart. "Aww. I kind of love that."

Leo blew out a breath. "Your advice, weirdo?"

"Their greatest fear is that there is something wrong with them that means they will always be left. Because of this fear, they lock their true selves away and hide behind their badass personas."

"Yeah. I know this."

"Getting through to them isn't about smashing down their walls, Leo. All that will do is make them lash out because they feel unsafe."

"I am not a subtle man, Kamilah."

She threw his own words back at him. "Yeah. I know this." She put a hand on his. "However, you're going to have to learn to be if you want a future with Sofi. You have to create a safe place for her, if you want her to emerge from her fortress, and you can't do it by scheming behind her back. You have to let her know that she's safe with you physically, mentally, emotionally. Her well-being is your priority."

"I tried to do that, but—"

Kamilah held up a hand, stopping him. "I know how hard this next part is, trust me. I struggle with this all of the time, but you're also going to have to be patient with her. Because even when she does come out from behind her walls, her first instinct will always be to hide behind them again when she feels vulnerable. It's not a reflection on you or her feelings for you. It's just her way of coping. So instead of getting mad or hurt or feeling defeated, you'll have to be patient and coax her out again."

"But, Kamilah, it shouldn't be that hard."

"Who says it's not hard? Movies? Songs? That's not real life. That's not how real relationships work. Real relationships are very hard. They require tremendous amounts of give-and-take, especially when the people in them are so different yet equally headstrong."

"I know relationships aren't easy, but I can't be the only one trying. That doesn't work either."

"You're one hundred percent right. You both need to put in the work, but all I'm telling you is that you can't expect her to just let down her guard completely and forever. You have to be willing to reassure her every time she tries to hide that you're still a safe place for her. If you can't or don't want to do that, then maybe it's best you two are done for real."

Leo looked down at his right hand which was holding his stress ball, but not squeezing—mostly because he couldn't. The last few days, he'd been doing a lot of thinking and one of his main thoughts was about changing. He'd felt like he'd changed a lot, but now he wasn't sure he had. At his core he was still the same person he'd always been, but he'd tried to at least make better choices for himself and his life. He guessed that was the most you could ask of people—for them to make better, less harmful choices. The same could be said for Sofi. He couldn't expect her to completely change her personality or way of interacting with the world. He could only be there for her as she tried to make those choices. She was never going to be this happy-go-lucky person with an open and trusting personality. He didn't want her to be. He loved her crotchety ass exactly how she was. So he needed to stop trying to change her.

He looked back up at his unexpectedly emotionally intelligent little sister. "So, like on a scale of zero to ten, how mad would you be if I hijack your wedding?"

She pursed her lips and tapped a finger on her chin. "Think about it like this: on a scale of zero to ten, how much do you like having at least one fully functional arm?"

"Okay. Okay. So wait until after your wedding is what I'm hearing."

"For the sake of your well-being that's probably the best idea. Yes."

Leo stood and made his way to the door. He paused at the threshold. "I just want to throw out that technically the reception is after the wedding. Okay. Love you. Bye." Then he took off running and ignored her yelling his name. He had an abuelo to see and a grand gesture to plan.

24

TOSTÓN LET OUT A PLAINTIVE WHINE. IT WAS HIS THIRD IN AS MANY minutes.

They were snuggled in bed, where they'd been for who knew how long at this point. Sofi hadn't left her bed unless it was to grab food from her mom's front door where it was left by a delivery person or to take Tostón for a walk. She knew she couldn't remain there for much longer, but she also wasn't ready to face the world yet.

Sofi lifted her hand and patted him on the head. "I know. I miss him too."

Tostón's head popped up. He stared in the direction of her front door, his head tilted like he was listening for something. Sofi's mom was picking up Abuela Fina after work to take her to the movies, so it wouldn't be her. Something that became perfectly clear when whoever it was knocked loudly.

Sofi held her breath. She wanted it to be Leo, but she also didn't. She wanted to see him, to ask about his arm, to hold him. At the same time she knew that it would only lead to more pain for them both. She needed to be strong no matter what.

Sofi hopped out of bed. She contemplated changing her clothes or at least brushing her teeth, but the knocking came harder, more insistent. She wrapped her blanket around herself, rushed to the door, and placed her hand on the knob. It started to turn. Sofi's stomach began to cramp.

The door swung open revealing a man, but not the one Sofi wanted. Her father stood in the doorway decked out in one of his designer suits. "What is wrong with you?" he asked. "Are you sick?"

Tostón started barking. He'd never met her dad. Sofi ignored the disappointment and told her dog to hush. "I'm taking a mental health day," she replied once Tostón quieted down.

"A mental health day? Qué ridiculez Americana es esa?"

Of course caring for her mental health was ridiculous to him. She stood straight. "I'm going through a lot right now and needed some time to myself."

"You haven't come to work in a week," he said, walking into her mom's house without her permission much like he always walked into her office. "You have important meetings coming up next week. We don't have time for you to be sitting in bed taking naps with a dog."

What the hell was he talking about? She didn't have anything coming up. She'd quit. Did he not know that? "Didn't Malorie tell you—"

He cut her off with a wave of his hand. "She said you told her that you quit, but I knew better. You were just mad and needed to cool off. You wouldn't really quit because some old guy made a pass at you. That's not how we do things. That's not the Rosario way."

"Papi, I did mean it. I really quit. I—"

"You think I want to work until I die? You're supposed to be learning how to run the company, but you always put what you want first. France, moving your abuela to Chicago, and then your friend's wedding. Everything comes before me."

That was it. The straw that snapped the camel straight in half, tore it into pieces, then set it on fire. Sofi stood, completely unconcerned that she was in a bralette and boy shorts. If he wanted her fully dressed he shouldn't have just shown up like he owned the place. "*I* put myself first? Are you joking? You must be joking. There's no way you're serious."

"Of course I'm serious. You think I came over here to waste my time?"

"You really have the audacity to sit there and tell me that when you're literally the most selfish person I have ever known?" She scoffed. "I don't know why I asked that. Of course you do. I don't think there is anyone less capable of self-reflection."

"Now wait a minute. You can't talk to me like that. I'm your father."

Sofi started laughing incredulously. "Oh, now you want to call yourself a father. This is rich."

"I *am* your father."

Sofi shook her head. "No. Fathers care about their children. You don't really give a shit about me. You only use me to make yourself look good."

He looked ready to respond, but Sofi didn't want to hear it. "Do you have any idea what you've done to me? I'm fucking *broken* because of you. I don't trust *anyone* because of you. I'm *miserable* with my life because of you."

"That's not fair," he said.

"I don't give a fuck about fair. I care about truth and the truth is that I don't believe anyone can truly love me or accept me, because *you never did*. How can I ever think that someone would put me first, protect me, want me despite my flaws, when you didn't? You were supposed to love me, to protect me, to be there for me when I needed you and even when I didn't, but you couldn't be bothered. You ripped my heart out of my chest the moment I was born and replaced it with a cracked shell of one. Every day another jagged piece of glass breaks off and digs into that wound."

"I know I screwed up when you were young, but I've apologized."

"I don't care that you apologized, because you didn't change. When you're really sorry for what you've done you learn from it and do better, be better. You didn't care until you needed my forgiveness to feel good about yourself, to make your parents not be ashamed of the way you treated me. That was why you apologized and even then it was lukewarm at best." She shook her head, tears dripping from her jaw to her chest.

"Lukewarm? I helped you go to school, I put you in a position of power, I'm trying to hand this company over to you."

"I don't want it! I never did! You forced it on me as a condition the one and only time I ever asked you for help. Because everything with you comes with strings. You are so fucking self-centered that you can't even help your only kid without getting something in return."

"And you are an ungrateful brat! What do you want from me? You want me to baby you? To hold your hand? That's not who I am. That's not the kind of man I am. I'm never going to sit there and coddle you. I'm busy. I have things to do. To accomplish. I thought you understood that."

"I know very well that I can't expect that from you, even if I wanted it, which I don't. All I've ever wanted from you is love and support. Why do you think I've stayed for as long as I have? Because I know that your love, attention, and support is conditional. I knew that if I'd told you that I never wanted to work at the company, you would've just brushed me off. You would've continued to ignore me. At least working at the company gave me some of your attention."

"Don't you dare try to blame me for everything! Your mother—"

Sofi cut that off before he could even finish. "Do *not* bring my mother into this."

"No. Let him talk," her mother's voice said from behind them.

Sofi spun to see Mami and Abuela Fina standing there with bags of takeout in their hands.

Mami wasn't looking at Sofi. She was looking at her dad. "Let him finish explaining how I'm the one to blame for any of this. I would love to see the gymnastics that will require."

"It'll be like watching the Olympics," Abuela Fina added.

Her mom shot Abuela Fina a look. "Mami, por favor."

"Fine, I'll just sit here quietly." Abuela Fina walked over to the kitchen and placed the bags on the counter before sitting on a stool. She crossed her legs and placed her hands on her knee, overlaid like a classy lady.

"I'm not here to fight with you, Alicia," her dad said. "I came to find out what is going on with our daughter since she hasn't come to work for days."

"Because I quit," Sofi said, but she was ignored. Her parents were busy glaring at each other.

Mami held a finger up as if to say, *Well, actually.* "See, now, that's where you're wrong." She used her finger to point at Sofi. "That smart, strong, fierce, and loyal woman standing there is *my* daughter. *I* raised her." She turned her finger to poke at her own chest as she continued, "I was the one to wake up in the middle of the night when she cried. I was the one who worried whenever she was sick or sad. I was the one who took her to school and helped her with her homework. I was the one who braided her hair and held her hand to cross the street. I was the one who hugged her when she cried every time you failed to show up. I was the one who broke my own heart in half so I could give it to the girl whose heart you broke. Sofia is my daughter and just like her mother, she doesn't need to jump through hoops for your attention. She deserves better than that."

"You never asked me for anything," he said. "So I didn't know what to do! I came when you let me and when she came to me for help, I gave it!"

"Ay, Jose, please. I never asked for anything because you made it very clear that I was on my own. But I never once prevented you from seeing her. All you had to do was show up, but you couldn't even do that unless your parents forced you to."

Abuela Fina scoffed and then muttered loudly in Spanish, "I can't believe this asshole is in his sixties and his balls still haven't dropped."

"Mami!" Sofi's mom turned back to her dad. "You have had her working with you every day for over ten years and yet she's still here brokenhearted and crying over your neglect. Do you have any idea how pathetic that is on your part? That in all that time you haven't managed to build a relationship with your only kid despite her showing up and busting her ass for you? You have failed her as a father, but she wanted you in her life anyway. Do fucking better, Jose."

"I was only doing what I thought best for her." He tried to defend himself.

"¡Ay ya!" Abuela Fina exclaimed. "Nos tienes hasta acá con tantas zanganerías." She waved a hand above her head as if saluting the sky. "Avanza y lárgate. Mira, mejor vaya pal carajo con todo y el trabajo."

There wasn't much to say after Abuela told him to go to hell and take his job with him.

Her father looked at her as if waiting for her to ask him to stay. Sofi kept her mouth shut. Mostly because she was doing her best to hold in her sobs, but also because she too wanted him to leave.

"That's what you want?" he asked.

Sofi nodded. "Maybe one day, I'll want to talk to you again, but not today."

He swallowed. "Well, you know where to find me." With that he left.

As soon as the door closed behind him, Sofi dropped to her knees. She buried her face in her hands and began bawling. She felt strong arms wrap around her and knew immediately who they belonged to, because they were as familiar to her as her own face.

Mami squeezed her tight and let her cry. At some point, Abuela Fina joined them. Her arms less strong, but no less comforting than her mother's.

"I'm still mad at you for working with Leo to manipulate me," she told Abuela Fina in between bouts of tears.

"I know, negrita. But I'm here for you anyway."

After a while Sofi ran out of tears to cry. She lifted her hands to wipe her face.

"Better?" Mami asked.

Sofi shook her head. "No, but I will be."

"There's my guerrera." Mami patted her on the back before standing and helping up Abuela Fina. "Now I have something for you and I want to make it clear that I'm giving it to you with no strings attached, so don't start freaking out on me." She walked over to her purse and pulled out a rectangle piece of paper. She handed it to Sofi.

Sofi looked at the paper and realized it was a check—for three hundred thousand dollars. She looked at the names and gasped when she saw her mother's name in the corner and her own name in the payee section. "What the hell is this?" Sofi asked.

"It's a check," Mami said helpfully.

"I can see that, but what are you doing?"

"I want you to use it to start your own business. The one you said."

"Mami, you don't have this kind of money."

Abuela Fina laughed. "Quien te dijo eso? Si tu mama es millonaría."

Sofi's jaw dropped. No way. Then she laughed. "Yeah okay. Mami's, a millionaire and so are you."

"I am," Abuela Fina said.

"What?" Sofi exclaimed. "There's no way!"

Abuela looked at her like she was a poor little idiot. "Nena, what do you think happened to all of your tío's baseball money?"

"I don't know. I figured he'd spent most of it and the rest went to his and Abuelo's funerals."

Mami shook her head. "Half went to your abuela and the other half went to me."

"If you're rich then why did we always live paycheck to paycheck?" Sofi asked.

"It wasn't a lot at first, a few hundred thousand, because Manny was reckless with his spending. I kept it in case of emergencies and for your school. But when you didn't need it, I invested it and it's been growing ever since."

"But you work so hard," Sofi said. "You cut coupons and only get the generic brand of stuff."

"Claro, I work hard because I love my job. It's important, and just because I have money doesn't mean I need to flaunt it."

"You're really telling me that I used to eat the same meal for days on end and learned to sew up the holes in my clothes for nothing?"

"You should've told me that you didn't want it or that you needed new clothes," Mami said.

Sofi gasped in outrage. "You should've told me that we weren't poor!"

"Vez, this is what happens when you close yourself off and try to do everything alone," Abuela Fina said. "You two are so much alike—stubborn and uncommunicative." She shook her head. "If you'd both just stop trying to be so damn independent, trying to not burden each other, you'd realize that you're only holding yourselves back."

"She's right," Mami said. "I've been trying for so long to keep you out of everything, to just handle all the difficult stuff so that you can live your life without worry. It never occurred to me that you'd draw your own conclusions and try to be the one protecting me instead."

"Of course, I'm going to want to protect you too. You're my mother. You're the most important person in my life. I want you to not worry about me and to be able to live your life too. That's why I try to do everything myself. I know that my childhood was hard for you because you were by yourself doing everything, so I want you to be able to live your life freely now. Why do you think I'm always trying to get you to take off work and do something fun? And you better believe that now that I know you two are loaded, I'm going to be badgering you to take more vacations."

"You don't have to badger me," Abuela Fina said. "I'll go on a cruise in a heartbeat."

"See? Look at that. You two can go on a nice long cruise to Hawaii or something. Maybe even a singles cruise!"

Mami grimaced. "I am *not* going on a singles cruise, especially with my mother. Besides, she's not even single anymore."

"Alicia!" Abuela Fina exclaimed, smacking Mami on the arm. "Why would you say such things?"

Sofi rolled her eyes. "If you think everyone doesn't already know about you and Papo Vega, you're delusional."

Abuela Fina actually blushed. It was adorable. "We are friends. Good friends."

Mami snorted. "Good friends who kiss."

"What?" Sofi exclaimed.

Mami smiled. "Yep. She didn't think I saw them in the arts

and crafts room, but I did. They were Frenching like two teen-agers under the bleachers."

Abuela swatted Mami again. "Que falta de respeto hacia tu madre, muchacha malcriada."

Mami laughed. "You're the one who raised me, so if I was raised wrong that's on you."

Abuela Fina stuck her tongue out at Mami. "Bye, Alicia," she said with a sassy neck roll and hand flip.

Sofi laughed. "It's 'bye, Felicia' and no one says that anymore. Besides, don't be mad at Mami when you're the one out here kissing boys in public, you light-skirt."

Abuela Fina gasped in outrage. "¿Mira, muchacha del diablo, como hablas así a tu abuela? You need to worry about yourself. I'm not the one locked in my room, crying, and smelling like dog."

"I knew it was only a matter of time before you brought that up!" Sofi exclaimed. "But since you did, let's talk about it. How dare you join forces with Leo and Papo to manipulate me like that?"

"If you think I'm going to tell you that I'm sorry I did it, I'm not. I know you. If we hadn't found ways to push you to-gether you would've kept stubbornly pushing him away. Except for sex, talk about light-skirts, and then lying to your best friend about it all."

"You don't know that," Sofi said.

Abuela laughed as if that were the funniest thing Sofi had ever said. "I know that because I know you. I know you even more now that I witnessed that fight with your sperm donor."

"Eww. Don't call him a sperm donor. That's gross."

"Well, I refuse to call him your father. He doesn't deserve that title. But that's not what we're talking about so don't try to distract me." She shook her finger at Sofi. "We're talking about you trying so hard to be strong and independent that you push everyone away. You're scared, negrita. You don't want to let anyone in because you think they will hurt you. I don't blame you for feeling that way, people have hurt you. They've left you. But you can't let that stop you from loving and being loved."

"You're an amazing daughter and amazing woman," Mami jumped in. "You have so much love inside you, Sofi. You'd walk through fire for the people you love, but you don't trust that they'd do the same for you. You think you're not worth it. That there is something wrong with you and you're broken." Mami grabbed her chin like she had done when Sofi was little and being scolded. "We are all broken in some way, Sofi. That is what makes us human. And what makes us beautiful is that we keep hoping and loving despite that. We all deserve love. You deserve love. You *have* love. You just need to let it in."

"I don't think I can, Mami," Sofi whispered. "I think I'll always be waiting for the other shoe to drop."

"And if it does?" she asked. "What then?"

Sofi blinked. "What do you mean 'what then'? I'll get hurt."

"And?"

"I don't want to be hurt."

Abuela Fina snorted. "Nobody wants to be hurt, boba."

"Be nice," Mami scolded her mother. Then she looked back at Sofi. "You've been hurt before. And you'll be hurt again. When your abuela dies, when I die, hell when this dog dies. Are you going to cut us out of your life now, so that you don't have to feel the pain, so that it will be less?"

"Of course not," Sofi said.

"Then why are you doing that to Leo? Do you love him more than you love us and so if he hurts you, you will die?"

"No," Sofi grumbled.

"Then what is stopping you, bebé? You know you will get hurt again. That's life. But that doesn't mean that you just give up, because then you miss out on the positive moments too."

"We do not let fear stop us," Abuela Fina decreed in Spanish. "We are Santanas and we look that fear in the eyes and tell it to fuck off. We're going to do what we want and we're going to have a great time doing it."

Sofi sat with the knowledge that had just been dropped on her. She appreciated that they hadn't tried to negate her fears or make it seem like they were unreasonable. However, she still wondered if they were right. Did she really just have to accept the future pain as something inevitable but survivable and that was that? It seemed too simple. But what was the alternative, to forever keep hiding from happiness out of fear of losing it? That was nonsense. "Leo told me that I look for things to go wrong to justify never giving them a chance."

Mami nodded. "A self-fulfilling prophecy."

"But I feel like everyone does that," Sofi said.

"True, but we aren't talking about everyone," Abuela Fina pointed out. "We're talking about you and how you want to live the rest of your life."

"What do you want, negrita? What does your future look like?"

Her future, if she let herself envision the perfect version, was something similar to what she'd experienced the last month— her, Leo, and Tostón enjoying their life together surrounded by their loved ones. In her ideal future she had a thriving event planning business and they maybe even had a couple of kids who'd grow up playing with all of their cousins, like Leo had. They'd take trips all over and explore the world. They'd all be together surrounded by love.

"That sounds achievable," Mami said, causing Sofi to realize she'd been speaking out loud.

"All you have to do is go grab it and work to hold on to it," Abuela Fina said.

Sofi voiced the question that replayed in her mind. "But what if I can't hold on? What if I lose it?"

"I did," Abuela Fina said. "And I'm not going to lie and tell you that it wasn't the worst pain I ever felt. I'm also not going to tell you that it still doesn't hurt. It does. Every day. But if you ask me if I'd do it all over again, knowing what I would lose, I wouldn't even have to think about it. My answer will always be yes."

Sofi tried to put herself in Abuela Fina's shoes. If she'd been the one to lose her husband and her son, would she have cursed the day she'd met the love of her life and wish it had never happened? No, of course not. She didn't regret being with Leo, not any of the times they were together. Her regret was that they weren't together now. She wanted to be with him even though it was hard and sometimes it hurt. "You're right. I'd rather have it all and lose it than to let it go without giving it a chance."

"Good," Mami said. "Now you have a lot of work to do, because I'm sick of holding down all the wedding stuff for you these last couple of days. Event planning is your thing, not mine."

Right. Sofi still had a wedding to pull off in a week. But after that, she'd figure out how to make sure Leo knew that this time, she was ready.

25

SOFI SWIPED A THIN COAT OF CLEAR GLOSS OVER KAMILAH'S
pinkish-nude lipstick to complete the shimmery makeup look
she'd spent the better part of the morning working on. The
look was perfect for Kamilah, natural enough that she still totally looked like herself, but with an extra glitter and glow to
match the aura she was practically blinding them all with.

"I must say, sometimes I surprise myself with how good I
am." Sofi placed the gloss back on the table. "Take a look."

But Kamilah didn't turn around. Instead, she stared up at
Sofi, her face serious. "I'm so glad you're here." Her light brown
eyes began to sparkle with unshed tears. "I tried to imagine
this day without you, but I couldn't."

Sofi would be lying if she said that she hadn't also struggled with the idea of missing Kamilah's wedding. It hurt her soul to think that she'd almost let her stubborn pride cause her to miss out on sharing this moment with her best friend. But now was not the time to talk about that. They had too much to do, so Sofi bit the inside of her lip and forcefully pushed back her own rising emotions. "Don't you start." She pointed a finger in Kamilah's face to prove just how serious she was. "That makeup has to make it through an entire day, so lock that shit down."

Beside them, Lucy laughed. "Only you would tell a bride that she's not allowed to cry on her wedding day." She fiddled with the tie at the waist of her gold sequin off-the-shoulder jumpsuit.

"Fine. Lock it down until after pictures," Sofi conceded, but she couldn't just leave it at that. She grabbed Kamilah's hand and gave it a squeeze. "Ride or die," she mumbled before spinning away.

The last week, working on Kamilah's wedding almost non-stop, had given Sofi clarity about herself and her relationship with Kamilah. Sofi thrived in chaos. It was a bit of a shock to her since she loved plans, organization, and peace. But taking something chaotic and systematically breaking down then rebuilding it into something beautiful was rewarding in a way she hadn't realized it would be, and the fact that this was for her best friend's wedding only made it that much more fun. She'd been like a kid in a candy store putting out fires as they emerged, creating crises plans for when she was busy doing her MOH duties, and shuffling all the pieces of the jigsaw puzzle into place. She'd gone all in and, despite the pressure, she'd felt better than she had in years. As for Kamilah, Sofi had seen her in a different light. At peace and simply grateful for whatever came her way, rather than trying to manage the emotions of everyone around her. It was refreshing to see and made Sofi more hopeful for their friendship's future.

The rest of the morning passed in a haze of laughter and pink lemonade mimosas as Sofi and the other four bridesmaids got ready. There was one brief touch-up needed to everyone's makeup after Valeria arrived and helped Kamilah put on her dress—a gorgeous cream-colored, mermaid style with an off-the-shoulder beaded bodice, softly sparkling lacelike embellishments that went from the draped sleeves through the long tulle train, and a sassy V-back that led to a row of tiny buttons.

None of them had been able to stop the waterworks after Valeria saw her only daughter completely ready for her wedding. Of course, Valeria was Valeria, so she had to throw in one comment about how she wished Kamilah had straightened her hair instead of wearing her long curls in a deep part with a golden floral comb holding back one side. However, Kamilah had only sighed happily and informed her mother that Liam had demanded her curls.

That became obvious to everyone as soon as they arrived at the distillery, the first location for their pictures, and Liam immediately pulled Kamilah into a tight embrace and buried his face in her hair. He pulled back and was clearly about to kiss her when Sofi jumped in.

"Hold up, lover boy! No kissing until after pictures!"

Liam drew back and shot her a glare.

"Speaking of pictures," Alex interjected. "Aren't we supposed to take these after the ceremony? Isn't it bad luck for the groom to see the bride before the wedding?"

"It's not bad luck when the photographer is costing me an arm and a leg and your cousin wants pictures taken of every single minute," Liam said.

Kamilah smacked his arm. "The whole point of taking pictures before the ceremony is so that we aren't rushing to get everything done in a one-hour block between the ceremony and the reception."

"But the reception is here, so why did we need to get here at the ass crack of dawn," Lucy asked with a yawn.

"It's almost eleven," Sofi pointed out.

"We needed to get the pictures in here done early so that Sofi's team can get in here to set up and decorate during the ceremony," Kamilah added.

Liam looked confused. "Set up in here? I thought everything was happening in the tent outside."

"Don't you listen?" his best man, Ben, asked. "The stage and dance floor are going to be in the tent and the dinner in here." He shook his head and turned to Kamilah. "It's not too late for you to dump this clown and marry me instead. We're both already dressed."

Kamilah laughed while Liam rolled his eyes and muttered a half-hearted "fuck off."

Deciding to get this show on the road before things resolved into absolute chaos, as was apt to happen whenever more than a few Vegas were around, Sofi handed Kamilah her huge bouquet of flowers in various pinks, peaches, and creams with sprigs of greenery and berries. "Let's get started," she said to the photographer who immediately took charge.

They took pictures all over Humboldt Park before finally making their way to the wedding church where they stopped for more photos on the carefully cultivated grounds.

Sofi was standing back watching the photographer position Kamilah's train just when she suddenly felt a tingle down her spine. She turned her head already knowing who she'd see staring back at her. This had been happening on and off all morning.

Leo stood a few feet away. Next to him Saint was listening intently to something Alex was telling them, but Leo wasn't listening to them at all. Instead his gaze tracked up Sofi's body from the tips of her stilettos to her leg, which peeked through the slit in her strapless fuchsia sequin dress, and up past her hips and breasts to her face. His tongue peeked out as he licked his bottom lip while his eyes blazed hungrily.

Everything in Sofi threatened to melt like an ice cube on hot pavement, but just like she had demanded of Kamilah earlier, she firmly locked that shit down. She was the wedding planner and she had a job to do. However, the fact that he couldn't take his eyes off her gave her hope that they'd be able to work everything out.

Hours later, after a few hiccups Sofi had rushed to solve before the bride or groom even heard about them, Kamilah and Liam were finally married. Dinner had been served, the cake had been cut, and the video of everyone's well-wishes that Sofi had gathered over the last few weeks played. Of course, it had ended with Killian's clip and there had been no dry eyes in the entire place. Even stoic Saint had been wiping at his eyes when digital Killian said, "I don't worry about having to keep your arses in check, because you two were made for one another. After all, you can't spell Kamilah without Liam," in his rusty Irish brogue.

It was true. They completed each other in a way that Sofi found both beautiful and terrifying. To give someone that much power, so much that you weren't even whole without the other person, that was insanity to her.

Kamilah and Liam were finishing up their first dance together as Leo sang "Creo en Ti" by Reik accompanied by two of his bandmates on guitars and their two teenage daughters playing violins. Sofi sat next to Valeria as she sobbed through the entire thing and repeated over and over how beautiful and perfect it was.

Sofi had to agree with Kamilah's mom. The song was about how someone had been struggling and suffering until the right person came along at the perfect moment. The love between them gave the singer hope, strength, and the ability to leave their difficult past behind. It was the perfect song for Kamilah and Liam, who'd been through a lot together and separately. Through it all, they'd held on to their love for each other even when they couldn't or wouldn't show it.

Sofi smiled and enjoyed the sight of Kamilah and Liam wrapped in each other's arms swaying to the music while they stared at each other with a love so strong it poured out of them, swept along the dance floor, and enveloped everyone else in the tent with them. It was the same feeling she'd gotten when the doors to the church opened and Kamilah stepped in on her dad's arm. Her gaze had locked immediately on Liam and Sofi had turned to see his reaction. Any negative feelings she'd harbored for the man had faded away when she'd witnessed Liam doing his best to stop the tears in his eyes from spilling down his cheeks.

As soon as the song finished Sofi was out of her chair. She knew what was coming next, so she went to find her mom, who'd been helping her hold everything down while Sofi was doing her maid of honor thing. Mami was sitting at a small table in the back with Abuela Fina, both of them looking gorgeous in dark pink dresses. Sofi slipped in between the two of them as Gio, the MC and DJ for the night, announced the father-daughter dance, "Llegaste Tú" by Luis Fonsi and Juan Luis Guerra. Sofi rested her head on her mom's shoulder and closed her eyes to try to prevent the tears from falling even though she knew it was futile. Anything father-daughter related always made Sofi cry. It hurt in a place deep down that nothing could reach. She'd tried her best to cure it, but there was no way. It opened up unexpectedly and bled like old scar tissue.

The music started and her mom gripped Sofi's hand. "I know, mi amor," Mami said as Sofi held her breath to stop any sobs from escaping. She kissed Sofi on the forehead. "I get it and I know."

Abuela Fina gripped Sofi's other hand and squeezed.

Sofi stayed there in between the two people she loved and trusted the most and let their love comfort her. They loved her without limits or conditions. They were there for her no matter what she said or did. That could be enough for her.

Suddenly the music changed to a salsa beat. Sofi opened her eyes to see Los Rumberos on stage with Papo, Saint, Eddie, and Cristian. Papo and Leo held microphones, but the other three held simple instruments like maracas, the guiro, and a cowbell.

"This is for you, Ojitos de Oro," Papo said into his microphone. "We want everyone to know that we are the men who loved you first."

On the dance floor Kamilah exclaimed in surprise and immediately started crying. Her dad held her in his arms as Leo and Papo began to sing a salsa version of "I'll Be There" by The Jackson 5. He dragged Kamilah into the dance steps and suddenly they were dancing while Kamilah still cried and the videographer caught every second.

"Fuck," Sofi exclaimed, burying her face in the handkerchief Ben had slipped her during the video. There was no way she'd keep it together now.

Mami wrapped her arms around Sofi and hugged her close. "Come on," she said. "Let's go get crumped."

Sofi laughed through her sobs. "It's 'crunk' not 'crumped' and no one says that anymore."

"Yeah," Abuela Fina said. "Now they say 'light.'"

"Lit," Sofi corrected. "And I don't know if they still say that either."

"Listen I don't care what it's called," Mami said. "All I know is that there is an open bar over there and I plan on using it. Now, are you coming or not?"

"Hell yes, I'm coming."

"Me too," Abuela Fina said. Tossing her napkin on the table and standing up.

They ordered three shots of tequila plus three of the signature cocktails Leo had created for the wedding. They'd just slammed their shot back when Lucy and Liza came up next to them holding hands and looking adorable in their matching gold sequin outfits: Lucy's jumpsuit and Liza's off-the-shoulder dress.

"Now this is what I'm talking about," Liza said. "Enough watching other people dance. I want to drink."

"Dear God, yes. Give me alcohol. All the alcohol," Lucy agreed.

Sofi passed Lucy her drink only to watch Lucy chug it in two seconds.

"My parents are bitching about our courthouse wedding again," she said in explanation. "My mom wants us to renew our vows so we can 'have a real wedding before those far-right dingbats make it illegal.'"

Sofi shook her head. "You mean you don't want to discuss politicians revoking your right to love and marry whomever you want at your cousin's hetero wedding?"

Lucy accepted a shot from Liza. "Shocking, I know," she said with a wry smile before she and her wife took their shots.

Kamilah came up to the group and threw her arms around Sofi. "Everything is so gorgeous. More beautiful than I ever imagined. Thank you so much. I love you."

Sofi returned her hug. "You're welcome, love. I'm happy you're having a good time and not stressing about anything."

"I stopped stressing as soon as you told me you'd take care of everything. I've been to your work events. I knew you'd kill it."

"Here," Mami offered, passing Kamilah a shot. "Take this."

"Alicia, this is why I love you," Kamilah said, accepting the drink. "You always know exactly what someone needs."

"It's because she's a nurse," Abuela Fina said with pride, her own shot in hand.

Someone handed Sofi a shot, so she raised it. "To Kamilah and Liam."

Kamilah shook her head. "No." She raised her shot glass. "This one's to badass women who build each other up!"

"Cheers!" everyone else yelled before slamming back their tequila.

"Okay." Sofi grabbed Kamilah's hand. "Ready for your outfit

change?" They'd gotten Kamilah a reception dress—a simple white tulle A-line with a corset top, thick shoulder straps, and a tea-length skirt. It was just the right amount of pretty, flowy, sexy, and classy. Plus, it was perfect for dancing.

"I am so ready. I love this dress, but it's heavy as hell and I feel like I can barely move." She shifted around as if trying to get comfortable. "But I had my mom put my other dress in Leo's place because the kids are already taking over mine."

Sofi knew she was asking if it was okay that they'd have to go to Leo's apartment. Sofi wasn't sure if it was. She'd been avoiding the place like the plague even though she still had stuff there. It just hurt too much to go in and know that it was no longer her home. It didn't matter that she'd stopped being a dumbass and decided to finally get out of her own way. She still didn't know how Leo felt, so she should be respecting his space. But this was Kamilah's wedding and what the bride says goes, so while it wasn't her first choice, she'd go up. Besides, she'd successfully spent the day around the actual man, going into his place was nothing in comparison. She tugged Kamilah through the tent, into the distillery, and then back past the door that led to Kamilah's place where the mini Vegas were playing board and video games and raiding the fridge. Sofi held Kamilah's train as they climbed the stairs.

When they opened the door to Leo's apartment, Sofi sucked in a breath. On the dining room wall, in place of the collage of wedding inspiration pictures she'd put there, was her and her tío Manny's map. It had been mounted in a frame and covered with glass. She walked closer and noticed that while all of the places she and her uncle had circled were under the glass, there were other places circled outside the glass—São Paulo in Brazil, Serengeti National Park in Tanzania, and most of Australia including the Great Barrier Reef. She turned to her best friend. "What's this?" she asked Kamilah.

"I don't know." Kamilah shrugged. "Leo must be doing something." She gestured to the dining room table.

Sofi looked down, shocked to see piles of travel books and brochures. They were spread out all over the place. Some were open and highlighted and annotated while others had colorful Post-it notes sticking out like piñatas.

"I can see you're going through something right now, so I'm just going to go get myself ready." Kamilah walked down the hall to one of the rooms.

Sofi kept swinging her head between the map on the wall and the books on the table. Had Leo really done this? What did it mean? Was she even supposed to know about this? Her mind whirled with more questions. Then something on the corner of the table caught her eye. Sofi picked it up and saw it was paperwork for a passport. She was thunderstruck to see Leo's information filled in. What did he need a passport for? He'd said that everything he needed was in Chicago. Was he going on some sort of trip? Why use her map?

"Ready to get our party on?" Kamilah asked, stepping back into the room in her new dress.

Sofi was ready for something, but not a party. She was ready for answers. She walked to the door and held out a hand for Kamilah. Together they rushed back out to the party.

Sofi was surprised to see almost everyone stopped and looking in their direction. "What the fuck is going on?" she whispered in an aside to Kamilah, while scanning the faces that seemed to be looking at her and not Kamilah.

"I don't know," Kamilah whispered back. "Maybe they needed me for something."

Sofi didn't think so.

Leo stood on the stage staring at her. "There you are," he said into the mic. "We've been waiting for you to come back. Get over here, bombón. I have something to say to you."

Sofi's heart kicked up.

"Fucking Leo," Kamilah whispered.

"Exactly," Sofi said.

Kamilah grabbed her hand and turned Sofi to face her. "You don't have to go up there if you don't want to."

Sofi was touched by the concern on her best friend's face, but she wasn't worried. Not exactly. "It's okay. I'm ready."

"Are you sure?"

Sofi nodded. "Yeah."

Kamilah smiled and leaned in to kiss her on the cheek. "I love you, bestie. Now go get your annoying-ass man."

Sofi chuckled but as soon as she turned the nerves came back. She swallowed thickly and walked forward. Everyone in the crowd moved out of her way until she was right in front of the stage. She looked up at Leo.

He crouched down, still wearing his emerald green wedding tux that made his eyes look like jade. "Hey."

Sofi arched a brow. Really? Did he think that was going to work?

He smirked as if reading her mind. "I have something to tell you."

"Something you need to tell me in front of everyone we know?"

He nodded. "Yep."

She swallowed hard. "Well, I have something to ask you first."

He raised a brow. "Something to ask me in front of everyone we know?"

She nodded. "Yep."

He waved his free hand, causing the microphone to make a wind noise. "Go ahead. I have nothing to hide. Not anymore."

"The map and the passport," she said. She was very proud of how breezy she sounded despite the way her heart was rampaging in her chest. "Why?"

He lifted the microphone to his lips. "Because no matter where you go, I want to go with you. If you want to go walk

The Great Wall, I'll walk it too. If you want to go do yoga by the Taj Mahal, I'll be there in warrior pose next to you. If you decide to go on a safari, I'll be your lion attack lookout. I want to be with you as you check off all those places you once marked on a map. And when you need to retreat to your safe place, I will always be waiting right outside for you. You know why?"

Sofi gulped. "Because you overcame your dislike of flying?"

He laughed. "No. But that's what drugs are for." He put the microphone back up to his mouth. "Because I love you and I'm going to do everything in my power to be the man you need. A man who doesn't see you as a conquest or a goal, but a person with all the complications humans have. One who supports you and puts your needs above his own. A man who realizes that sometimes you're going to need space to figure things out, but that doesn't mean you're rejecting me or thinking that I'm not enough."

She felt sweaty, breathless, and weirdly amped up, as if she'd just finished a high intensity Zumba class. At least that was how she felt physically; emotionally was a different story. She wasn't exactly sure how she was feeling emotionally. On the one hand she was pissed at Leo for being so indiscreet. At the same time, she was…excited? Giddy? It was the constant back-and-forth that had her adrenaline spiking. She was so sick of being at constant war with herself and her feelings. She knew what she wanted now even though she was a bit late.

But Leo had always known. He knew her so well. In so many ways he knew her better than she knew herself. He was always striving to give her exactly what she wanted, even when it was probably not what he needed. He'd been doing it for years, letting her hide from her emotions and while she offered him only the smallest part of herself.

Yet here he was reaching out to her again and accepting blame, despite the fact that she was the one who'd really messed up. She was the one who'd pushed him away and refused to give them an honest chance. She was the coward who'd tried to keep everything surface level. He'd always been the one willing to go all in.

It was time for Sofi to show him that she was all in too. She wasn't going to leave him alone in this anymore.

26

AS SOFI JUST STOOD THERE STARING AT HIM, LEO'S STOMACH
dropped. *Fuck.* He'd embarrassed Sofi in front of everyone. She
definitely wouldn't forgive him. *Stupid, Leo. Stupid. Idiotic. Asi-
nine.* He berated himself as he tried to quell the rising panic in his
chest. He shut his eyes and shook his head wondering how he'd
managed to mess up already.

A hand tapped him on the knee and his eyes flew open. A
soft, brown hand covered in gold jewelry and tipped with long
pointy nails decorated with gold flecks and rhinestones made a
give me motion at him.

Sofi.

"Give me the mic and help me up," she told him.

He did exactly as she asked, ignoring his discomfort. Then

she was standing next to him. They were practically the same height thanks to the tall heels he'd been checking out at random intervals all night when he salivated over her exposed leg. She looked absolutely stunning. She'd been the only one of the bridal party in a rich pink dress instead of gold. The color was magic and brought out the warm undertone of her brown skin while also shimmering in all the different kinds of light. It had no sleeves so her collarbone and chest were on display and that fucking thigh-high slit was killing him. He'd envisioned sliding his hand in it way too many times for a man surrounded by his family and close friends. Everything about her from her head to her toes was flawless. She was just perfect. She made his heart beat erratically every time.

When she lifted the mic to her lips, he barely paid attention because he was so focused on her mouth. He loved that sassy, pouty mouth of hers. "I have something to say," she began, but then she kind of froze.

Leo finally noticed the way the mic shook in her hand and the sweat beading along her hairline. He remembered her confession about fearing public speaking. "You don't have to do this, bombón. Not here or like this."

At the sound of his voice she appeared to come to. She blinked and looked at him. "Yes, I do. I need to face my fears instead of hiding from them." She turned and faced the crowd in the tent. "I thought I was going to get through this without having to talk in public, but it appears that life had other plans." There were some chuckles in the audience. "The truth is that I hate speaking in public. It's why I quit competing in pageants and why I have to prepare weeks in advance before a presentation. Of course, I didn't prepare tonight, but I guess that's okay. I mean it's not okay. My knees are quaking like I'm a baby giraffe and I'm probably going to sweat out this silk press." She paused briefly. "I guess that's more information that y'all didn't need." She looked at Leo. "What was I talking about?"

"Your fears."

She nodded. "Right. My fears." She turned back to the crowd. "Most of you have known me for a long time. Even so, I know a lot of you will be surprised to know that public speaking is not the only thing I'm scared of. There are tons, but I got really good at hiding them all. I never wanted anyone to see me as weak or foolish, but I guess I already ruined that tonight. And oh shit is that, Chord Bailón?"

She looked at him for confirmation.

Leo nodded. "He came with Eva."

"I'm making an ass of myself in front of Chord Bailón. Cool, cool, cool." She would've been whispering that to herself if it weren't for the mic. She paused again. Her brow furrowed. "I think, I should be more upset about that, but I'm not. It's kind of a relief." She shook her head. "No, it *is* a relief." She took a breath. "I'm Sofia Santana and I'm a coward who hides from the things that scare me instead of facing them." She turned to him. "And you, Leo, are the scariest thing I've ever faced."

Leo watched her throat bob as she swallowed thickly.

"From the moment we met, you've seen me. The real me. Not the facade that I show the rest of the world. You poke and prod and push and piss me off like no other." She clenched her jaw like just thinking about it made her mad. Then she blew out a breath. "That's because you dare me to be my true self and that's terrifying to me. I don't know how you do it all the time. But you've always been braver than I am. You are ready to face anything and to go all in while I want to hide like a turtle in my shell, but I can't continue to hide. It's not fair to you. So here's my truth." She licked her lips. "I love you, Leo Vega. I've loved you since the night you knocked on my window, took me to The Bean, and forced me to feel my emotions, because you knew that's what I needed." Her eyes began to glisten with unshed tears. "Probably before then actually, but that was the night I knew for sure. Anyway, you've always done that for me, given me what I didn't know I needed. In return, I haven't done the same for you. I've pushed you away and made you seem unimportant and I'm so sorry for that." Her voice cracked and a single tear rolled down her cheek.

Leo couldn't take it anymore. He reached for her right as she opened her mouth again.

"I—"

His lips crashed into hers. He kissed her like he'd never kissed her before and she returned it with just as much zeal. Distantly, he heard the cheers of their loved ones and the awful screech the mic made when it fell and rolled too close to the amp. But his attention was solely on Sofi and the kiss that was threatening to burn down the tent around them. They kissed how he'd once caught his parents kissing in the pantry of the kitchen, or frequently witnessed between Liam and Kamilah since they had no shame, or how Lola was prone to kissing Saint whenever she thought they were alone. They kissed with the entirety of their beings.

She pulled away first. "You didn't let me finish saying what I wanted to say and now I don't remember what it was."

Leo smirked. "It doesn't matter, because you had me at 'quaking baby giraffe knees.'"

Sofi let out a laugh and smacked him on the arm. "You are so damn cheesy," she said before pulling him in for another quick kiss. She pulled away and held up a finger. "But don't think for one second that we aren't going to have words about you calling me out in front of everyone—"

Leo cut her off with another kiss. This time he pulled her close and then dipped her back into the kind of kiss that never failed to turn her brain to putty. He knew he'd succeeded when he lifted her up to release her, only to have her body collapse against his like her legs wouldn't work right. All while staring at him like he hung the stars in the sky. "We'll have plenty of words, but the only ones I want to hear or say right now are these... I love you. Te amo. And that's all the ways I know right now, but you better believe that I'll learn more from every country we visit."

"Here's a freebie. Je t'aime," she purred in that sexy French she now spoke. He really had no idea if she was fluent, but he didn't care. They both knew the most important words and that was all that mattered.

"Je t'aime," he told her back before they kissed until they got kicked off the stage.

Hours later, drinks had been consumed, high heels had been left abandoned under tables, ties were off, and suit jackets were missing. The children were gone, but the party was still in full swing and if there was one thing his family knew how to do, it was party. Gio was hitting the '90s hip-hop and R&B really hard at the moment and everyone was showing off their old-school dance moves. Leo smiled as he watched Kamilah holding the full fluffy skirt of her second dress out of the way so she could do the Kid 'n Play with Lucy as they danced and sang to "Poison" by Bell Biv DeVoe in the middle of a circle. Everyone around them was yelling and cheering them on as they danced along.

Gio did some DJ magic and all of a sudden "Poison" was now "Gasolina" by Daddy Yankee. Unsurprisingly, a bunch of the women screamed and joined Kamilah in the middle of the circle. It appeared that '90s time was over and it was now time for perreo. Leo would join them in a minute. He needed to hydrate after his epic dance-off with Ricky and a bunch of their other cousins. That Chicago footwork was getting hard. He was getting old. All that mattered was that he won though. At least, he'd proclaimed himself the winner.

"I hope you got me some water too," Sofi said from behind him.

"Of course." He handed her a bottle. "How was Tostón?"

"Happily passed out in Kamilah and Liam's bed with all your nieces and nephews, including Omar." She opened the bottle and took a long drink.

"They all fit?" Leo asked.

She swallowed. "Barely," Sofi said with a smile. "They were either piled on top of each other or hanging off the sides. I took, like, twenty pictures."

Leo wrapped his arms around her waist. "Aww. You're already a proud tití."

She wrapped her arms around his neck. "I've been around since they were all born. Of course, I'm their tía. Even if we weren't together."

"But we are together," Leo said. "And we will be for the rest of our lives."

"Yes."

Suddenly they heard shouting coming from the dance floor. They turned in unison.

Abuelo Papo was in the middle of the circle with Doña Fina and they were dancing to "Dile" by Don Omar.

"Oh hell, no!" Leo exclaimed in glee. He grabbed Sofi's hand and dragged her out onto the dance floor where everyone was surrounding the couple and cheering or catcalling.

"Ohh!!!"

"Go! Go! Go!"

Suddenly Doña Fina dropped it like it was hot and everyone lost their minds.

"Oh shit! Your grandma got them Megan knees," Leo shouted to Sofi.

Sofi was too busy laughing and shaking her head in disbelief to respond to him.

"Hey! Hey! Hey!" everyone started cheering.

Of course, that only pumped up the two attention whores on the floor.

"Oh my God," Kamilah said from next to him. "And I thought you and Sofi were going to be the most extra couple!"

"We are," Leo said. He looked at Sofi, who nodded.

"Just wait until they play the next bachata," she told Kamilah. "Y'all are going to get sick of us."

"Exactly," Leo agreed. "If we aren't actively making you all regret us getting together, then we aren't doing enough."

"Oh God," Kamilah said. "I already regret it."

"Too late," Sofi said. "You should've thought about that before you encouraged his shenanigans."

"I did no such thing," Kamilah said.

"She actually threatened me if I hijacked her wedding," Leo told Sofi.

Sofi shook her head at him. "And of course that only made you more determined to do it."

"Well, duh. I mean, she was obviously trying to tell me to do it in a way that couldn't get her in trouble if you hated it."

Sofi looked at Kamilah, who suddenly turned to dance with their cousins.

"Ugh. Your sister is a pain in my ass," Sofi grumbled.

"Tell me about it," Leo said. "But she's also your biggest fan."

Sofi smiled. "And she's my first official client, even though I did this all pro bono."

"What do you mean 'official client'?"

"I'm opening my own event planning company. You are looking at the founder and CEO of Sofia Maria Events."

"Wepa!" Leo cheered. He pulled her in for a hug. "I'm so proud of you! That's amazing."

She beamed at him. "What about you? What did you decide about the CFD?"

"I'm done with that. I don't have to put my body through hell just to prove I can be successful. My new goal is to be the best manager Kane Distillery Tasting Room has ever seen, even if I'll be the only one."

"Look at us," Sofi exclaimed. "We've only been a couple for a few hours and we're already killing it like Jay-Z and Beyoncé."

"Of course we are," Leo said. He'd known they were meant to be from the moment he'd found out that Sofi's birthday was the day after his. His new goal was to prove it every year for the rest of their lives. "Wait until they see what I have planned for our birthdays next week…sky writing may be involved."

Sofi winced, but the twinkle in her eyes told him how she truly felt. "Oh God, I just realized that we're two dramatic ass Leos in a relationship together. We're going to piss everyone off."

Leo shrugged. "Haters gonna hate."

Sofi laughed and wrapped her arms around his neck. "So, about those travel books and brochures. Did you actually read them or was that all a setup for me to see when I helped Kamilah change? Because, I mean, we both know that you don't study or make lists."

Her smart-ass smirk made his heart race. God, he loved this woman. She'd never make anything easy for him, but that was exactly the way he wanted it. If it wasn't a challenge then it wasn't worth it. "I do for you, bombón," he told her. "I do it all for you and only you."

"Cheesy," she accused again, but then she leaned in and kissed him until he was the one suffering from quaking baby giraffe knees.

EPILOGUE

PAPO VEGA STOOD AT THE BACK OF THE TENT WATCHING EVERYONE he loved enjoying themselves and feeling more than a little smug. He was three for three when it came to his matchmaking. His family was celebrating Liam and Kamilah's wedding right now because of his and Killian's machinations. Saint and Lola were happily awaiting the arrival of their first biological kid together because of his input. Now Leo and Sofi were together for real all due to the push Papo had given them.

"I don't know that I like the look on your face right now," Leo told him as he walked up. "You look the same way Tostón did after his begging got Doña Fina, Sofi, and Alicia to give him pieces of their filet mignon."

"Those Santana women are really something," Papo said, thinking about one in particular.

"Does that mean you're finally ready to admit that you and

Doña Fina are dating? Or whatever the old person version of it is."

Papo fussed with the sleeves of his tuxedo jacket. He was nervous to hear what his grandson thought of his budding relationship. He and Fina were truly just friends at the moment, but Papo couldn't deny that he wanted more. He would never love anyone like he loved his Rosa Luz, but that didn't mean that he needed to live the rest of his life alone—especially now that Killian, his only other companion, had also passed. Fina felt the same about her own husband. But she too was willing to give this a shot. "What would you say if I am? Would that bother you?"

Leo shook his head. "I think everyone here would agree that you deserve to be happy, Abuelo. If she makes you happy, I can't see anyone disapproving of your relationship."

"Gracias, mijo." Papo's eyes were glassy as he put a hand on Leo's shoulder and gave it a rough shake. "That means everything to me."

Leo wrapped an arm around Papo's shoulders and gave him a one-armed hug. "I love you, Abuelo. You're my favorite person."

"I love you too."

"This is where you tell me that I'm your favorite too."

Papo loved all of his grandchildren equally, which is why he busted his butt to make them happy. Not that he was finished with that goal by any means. "Nah uh," he told Leo with a wag of his finger. "Nice try."

"Fine, don't say it out loud, but we both know it's true."

Papo ignored his nonsense. "I have an idea for how to close out this party, but I need your help."

His clone didn't even hesitate. "Whatever it is, I'm in."

Within moments Papo was onstage with Leo and the rest of the band Papo had founded in his youth.

"What are we doing?" Leo asked.

"Just follow along," Papo said before holding the mic to his mouth and addressing the crowd. "Leo and I want to sing one more song tonight. Ya se me está acabando la gasolina."

"Of course you're running out of gas," Leo said into his own mic. "You were dropping it all over the dance floor with Doña Fina."

Chuckles arose.

Papo shot him a look that told him to remember his place. Papo was the star here. "Anyway, before we sing. I just wanted to say a few things. I'm so proud of this family. We've been through a lot together from losing mi amada, Rosa, to almost losing my mini-me." He pointed at Leo. "But everything we've gone through has only made us stronger, closer, and better. I know that there will be difficult times in our future, but I also know we will be okay because we'll always have each other to help us through everything. Los amo con todo mi corazón."

Cheers and calls of "We love you too" thundered through the tent.

Papo smiled widely. "Canten con nosotros." He signaled to the band.

The band began to play and everyone immediately recognized the song. "Vivir Mi Vida" by Marc Anthony. It was perfect. It was all about continuing to enjoy life despite the troubles everyone inevitably faces.

Papo began singing the first verse about how those things that seemed negative could actually be something positive. As he sang, Papo searched the crowd. His entire family, including the people he wasn't actually related to but loved all the same, stood on the dance floor dancing and singing along. When he sang the bridge about the pointlessness of crying over things when everything will eventually pass, he did it with everything in him.

Leo joined him in singing the chorus. Together in perfect harmony they sang about how they were going to laugh, dance, have fun, and live their lives.

Papo put all the emotion he could into his voice. If he had a theme song, this would be it. He knew better than most that life was for laughing, singing, dancing, dreaming, loving, and living. Life was for moving forward with hope and happiness. Thanks to the love of everyone in the crowd, Papo was always able to do so.

★ ★ ★ ★ ★

ACKNOWLEDGMENTS

From the moment I first created the Vega family, something about Sofi and Leo captured my imagination to the fullest. I waited, with barely leashed anticipation, for years to write their story. Now their story has been written and I'm actually sad. I love these two and their relationship so much. I wish I could simply continue to tell their love story—every moment from traveling the world, to getting married, to having/raising kids, to being empty nesters enjoying their golden years surrounded by grandkids, and every fight plus subsequent make-up in between. I can only hope that you, the readers, love my two clueless babies as much as I do.

This book required so much patience, optimism, and dogged tenacity to complete (not all of it mine). To that end, I must thank April Osborn, my editor, for being patient with me when it was unclear when, or if, my health would allow me to get words on the page. Seriously, April, thank you! Working with you has helped me grow so much as an author! To the rest of the MIRA team, Ashley MacDonald and Puja Lad for marketing; Justine Sha for publicity; and Alexandra Niit for art direction, I owe you all many many thanks. This book would not have happened without any of you.

To the cover artist, Andressa Meissner, I continue to be in awe of your ability to create such perfect depictions of my characters and stories. Each and every cover design holds a special place in my heart. Obrigada por compartilhar seu talento incrível comigo.

I am so grateful to my agent, Jessica Watterson, for having my back since the moment we signed. I know we are going to make so many more stories together!

Again, I have to thank my family. Your love for me, our culture, and each other was the catalyst for the invention of the Vega family. Although, there are no exact comparisons (stop looking) you all continue to be what inspires me to keep writing.

Thank you to every single person, including many of my fantastic author friends, who displayed enthusiasm for Sofi and Leo's story. Your zealous demands for more Leo kept me going when I could barely function. I hope I lived up to your expectations!

Lastly, I must thank every reader who has reached out to me to let me know how my stories have touched you and spoken to something in you. This goes double for my Latine readers. I strive to provide you with honest and accurate representation while making y'all proud to be a part of la comunidad. I aspire to continue doing so for many years to come and hope you will all come along on that journey with me.

Love you all,
Natalie